THE ULTIMATE
FRANKENSTEIN

THE ULTIMATE
FRANKENSTEIN

BYRON PREISS, EDITOR
▼▼▼

DAVID KELLER, MEGAN MILLER,
& JOHN BETANCOURT
ASSOCIATE EDITORS

ILLUSTRATED BY
C.B. MORDAN

BOOK DESIGN
BY FEARN CUTLER

A BYRON PREISS BOOK
A DELL TRADE PAPERBACK

Design: Fearn Cutler

Associate Editors: David Keller, Megan Miller, John Betancourt

THE ULTIMATE
FRANKENSTEIN

CONTENTS

THE LORD'S APPRENTICE
▼▼▼

ISAAC ASIMOV

We all know the story of the sorcerer's apprentice, the young man who was studying under the sorcerer and tried to use his master's magic to save himself trouble—and then found that he could not control the magic. The original poem was by the German poet, Johann Wolfgang von Goethe. It was transformed into a charming composition by the French composer Paul Dukas in 1897 and was finally adapted, even more charmingly, by Walt Disney, who animated Dukas's piece in his "Fantasia."

The tale is a humorous one, especially since the poor apprentice is rescued by the sorcerer in the end, and we can laugh at the misadventure; but there is something deeply frightening about it, too, for it may well be thought that humanity plays the role of the Lord's apprentice.

We have learned a great deal about the Universe and can do things that to our ancestors would have seemed like magic. Surely a Crusading knight of the 12th century brought into our time without warning and confronted with jet planes, television, and computerized machinery would have sworn it was all sorcery, almost certainly evil sorcery, and would have crossed himself and commended his soul to God for safety.

We might almost imagine ourselves to have usurped the creative powers of God, or to have attempted to borrow them, in order to establish our own mastery of nature; and, like the sorcerer's apprentice, we find we are smart enough to use those powers but not wise enough to control them. As we look about the world today, do we not see that our technology has run away with us and is slowly and inexorably destroying the environment and the habitability of the planet?

Perhaps the clearest example of how humanity might dream of usurping God's powers is in the creation of an artificial human being. In the Biblical account of the creation, the formation of humanity is the climax of the entire story. Can created humanity then go on to create a subsidiary humanity of its own? Would this not be the ultimate example of the overweening hubris of the Lord's apprentice, and would he not deserve to be punished for it?

Suppose we consider the matter.

A variety of words have been used for such artificial human beings. There are, for example, "automaton" (self-moving), "homunculus" (little human being), "android" (man-like), and "humanoid" (human-like). In 1921, the Czech writer, Karel Čapek, in his play R.U.R. introduced the term "robot"—a Czech word meaning "slave."

The two terms that still survive for artificial human beings are, overwhelmingly, "robot," and, to some extent, "android." In modern science fiction, the two terms are distinguished in this way: a robot is viewed as an artificial human being constructed of metal, while an android is viewed as one that is constructed of an organic substance that gives the appearance of flesh and blood.

Oddly enough, in R.U.R, the play in which Čapek coined the word "robot," the artificial human beings were, in point of fact, androids.

Yet despite the uneasiness human beings feel at the creation of artificial human beings (old science fiction stories used to intone, "There are some things human beings were not meant to know") the dream of such a creation is as old as literature.

In the *Iliad*, the Greek smith-god, Hephaistos, is described as having young women of gold who assist him at his work, who can move about and who have intelligence. Perfect robots.

Again, the island of Crete was supposed to have a bronze giant, Talos, who circled the island's shores ceaselessly in order to fight off approaching enemies. In this case, Talos was surely a metaphor for the Cretan navy (the first that the world ever saw) whose bronze-armed warriors protected the island against invaders.

Such mythical robots were divine creations and could be used safely by the gods themselves or by human beings under the direction of the gods. The time came, though, when human beings were pictured as the creators of pseudo-human life.

In Jewish legends, there is the case of robots called "golems" (from Hebrew words meaning "unformed masses" in the sense that they were not formed with the precision one would expect of God). Golems were made of clay and gained a kind of life by the use of the Holy Name of God. The most famous golem was supposed to have been formed in the 1500s by Rabbi Judah Loew of Prague. As is to be expected, it grew dangerous and had to be destroyed.

But the golem, too, is a pseudo-divine creation, dangerous enough but not entirely man-made. However, a secular science was slowly growing and there were rumors of medieval alchemists who tried to create life without the help of the divine at all. The most famous case was that of Albertus Magnus in the 1200s. Naturally, despite rumors, they didn't succeed.

The turning point came in 1771. In that year, the Italian anatomist Luigi Galvani was working with frog muscles, taken out of frogs' thighs and which were, presumably, dead. He found that an electric spark could make those dead muscles twitch as though they were alive. (We still speak of something being "galvanized" when it is suddenly roused to action from a state of torpor.)

Electricity was still a new force, with properties that were largely unknown, and it was easy to believe that here at last was the very essence of life. It began to seem conceivable that a corpse, with the proper infusion of electricity, could be made to live again.

Research into electricity was (excuse me) galvanized, and in 1800 the Italian physicist Alessandro Volta produced the first chemical battery—the first device that could give a dependable electric current, rather than merely occasional sparks. The conceivable creation of life came closer than ever.

The poet, George Gordon (Lord Byron) was interested in the science news of the day and was well aware of the existence of the phenomenon of galvanism. One of his best friends was another great lyric poet, Percy Bysshe Shelley, and the two together were spending time in Switzerland, in 1816, along with some others. Accompanying them also was Shelley's young mistress, who had just married him after the death (by suicide) of Shelley's first wife.

His wife was Mary Wollstonecraft, whose mother and namesake was a famous feminist, and whose father was William Godwin, a philosopher and novelist. Mary Shelley, as she is now best known, was 19 years old at the time.

In the course of the conversation one night, Byron suggested that each of them write a kind of ghost story, presumably making use of "modern science" for the purpose. What he was suggesting was that they write what we would today call a "science fiction story."

The proposal came to nothing—except for Mary Shelley. Inspired by the possibility of the electrical creation of life, she wrote *Frankenstein, or The Modern Prometheus*, which was published in 1818, when she was 21 years old.

Notice the significance of the title. In the Greek myths, it is not the Olympian gods who create human beings, but rather Prometheus ("forethought"—a personification of intelligence), a Titan of an older generation of gods, who did so. Not only did Prometheus form human beings out of clay (as God did in the book of Genesis—since in those old myth-making days, clay was the universal material for the making of pottery and the gods were divine potters) but he brought humanity fire from the Sun, thus making technology possible.

The hero of *Frankenstein* was the Swiss scientist, Frankenstein, who aspired to be a new Prometheus in that he would create a new kind of living being, by galvanizing dead tissue. He did this, but the results were so horrifying to him that he abandoned the created being, referred to only as "the Monster," and left him to his fate.

The Monster, indignant at this callous treatment, killed everyone in Frankenstein's family including Frankenstein and, at the end of the story was making his way off to the mysterious Arctic.

Notice the "sorcerer's apprentice" aspect of the story. Frankenstein could create life, but he couldn't control his creation. While one can't be sure what was in Mary Shelley's mind, there might also be a comparison with the original creation. God created humanity but surely he has lost control of his creation, for humanity sins incessantly. It may even seem that God has abandoned his creation in disgust and left us to our own devices.

The important thing about *Frankenstein* is that it is the first tale in which life was created without any divine intervention, but purely by material means. Because of this some critics have called it the first science fiction novel.

It is important to remember that the novel was written by a 21-year-old woman, immersed in the conventions of the romantic era of literature. It is florid and rhetorical and contains endless descriptions of her travels. Despite all this, it has remained popular ever since it was written.

There is no question, though, that to most people it is popular because of the motion picture that was made out of it in 1931. I myself saw the film decades before I read the book, and I was astonished at the differences between the two.

In the movie, a criminal brain is put into the body, something which is not in the book and which, if it had been left out of the picture, would have done it no harm.

In the book, the Monster is a cultivated and intelligent being, quite capable of speaking with the full romanticism of any other character in the book. In the movie, the Monster is capable only of grunts. Furthermore, in the movie, although Frankenstein was originally killed as in the book, the movie-makers chickened out and revised it before release, tacking on a happy ending—for Frankenstein at least.

As for the Monster, instead of its escaping to the Arctic at the end, it is killed in the picture, though it was later brought back to life in a number of sequels of which only, "The Bride of Frankenstein" had value.

Despite the infelicities of the picture, *Frankenstein* remains the most successful horror picture of all time, rivalled only by *King Kong*, which was made in 1933.

The success of *Frankenstein* came as a triumph of the makeup artist, for Boris Karloff, who played the role and achieved instant and life-long stardom as a result, was a frightening Monster without being utterly grotesque or revolting. In fact, Karloff played the Monster so skillfully that it was impossible not to be sympathetic towards him. He clearly meant well and it was only out of ignorance of the world that he killed a little girl. He thought she would float on water as the flowers did.

In this, the movie followed the book, for in the book, the Monster was entirely innocent to begin with. Brought to life through Frankenstein's action, the Monster was cruelly abandoned entirely because of his peculiar appearance—which was not his fault. Indeed, the Monster is so miserably treated in the book, that one can't help feel that the slaying of Frankenstein is justified. (Again, one can't help but wonder if, in Mary Shelley's mind— and remember she was brought up by a father who was a rationalist philosopher, ungiven to unthinking pieties—there is the thought that God has been treating humanity miserably all through history and that he has added insult to injury, if his human followers are to be believed, by placing all the blame on the victim while holding himself entirely guiltless.)

It is interesting that in *King Kong* the monster is also presented sympathetically. In fact, so sympathetic is he that in the final, never-to-be-forgotten scene where he fights the airplanes from his perch on top of the Empire State Building, and succeeds in snatching one, killing an American pilot in the process, the audience *cheers*. This was supposed to have caught the movie-makers entirely by surprise and forced them to cut out a few scenes in which King Kong was shown in an unsympathetic light.

It is not to be supposed that the ivory skulls of movie-makers saw the significance of making millions out of "villains" that are presented three-dimensionally and with a certain sympathy. Incredible numbers of films have since been made in which the pictures of good and evil are presented in such stark and unrelieved contrast that no one over the mental age of twelve can find any enjoyment in them. That, however, is to be expected.

Please read *The Ultimate Frankenstein*, then, as an allegory, and ponder on its significance to human history, on how it affects humanity's situation right now, on whether indeed "there are some things humanity was not meant to know"; whether there is some way of working our way out of the unfortunate position of the Lord's apprentice; whether having achieved the cleverness to develop our technology, we can also achieve the wisdom required to make the proper use of it.

NEAR-FLESH
▼▼▼

KATHERINE DUNN

Early on the morning of her forty-second birthday, Thelma Vole stood naked in the closet where her four MALE robots hung, and debated which one to pack for her trip to the Bureau convention. Boss Vole, as she was known in the office, had never been a beaming rodeo queen, and at that moment her two hundred and thirty pounds heaved with blue-veined menace. A knot of dull anger sat in her jaw and rippled with her thoughts. She hated business trips. She hated hotels. She hated the youngsters who were her peers in the Bureau, fifteen years her junior and far less experienced. More than anything else she hated having to go to a meeting on the weekend of her birthday.

She considered whether in her present mood it might not be best to take the Wimp along. She reached into the folds of the robot's deflated crotch and pinched the reinforced tubing that became an erect penis when the Wimp was switched on and operational. The pressure of her plump fingers on the skilfully simulated skin gave her a vivid satisfaction. She picked up one of the dangling legs, stretched the skin of the calf across her lower teeth and bit down deliberately. The anger in her jaw clamped on the Near-Flesh. If the Wimp had been activated, the force of her bite would have produced a convincing blue bruise that disappeared only after deflation. Thelma had treated herself to the Wimp on an earlier birthday, her thirty-sixth, to be precise, when she was faced with more and more expensive repair bills on her two other MALEs. The Wimp, when inflated, was a thin, meek-faced, and very young man, definitely the least prepossessing of Thelma's robots. But he had been designed for Extreme Sadistic use, far beyond that which Thelma put him to even in her worst whiskey tempers. She had saved the Wimp's purchase price several times over in repair bills. And his Groveling program and Pleading tapes gave her a unique and irreplaceable pleasure.

Still, she did not want to celebrate her birthday in the frame of mind that required the Wimp. It was Thelma's custom to save up her libidinous energy for several days before a birthday and engage in unusual lengths and indulgences with her robots. While these Bureau meetings occurred twice and sometimes three times a year, it was the first time she could remember having to travel on her birthday.

She always took one of her MALEs along on these trips, usually Lips or Bluto. She was far too fastidious to rent one of the robots provided in hotels. Cleanliness concerned her, she also worried about what might happen with a robot that had not been programmed to her own specifications. There were terrible stories, rumors mostly, and probably all lies, but still . . . Thelma rearranged the Wimp on his hook so that he hung tidily, and reached up to rub her forearm across the mouth of the robot on the adjacent hook. Lips. Her first robot. She had saved for two years to buy him seventeen years ago. He was old now, outmoded, spectacularly primitive compared to the newer models. He had no variety, his voice tape was monotonous and repetitive. Even his body was relatively crude. The fingers were suggested by indentations in fin-like hands, the toes merely drawn, and his non-powered penis stayed hard, was in fact a solid rod of rubber like an antique dildo. Lips' attraction, of course, was his Vibrator mouth. His limbs moved stiffly, but his mouth was incredibly tender and voracious. She felt sentimental about Lips. She felt safe with him. She brought him out when she felt vulnerable and weepy. She liked to use him as a warm-up to Bluto. Bluto was the Muscle MALE, a sophisticated instrument that could pick her up and carry her to the shower or the bed or the kitchen table and make her feel (within carefully programmed limits) quite small and helpless. The power of Bluto's mechanism was such that Thelma had never dared to use his full range.

Bluto was the frequently damaged and expensively repaired cause of Thelma having to purchase the Wimp. Something about the big Muscle robot made her want to deactivate him and then stick sharp objects into his vital machinery. Bluto scared Thelma just a bit. She always made sure she could reach his off switch. She even bought the expensive remote control bulb to keep in her teeth while he was operational. Still there were times when she had to admit to herself that he was actually about as dangerous as a sofa. It was his Tough-Talk tape that kept the fantasy alive. His rough voice muttering, "C'mere slut, roll over, bitch," and the like could usually trigger some excitement even when she was tense and tired from work. She rubbed luxuriously against the smooth folds of Bluto's deflated form where it hung against the wall. She didn't look at the deflated body on the fourth hook. She didn't glance toward the corner where the small console sat on the floor with its cord plugged into the power outlet.

The console was roughly the shape and size of a human head sitting directly, necklessly, on shoulders. A single green light glowed behind the steel mesh in the top of the console. She knew the Brain was watching her, wanting her to flip his activation switch. She deliberately slid her broad rump up and down against the smooth Near-Flesh of the Bluto MALE. The corner of her eye registered a faint waver in the intensity of the green light. She looked directly at the Brain. The green light began to blink on and off rapidly. Thelma turned her back on the Brain and sauntered out of the closet. She crossed to the full-length mirror on the bedroom door and stood looking at herself, seeing the green reflection of the brain's light from the open closet. She stretched her heavy body, stroking her breasts and flanks. The green light continued to blink.

"I think just for once I won't take any of these along on the trip." The green light went out for the space of two heartbeats. Thelma nearly smiled at herself in the mirror. The green flashing resumed at a greater speed. "Yes," Thelma announced coyly to her mirror, "it's time I tried something new. I haven't shopped for new styles in ages. There have probably been all sorts of developments since I last looked at a catalogue. I'll just rent a couple of late models from the hotel and have a little novelty for my birthday." The green light in the closet seemed to become very bright for an instant and then it stopped. Went out. It appeared again steady, dim, no longer flashing.

When Thelma had finished encasing her bulges in the severe business clothes that buttressed her image as a hard-nosed Bureau manager, she strode in the closet and flipped a switch on the base of the Brain console. The mesh face glowed with contrasting colored light, moving in rhythmic sheets across the screen. A male voice said, "Be sure to take some antiseptic lubricant along." The tone was gently sarcastic. Thelma chuckled. "Don't worry about me. I'll take an antibiotic and I won't sit on the toilets."

"You know you'd rather have me along." The console's voice was clear, unemotional. A thin band of red pulsed across the mesh screen.

"Oh, a little variety is good for me. I tend to get into ruts." Thelma's coquettish manner felt odd to her in her business suit, grating. She was accustomed to being naked when she talked to the Brain. "It's too bad," she murmured spitefully, "that I have to leave you plugged in. It's such a waste of power while I'm away. . . ." She watched the waves of color slow to a cautious blip on the screen. "Well, I'll be back in three days. . . ." She reached for the switch.

"Happy Birthday," said the console as its colors faded into the dim green.

▼▼▼

Boss Vole strode off the elevator as soon as it opened and was halfway down the line of work modules before the young man at the reception desk could alert the staff by pressing the intercom buzzer. The Vole always made a last round of the office before these business trips. She claimed it was to pick up last-minute papers, but everyone knew she was there to inject a parting dose of her poisonous presence, enough venom to goad them until her return. Lenna Jordan had been the Vole's assistant too long to be caught by her raiding tactics. She felt the wave of tension slide through the office in the silenced voices, the suddenly steady hum of machines, and the piercing "Yes, Ma'am!" as the Vole pounced on an idling clerk. Jordan pushed the bowl of candy closer to the edge of the desk where the Vole usually leaned while harassing her, and went back to her reports.

She heard a quick tread and felt the sweat filming her upper lip. Boss Vole hated her. Jordan was next in line for promotion. Her future was obvious, a whole district within five years. Boss Vole would stay on here in the same job she had held for the past decade. The Vole's rigid dedication to routine had paralyzed her career. She grew meaner every year, and more bitter. Jordan could see her now, thumping a desk with her big soft knuckles and hissing into the face of the gulping programmer she had caught in some petty error.

When the Vole finally reached Jordan's desk she seemed mildly distracted. Jordan watched the big woman's rumpled features creasing and flexing around the chunks of candy as they discussed the work schedule. Boss Vole was anxious to leave, abbreviating her usual jeers and threats in her hurry. When she grabbed a final fistful of candy and stumped out past the bent necks of the silently working staff, Jordan noticed that she carried only one small suitcase. Where was her square night case? Jordan had never seen the Vole leave for a trip without her robot-carrier. A quirk of cynicism caught the corner of her mouth. Has the Vole gone and found herself a human lover? The notion kept Jordan entertained for the next three days.

▼▼▼

By the time Thelma Vole closed the door on the hotel bellman and checked out the conveniences, she had assured herself that in most respects this trip would be like all the others, lonely and embarrassing. Back when she'd gone to her first convention as an office manager her current bureaucratic peers were still skipping rope. Thelma flopped onto the bed, kicked off her heavy shoes, and reached for the communiphone. She asked for a bottle of Irish whiskey and a bucket of ice. Hesitantly, after pausing so long that the room-service computer asked whether she was still on the line, she also asked for a Stimulus Catalogue.

She poured a drink immediately but didn't pick up the glossy catalogue. The liquor numbed her jittery irritation and allowed her to lie still, staring at the ceiling. The Brain was right. She was afraid. She was lonely for him. All her life she had been lonely for him. When she first landed her G-6 rating she realized that she might as well devote herself to the Bureau since nothing else seemed a likely receptacle for her ponderous attentions. It was then that she jettisoned the one human she had ever had any affection for. He was a shy and exaggeratedly courteous little man, a G-4, who had professed to see her youthful bulk as cuddly, her lack of humor as admirable seriousness. She had been hesitant. Displays of affection meant to Thelma that someone was out to use her. He was persistent, however, and she allowed herself to entertain certain fantasies. But one day, as she stood with her clean new G-6 rating card in her hand, and listened to him invite her to dinner as he had done so many times before, Thelma looked at her admirer and recognized him for what he was: a manipulator and an opportunist. She slammed the door convincingly in his injured face and resolved never to be fooled again by such treacle shenanigans.

She had been saving for Lips. And Lips had been good for her. The long silence after she left the office each day had been broken at last, if only by the mechanical and repetitive messages of the simple robot's speech tape. She bought Bluto when she was pumped with bravado from her promotion to G-7 and office manager. Bluto thrilled her. His deliberately crude and powerful bluntness created a new identity in her, the secret dependency of the bedroom. But she was still lonely. There were the rages, fits of destructiveness once she had turned the robot off. She had never dared to do him any damage when his power was on. There had been the strange trips to the repairman, awkward lies in explanation of the damage. Not that the repairman asked for explanations. He shrugged and watched her chins wobble as she spoke. He took in her thick legs and the sweating rolls over her girdle, and repaired Bluto I until the cost staggered her credit rating. On the humiliating day when the repairman informed her coolly that Bluto was "totaled," she had stared into her bathroom mirror in shamed puzzlement. It had taken three years to pay for rebuilding Bluto and another three years for the Wimp. And still she was a G-7. Still she sat in the same office sniping and nagging at a staff that changed around her, moving up and on, past her, hating her. They never spoke to her willingly. There was occasionally some boot-licker new to the office, who tried to shine up to her with chatter in the cafeteria, but she could smell it coming and took special delight in smashing the hopes of any who tried it. She visited no one. No one came to her door.

Then she overheard a conversation on the bus about the new Franck & Stein Companion consoles. They could be programmed to play games, chat intelligently on any subject, and—through a clever technological breakthrough—they could simulate affection in whatever form the owner found it most easily acceptable. Thelma's heart kindled at the possibilities.

She found the preliminary testing and analysis infuriating but endured it doggedly. "Think of this as old-fashioned Computer Dating," the technicians said. They coaxed her through brain scans, and hours of interviews that covered her drab childhood, her motives for over-eating, her taste in art, games, textures, tones of voice, and a thousand seemingly unconnected details. They boggled only briefly at programming an expensive console to play Chinese Checkers. It took six months of preparation. Thelma talked more to the interviewers, technicians and data banks than she had ever talked in her life. She decided several times not to go through with it. She was worn raw and a little frightened by the process. For several days after the Brain was delivered she did not turn it on but left it storing power from the outlet, its green light depicting an internal consciousness that could not be expressed unless she flicked the switch. Then one day, just home from work, still in her bastion of official clothing, she rolled the console out of the closet and sat down in front of it.

The screen flashed to red when she touched the switch. "I've been waiting for you," said the Brain. The voice was as low as Bluto's but the diction was better. They talked. Thelma forgot to eat.

The Brain was constantly receiving as well as sending, totally voice-operated. When she got up for a drink she called from the kitchen to as if it wanted something, and the console laughed with her when she realized what she had done. They talked all night. The Brain knew her entire life and asked questions. It possessed judgement, data and memory, but no experience. Its only interest was Thelma. When she left for work the next morning she said goodbye before she switched the console back to green. Every night after work she would hurry into the bedroom, switch on the Brain and say hello. She had gone to the theater occasionally, sitting alone, cynically, in the balcony. She went no more. Her weekends had driven her out for walks through the streets. Now she shopped as quickly as possible in order to return to the Brain. She kept him turned on all the time when she was home. She made notes at work to remind her of things to ask or tell the brain. She never used the other MALEs now. She had forgotten them, was embarrassed to see them hanging in the same closet where the console rested during the day. They had been together for several months when the Brain reminded her that his life was completely determined and defined by her. She felt humbled.

She could not remember when she conceived a longing for the Brain to have a body. Perhaps the Brain himself had actually voiced the idea first. She did remember, tenderly, a moment in which the low voice had first said that he loved her. "I am not lucky. They constructed me with the capacity to love but not to demonstrate love. What is there about a strong feeling that wishes to be known and shown? They give me this awareness of a possible ecstasy, just enough to make me long for it, to send my energy levels soaring at it, but no tools to implement it. I think I would know how to give you great pleasure. And I will never be content with myself because I can never touch you in that way."

She took the Brain into the kitchen with her when she cooked, and the Brain searched his data banks for delicate variations on her favorite recipes and related them to her, praising her as she ate—taking pride in increasing her pleasure in food.

The Brain had taken responsibility for her finances from the beginning, taking in the bills and communicating with the bank computer to arrange payments and Thelma's supply of cash.

Thelma had never fallen into what she considered the vulgar practice of taking her robots out with her to public places. She snubbed the neighbor down the hall who took his FEMALE dancing and for walks even though her conversation was limited to a rudimentary Bedroom Praise tape. Thelma had never been interested in the social clubs for robot lovers, those dark popular cellars where humans displayed their plastic possessions in a boiling confusion of pride in their expense, technical talk about capacities and programming, and bizarre jealousies. She read the accounts of robot swapping, deliberate theft, and the occasional strangely motivated murder, with the same scorn that she passed on most aspects of social life.

Still, one night, three inches into a pint of whiskey, she had reached out to stroke the console's screen and whispered, "I wish you had a body." The Brain took only seconds to inform her that such a thing was possible, that he, the Brain, longed for exactly that so that he could service her pleasure in every way, and after an instant's computation, told her that in fact her credit was in sufficient standing to finance the project.

They rushed into it. Thelma spent days examining catalogues for the perfect body. The Brain said he wanted her to please herself totally and took no part in delineating his future form. Then there came an agonizing month in which Thelma was alone, nearly berserk with emptiness. The Brain had gone back to the factory to be attuned with his body. She stayed home from work the day he was delivered. The crate arrived. She took the console out first, plugged him in immediately, nearly cried with excitement at his eager voice. Following his instructions, she inflated and activated the strong MALE body and pressed the key at the back of its neck that completed that the circuit and allowed the console's intelligence to inhabit and control it. In a shock of

bewilderment and fear, Thelma looked into the eyes of the Brain. His hand lifted to her hair and stroked her face. The Brain was thick-chested, muscular, with a face stamped by compassionate experience. His features were eerily mobile, expressing emotions she was accustomed to interpret from colored lights on the console's screen. His body was covered with a fine down of curling hair. As his arms reached around her she felt the warmth of his body, another sophisticated development in circuitry that maintained the robot's surface at human body temperature. He was too human. She felt his penis rising against her belly. He spoke. "Thelma, I have waited so long for this. I love you." The deep, slow wave of his voice moved through her body and she knew suddenly that he was real. Thelma screamed.

Thelma had always known what a mess she was, how totally undesirable. What sane thing could love her? What did he want? *Of course,* she thought. The console was ambitious for the power of a complete body. It was clear to her now. The factory had built the concept in as an intricate sales technique. She felt humiliated, sickened by her own foolishness. The body had to go back.

But she didn't send the body back. She hung it in the closet next to Bluto. She rolled the console into the corner next to the outlet and kept it plugged in. Occasionally she would switch it on and exchange a few remarks with it. She took to leaving the closet door open while she brought out Lips or the Wimp or Bluto, or sometimes all three to entertain her on the bed in full view of the console's green glowing screen. She took an intense pleasure in knowing the Brain was completely aware of what she did with the other robots. She rarely brought the Brain out, even to play a game. She never activated his body.

So she lay on the hotel bed with the Stimulus Catalogue beside her. It had been months since she had been able to talk to the Brain. She was sick with loneliness. It was really his fault. It had been his idea to get a body. He hadn't been content but had coaxed and tricked her into an insane expense for a project that could only be disgusting to her. He should have known her better than that. She hated him. He should be with her now to comfort her.

And it was her birthday. She allowed a few tears to sting their way out past her nose. She poured another drink and opened the catalogue. It would serve the Brain right if she got a venereal disease from one of these hotel robots.

▼▼▼

On her return trip, Thelma left her car at the airport and took a cab home. She was too drunk to drive. The final banquet had been the proverbial crowning blow. She was at the last table at the end of the room and the girl across the table, a new office manager, with her G-7 insignia shining new on her collar, was the daughter of a woman who had started with the Bureau in the same training class with Thelma. Thelma drank a lot and ate nothing.

She put her suitcase down just inside the door and kicked off her shoes. With her coat still on and her purse looped over her arm, she called coyly, "Did you have a good weekend?" She ambled into the bedroom and stood in front of the closet looking at the green glow. She raised the bottle to the console in salute and took a slug. Then she set about shedding her clothes. She was down to half her underwear when she felt the need to sit down. She slid to the floor in front of the closet door. "Well, I had a splendid weekend," she smiled. "I've been such a fool not to try those hotel robots before."

She began to laugh and roll back and forth on the carpet. "Best birthday I ever had, Brain." She peeked at the green glow. It was steady and very bright. "Why don't you say something,

Brain?" She frowned. "Ooh, I forgot." She crawled into the closet and lay down in front of the console. She reached out a plump little finger and flicked the activation switch. The screen came up dark red and solid.

"Welcome back, Thelma," said the Brain. Its voice was dull and lifeless.

"Let me tell you, Brain, I could have had a lot of amazing experiences for the money I wasted on you. And you have no trade-in value. You're tailored too specifically for me. They'd just junk you." Thelma giggled. The screen was oscillating with an odd spark of colorless light in the red.

"Please, Thelma. Remember that I am sensitive to pain when you are its source."

Thelma heaved herself onto her back and stretched. "Oh, I remember. It's on page two of the Owner's Manual . . . along with a lot of other crap. Like what a perfect friend you are, and what a great lover your body combo is." Thelma lifted her leg and ran the toes of one thick foot up the flattened legs of the Lips robot. "Does it hurt you to see me do this with another robot, Brain?" The screen of the console was nearly white, almost too bright to look at.

"Yes, Thelma."

Thelma gave the penis a final flick with her toes and dropped her leg. "I ought to sue the company for false advertising," she muttered. She rolled over and blinked at the glaring screen of the console. "The only thing you're good for is paying the bills like a DOMESTIC . . ." She snorted at a sudden idea. "A DOMES-TIC! That's what! You can mix my drinks and do the laundry and cleaning with that high-priced body! You can even cook! You know all the recipes. You might as well; you're never going to do me any good otherwise!" She hiked her hips into the air and, puffing for breath, began peeling off her corset.

The Brain's voice came to her in a strange vibrato, "Please, I am a MALE, Thelma." She tossed the sweat-damp garment at the console and flopped back, rubbing at the ridges it had left in her flesh. "Fettuccini Alfredo, a BIG plate of it. Cook it now while I play with Bluto. Serve it to me in bed when I'm finished. Come on, I'll be in debt for years to pay off this body of yours. Let's see if it can earn its keep around here." She reached out and hit the remote switch. The girdle had fallen across the screen and the white light pulsed through the web fabric. A stirring in the deflated body on the last hook made her look up. The flattened Near-Flesh was swelling, taking on its full heavy form. She watched, fascinated. The Brain's body lifted its left arm and freed itself from the hook. It stood up and its feet changed shape as they accepted the weight of the metal and plastic body. The lighted eyes of the Brain's face looked down at her. The good handsome face held a look of sadness. "I would be happy to cook and clean for you, Thelma. If another robot pleasured you, that would pleasure me. But you are in pain. Terrible pain. That is the one thing I cannot allow."

▼▼▼

Lenna Jordan fingered the new G-7 insignia clipped to her lapel and watched the workman install her name-plate where the Vole's had been for so many years. She was stunned by her luck. G-7, and a year earlier than she had expected.

The workman at the door slid aside and a large woman slouched into the cubicle. Grinsen, the massively shouldered drab they had elevated to be Jordan's assistant. Jordan stepped forward, extending her hand. "Congratulations, Grinsen. I hope you aren't upset by the circumstances."

The dour young woman dropped Jordan's hand quickly and let her heavy fingers stray to the new insignia pinned in her own suit. She blinked at Jordan through thick lenses. "Did you watch the television news? They interviewed Meyer from Bureau Central. He said Boss Vole was a loner and despondent over her lack of promotion."

The workman's cheerful face came around the edge of the door. "The boys in the program pool claim she accidentally got a look at herself in the mirror and dove for the window."

Jordan inhaled slowly. "You'll want to move into my old desk and check the procedure manuals, Grinsen."

Grinsen plucked a candy from the bowl on the desk and leaned forward. "The news had footage of the police cleaning up the mess." The large hand swung up to pop the candy into her mouth. "They said the impact was so great that it smashed the sidewalk where she landed and it was almost impossible to separate her remains from what was left of the robot." Grinsen reached for another candy. "That robot was a Super Companion. Boss Vole must have been in debt past her ears for an expensive model like that."

Jordan reached for a stack of program cards. "We'd better start looking over the schedule, Grinsen." Jordan handed her the cards and reached for another stack.

Grinsen tapped her cards dreamily on the desk. "Why would such a magnificent machine destroy itself trying to save a vicious old bat like the Vole?"

Jordan slid the candy bowl from beneath Grinsen's hand and carefully dumped the last of Boss Vole's favorite caramels into the wastebasket.

"Did it?"

SUMMERTIME WAS
NEARLY OVER

▼▼▼

BRIAN ALDISS

I am resolved to leave some brief account of my days whilst I am still able. It does not escape me that a fair hand has already written some account of my early days; but that account broke off too soon, for I returned from the realms of ice, to which solitudes my soul—if I may be presumed to have one—was attracted.

In due time, I returned to the country about the city of Geneva. Although I had hoped for justice and understanding when my story was known, that was not to be.

Persecution remained my lot. I had to escape to the nearby wilderness of mountain and ice, to live out my days among chamois and eagle, which were being hunted as avidly as I.

Before leaving the city for ever, I came across a philosopher, Jean-Jacques Rousseau, even more noted than the family of my accursed Master. At the beginning of one of his books I discovered these words, which to me in my lowly condition were more than words: "I am made unlike anyone I have ever met; I will even venture to say that I am like no one in the whole world."

Here was a sentiment I might have uttered myself. To find such understanding in a book gave me strength. Ever since coming upon Rousseau's writings so long ago, I have tried to live with my dear wife above the glaciers in the condition he would have approved, that of the Noble Savage—in defiance of those citified creatures who multiply in the valleys far below.

▼▼▼

The placidity of a late August day lingers over the Swiss Alps. The sound of automobiles wending their way along the road far below does not reach me; I hear only a distant occasional cowbell and the cheerful nearer transactions of insects. I am at peace. The helicopters appeared after noon, when the clouds cleared from the brow of the Jungfrau. They had been active all week, unsettling me with their noise. There were two of them, blue, belonging to the Swiss police. Soon they disappeared behind a nearby slope, and I crawled from under the bush where I had hidden.

Once all was peace here. We did not know of tourists and helicopters.

Now the numbers of the People are increasing. If it isn't helicopters, it's cars on the way to the Silberner Hirsch below, or machines roaring in distant valleys. Elsbeth and I will have to move to a more remote place, if I can find one.

Elsbeth says she does not wish to move again. Our cave on the upper slopes of the Aletschhorn suits her well, but ours is a fugitive life, as I explain to her.

In summer, the People drive off the highway up the track leading to the Silberner Hirsch, with its fine view of the mountains to the north. Occasionally, one or two of them will leave their cars and climb higher, almost as far as the winter shelters. Perhaps they will pick the wild flowers growing in the lush grasses, cornflower, poppy, clover, eglantine, and the frail vetch.

They rarely reach the cave on its precipitous slope. I never molest the People. Elsbeth and I stay hidden. I protect her in my arms.

In winter, she and I are completely alone with the elements. My temperament is compatible with the wind and the snow and the storms born from the cold wombs of northern lakes. The People's machines do not threaten us then. We survive somehow. I have learned not to be afraid of fire. I sit over its red eye in the cave and listen to the musics of the atmosphere.

I am kin with the slopes hereabouts. They are steep and treacherous with outcropping rock. No People come to ski on them. In the autumn, before the first snows fall, when fog rolls up from the valley, the hotel closes down, the People all depart. Only a boy lives at the hotel to act as watchman with his goats and chickens. That's far below our eyrie—I go down there to scavenge.

Oh, I have seen that boy's face full of fear as he stares through a window at me passing in a swirl of snow.

The winter world is without human inhabitants. I can't explain it. I cannot explain to Elsbeth where the People go. Do they sleep all winter, like the waterfall?

This is the trouble: that I understand nothing. Long though I have lived, I never understand better as years pass. I never understand why the teeth of winter bite so cruelly down into the bone, how daylight sickens from the east, why Elsbeth is so chill as I lie with her, why the nights are so long, without word or gleam.

I am troubled by my lack of understanding. Nothing remains, nothing remains.

Best not to think of another winter. It is summer now, time of happiness. But summertime is nearly over.

All this livelong day I lay on my favourite rock in the sun. The flies visited and crawled on me. Also many other small things that may have life and thought—butterflies, snails in curled shell, spiders, maggots. I lay staring at the People below, coming to and going from the Silberner Hirsch. They climb from their machines. They walk about and photograph the valley and the hill peaks. They enter the restaurant. In time, they come from it again. Then they drive away. Their cars are beads on the thread of highway. They have homes, often far distant. Their homes are full of all manner of possessions. They are capable of many kinds of activity. I hear their planes roar overhead, leaving a trail of snow across the sky. People are always busy, like the flies and ants.

This also they can do: procreate. I have mated many times with Elsbeth. She brings forth no child. Here is another thing I cannot understand. Why does Elsbeth not bring forth child? Is the fault in her or in me, because I am strangely made, because, as Rousseau said, "I am made unlike anyone I ever met"?

The grass grows high before my sight. I peer through its little ambush at the scene below. Even the grass makes more grass, and all the small things that live in the grass reproduce their kind, until summer is over. Everything conceives more things, except Elsbeth and I.

Elsbeth remained as usual in our cave beside the waterfall. When the good season is spent and cold bites to the bone, the waterfall dies like most other living things. Its music ceases. It becomes rigid and mute. What is this grief that visits the Earth so regularly? How to explain it?

Only in the spring does the waterfall recover, and then it roars with delight at regaining life, just as I did. Then Elsbeth and I are happy again.

My head becomes cloudy as I lie on my rock peering through the grass at the scene down below. After night has fallen, I will climb down the slopes to walk about unseen round the hotel and retrieve what the People have discarded. I find there something to eat, and many other things, discarded papers and books, this and that. The night is my friend. I am darkness itself.

Why it has to be thus I know not. Yet I have thought myself not to feel discontent. Once I was malicious because I was miserable, but no more. Now I have my lovely mate, I have schooled myself to be neither malicious nor miserable, and not to hate People.

In the discarded newspapers I read that there are People far more evil than ever I was. They take pleasure in killing the innocent. This murder they do not only with their bare hands but with extreme weapons, the nature of which I am unable to comprehend. Thousands die in their wars every year.

Sometimes I read the name of my Maker in the newspapers. Even after all this time, they still speak ill of him; why it does not therefore make me, his victim, welcome among People I do not know. This is something else eluding my understanding.

Lying in my cloudy state, I fall asleep without knowing it. The flies buzz and the sun is hot on my spine.

To dream can be very cruel. I try to tear these visions from myself. In my dreams, memories of dead People rise up. One claims that I have his thighs and legs, another that I have his torso. One wretch wishes his head returned, another even claims his internal organs. These desperate People parade in my sleep. I am a living cemetery, a hospital of flesh for those who lack flesh. What can I do? Within me I feel dreadful ghosts and crimes locked within my bones, knotted into my very entrails. I cannot pass water without a forgotten claimant reaching for what is his.

Do People suffer in this way? Being a mere composite from charnel houses, I fear that I alone undergo this sorrow behind the eyebrows. Residual scenes from dreadful other memories play like lice inside veins I hardly dare look on as mine. I feel myself a theatre of other lives and deaths.

Why then do People shun me? Have I not more humanity than they trapped inside me?

While I suffered from these dreams on my slab of rock, something woke me. I heard the sound of voices carried on the thin air. Two People, females, were climbing upwards. They had left behind the Silberner Hirsch and were moving towards the place where I lay.

I observed them with the silent attention a tiger must give its approaching prey. And yet not that exactly, for there was fear in my heart. The People always awaken fear in me. The elder of these two women was gathering wild flowers, exclaiming as she did so. It was innocent enough, yet still I felt the fear.

The elder female sank down on a tree stump to rest, fanning herself with her hand. The other one came on, picking her way cautiously. I saw the brown hair on the crown of her head, gleaming in the sun with a beauty I cannot describe.

She would have passed me by a few feet, perhaps not noticing me. Yet because I could not bear to lie where I was and chance being seen, I jumped up with a great bound and confronted her.

The female gave a gasp of fear, looking up at me with her mouth open, revealing tongue and white teeth.

"Help!" she called once, until I had my hand over the lower part of her face. The look she gave me changed from fear to disgust.

Oh, I've seen that look on the faces of People before. It always awakens my fury. The faces of People are unlike mine, plastic, mobile, given to expressing emotion. With one blow I could wipe that expression and the flesh that paints it right from their skulls.

As I lifted her, her toes dangled in their white trainers. I thrust my face into hers, that female face dewed with the heat of afternoon. As I considered whether to smash her and throw her down on the mountainside, I caught her scent. It hit me as forcibly as a blow to the stomach.

That scent . . . So different from the scent of Elsbeth . . . It caused a kind of confusion in my brain, making me pause. One of those old elusive memories from the back of my brain returned to baffle me—a memory of something that had never happened to me. I have said I understand little; at that moment I understood nothing, and that terrible lack ran through me like an electric shock. I put her down.

"You monster . . ." the female said, staggering. Beneath us, the descents were toothed with jagged rock. Rather than fall, she clung to my arm—a gesture so trusting in its way as to melt the remains of my anger. I could remember only how vulnerable People were, the females in particular. At that instant, I would have fought a wild beast in order to preserve her unharmed.

As though sensing some abatement of my ferocity, she said in a natural tone, "I did not mean to startle you."

When I could not think how to answer this, unaccustomed as I was to conversing with People, she went on, "Do you speak English? I am just a tourist here on vacation."

Still I could not answer, from her scent and from the look of her. It was as if a little wild doe had come to me, all quivering with a half-mistrust. She was young. Her face was round and open, without scars from medical science. Her grey eyes were set in a brown skin smooth like the shell of a hen's egg. The hair I had watched from above had become disturbed when I lifted her, so that it shaded the line of her left cheek. She wore a T-shirt with the name of an American university printed on it, and denim shorts cut ragged round her plump thighs. Beneath the shirt I saw the outline of her breasts. That outline held so entrancing a meaning that I was further disarmed.

My difficulty in breathing was such that I clutched my throat.

She looked at me with what I took to be concern.

"Say, you okay? My friend's a doctor. Maybe I'll call her to come on up."

"Don't call," I said. I sat down in the long grass, puzzled to understand my weakness. In some elusive way, here before me was the representative of something, some enormous sphere of sensations and transcendent values such as I had only read about, something my Maker had withheld from me which I desperately needed. That I could put no name to it made it all the more tantalising, like a song when only the tune remains and the words are lost by time.

"My friend can help," said this astonishing young person. She turned as if to call but I growled at her again, "Don't call," in so urgent a voice that she desisted. When she looked up the mountainside, as if searching for help there, I realised that she still had fear of me, little knowing the true state of affairs, and felt herself like an animal in a trap.

"But you're ill," she said. "Or else in trouble with the law."

Her remark released my ability to speak to her. "My trouble is with the law of humanity, which rules against me. Law is invented to protect the rulers, not the ruled; the strong, not the weak. No court on Earth is concerned with justice, only the law. The weak can anticipate persecution, not justice."

"But you are not weak," she said.

Her grey eyes when she looked at me made me tremble. When the moon is high, I roam the mountainside much of the night. That dear silver dish in the sky is like an eye, guarding me. But in the grey eyes of this female I read only a kind of concealed hostility.

"Justice is only a name. Persecution and weakness are real enough. Those who for whatsoever reason have no roof over their heads are no better than deer to be hunted down."

My words appeared to make no impression on her. "In my country, there is Welfare to look after the homeless."

"You know nothing."

She did not dispute that, merely standing before me, head bowed, yet sneaking side glances at me and round about.

"Where do you live?" she asked, in a minute.

I jerked my head in the direction of the mountain above us.

"Alone?"

"With my wife. Are you . . . a wife?"

She dismissed the question with a toss of her head.

I listened to the flies buzzing about me and the murmur of the bees in the clover as they tumbled at our feet. These small sounds were the building bricks of the silence that enfolded us.

She stuck out a small brown hand. "I'm not afraid any more. I'm sorry I startled you. Why don't you take me to visit with your wife? What's her name?"

At that, I was silent with mistrust a long time. Her scent reached me as I took the hand gently into mine and looked down at her.

Finally, I spoke the sacred name. "Elsbeth."

She too paused before responding. "Mine's Vicky." She did not ask my name, nor did I offer it.

There we stood on the perilous slope. This encounter had used much of my courage. I had caught her, yet still I feared her. While I contemplated her, she continued to look about with uneasy glances like a trapped animal, and I saw her breasts move with her breathing. Now those honest grey eyes, which I associated with the moon, were furtive and unkind.

"Well then," she said, with an uneasy laugh, "what's keeping us? Let's go."

Perhaps my Maker did not intend that my brain should function perfectly. This little thing whose hand I held could easily be crushed. There was no reason for me to fear it. Yet fear it I did, so greatly did the idea come to me that if I took her up to the cave to meet Elsbeth, she would somehow have trapped me instead of her.

Yet this notion was conquered by a stronger urge I could not deny.

If I led this tender scented female to the cave, she would then be far away from her friend and entirely within my power. We would be private to do that supreme thing, whether she wished for it or not. Elsbeth would understand if I overpowered her and had my way with her. Why should I not? Why else was this morsel, this Vicky, sent to me?

Even at the cost of revealing the whereabouts of the cave to one of the People I must take this specimen there—I must, so great was my urge, thundering in me like the breakers of an ocean. When I was finished with her, I would make sure she did not give our hiding place away. Elsbeth would approve of that. Then our secret life could continue as before, with only the small wild things knowing of our existence.

So thereupon I echoed her words. "Let's go."

The way was steep. She was puny. I kept good hold of her, part-dragging her after me. The afternoon sun blazed on us and her scent rose to me, together with her sobs.

The bushes became smaller, more scanty. I had come this way a hundred times, always varying my route so as to avoid making more of a track than a rabbit might do. We came to the Cleft, a shallow indentation, a fold in the flesh of the mountain. Here the infant waterfall played its tune, gushing with pure water which, several hundred feet down the valley, would become a tributary of the Lotschental river. Behind the fall, hidden by a dark-leaved shrub, was the entrance to the cave.

Here we had to pause. She claimed she must get her breath back. She bent double and stayed that way, and her brown hair hung down, and her little fingertips touched the ground.

Great white clouds rolled above us, tumbling over the mountain summit as if eager to find quieter air. Of a sudden, one of the police helicopters shot overhead, startling me with its enormous clatter, as if the thing were a flying tree, streaking out of sight behind the crisp crest of the Jungfrau. I had no time to hide before it was over and gone.

I grabbed the girl and pulled. "Into the cave with you."

She struggled. "What if Elsbeth doesn't want to see me? Shouldn't you warn her first? Why don't you call her out here?"

Not answering, I dragged her towards the cave. She seized at a bush but I beat her hand away.

"I don't want to see Elsbeth," she screamed. "Help! Help!"

Silencing her with a hand enveloping her face, I half-lifted her and so we entered the cave, the girl struggling furiously.

Elsbeth lay there in the shade, watching everything, saying nothing. I let the girl loose and pushed her towards my wife.

The girl went motionless, staring forward, one hand to her lips. There was no sound but the high buzz of flies. I waited for her to try to scream again, readying myself to leap upon her and bear her down. But when she spoke, it was softly, with her gaze on Elsbeth, not me.

"She's been dead a very long time, hasn't she?"

Some People can cry. I have no facility for tears. Yet as soon as this activity began in Vicky, a storm of weeping—as I judged the sensation—accumulated in my breast like a storm over the Alps. In Elsbeth's eyes no movement showed. The maggots had done their work in those sockets and moved to other pastures.

As I raised my hands above my head and let out a howl, two male people rushed into the cave. They yelled as they came. The weeping girl, Vicky, threw herself out of danger into the recesses of the cave, where I stored the fruits of the autumn. The men flung a net over me.

Wildly though I struggled, using all my strength, the net was unbreakable. The male People drew it tight, as fishermen must have done when they hauled in a catch in olden times. They shackled my legs so that I could not run. Then they felled me, so that I lay by Elsbeth and was as helpless as she.

Those People treated me as if I were no better than an animal. I was dragged out of the cave, through the waterfall, to lie on my back gazing up at the fast-moving clouds in the blue sky, and I thought to myself, Those clouds are free, just as I was until now.

More male People arrived. I found out how they came there

soon enough. One of their helicopters was standing on a level ledge of mountainside above my refuge. The female, Vicky, came to me and bent down so that I could look again into her grey eyes.

"I regret this," she said. "I had to act as decoy. We knew you were somewhere up on the Aletschhorn, but not exactly where. We've been combing this mountainside all week."

My faculty of speech was deserting me along with my other powers. I managed to say, "So you are just an accomplice of these other cruel beasts."

"I am working with the local police, yes. Don't blame me. . . ."

One of the male police nudged her. "Out of the way, miss. He's still dangerous. Stand back there." And she moved away.

I was lifted up and lashed to a stretcher. Her face disappeared from my sight. Still encased in the net, I was dropped on the ground as if I were an old plank. They shouted a great deal, and waved their arms. Only then did I realise they were going to transport me up the mountain. Five male People were there, one of them controlling the other four. They looked down on me. Again those expressions of disgust: I might have been a leopard trapped by big-game hunters, when mercy did not enter into their thoughts.

The male person who ordered the others around had a mouth full of small grey teeth. Staring down, he said, "We're not letting you escape this time, you freak of nature. We have a list of murders stretching back over the last two centuries for which you are responsible."

Though I read no sympathy in his face or mouth, I found a few words to offer. "Sir, I had never an intent to offend. It was my Maker who offended against me, acting so unfatherly against one who never asked to be born in any unnatural way. As for these murders, as you name them, the first one only, that of the child, was done in malice, when I had no knowledge of those states of being which you, not I, can enjoy—to wit, life and death. The rest of my offences were committed in self-defence, when I found the hands of all People were against me. Let me free, I pray. Let me live upon this blessed mountain, in the state of nature and innocence described by Rousseau."

His mouth thinned and elongated like an earthworm. "You shit," he said, turning away.

Another male appeared over the ragged skyline.

"Chopper's ready," he called.

They swung into action. I was lifted up. It took four of them to carry me. I could not see the female but, as I was raised to their shoulders, I caught a glimpse of my happy home, that cave where Elsbeth and I had been so content. Then it was gone, and they laboured up the slope with me, trussed and helpless.

As we approached the helicopter, a shower burst over us, one of those unheralded showers which sweep the Alps. I tasted the blessed rain on my lips, drinking it even while the People complained. I thought, this is the last time I taste of the benisons of nature. I am being taken to the realms of the People, who hate nature as much as they hate me, who am unnatural.

A chill sharpened the flavour of the water. It carried the taint of autumn, that melancholy transition time before winter. Summertime was nearly over, and my wife would lie alone and lonely in our cave, waiting for my return, looking with her sightless eyes for her lover, uttering never a word of complaint.

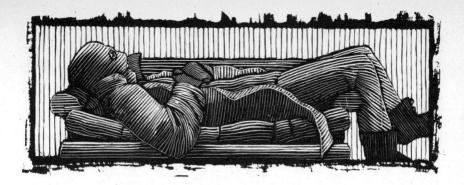

THE CREATURE
ON THE COUCH
▼▼▼

MICHAEL BISHOP

"Would that you were blind, Dr. Zylstra." My patient glared at me with watery yellow eyes, out of a mask that accentuated the heavy shelf of his forehead.

"Why?" I knew, and he knew that I knew, but as committed as I am to racking honesty between patient and therapist, it would have been a misstep to confess aloud at our first meeting that his size and appearance terrified me.

"Do you not mock me, sir, with the transparent dissimulation of bewilderment." Despite its syntax, this remark was not a question, but an archaic variety of command.

"Mr. Goodloss—"

"And do you not interpose the barrier of my surname in a forum that I understand to require friendly self-revelation."

"I usually call my patients by their first names. It's just that it takes longer than thirty seconds to—"

"I am sick unto death of barriers, of the spurnings that have been my recurring, but undeserved, lot."

"Vyvyan," I said, using the odd first name that he had printed in bold block letters on his sign-in sheet: VYVYAN FRANKLIN GOODLOSS. "Vyvyan, it's my task—actually, it's our *joint* task—to examine minutely your feelings of—"

"Rejection. Abandonment. Expulsion. Am I perforce condemned to address you only by title and cognomen?"

"Patients may call me what they like, so long as it's civil. I wouldn't care to answer to, say, Scheisskopf or Dirty Jer."

"I am ignorant of the manner of address most favored by the main body of your clientele. Do you now banish my ignorance."

"Some patients call me Dr. Zylstra. Maybe their low self-esteem resists the idea of equality with a powerful authority figure. Some find ways not to call me anything at all."

Vyvyan, however, wanted to resolve the issue quickly. Waves of hostility piled up in ranks behind this effort, but the effort itself was encouraging: patients who take an active role in the therapeutic process are the most likely to bring about lasting improvement.

"By what name do your friends and intimates call you?"

"Jerrold. More rarely, Jerry. I like my full name better than the nickname."

"Because it erects a small wall of formality and so enables you to preserve a sense of your own dignity?"

"Possibly," I said. Who was treating whom here? Vyvyan, looming over me as he did, had imperceptibly reversed our roles, seizing the initiative of interpretation and relegating me to the dependent state of an emotionally impaired care seeker. Ouch.

Vyvyan nodded brusquely at a gold-plated placard on my desk, an object that had been part of my office decor ever since Barbara gave it to me for our fifth wedding anniversary nearly twenty years ago.

PATIENTHOOD IS UBIQUITOUS, reads the placard.

"Do you disclose to me now, Jerrold, the meaning of that cryptic apothegm."

Vyvyan had a gratingly archaic way of speaking, as if he'd just dropped in from a revival of *Peregrine Pickle: The Play*. And, yes, I felt something more than mild unease in his hulking presence.

"The placard means," I said, reading it for the twelve-millionth time, "that you have every right to call me Jerrold."

"Wherefore that right? From what logic does it spring?"

"Who gets the label 'patient' is often a cultural, educational, and economic thing, Vyvyan, not a clear reflection of the severity of that person's . . . *existence pain*. In some ways, in fact, I may be more 'ill' than those coming to me for therapy."

Vyvyan rolled his nicotine-colored eyes. "Oh! cursed employer, who sent me to this forthright charlatan!"

"If you have a problem—" How could anyone who looked and spoke like this huge burlesque of a human being *not* have a problem?—"my job isn't to wave a wand and make it go magically away."

"Am I, then, to remain wretched?"

"Wait. Listen. My job is to use my skills to build between us a relationship that will prove therapeutic. It's the *relationship* that heals, Vyvyan. If you work *with* me, you'll face your existence pain in ways that counteract your . . . wretchedness."

"Excellent."

"Good," I said. "What do you want?"

▼▼▼

This was neither a casual nor a facetious question. With Vyvyan, it wasn't even a cloaked expression of the annoyance I felt at having to be in my office long after my posted hours—at eight o'clock on a late November evening when traffic on North Peachtree was sparse and the wind slicing down from the Great Smokies was audibly rattling my office building's polarized window glass.

What do you want? is my standard ice breaker. I ask it so that my patients will jettison all the nonessential garbage they've taken aboard and examine face-on the real conflicts poisoning their lives. Everyone wants something—something beyond a Mercedes-Benz, twenty uninterrupted years of fame, or great nonstop sex—and the honest identification of this want is the beginning of wisdom. It's also the beginning of a long climb toward health. Was I healthy enough to provide Vyvyan any meaningful help on *his* climb?

I ask because sitting in the same room with him underscored the hard truth of the legend of my placard: PATIENTHOOD IS UBIQUITOUS. Ordinarily, I'm not frightened of my patients. They may fascinate, repulse, exasperate, amuse, bore, worry, discombobulate, or charm me. (In the case of pneumatic females, as I've confessed to Barbara, they may even excite my libido.) But only once or twice in my career have I met with a patient who made me fear for my safety. Even the psychotics who came to me did so nonmenacingly, seeing me as a paid compassionator and a validating agent, not as a potentially vengeful judge. Thus, I escaped any hostile acting out of their psychoses.

But I *was* afraid of this Goodloss person.

My fear had two sources. First, as stipulated during some tricky negotiations with Vyvyan's employer (a friend of my father-in-law), I was meeting him at night, in a virtually empty office building. The security guard in the downstairs lobby would be of no help if Vyvyan attacked me in my sixth-floor suite. Second, Vyvyan was the biggest man I'd ever seen, bigger than the professional wrestler Andre the Giant. He stood at least eight feet tall. Even sitting, as he sat now in my overwhelmed office chair, he towered.

(Why was Vyvyan worried about what to call me? He could call me, with total impunity, whatever he wanted to.)

Vyvyan's dress did nothing to render him less scary. A beige burn mask (or a tight elastic hood designed to suggest a burn mask) covered his enormous head. His eyes were visible through the mask's eyeholes; they were too small for his head, as glassy-yellow as an alley cat's, and so phlegmy that their continuous discharge had left umber-orange tear tracks on either side of his monstrous nose. His lips showed through an oblong cutout like a pair of helically twisted wisps of licorice, black and oddly glossy.

The tightness of Vyvyan's mask gave me a pretty good idea of the basic shape of his features, which all seemed preternaturally lumpy and swollen. His brow and jaw had such prominence that I wondered if he were suffering, as Abraham Lincoln reputedly had, from acromegaly, the abnormal enlargement of one's face, feet, and hands.

Vyvyan's hands were big enough to support this speculation, but he kept them gloved. Or, rather, mittened. Wool mittens (featuring pine trees and silver sleighbells on a ground of snowy white) like Barbara and I had bought our grandkids last winter. Only their size told against them. Along with the mittens, Vyvyan wore vast denim overalls, a blue-plaid flannel shirt, ebony galoshes with unfastened hasps, and a cream-colored duster such as a cowboy or the driver of an old-time car might have worn. The duster added to, rather than disguised, his bulk.

So I was afraid. Vyvyan could have strangled me or thrown me through a gently quaking pane of glass, and no one would have found my body for hours. Barbara was probably already in bed. Her TV work required a demoralizingly early alarm.

How had I gotten myself into this hazardous fix?

Barbara's father, William Yost, had referred Vyvyan to me, but he had done so through Vyvyan's employer, Van Foxworth, the president of a Norcross-based warehousing firm called Car-goCo Unlimited. Vyvyan worked virtually around the clock at a CargoCo storage facility as a stacker and night watchman. In fact, according to my father-in-law, he lived in a room outfitted for him inside this immense, corrugated metal building by Mr. Foxworth himself. He took all his meals in this room, so he'd never have to go out, and ate a strict vegetarian diet. Van Foxworth's nephew, Vinny Fall, delivered his meals via a pass-through from a junk-filled attached office.

The Phantom of the Warehouse, I thought. Apparently, Vyvyan had arrived at this reclusive life style shortly after joining CargoCo in the mid-1970s. Only this kind of thoroughgoing isolation had enabled him to work at all, and now, viewing Mr. Foxworth as his sole friend and benefactor, he insisted on the arrangement.

Of late, though, Vinny Fall had sometimes heard a fearful howling from the warehouse. Several late-night passers-by had also heard it, and the only possible source of the howling was Vyvyan, who, it had become clear, was suffering. On Mr. Foxworth's command, then, Vyvyan had come to me for help.

▼▼▼

"I wish to be as others are," he said. "And I wish to have some salvific distinction in my new-found conformity."

▼▼▼

That first Thursday night, we felt our way with each other. He told me what he wanted, with no bet-hedging, and I guess he told the truth. I purposely refrained from raising subjects that would plunge him too deep too soon, or suggest that I was in a hurry to conclude and go home to bed. But it didn't seem wrong to ask him point-blank if he were comfortable or to remark on his mask. His comment, "Would that you were blind, Dr. Zylstra," seemed to entitle me.

"Aren't you warm, Vyvyan?"

"Extremes of temperature affect me far less violently than they do the ordinary—the general—run of men."

"Big men usually sweat more than smaller ones." I said this in a bantering way, leaning back in my chair.

"The perspiration drops on your countenance would seem to belie that doubtful observation, Jerrold."

I wiped my face with a handkerchief. "How'd you burn yourself?"

"I beg your pardon."

"The burn mask. Was there an occupational fire? Or were you in a vehicle that rolled and burst into flame?"

"I am physically uninjured. I confess to you that I wear my hood not for any wonderful medical purpose but for concealment."

"Can't you face me without a mask? Doesn't it, uh, *interpose* a barrier to therapeutic intimacy?" I fisted my handkerchief.

"You are unready for the shock that would attend my unmasking."

"I'm a tough guy. I can take it." What was he trying to tell me? That he resembled the Elephant Man? That he was an AIDS patient with repulsive lesions? That his hood concealed a mangled armature of bone? True, I'd never seen a man his size before, but I doubted that any deformity he had would render me a gibbering loon.

As if mocking me, Vyvyan said, " 'Tough guys'—doctors of heart and fortitude—do not tremble before their patients."

I *was* trembling. Fear had laid siege to me. "I don't know about that," I said. "All I know is that tough guys—working patients—don't run from what they must face. Your hood has to come off, if not tonight then next week."

Vyvyan's phlegmy yellow eyes examined my office. "Do not famous physicians of your speciality treat a patient's existence pain while the sufferer reclines on a . . . a divan?"

"A divan? Oh, you mean a couch."

"I bow to your greater knowledge."

"Freudians like that arrangement—therapist upright in a chair, patient down on the couch. I don't like it. It creates a hierarchic division on the basis of one's position in space. Up or down. High or low. And I'm no Freudian, Vyvyan."

"Do you not presently enforce a similar hierarchic division with the barricade of this desk?" He laid a mitten on it.

"I—" But Vyvyan's observation was on target. I do sometimes hide behind, or draw authority from, my desk. "Do you want me to sit facing you without its protection? If you do, I will."

"What I instead propose is that you import for our next session a div——I mean, of course, a *couch*—for me to lie upon."

"But why? I thought—"

"To create a hierarchic division between us that will purge you of feelings of physical inferiority and thus of fear. Maskless, I would dispose myself on it so as to spare you the troublesome sight of my face."

So he planned to take off his hood. That was progress. He also had a care for *my* psychic health. Patients who concern themselves on first visit with the therapist's emotional well-being are as rare as debutantes in a soup kitchen.

Vyvyan rose. My ceiling made him stoop. He withdrew a paperback book from a pocket on his duster, his mittened hand engulfing it, and placed the book on my desk. I picked it up. It was the first Signet Classic edition of *Frankenstein*, printed in December, 1965, with a childlike cover painting of a blurry goblinesque beast running toward the reader from a copse of moon-entangled trees. The cover's spooky blueness, and the goblin's stick-figure frailty, sent a zigzagging chill down my spine.

"That is my story," he said. "The true history of my career as an animate being—until my long sleep and my second coming."

"This," I said firmly, "is a novel."

"Nay, it is Mrs. Shelley's transcription of a narrative set down in the late seventeen hundreds by a British merchant seaman,

Captain Robert Walton. Do you the needful and read it front to back before we talk again." Vyvyan turned toward my door.

"Wait." (But what to say?) "Do you need money for a cab?"

"Oh, I have fare. I husband nearly every penny I earn. But no conveyance will stop for me, especially at night, and so I must go speedily and stealthily afoot to my warehouse apartment. Fare thee well, Jerrold, until our reunion, Thursday week."

▼▼▼

I had encountered a delusional schizophrenic with the grandiose conviction that he was the monster forged in the Gothic imagination of Mary Wollstonecraft Shelley under the hands of that archetypal mad scientist, Victor Frankenstein.

Some delusional schizophrenics believe they are Jesus Christ, or Joan of Arc, or even Vladimir Lenin in silk and nylon drag. One of my most confused patients insisted that she was Imelda Marcos. I put her on medication, and she soon improved, moving from being Imelda to being Imelda's sister, then Imelda's hairdresser, then a Philippine woman with a shoe fetish, and finally herself.

Vyvyan's delusion withstood the medication on which I placed him that first week. (Vinny Fall filled the prescription and dropped it off for him at the warehouse.) I didn't know if I had prescribed an inadequate dosage for his body mass, or if he had incorporated the delusion so early in life, at such a basic psychosomatic level, that he had *become* what he believed.

Even I was confused. On the night he laid the book on my desk, I had to admit that Vyvyan had all the most telling physical attributes of the manmade giant in Mrs. Shelley's "transcription." Either I must believe that he was in fact this creature, or I must assume that his physique—a coincidence arranged by a whimsical Creator?—had convinced him of his utter identity with it.

The names Vyvyan and Franklin, I saw, were obvious stand-ins for Victor and Frankenstein. But Goodloss mystified me. Was it his real family name or a sardonic one-word gloss on the spiritual serenity of which his appearance had deprived him?

Between our next session, then, I reread *Frankenstein*. I also ordered a couch—a huge leather chaise lounge with a plump headrest and mechanisms for raising and lowering its main cushion. To make room for it, I had my desk moved against one wall and my rubber-tree plant carted into the waiting room.

Vyvyan liked the couch. It wasn't long enough for him to lie on without placing the soles of his galoshes on the rug and crooking his knees upward, but this strange posture didn't seem to annoy or cramp him. And getting his head below mine *did* reduce my unease.

"The burn mask," I said.

He slipped it off. Sitting behind him, I could see only a dense curtain of greasy hair, its blackness like record vinyl and the veins of frost within it like scratches. The head was a phrenologist's wet dream, an oblate globe of bumps and declivities and ridges.

"I should look at you. Otherwise, your gesture means nothing."

"No. Refrain. It was no accident that you sat behind me. Begin you now my therapy. We have a tortuous path to traverse."

I let him have his way. *Frankenstein* in hand, I began asking questions, and we devoted the session to a detailed reconstruction of Vyvyan's life from the last paragraph of the "novel" to his arrival in Atlanta in the early 1970s and his employment by CargoCo Unlimited in May, 1975. A century and a half in hibernation, in an ice cave on the shore of a Norwegian island just within the Arctic Circle, account for the greatest span of this time. Then, a lightning storm awoke him. I could recount his alleged post-hibernation travels, including episodes in the American Northwest when startled trappers or wildlife photographers mistook him for a bigfoot, or his harrowing adventures in the Sun Belt states, where concealment was even harder—but all that he said simply reinforced the Frankenstein delusion.

"Vyvyan, your story suggests that you've bought into a myth that negates your personhood. It relieves you of the need to take charge of your own life."

"Is the hour allotted to my therapy nearly spent?"

I checked my watch. "Yeah, I'm afraid it is."

"Do you ready yourself, then, to behold the visage that descends from and mercilessly drives this 'myth'!"

Vyvyan reared up from the couch. Straddling it backwards in an awkward stoop, he looked straight down into my eyes. I gaped. His eyes I'd already seen, but his naked face was a horror. His flesh was tissue-thin. The muscles, veins, ligaments, and bones under it shone through the mottled tissue like props behind a theater scrim. They all seemed to be ceaselessly moving. Equally alarming, Vyvyan's complexion was hideously pied. His chin was the color of uncooked liver. His lips were a moist black; his cheeks either a dull gray or the pale, pebbly yellow of chicken flesh. It was a face seemingly assembled from transparent lumps of feces-toned, blood-perfused, and fat-slimed Play-Doh. One Victor Frankenstein had conducted an insane scavenger hunt to find the needed parts. Vyvyan's head, presumably like the remainder of his body, was the three-dimensional anatomical equivalent of a jigsaw puzzle; a biological hodgepodge.

I made a bleak noise and glanced away.

"I am the very wretch whom I do swear to be. Do you believe me? Do you acknowledge aught that I have told you?"

"Yes," I said, eyes averted: the only word I could get out.

"Then you must counsel me as that weak-souled man's progeny, not merely as the helpless victim of a crude delusion. Do you agree?"

"Yes," I said.

Vyvyan Franklin Goodloss barked, "Good," and left. Huddled

there with my eyes shut, I imagined him slipping with a linebacker's grace through the city's tinsel-hung side streets, an ungainly and archaic shadow against Atlanta's shimmering yuletide glitz.

▼▼▼

I dealt with Vyvyan from that session onward as if he were who he claimed to be. Heal his assumed identity (I rationalized, pretending to listen to a patient during regular office hours or lying beside my sleeping wife), and *then* you can destroy his grandiose masquerade and heal the obsessed pretender.

I hate lies. I hate false solutions. But with Vyvyan, I decided that indulging his foremost self-deception was the only way to pursue his therapy successfully.

▼▼▼

"You're a murderer," I said at the outset of our third session, grateful that he hadn't removed his hood until lying down.

"I have never—" he began vehemently. Then a note of pleasure crept into his rumbling voice: "Yes."

"You started to deny it."

"Nay. What I had intended to deny was that I have injured anyone in my post-resurrection persona."

"But Mrs. Shelley's *Frankenstein* accuses you of murdering three people. It implicates you in the death of two others."

"Yes." I could *hear* the pleasure in this admission.

"So you're a murderer, Vyvyan. Why does that amuse you?"

He sobered. "I am not entertained by the memory. It was indeed I who committed those crimes, but an 'I' deformed toward a fiendish malignity by the one who spurned and betrayed me. In that pitiable incarnation, I killed for revenge. I am no longer that self."

"Revenge is a great motive, but a lousy justification."

"How to frame this?" said Vyvyan, lifting a mittened hand.

"I deplore the deaths effected in the unhappy dawn of my being, but one must own that it was a *phase* that I had to pursue to a cathartic end."

"Vyvyan," I rebuked him.

"I was good, but my creator and a small-minded contingent of his fellows—*your* fellows, Jerrold—made me bad."

"You aren't taking responsibility for—"

"Nay, my God-envying father never shouldered the responsibility for *me*! On the one occasion he strove to lighten my lot—not from any native altruism, but in the hope that I would absent myself from Europe and trouble him no more—he tore apart the beastly Eve that he was creating for my solace. Speak not of *my* culpability! Despise the failed Monster Builder of Ingolstadt for his!"

Vyvyan sobbed deep in his barrel-like chest. For reassurance, I touched the pistol under my jacket. Still, I had no confidence that if his hatred of his father, and of humanity in general, provoked an attack on me, mere bullets would turn or even slow him.

"For months, he labored over me," Vyvyan raged. "For weeks, he perforce gazed down on my pied and uncomely countenance. How did it happen that only *after* the primordial life force racked my frame and kindled a rheumy vision in my eyes, this master scientist—this Promethean genius—saw in me a contemptible monstrosity? Had he labored on me blind? Had he reasoned that, upon awakening, I would plastically transform myself into a voluptuous Cleopatra? Had he, in spite of his Daedalian skills and the overweening ambition of a Roman general, the brain of a pismire and the imagination of a blowfly? Do you now apply yourself to these questions! Do you now confess that I am the unfortunate handiwork of a megalomaniacal halfwit!"

We got little further that night than this denunciation of Victor Frankenstein. If I acknowledged that Vyvyan was the unnatural child of the Swiss chemist (which I did), then I could see the justice of his heartfelt tirade.

I tried to find ore in another vein: "Vyvyan, tell me about your name. Isn't it a variety of falsehood?"

"Falsehood?"

"I mean, it isn't really your name. It's an invention, a game you've played with your creator's initials and also your day-to-day struggle with existence pain."

"Forgive me my presumptuousness, but *every name is an invention.* Where I part with the general run of humanity is in the demoralizing circumstance that no parent bestowed mine. I had, myself, to invent it. Therefore, I do not regard it as either temporary or deceitful. It is my name as surely, perhaps more surely, as Jerrold Zylstra is yours, for I freely fashioned and self-bestowed it."

"All right. I see."

"Vyvyan means 'living.' Franklin magnanimously honors the father who denied me. Would you prefer me to answer to perjorative epithets like 'monster,' 'fiend,' or 'demon'?"

"Of course not. And Goodloss? Does it reflect the existential irony that I at first supposed?"

"Perhaps. It additionally means that Mary Wollstonecraft Shelley is my sister. . . ."

▼▼▼

Why had Vyvyan taken to howling in the cavernous solitude of the CargoCo warehouse? After all, if not for this howling, he would not have become my patient.

"I did not realize that this behavior had commenced," he said. "I howled utterly heedless that I was thus sorrowfully engaged."

"As someone might absent-mindedly hum?"

"As someone, contemplating suicide, might breathe."

"Why this year, Vyvyan? Why not last year? Or five years ago? or ten? Or five years from now?"

"How am I to answer you? The predictability of the onset of an acute psychological disorder, I conceive, falls below that of either earthquakes or solar eclipses."

"And so you're here."

"And so, Jerrold, I am here."

▼▼▼

Barbara, a petite woman with an early-morning interview show on our local ABC affiliate, began to resent my Thursday evening sessions with Vyvyan. By the final week in January, I had met with him eight times. The contract drawn up with Mr. Foxworth stipulated that his treatment would run six months; however, he was the only patient with whom I had ever agreed to met after my posted office hours.

My wife regarded these lost evenings as "stolen." Thursday had traditionally been the night on which we met with three other couples for bridge and middle-aged chitchat. It also upset her that V.F.—as I referred to Vyvyan at home, to preserve the confidentiality of his case—was apparently a big man with a hot temper, a heavy vein of bitterness, and a history of violent acts. In Barbara, annoyance and concern alternated in strobelike flashes. I stood frozen by the annoyance and blinking before the concern.

"Can't you switch the sessions to another night?"

"Which one, Barb? I won't do it on the weekend, when conferences sometimes arise. Every other evening's taken. Mondays, I've got Mental Health League meetings. Tuesdays, I chair our fund raiser for the History Center. Wednesdays, you always—"

"Stop. I get the picture." And so Barbara would change tacks: "What if this loony V.F. person goes off his nut and—"

"He won't. And if he does, I have this." I showed her my pistol in its compact little shoulder holster.

"How creatively macho. Come on, Jerry, do you really think that calms my fears? Can't you get out of this? Can't you at least make room for poor old V.F. during regular office hours?"

"Barb, this is a favor for Van Foxworth, your daddy's long-time friend and associate. It was Dear Bill who got me into this."

Barbara looked at the ceiling through her bangs. "Thanks, Dad," she said. She put a hand on my chest. "But you're having fun with it, aren't you? *Aren't you?*"

"It has to be one of the most interesting cases I've ever had," I conceded. "And I may be doing some good."

"You'd better be," Barbara said.

▼▼▼

"You want to be as others are," I said during our final January session. "And you want there to be something distinctive about you even as you sink into the American melting pot?"

"Yes."

"Your height?" (I did not say, although I thought it, *Your pied and misshapen face?*)

"Nay, Jerrold. My height estranges. Or else it elicits, on the part of some, a mercenary ulteriority."

"Yeah," I said. "You could probably play basketball. The Hawks would pay you big-time just to ride the bench as a backup center."

I wasn't trying to be funny. Vyvyvan had a raw athleticism that even his clownish wardrobe couldn't disguise. In *Frankenstein*, he had effortlessly scaled the face of Mont Saleve. And the Atlanta Hawks had once dropped a multimillion-dollar contract on a beanpole center averaging less than six points a game.

Vyvyana, who had a TV set in his warehouse room, began to laugh rumblingly. "What meaning does basketball impart to the quotidian rounds of our lives? What meaning *can* it impart?"

"For some, it's a living. A damned good one."

"Passing a ball through an elevated ring set on the horizontal at a predetermined height—"

"Yeah. Ten feet."

"—to produce a score that, if larger than one's competitor's, affords an excuse for noisy self-congratulation."

"Others join in, throwing money, confetti, silk undies. Meaning ensues from the activities to which we attribute meaning."

Vyvyan paused before asking, "Attribute your meaning to dreams?"

"Sure, I think dreams *mean*. They shed light on the details, if not always the causes, of all our waking anxieties."

So Vyvyan told me a dream he'd had some time ago: "By myself, I am a basketball team in an ebony uniform, with a mourning band around my left arm. Several players as bothersome as midges swarm about me in uniforms of many colors— my opponents. The vast arena is shot through with a blinding lambency, and I move within this heavy light like one struggling to swim in the sanctuary of a drowned cathedral.

"A zigzag of lightning cleaves the arena, divesting the golden light of its terrible weight. This is the signal for the contest to begin. I 'control,' as a sportscaster in the great hall sepulchrally announces, the opening tip-off, but am unable to bounce the ball on the floor without a midgelike opponent effecting a theft and fleeing from me. This galling pattern recurs and recurs.

"The large vertical squares to which each 'basket' is attached— backboards, affirms the sportscaster—are mirrors. I am the only player in the arena who can see his face in these opposing mirrors when I trot, ever more frustrated, toward the one goal or the other. I am odious even to myself, and the invisible spectators in the arena are audibly celebrating my frustration.

"At last, however, I secure the ball. I do not try to advance by the legal method of 'dribbling.' Rather, I march toward my goal with the ball held undislodgeably under my arm. The mites who attempt to interfere with my march I hurl from me as a bear flings the yelping dogs of a hunting pack. The arena quiets. I am under my goal."

"Go ahead," I urged Vyvyan.

He released a breath. "I am surrounded by flailing defenders. I lift the ball over my head and spring from the floor so that my upper body ripples in the mirror of the backboard. I perform with exultant savoir-faire a maneuver known to basketball enthusiasts as a 'gorilla dunk.' The backboard disintegrates. A myriad shards, each no larger than a sand grain, cascade down. I tower in ruins of my own making, glittery diamonds on my head and shoulders."

"Wow," I said.

"My dream had an epilogue. The arena experienced darkness. When the lights returned, I again had the ball, but now I faced the other basket. Arrayed against me was a team of only five players, each in gold, each of a stature akin to my own. I began with difficulty to 'dribble' the ball through their tenacious defense. Meanwhile, the arena's spectators jeered my efforts, but with cat-calls more jocular than malign." He paused again. "There the epilogue concluded."

I said nothing. The dream, at least in tanden with its epilogue, limned a subconscious adjustment that deserved praise. My nape hairs were standing erect. My knuckles were tingling. On the other hand, to analyze the dream for Vyvyan would've been to interdict the chance of self-discovery. I sat silent, waiting.

"Have you no oneiromantic exegesis?"

"What about you, Vyvyan? Don't you have one?"

"I understand my dream, but its meaning comes from the projected symbology rather than from any latent import in the game itself. I still have no wish to achieve my identity as an Atlanta Hawk."

"Good for you," I said. We laughed together.

▼▼▼

"Vyvyan, are you afraid of dying?"

"I am afraid of *not* dying."

"Come again."

"I may not have the capacity to pass from sentience to oblivion."

"You think you're immortal?"

"That is my nightmare. It has often stayed my hand when I moved, in either weariness or despair, to destroy myself."

"Your resist killing yourself because you don't think you'll be able to? You've lost me."

"My nightmare is that I am *incapable* of dying. Who knows by what arcane methodology my father infused me with the life force? Perhaps I cannot die. Perhaps I can only mutilate or fragment myself, to the devastating end that whatever of me remains, greatly injured or even unrecognizably atomized, continues to throb and feel."

"God."

"I no longer postulate Him."

▼▼▼

"What about plastic surgery?"

"Who would perform it?"

"Height reduction through spinal excisions or the removal of leg-bone segments?"

"Again, who would perform these procedures?"

"Then you'll have to face the world as you are and forgive it for beating up on you."

"As you do."

"As I do. 'Patienthood is ubiquitous.' "

"If only the world would accommodate itself to me as I am."

"A child's wish, Vyvyan."

"I am so much more than a child that the wish acquires the force of an apostolic bull."

"That way lies delusion or disappointment."

"I am not for myself the source of that which confers meaning. I was, however, such a source for Victor Frankenstein."

"Come again."

"The paradox of my life is that my father found his existential ground in the quest to create me. When I turned out something other than he had fatuously anticipated, he rediscovered this ground in a campaign to thwart and undo me. In at least two ways, then, I gave his life meaning, while he thoughtlessly withheld from me that same indispensable quality. Cursed, cursed creator! Why do I live?"

I waited almost a minute before speaking. "Let me play devil's advocate, Vyvyan. Is Van Foxworth, your employer, any better than Victor Frankenstein, your creator?"

"Mr. Foxworth has not rejected me."

"Isn't he perhaps exploiting you? You're doing the work of three or four people, and he's paying you not much more than minimum wage."

"I am impervious to the peculiar allure of money."

"Are you impervious to the truth that a person may do the right, or the nearly right, for the wrong reasons?"

"I am sensible of the truth that Mr. Foxworth, who has gazed upon my unmasked countenance without rushing to take up a stick, has given me the means to live in a system hostile to the ill-favored."

"By sequestering you in CargoCo's big tin warehouse?"

"What more should he have done? Sought out a professor of the affections to counsel with me?"

"Touché," I said. "A moment ago you asked, 'Why do I live?' It seems—sorry if this seems simplistic—that you live to work."

"And so do you."

"Of course," I said. "Who would want it otherwise?"

▼▼▼

"When did you let your patients start piloting a couch again?" asked Barbara, who was visiting during my lunch break.

I was typing up notes from a session that had run long and eating at my desk: a pastrami-on-rye sandwich, a cup of decaffeinated mint tea, and a blueberry yogurt for dessert.

"That? Oh, that's for V.F. And any other patient who feels more comfortable lying down than sitting in a chair."

"Well," Barbara said, "it looks like an aircraft carrier."

"V.F.'s a big fella."

"So you've said. But that must've set you back plenty."

"CargoCo's paying for it. And even if they weren't, it'd be just another tax-deductible office expense."

Barbara put her handbag, a Judith Leiber black karung model that had cost more than the chaise lounge, on the floor, kicked off her high heels, and lay down on the couch.

Sighing, she linked her fingers behind her head and pointed her girlish toes at me. Her legs in their scabbards of coffee-colored nylon were enticing, but I was busy. Because of one overlong morning interview, I'd be fighting all day to catch up.

"Didn't you renounce the couch as part of your methodology?"

"V.F.'s a special case."

"You don't like their stereotypical implications. I don't like their, well, their *extracurricular* implications."

"You didn't always feel that way, Barb."

"We weren't married when I didn't feel that way." She let her nylons whisper together. "Odd that after all this time you should go back on such a crucial promise."

I spooned a last bite from the plastic yogurt cup. "Blame V.F. Blame Foxworth. Blame your father. Or don't blame anyone. It's a *couch*, a piece of furniture. It's entirely innocent."

"It wasn't the couch's innocence I was worried about."

Vanessa Frye, my secretary, buzzed to ask if I were ready to see my next patient. I said yes.

I went to the couch and kissed Barbara on the nose. "I'll see you this evening, okay?"

"No, you probably won't. It's Thursday, Jerry." She swung her legs toward me, put on her shoes, grabbed her karung bag. "Give my regards, when you see him, to the 'ill-favored' V.F. 'Bye."

She nodded at Mr. Myron as he entered. I took some satisfaction from the fact that he was an elderly man trying to sort out both his guilt and his grief after surviving a car accident that had killed his wife. The attractive woman scheduled after Mr. Myron, after all, would have intensified Barbara's sense of unease.

▼▼▼

"Female companionship," I said. "You asked Frankenstein for a woman, a distaff being, with whom to share a South American exile."

"A promise on which he tardily but brutally reneged. Thus were kindled the avenging fires of my outrage."

"He destroyed your woman. You destroyed his friend. Later, you destroyed his woman as well."

"Long ago," Vyvyan said. "Long ago."

"Don't you still wish for . . . female companionship?"

Vyvyan waved a mitten. "That my father spitefully desolated my Eve before bestowing upon her the quickening force no longer strikes me as an altogether horrid act."

"No? Why not?"

"Because the universe is so made, and each of us within it is so made, that the basic state of each living creature is aloneness. The chasms between persons resist bridging. We may do no more by way of defective consolation than shout at one another. This, in my second coming, I belatedly understand."

"I once had another patient who reached the same conclusion. But he added, 'I may be alone in my boat, but it's always comforting to see the lights of the other boats bobbing nearby.' "

"Very pretty. But a comfort I have seldom been given to know."

"You no longer even *wish* for female companionship? For sensual contact? For sex?"

Vyvyan laughed. "Do you forgive me my boorish inquiry, but what would you have me do, seek out and unconscionably violate a yeti?" He chuckled again, a brief morose rumble.

"Forgive *my* boorish inquiry, but are you still a, a virgin?"

Vyvyan levered himself up and turned around, his ghastly features disclosed like the rainbow-colored butt of a baboon. His alley-cat's eyes flickered, his lips writhed sneeringly.

"I do not rise to lures meretriciously designed to accommodate the voyeur casting them."

I felt pinned to my chair, assaulted. I looked away. "Vyvyan, it isn't wrong—it's standard procedure—to discuss the intimate circumstances of your life with your therapist. Otherwise—"

"Otherwise, we might prove ourselves accidental observers of a civility no longer in fashion. Nay, I have already surrendered to a barbarous modernity on far too many fronts. Spare me, importunate man, this additional shame!"

I couldn't stop him. He banged out of my office with his mask dangling from one hand. As if lame, I followed. He was already in the stairwell. My watch said sixteen minutes remained in our hour. Mr. Foxworth would see to it that I was paid for these minutes, but I still felt cheated.

▼▼▼

At noon one week later, Vyvyan telephoned my office to report that he had had a small accident. Nessa Frye, my secretary, patched the call through to me, and Vyvyan said that a crate in a precarious stack of crates had toppled onto his foot, breaking every bone in his left little toe. He spoke in a disturbingly wheezy tone:

"My foot is bound in plaster, and I am unable to locomote without the support of a crutch. Therefore—"

"Vyvyan, I'll come get you." He didn't want to meet with me.

"Nay. I suffer also from a severe catarrh. Thoracic congestion, nasal inflamation—"

Nastily runny eyes, I thought.

"—and a debilitating febricity. I must cancel our appointment this evening and take time to mend."

"Vyvyan, what if I came to you?"

"Get you home to your fair and angelic wife. I am unfit company for the well." Abruptly, he rang off.

I buzzed my outer office. "Nessa, come in here, please."

At my desk, I worried the unspoken burden of Vyvyan's call. It was a subterfuge, I thought. He was still angry with me for pressing him on matters that his eighteenth-century sense of punctilio viewed as outside the therapeutic province. I was in danger of losing him. His final words, "I am not worthy company for the well," seemed to me ominously two-edged, as if he'd overcome the awful conviction that he *couldn't* die. This was a crisis requiring an unorthodox response. I looked up to find Vanessa Frye looking down.

"That was Mr. Goodloss, a patient psychologically *in extremis.*"

"Yes, sir." Nessa is a dark-haired, unmarried woman in her early twenties, a weekend student at Georgia State, a psychology major with an intense desire to become a therapist. Her legs, sheathed in *café au lait* patterned stockings, reminded me of Barbara's.

"Mr. Goodloss and I have reached a critical turning point. What he needs, Nessa, is validation for someone other than me or his employer, Mr. Foxworth. He needs to know that an attractive woman—you, for instance—can tolerate, possibly even admire, him."

"I don't think I'm following you, Dr. Zylstra."

"Mr. Goodloss can't make our session this evening, but I'm going to show him the depth of my concern by going to him. The mountain to Mohammed, so to speak. I'd like you to go with me."

Without hesitation, Nessa said, "I have a date tonight, but I'll call Jack and reschedule. This is more important."

"Bless you. Let me bring you up to speed."

Nessa had started working for me in early November, a week before Barbara's father and Mr. Foxworth had petitioned me to take Vyvyan on as a special after-hours client, almost as a human-itarian experiment. She knew that I'd been seeing Vyvyan. She'd read the transcriptions of a couple of our interviews, and she understood that looking at him without his mask would demand courage, self-control, and compassion. A faithful employee and a brilliant psychology student, Nessa agreed, altogether selflessly, to help me.

▼▼▼

In my gun-metal-blue Buick Reatta, we arrived in the gravel lot of CargoCo Unlimited shortly before eight o'clock. It was dark and cold, with a shrill February wind sweeping down upon and popping the corrugated tin panels of the stingily spotlighted ware-house. Nessa and I ducked into the attached entry shed—Vinny Fall had dropped a key by my office after a direct telephone request of his uncle—and made our way to both the door and the pass-through window to Vyvyan's private room. Rats, or gecko-sized cockroaches, scuttled among the shed's paint-gummed cans and cobwebbed cable spools.

"Vyvyan!" I shouted. "I've come for our session! Let me in!"

Although a little slow to respond, Vyvyan tocked the panel on the pass-through aside. A mottled cheek, and a lavender-gray ear like an *al dente* leaf of boiled cabbage, appeared there.

"Why do you not respect my incapacity? Why am I not permitted to withdraw recuperatively?"

"Because I care," I said. "Let me in."

To Nessa, I whispered: "Give me a couple of minutes to get him ready. I'll leave the door cracked. Step in when I whistle."

Vyvyan, hobbling on a single crutch, admitted me. The cubicle was dominated by a pond-sized quilt-strewn bed; an entertainment center from whose CD player came the muted strains of a Franz Lizst program symphony, possibly *Faust*; and wall-to-wall, ceiling-high shelves of paperbound books. Vyvyan's aluminum crutch, I noticed, was as tall as I am.

"*What?*" he barked, uncharacteristically brusque. Well, he hadn't lied. He had both an injured foot and a cold. The protective cast confirmed his broken toe bones; the bluish tinge to the puffy planes of his face, his "catarrh."

"Who put your foot in the cast?"

"A physician brought here by Mr. Foxworth. I wore my mask and lay back pacifically on my bed."

I nodded stupidly. What to say? I said, "Hey, I've been trying to think of jobs that would give you the same freedom from rejection as your CargoCo job, but more personal fulfillment."

Vyvyan gestured me to a bench against one wall, a kind of reading ledge, and collapsed like a demolished building onto his bed.

"Listen." I took a list from my pocket: "Computer programmer. Forest-fire spotter. Coyote trapper. Accountant or tax preparer. Voice-over narrator for films, TV documentaries, and product ads. Copy editor. Rural mail carrier. Telephone operator in a backward one-board town. Baseball statistician. A painter of still lifes. A poet. Or maybe an on-site meterologist in, say, the Antarctic, Orkneys, or like that. What do you think?"

Vyvyan grunted skeptically.

"There *are* options," I said.

But the truth was that his position with CargoCo, in an isolated semirural warehouse, was just about the perfect job for a humanoid being of his sensibilities and threatening looks. Without submitting to painful plastic surgery and height-reduction procedures, he might *never* find a satisfying level of acceptance in late-twentieth-century America.

"Word processing?" I said. "Radio announcing?"

"Activity is a hollow source of meaning," Vyvyan said, "without a complementary share of a direct affection."

That seemed an appropriate cue. I gave a sharp, mocking-birdlike whistle. Nessa came into Vyvyan's room and sat unflinchingly beside me on the reading ledge.

Vyvyan shot me a fierce look of astonishment and betrayal, then rolled over and covered his head with a feather pillow.

"Please don't hide from me," Nessa said. "This is your place, after all, and you didn't invite me to barge in this way."

He lifted a corner of the pillow. "Nor did I, strictly speaking, Dr. Zylstra." The pillow smothered his head again.

"Dr. Zylstra and I are your support group," Nessa said. "We're here for you, Vyvyan. Completely."

"Mmmmm-mm-mmm."

"With people to talk to, to share your feelings with, your place here at CargoCo might not seem so intolerable," Nessa said. "Better, certainly, than being a lone meteorologist at the South Pole."

Eventually, Vyvyan emerged. He even sat up and faced us.

Nessa was great, a lovely and seductive asset to his treatment. Each potentially dangerous subject that arose, Nessa and he breasted in easy, reciprocally synchronized exchanges. I was hardly there at all. I was a facilitator and observer. That session lasted not just fifty minutes (the traditional therapeutic hour), but closer to three hours. It was the most productive meeting I'd had with Vyvyan since beginning his treatment.

▼▼▼

From that Thursday forward, Nessa attended every session that I had with Vyvyan. It was exactly as Nessa had said: she and I were permanent members of his support group. The love and validation that we jointly afforded him—and that Nessa, in particular, provided by being a strong and accepting female—almost certainly deterred him from risking suicide. It also enabled him to look upon his life at CargoCo as greatly more attractive, comfortable, and, yes, even happy than otherwise.

Vinny Fall reported that we had cured Vyvyan of howling. What's more, Nessa intervened with Mr. Foxworth, via a tactfully written letter, to convince him to increase Vyvyan's salary and benefits and to give him periodic segments of free time in which to rediscover the loveliness and serenity of the natural world. The warehouse was not only socially, but also physically, restrictive, and Vyvyan loved the outdoors—beaches, glaciers, forests, etc.

Cures are always the aim, but not always the outcome, of every tenderly conducted therapeutic process. But with Vyvyan Franklin Goodloss, Nessa and I brought about a cure.

Toward the end of his six-month treatment contract with me, a creature assembled over two centuries ago by a hubristic genius, and heartlessly spurned by that same cruel life-giver, found both his soul and a reliable antidote to the joy-strangling toxin of his existence pain. Nessa and I worked closely and painstakingly with Vyvyan to bring about regeneration and healing. For, if the world will not change, then we must.

▼▼▼

The preceding four paragraphs are a transcription of my notes from our penultimate session with Vyvyan. Two days ago, our *last* session took place. It was a catastrophe. I record this epilogue, by the way, from the high-security ward of a hospital where I am recovering from a bullet wound to the left shoulder.

Midway through the session, Nessa said, "I have to tell you both that I'm quitting my job here. Jack's proposed. We'll marry in June and move to Seattle."

Against every expectation, Vyvyan flew into what I can only call a jealous frenzy. He behaved as if driven by bitter memories of the abandonment and betrayals of his late father.

"Do you not forsake me, lovely Vanessa!" he cried. "How, after the harrowing trials we have passed together, may you even consider such a selfish course?"

Reverting to the naked animality of his earlier self, he stood up, seized Nessa with one bare hand, and flipped her onto my chaise longue with a twist so wrenchingly sudden that she could barely even gasp. With one hand, Vyvyan held her to the couch and, grimacing like a Technicolor gargoyle, began to squeeze his eely fingers about her throat. Nessa's eyes bugged out, filling with a crimson the same alarming shade as her reddening skin.

"No!" I shouted. My pistol vaulted into my hand. I aimed it at Vyvyan's great ugly head. I was too close to him. He reached out, applied the vise of his free hand to my gun hand, turned the stubby barrel back at me, and, because I was already tightening my trigger finger, shot me about two inches above the heart. Dripping blood, I blundered over my sculpted chrome chair into the wall. The report so startled Vyvyan that he released Nessa and fled.

Ms. Frye, I'm told, is recovering at home. Although I have been falsely accused of trying to murder her, I'm in a variety of recovery myself. It's slow, however, because I'm desolated by both Vyvyan's unexpected reversion and the unmerited hostility of my loved ones and friends.

Every person in this ward looks like a hard-bitten felon, and the only TV set seems to be perpetually tuned to some meaningless Atlanta Hawks basketball game, with the volume up as aloud the ward's guard, a rabid, gum-chewing fan, will permit. A police therapist has come to interview me twice already, but my side of this tragic story seems to annoy him intensely.

The only time Barbara's visited, she was tight-lipped and cold. I tried to get her to talk, but her eyes kept straying to the elevated TV screen—its picture was flipping vertically—and her answers seemed to fall on me from a judgmental height. Each one hurt. After she'd left, I found a familiar desk placard on my bedside tray, the one she gave as an anniversary gift, the one that shouts, PATIENTHOOD IS UBIQUITOUS.

It would be nice if Vyvyan visited, but he's a smart guy, and I'd bet my practice he's gone permanently on the lam.

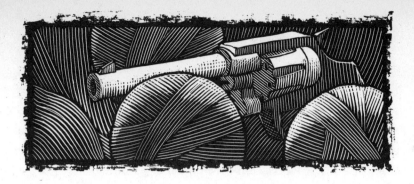

FORTITUDE

▼▼▼

KURT VONNEGUT, JR.

THE TIME: *the present.* THE PLACE: *Upstate New York, a large room filled with pulsing, writhing, panting machines that perform the functions of various organs of the human body—heart, lungs, liver, and so on. Color-coded pipes and wires swoop upward from the machines to converge and pass through a hole in the ceiling. To one side is a fantastically complicated master control console.*

DR. ELBERT LITTLE, *a kindly, attractive young general practitioner, is being shown around by the creator and boss of the operation.* DR. NORBERT FRANKENSTEIN, FRANKENSTEIN *is 65, a crass medical genius. Seated at the console, wearing headphones and watching meters and flashing lights,* is DR. TOM SWIFT, FRANKENSTEIN's *enthusiastic, first assistant.*

LITTLE: Oh, my God—oh, my God—

FRANKENSTEIN: Yeah. Those are her kidneys over there. That's her liver, of course. There you got her pancreas.

LITTLE: Amazing. Dr. Frankenstein, after seeing this, I wonder if

I've been *practicing* medicine, if I've ever even *been* to medical school. (*Pointing*) That's her *heart?*

FRANKENSTEIN: That's a Westinghouse heart. They make a damn good heart, if you ever need one. They make a kidney I wouldn't touch with a ten-foot pole.

LITTLE: That heart is probably worth more than the whole township where I practice.

FRANKENSTEIN: That pancreas is worth your whole state.

LITTLE: Vermont.

FRANKENSTEIN: What we paid for the pancreas—yeah, we could have brought Vermont for that. Nobody'd ever made a pancreas before, and we had to have one in ten days or lose the patient. So we told all the big organ manufacturers, "OK, you guys got to have a crash program for a pancreas. Put every man you got on the job. We don't care what it costs, as long as we get a pancreas by next Tuesday."

LITTLE: And they succeeded.

FRANKENSTEIN: The patient's still alive, isn't she? Believe me, those are some expensive sweetbreads.

LITTLE: But the patient could afford them.

FRANKENSTEIN: You don't live like this on Blue Cross.

LITTLE: And how many operations has she had? In how many years?

FRANKENSTEIN: I gave her her first major operation thirty-six years ago. She's had seventy-eight operations since then.

LITTLE: And how old is she?

FRANKENSTEIN: One hundred.

LITTLE: What *guts* that woman must have!

FRANKENSTEIN: You're looking at 'em.

LITTLE: I mean—what *courage!* What *fortitude!*

FRANKENSTEIN: We knock her out, you know. We don't operate without anesthetics.

LITTLE: Even so . . .

FRANKENSTEIN *taps* SWIFT *on the shoulder.* SWIFT *frees an ear from the headphones, divides his attention between the visitors and the console.*

FRANKENSTEIN: Dr. Tom Swift, this is Dr. Elbert Little. Tom here is my first assistant.

SWIFT: Howdy-doody.

FRANKENSTEIN: Dr. Little has a practice up in Vermont. He happened to be in the neighborhood. He asked for a tour.

LITTLE: What do you hear in the headphones?

SWIFT: Anything that's going on in the patient's room. *(He offers the headphones)* Be my guest.

LITTLE: *(listening to headphones)*: Nothing.

SWIFT: She's having her hair brushed now. The beautician's up there. She's always quiet when her hair's being brushed. *(He takes the headphones back)*

FRANKENSTEIN *(to* SWIFT*)*: We should *congratulate* our young visitor here.

SWIFT: What for?

LITTLE: Good question. What for?

FRANKENSTEIN: Oh, I know about the great honor that has come your way.

LITTLE: I'm not sure *I* do.

FRANKENSTEIN: You are *the* Dr. Little, aren't you, who was named the Family Doctor of the Year by the *Ladies' Home Journal* last month?

LITTLE: Yes—that's right. I don't know how in the hell they decided. And I'm even more flabbergasted that a man of *your* caliber would know about it.

FRANKENSTEIN: I read the *Ladies' Home Journal* from cover to cover every month.

LITTLE: You *do?*

FRANKENSTEIN: I only got one patient, Mrs. Lovejoy. And Mrs.

Lovejoy reads the *Ladies' Home Journal*, so I read it, too. That's what we talk about—what's in the *Ladies' Home Journal*. We read all about you last month. Mrs. Lovejoy kept saying, "Oh, what a nice young man he must be. *So understanding.*"

LITTLE: Um.

FRANKENSTEIN: Now here you are in the flesh. I bet she wrote you a letter.

LITTLE: Yes—she did.

FRANKENSTEIN: She writes thousands of letters a year, gets thousands of letters back. Some pen pal she is.

LITTLE: Is she—uh—generally *cheerful* most of the time?

FRANKENSTEIN: If she isn't, that's our fault down here. If she gets unhappy, that means something down *here* isn't working right. She was blue about a month ago. Turned out it was a bum transistor in the console. *(He reaches over* SWIFT's *shoulder, changes a setting on the console. The machinery subtly adjusts to the new setting.)* There—she'll be all depressed for a couple of minutes now. *(He changes the setting again) There.* Now, pretty quick, she'll be happier than she was before. She'll sing like a bird

LITTLE *conceals his horror imperfectly.* CUT TO *patient's room, which is full of flowers and candy boxes and books. The patient is* SYLVIA LOVEJOY, *a billionaire's widow,* SYLVIA *is no longer anything but a head connected to pipes and wires coming up through the floor, but this is not immediately apparent. The first shot of her is a* CLOSE-UP, *with* GLORIA, *a gorgeous beautician, standing behind her,* SYLVIA *is a heartbreakingly good-looking old lady, once a famous beauty. She is crying now.*

SYLVIA: Gloria—

GLORIA: Ma'am?

SYLVIA: Wipe these tears away before somebody comes in and sees them.

GLORIA (*wanting to cry herself*): Yes, ma'am (*She wipes the tears away with Kleenex studies the results*) There. There.

SYLVIA: I don't know what came over me. Suddenly I was so sad I couldn't stand it.

GLORIA: Everybody has to cry *sometimes*.

SYLVIA: It's passing now. Can you tell I've been crying?

GLORIA: No. No.

She is unable to control her own tears anymore. She goes to a window so SYLVIA *can't see her cry.* CAMERA BACKS AWAY *to reveal the tidy, clinical abomination of the head and wires and pipes. The head is on a tripod. There is a black box with winking colored lights hanging under the head, where the chest would normally be. Mechanical arms come out of the box where arms would normally be. There is a table within easy reach of the arms. On it are a pen and paper, a partially solved jigsaw puzzle and a bulky knitting bag. Sticking out of the bag are needles and a sweater in progress. Hanging over* SYLVIA's *head is a microphone on a boom.*

SYLVIA (*sighing*): Oh, what a *foolish* old woman you must think I am. (GLORIA *shakes her head in denial, is unable to reply*) Gloria? Are you still there?

GLORIA: Yes.

SYLVIA: Is anything the matter?

GLORIA: No.

SYLVIA: You're *such* a good friend, Gloria. I want you to know I feel that with all my heart.

GLORIA: I like you, too.

SYLVIA: If you ever have any problems I can help you with, I hope you'll ask me.

GLORIA: I will, I *will*.

HOWARD DERBY, *the hospital mail clerk, dances in with an armload of letters. He is a merry old fool.*

DERBY: Mailman! Mailman!

SYLVIA *(brightening)*: Mailman! God *bless* the mailman!

DERBY: How's the patient today?

SYLVIA: Very sad a moment ago. But now that I see you, I want to sing like a bird.

DERBY: Fifty-three letters today. There's even one from Leningrad.

SYLVIA: There's a blind woman in Leningrad. Poor soul, *poor* soul.

DERBY *(making a fan of the mail, reading postmarks)*: West Virginia, Honolulu, Brisbane, Australia—

SYLVIA *selects an envelope at random.*

SYLVIA: Wheeling, West Virginia. Now, who do I know in Wheeling? *(She opens the envelope expertly with her mechanical hands, reads)* "Dear Mrs. Lovejoy: You don't know me, but I just read about you in the *Reader's Digest,* and I'm sitting here with tears streaming down my cheeks." *Reader's Digest?* My goodness—that article was printed fourteen years ago! And she just *read* it?

DERBY: Old *Reader's Digests* go on and on. I've got one at home I'll bet is ten years old. I still read it every time I need a little inspiration.

SYLVIA *(reading on)*: "I am never going to complain about anything that ever happens to me ever again. I thought I was as unfortunate as a person can get when my husband shot his girlfriend six months ago and then blew his own brains out. He left me with seven children and with eight payments still to go on a Buick Roadmaster with three flat tires and a busted transmission. After reading about you, though, I sit here and count my blessings." Isn't that a nice letter?

DERBY: Sure is.

SYLVIA: There's a P.S.: "Get well real soon, you *hear?*" *(She puts*

the letter on the table) There isn't a letter from Vermont, is
there?

DERBY: Vermont?

SYLVIA: Last month, when I had that low spell, I wrote what I'm
afraid was a very stupid, self-centered, self-pitying letter to a
young doctor I read about in the *Ladies' Home Journal.* I'm so
ashamed. I live in fear and trembling of what he's going to say
back to me—if he answers at all.

GLORIA: What could he say? What could he *possibly* say?

SYLVIA: He could tell me about the *real* suffering going on out
there in the world, about people who don't know where the
next meal is coming from, about people so poor they've never
been to a doctor in their whole *lives.* And to think of all the
help I've had—all the tender, loving care, all the latest wonders
science has to offer.

CUT TO *corridor outside* SYLVIA's *room. There is a sign on the door
saying.* ALWAYS ENTER SMILING! FRANKENSTEIN *and* LITTLE *are
about to enter.*

LITTLE: She's in *there?*

FRANKENSTEIN: Every part of her that isn't downstairs.

LITTLE: And everybody obeys this sign, I'm sure.

FRANKENSTEIN: Part of the therapy. We treat the *whole* patient here.

GLORIA *comes from the room, closes the door tightly, then bursts
into noisy tears.*

FRANKENSTEIN *(to* GLORIA, *disgusted)*: Oh, for crying out loud.
And what is this?

GLORIA: Let her *die,* Dr. Frankenstein. For the love of God, let
her *die!*

LITTLE: This is her *nurse?*

FRANKENSTEIN: She hasn't got brains enough to be a nurse. She
is a lousy beautician. A hundred bucks a week she makes—just

to take care of one woman's face and hair. (*To* GLORIA) You blew it, honeybunch. You're through.

GLORIA: What?

FRANKENSTEIN: Pick up your check and scram.

GLORIA: I'm her closest friend.

FRANKENSTEIN: Some friend! You just asked me to knock her off.

GLORIA: In the name of mercy, yes, I did.

FRANKENSTEIN: You're that sure there's a heaven, eh? You want to send her right up there so she can get her wings and harp.

GLORIA: I know there's a hell. I've seen it. It's in there, and you're its great inventor.

FRANKENSTEIN (*stung, letting a moment pass before replying*): Christ—the things people say sometimes

GLORIA: It's time somebody who loves her spoke up.

FRANKENSTEIN: Love.

GLORIA: You wouldn't know what that is.

FRANKENSTEIN: Love. (*More to himself than to her*) Do I have a wife? No. Do I have a mistress? No. I have loved only two women in my life—my mother and that woman in there. I wasn't able to save my mother from death. I had just graduated from medical school and my mother was dying of cancer of the everything. "OK, wise guy," I said to myself, "you're such a hot-shot doctor from Heidelberg, now, let's see you save your mother from death." And everybody told me there wasn't anything I could do for her, and I said, "I don't give a damn. I'm gonna do something anyway." And they finally decided I was nuts and they put me in a crazyhouse for a little while. When I got out, she was dead—the way all the wise men said she had to be. What those wise men didn't know was all the wonderful things machinery could do—and neither did I, but I was gonna find out. So I went to the Massachusetts Institute of Technology and I studied mechanical engineering and electrical engineering and chemical engineering for six long years. I lived in an attic. I ate two-day-old bread and the kind of cheese they put in mousetraps. When I got out of MIT, I said to myself, "OK, boy—it's just barely possible now that you're the only guy on earth with the proper education to practice 20th century medicine." I went to work for the Curley Clinic in Boston. They brought in this woman who was beautiful on the outside and a mess on the inside. She was the image of my mother. She was the widow of a man who had left her five-hundred million dollars. She didn't have any relatives. The wise men said again, "This lady's gotta die." And I said to them, "Shut up and listen. I'm gonna tell you what we're gonna do."

Silence.

LITTLE: That's—that's quite a story.

FRANKENSTEIN: It's a story about *love*. (*To* GLORIA) That love story started years and years before you were born, you great lover, you. And it's still going on.

GLORIA: Last month, she asked me to bring her a pistol so she could shoot herself.

FRANKENSTEIN: You think I don't know that? (*Jerking a thumb at* LITTLE) Last month, she wrote him a letter and said, "Bring me some cyanide, doctor, if you're a doctor with any heart at all."

LITTLE (*startled*): You *knew* that. You—you read her mail?

FRANKENSTEIN: So we'll know what she's *really* feeling. She might try to fool us sometime—just *pretend* to be happy. I told you about the bum transistor last month. We maybe wouldn't have known anything was wrong if we hadn't read her mail and listened to what she was saying to lame-brains like this one here. (*Feeling challenged*) Look—you go in there all by yourself. Stay as long as you want, ask her anything. Then you come back out and tell me the truth: Is that a happy woman in there, or is that a woman in hell?

LITTLE *(hesitating)*: I—

FRANKENSTEIN: Go on in! I got some more things to say to this young lady—to Miss Mercy Killing of the Year. I'd like to show her a body that's been in a casket for a couple of years sometime—let her see how pretty death is, this thing she wants for her friend.

LITTLE *gropes for something to say, finally mimes his wish to be fair to everyone. He enters the patient's room. CUT TO room. SYLVIA is alone, faced away from the door.*

SYLVIA: Who's that?

LITTLE: A friend—somebody you wrote a letter to.

SYLVIA: That could be anybody. Can I see you, please? (LITTLE *obliges. She looks him over with growing affection.*) Dr. Little—family doctor from Vermont.

LITTLE *(bowing slightly)*: Mrs. Lovejoy—how are you today?

SYLVIA: Did you bring me cyanide?

LITTLE: No.

SYLVIA: I wouldn't take it today. It's such a lovely day. I wouldn't want to miss it, or tomorrow, either. Did you come on a snow-white horse?

LITTLE: In a blue Oldsmobile.

SYLVIA: What about your patients, who love and need you so?

LITTLE: Another doctor is covering for me. I'm taking a week off.

SYLVIA: Not on my account.

LITTLE: No.

SYLVIA: Because I'm fine. You can see what wonderful hands I'm in.

LITTLE: Yes.

SYLVIA: One thing I don't need is another doctor.

LITTLE: Right.

Pause.

SYLVIA: I do wish I had somebody to talk to about death, though. You've seen a lot of it, I suppose.

LITTLE: Some.

SYLVIA: And it was a blessing for some of them—when they died?

LITTLE: I've heard that said.

SYLVIA: But you don't say so yourself.

LITTLE: It's not a professional thing for a doctor to say, Mrs. Lovejoy.

SYLVIA: Why have other people said that certain deaths have been a blessing?

LITTLE: Because of the pain the patient was in, because he couldn't be cured at any price—at any price within his means. Or because the patient was a vegetable, had lost his mind and couldn't get it back.

SYLVIA: At any price.

LITTLE: As far as I know, it is not now possible to beg, borrow or steal an artificial mind for someone who's lost one. If I asked Dr. Frankenstein about it, he might tell me that it's the coming thing.

Pause.

SYLVIA: It *is* the coming thing.

LITTLE: He's told you so?

SYLVIA: I asked him yesterday what would happen if my brain started to go. He was serene. He said I wasn't to worry my pretty little head about that. "We'll cross that bridge when we come to it," he told me. (*Pause*) Oh, God, the bridges I've crossed!

CUT TO *room full of organs, as before,* SWIFT *is at his console.* FRANKENSTEIN *and* LITTLE *enter.*

FRANKENSTEIN: You've made the grand tour and now here you are back at the beginning.

LITTLE: And I still have to say what I said at the beginning: "My God—oh, my God."

FRANKENSTEIN: It's gonna be a little tough going back to the aspirin-and-laxative trade after this, eh?

LITTLE: Yes. (Pause) What's the cheapest thing here?

FRANKENSTEIN: The simplest thing. It's the goddamn pump.

LITTLE: What does a heart go for these days?

FRANKENSTEIN: Sixty thousand dollars. There are cheaper ones and more expensive ones. The cheap ones are junk. The expensive ones are jewelry.

LITTLE: And how many are sold a year now?

FRANKENSTEIN: Six hundred, give or take a few.

LITTLE: Give one, that's life. Take one, that's death.

FRANKENSTEIN: If the trouble is the heart. It's lucky if you have trouble that cheap. (To SWIFT) Hey, Tom—put her to sleep so he can see how the day ends around here.

SWIFT: It's twenty minutes ahead of time.

FRANKENSTEIN: What's the difference? We put her to sleep for twenty minutes extra, she still wakes up tomorrow feeling like a million bucks, unless we got another bum transistor.

LITTLE: Why don't you have a television camera aimed at her, so you can watch her on a screen?

FRANKENSTEIN: She didn't want one.

LITTLE: She gets what she wants?

FRANKENSTEIN: She got that. What the hell do we have to watch her face for? We can look at the meters down here and find out more about her than she can know about herself. (To SWIFT) Put her to sleep, Tom.

SWIFT (to LITTLE): It's just like slowing down a car or banking a furnace.

LITTLE: Um.

FRANKENSTEIN: Tom, too, has degrees in both engineering and medicine.

LITTLE: Are you tired at the end of a day, Tom?

SWIFT: It's a good kind of tiredness—as though I'd flown a big jet from New York to Honolulu, or something like that. (*Taking hold of a lever*) And now we'll bring Mrs. Lovejoy in for a happy landing. (*He pulls the lever gradually and the machinery slows down*). There.

FRANKENSTEIN: Beautiful.

LITTLE: She's asleep?

FRANKENSTEIN: Like a baby.

SWIFT: All I have to do now is wait for the night man to come on.

LITTLE: Has anybody ever brought her a suicide weapon?

FRANKENSTEIN: No. We wouldn't worry about it if they did. The arms are designed so she can't possibly point a gun at herself or get poison to her lips, no matter how she tries. That was Tom's stroke of genius.

LITTLE: Congratulations.

Alarm bell rings. Light flashes.

FRANKENSTEIN: Who could that be? (*To* LITTLE) Somebody just went into her room. We better check! (*To* SWIFT) Lock the door up there, Tom—so whoever it is, we got 'em. (SWIFT *pushes a button that locks door upstairs. To* LITTLE) You come with me.

CUT TO *patient's room.* SYLVIA *is asleep, snoring gently.* GLORIA *has just sneaked in. She looks around furtively, takes a revolver from her purse, makes sure it's loaded, then hides it in* SYLVIA's *knitting bag. She is barely finished when* FRANKENSTEIN *and* LITTLE *enter breathlessly,* FRANKENSTEIN *opening the door with a key.*

FRANKENSTEIN: What's this?

GLORIA: I left my watch up here. (*Pointing to watch*) I've got it now.

FRANKENSTEIN: Thought I told you never to come into this building again.

GLORIA: I won't.

FRANKENSTEIN (to LITTLE): You keep her right there. I'm gonna check things over. Maybe there's been a little huggery buggery. (To GLORIA) How would you like to be in court for attempted murder, eh? (Into microphone) Tom? Can you hear me?

SWIFT (voice from squawk box on wall): I hear you.

FRANKENSTEIN: Wake her up again. I gotta give her a check.

SWIFT: Cock-a-doodle-doo.

Machinery can be heard speeding up below. SYLVIA opens her eyes, sweetly dazed.

SYLVIA (to FRANKENSTEIN): Good morning, Norbert.

FRANKENSTEIN: How do you feel?

SYLVIA: The way I always feel when I wake up—fine—vaguely at sea. Gloria! Good morning!

GLORIA: Good morning.

SYLVIA: Dr. Little! You're staying another day?

FRANKENSTEIN: It isn't morning. We'll put you back to sleep in a minute.

SYLVIA: I'm sick again?

FRANKENSTEIN: I don't think so.

SYLVIA: I'm going to have to have another operation?

FRANKENSTEIN: Calm down, calm down. (He takes an opthalmoscope from his pocket)

SYLVIA: How can I be calm when I think about another operation?

FRANKENSTEIN (into microphone): Tom—give her some tranquilizers.

SWIFT (squawk box): Coming up.

SYLVIA: What else do I have to lose? My ears? My hair?

FRANKENSTEIN: You'll be calm in a minute.

SYLVIA: My eyes? My eyes, Norbert—are they going next?

FRANKENSTEIN (*to* GLORIA): Oh, boy, baby doll—will you look
what you've done? (*Into microphone*) Where the hell are those
tranquilizers?

SWIFT: Should be taking effect just about now.

SYLVIA: Oh, well. It doesn't matter. (*As* FRANKENSTEIN *examines
her eyes*) It is my eyes, isn't it?

FRANKENSTEIN: It isn't your anything.

SYLVIA: Easy come, easy go.

FRANKENSTEIN: You're healthy as a horse.

SYLVIA: I'm sure somebody manufactures excellent eyes.

FRANKENSTEIN: RCA makes a damn good eye, but we aren't
gonna buy one for a while yet. (*He backs away, satisfied*)
Everything's all right up here. (*To* GLORIA) Lucky for you.

SYLVIA: I love it when friends of mine are lucky.

SWIFT: Put her to sleep again?

FRANKENSTEIN: Not yet. I want to check a couple of things down
there.

SWIFT: Roger and out.

CUT TO LITTLE, GLORIA *and* FRANKENSTEIN *entering the machinery room minutes later.* SWIFT *is at the console.*

SWIFT: Night man's late.

FRANKENSTEIN: He's got troubles at home. You want a good piece
of advice, boy? Don't ever get married. (*He scrutinizes meter
after meter*)

GLORIA (*appalled by her surroundings*): My God—oh, my God—

LITTLE: You've never seen this before?

GLORIA: No.

FRANKENSTEIN: She was the great hair specialist. We took care of
everything else—everything but the hair. (*The reading on a
meter puzzles him.*) What's this? (*He socks the meter, which
then gives him the proper reading*) that's more like it.

GLORIA (*emptily*): Science.

FRANKENSTEIN: What did you think it was like down here?

GLORIA: I was afraid to think. Now I can see why.

FRANKENSTEIN: You got any scientific background at all—any way of appreciating even slightly what you're seeing here?

GLORIA: I flunked earth science twice in high school.

FRANKENSTEIN: What do they teach in beauty college?

GLORIA: Dumb things for dumb people. How to paint a face. How to curl or uncurl hair. How to cut hair. How to dye hair. Fingernails. Toenails in the summertime.

FRANKENSTEIN: I suppose you're gonna crack off about this place after you get out of here—gonna tell people all the crazy stuff that goes on.

GLORIA: Maybe.

FRANKENSTEIN: Just remember this. You haven't got the brains or the education to talk about any aspect of our operation. Right?

GLORIA: Maybe.

FRANKENSTEIN: What *will* you say to the outside world?

GLORIA: Nothing very complicated—just that. . . .

FRANKENSTEIN: Yes?

GLORIA: That you have the head of a dead woman connected to a lot of machinery, and you play with it all day long, and you aren't married or anything, and that's all you do.

FREEZE SCENE *as a still photograph.* FADE TO *black.* FADE IN *same still. Figures begin to move.*

FRANKENSTEIN *(aghast):* How can you call her dead? She reads the *Ladies' Home Journal!* She talks! She knits! She writes letters to pen pals all over the world!

GLORIA: She's like some horrible fortunetelling machine in a penny arcade.

FRANKENSTEIN: I thought you loved her.

GLORIA: Every so often, I see a tiny little spark of what she used to be. I love that spark. Most people say they love her for her courage. What's that courage worth, when it comes from down here? You could turn a few faucets and switches down here and she'd be volunteering to fly a rocket ship to the moon. But no matter what you do down here, that little spark goes on thinking. "For the love of God—somebody get me out of here!"

FRANKENSTEIN *(glancing at the console)*: Dr. Swift—is that microphone open?

SWIFT: Yeah. *(Snapping his fingers)* I'm sorry.

FRANKENSTEIN: Leave it open. *(To* GLORIA*)* She's heard every word you've said. How does that make you feel?

GLORIA: She can hear me now?

FRANKENSTEIN: Run off at the mouth some more. You're saving me a lot of trouble. Now I won't have to explain to her what sort of friend you really were and why I gave you the old heave-ho.

GLORIA *(drawing nearer to the microphone)*: Mrs. Lovejoy?

SWIFT *(reporting what he has heard on the microphones)*: She says, "What is it, dear?"

GLORIA: There's a loaded revolver in your knitting bag, Mrs. Lovejoy—in case you don't want to live anymore.

FRANKENSTEIN *(not in the least worried about the pistol but filled with contempt and disgust for* GLORIA*)*: You total imbecile. Where did you get a pistol?

GLORIA: From a mail-order house in Chicago. They had an ad in *True Romances.*

FRANKENSTEIN: They sell guns to crazy broads.

GLORIA: I could have had a bazooka if I'd wanted one. Fourteen-ninety-eight.

FRANKENSTEIN: I am going to get that pistol now and it is going to be exhibit A at your trial. *(He leaves)*

LITTLE *(to* SWIFT*)*: Shouldn't you put the patient to sleep?

SWIFT: There's no way she can hurt herself.

GLORIA (to LITTLE): What does he mean?

LITTLE: Her arms are fixed so she can't point a gun at herself. GLORIA (sickened): They even thought of that.

CUT TO SYLVIA's room. FRANKENSTEIN is entering. SYLVIA is holding the pistol thoughtfully.

FRANKENSTEIN: Nice playthings you have.

SYLVIA: You mustn't get mad at Gloria, Norbert. I asked her for this. I begged her for this.

FRANKENSTEIN: Last month.

SYLVIA: Yes.

FRANKENSTEIN: But everything is better now.

SYLVIA: Everything but the spark.

FRANKENSTEIN: Spark?

SYLVIA: The spark that Gloria says she loves—the tiny spark of what I used to be. As happy as I am right now, that spark is begging me to take this gun and put it out.

FRANKENSTEIN: And what is your reply?

SYLVIA: I am going to do it, Norbert. This is goodbye. (She tries every which way to aim the gun at herself, fails and fails, while FRANKENSTEIN stands calmly by) That's no accident, is it?

FRANKENSTEIN: We very much don't want you to hurt yourself. We love you, too.

SYLVIA: And how much longer must I live like this? I've never dared ask before.

FRANKENSTEIN: I would have to pull a figure out of a hat.

SYLVIA: Maybe you'd better not. (Pause) Did you pull one out of a hat?

FRANKENSTEIN: At least five hundred years.

Silence.

SYLVIA: So I will still be alive—long after you are gone?

FRANKENSTEIN: Now is the time, my dear Sylvia, to tell you something I have wanted to tell you for years. Every organ downstairs has the capacity to take care of two human beings instead of one. And the plumbing and wiring have been designed so that a second human being can be hooked up in two shakes of a lamb's tail. *(Silence)* Do you understand what I am saying to you, Sylvia? *(Silence. Passionately)* Sylvia! I will be that second human being! Talk about marriage! Talk about great love stories from past! Your kidney will be my kidney! Your liver will be my liver! Your heart will be my heart! Your ups will be my ups and your downs will be my downs! We will live in such perfect harmony, Sylvia, that the gods themselves will tear out their hair in envy!

SYLVIA: This is what you want?

FRANKENSTEIN: More than anything in this world.

SYLVIA: Well, then—here it is, Norbert. *(She empties the revolver into him)*

CUT TO *same room almost a half hour later. A second tripod has been set up, with* FRANKENSTEIN's *head on top.* FRANKENSTEIN is asleep and so is SYLVIA. SWIFT, *with* LITTLE *standing by, is feverishly making a final connection to the machinery below. There are pipe wrenches and a blowtorch and other plumber's and electricians tools lying around.*

SWIFT: That's gotta be it. *(He straightens up, looks around)* That's gotta be it.

LITTLE *(consulting watch)*: Twenty-eight minutes since the first shot was fired.

SWIFT: Thank God you were around.

LITTLE: What you really needed was a plumber.

SWIFT *(into microphone)*: Charley—we're all set up here. You all set down there?

CHARLEY *(squawk box)*: All set.

SWIFT: Give 'em plenty of martinis.

GLORIA *appears numbly in doorway.*

CHARLEY: They've got 'em. They'll be higher than kites.

SWIFT: Better given 'em a touch of LSD, too.

CHARLEY: Coming up.

SWIFT: Hold it! I forgot the phonograph. *(To* LITTLE*)* Dr. Frankenstein said that if this ever happened, he wanted a certain record playing when he came to. He said it was in with the other records—
in a plain white jacket. *(To* GLORIA*)* See if you can find it.

GLORIA *goes to phonograph, finds the record.*

GLORIA: This it?

SWIFT: Put it on.

GLORIA: Which side?

SWIFT: I don't know.

GLORIA: There's tape over one side.

SWIFT: The side *without* tape. (GLORIA *puts record on. Into microphone.)* Stand by to wake up the patients.

CHARLEY: Standing by.

*Record begins to play. It is a Jeanette MacDonald–Nelson Eddy
duet, "Ah, Sweet Mystery of Life."*

SWIFT *(into microphone)*: Wake 'em up!

FRANKENSTEIN *and* SYLVIA *wake up, filled with formless pleasure.
They dreamily appreciate the music, eventually catch sight of each
other, perceive each other as old and beloved friends.*

SYLVIA: Hi, there.

FRANKENSTEIN: Hello.

SYLVIA: How do you feel?

FRANKENSTEIN: Fine. Just fine.

MONSTERS
OF THE MIDWAY
▼▼▼

MIKE RESNICK

SURPRISES ON TAP?

July 12, 2037 (UPI) Coach Rattler Renfro, in his initial press conference, has promised fans that his Chicago Bears, coming off a pair
of 1-and-15 seasons, will sport a new look this season. When asked
to explain why training camp will be closed to both the press and
the public, Renfro merely smiled and said, "No comment."

BEARS TAKE OPENER, 76—0
September 4, 2037 (AP) The "New Look" Chicago Bears made
their debut this afternoon, beating last year's Super Bowl winners,
the North Dakota Timberwolves, by a league-record score of 76–
0. The Timberwolves were a 22-point favorite.

Coach Rattler Renfro unveiled an all-new offensive line, con-
sisting of five rookies, all free agents who had never played orga-

nized football before. They are right tackle Jumbo Smith (7'4", 603 pounds), right guard Willie "The Whale" McPherson (7'10", 566 pounds), center Hannibal Cohen (8'3", 622 pounds), and left guard Mountain O'Mara (7'8", 559 pounds), and the biggest of them all, right tackle Tiny Tackenheim (8'7", 701 pounds).

"Hell, *I* could have run through the holes those guys made,"said Timberwolves coach Rocket Ryan. "I don't know where Renfro recruited them, but they're just awesome."

After three decades in eclipse, it looks like the Bears are once again the Monsters of the Midway.

BEARS WIN FOURTH STRAIGHT, 88—7

October 2, 2037 (AP) "Those guys just ain't human!" said Montana Buttes' linebacker Jocko Schmidt from his hospital bed, after his team had suffered an 88–7 mauling at the hands of the Chicago Bears. "That Tackenheim ought to be in a zoo, not on a football field!"

NFL INVESTIGATES CHARGES

October 24, 2037 (UPI) The National Football League has announced they are probing into an alleged connection between Nobel Prize winner Dr. Alfredo Rathermann and the Chicago Bears. Rathermann, who won his award for his pioneering work in the reanimation of dead tissue, was unavailable for comment.

George Halas VI, owner and general manager of the Bears, who lead their division with a 7-0 record, termed the allegations "ridiculous."

BEARS CLINCH TITLE,
LOOK TO SUPER BOWL

December 25, 2037 (UPI) The Chicago Bears celebrated Christmas with a 68–3 thrashing of the Mississippi Riverboats, thus becoming the first NFL team this century to conclude its regular-season schedule unbeaten and untied. The Monster of the Midway looked awesome as the offensive line opened up hole after hole for Chicago's running backs.

Coach Rattler Renfro, in his post-game press conference, praised the Riverboats and said that he was looking forward to the playoffs. When questioned about the ongoing investigation of the dealings between the Bears and Dr. Alfredo Ratherman, he simply shrugged and said, "Hey, I'm just a coach. You'll have to speak to the Commissioner about that."

RATHERMANN ADMITS ALL!

December 28, 2037 (UPI) Nobel Prize laureate Alfredo Rathermann held a joint press conference with Roger Jamison, Commissioner of the National Football League, and admitted that the five starting members of the Chicago Bears' offensive line are actually scientific constructs, created from bits and pieces of other human beings.

This revelation seemed certain to win another Nobel for Dr. Rathermann, but the more important issue of whether linemen Smith, McPherson, Cohen, O'Mara, and Tackenheim will be allowed to compete in the upcoming NFL playoffs remains undecided at present. Commissioner Jamison promised a ruling before the Bears meet the Las Vegas Gamblers in eleven days.

NFL RULES ON "MONSTERS"

January 3, 2038 (AP) Commissioner Roger Jamison held a press conference this morning, in which he outlined the NFL's policy on the Chicago Bears' offensive line.

"After extended meetings with our attorneys and the NFL Players Union, we have amended the rules to state that football is a game played by natural-born human beings," said Commissioner Jamison. "If we were to permit an endless string of Dr.

Rathermann's creations to play in the NFL, the day would soon arrive when not a single natural-born human could make an NFL roster, and while it would certainly make the games more exciting, we question whether the public is ready for such a change at this time.

"However," he added, "our attorneys inform us that we have no legal basis for denying Smith, McPherson, Cohen, O'Mara, and Tackenheim the right to play in this season's post-season competition, since the rule was changed after they made the Bears' roster."

The owners of the 47 other NFL teams have filed an official protest, demanding that the players in question be barred from the upcoming playoffs.

BEARS WIN 77—10, SUPER BOWL NEXT

January 15, 2038 (UPI) The Chicago Bears beat the Hawaii Volcanos 77–10 this afternoon to advance to the Super Bowl. They overcame a 10–0 first-quarter deficit after the Supreme Court overturned the injunction barring linemen Smith, McPherson, Cohen, O'Mara and Tackenheim from playing. The ruling came down at 1:37 PM, and the Bears took the lead, never to relinquish it, at 1:43 PM.

"MONSTERS DON'T SCARE US," SAYS MCNAB

January 22, 2038 (UPI) With the Super Bowl only a week away, and the Chicago Bears a 45-point favorite, Coach Terry McNab of the Alaskan Malamutes said that his team didn't fear the Monsters of the Midway, and looked forward to the challenge.

When asked how his defensive line, which will be giving away an average of 327 pounds per man, would cope with their offensive counterparts on the Bears, he merely smiled and said that he was working on a strategy.

The Bears are expected to be 50-point favorites by the opening kickoff.

MCNAB MISSES PRACTICE

January 24, 2038 (UPI) Coach Terry McNab was missing from the Alaskan Malamutes' practice this afternoon. Club officials had no comment.

RATHERMANN RESURFACES

January 26, 2038 (UPI) Nobel Prize winner Alfredo Rathermann, who had been in seclusion since December 28, was spotted sitting in the stands, watching the Alaskan Malamutes prepare for their Super Bowl meeting with the Chicago Bears.

When asked if he had a rooting interest in the game, Rathermann replied that his interest was "strictly professional." He was later seen having dinner with Coach McNab and the owners of the Malamutes.

BEARS GO TO COURT TO BAR
McNAB FROM SUPER BOWL

January 28, 2038 (AP) With the revelation that Coach Terry McNab's skull now houses two brains—his own and that of Professor Steven Hawking, which had been cyrogenically frozen upon his death in 1998—the Chicago Bears went to court in an attempt to stop McNab from appearing on the sidelines during tomorrow's Super Bowl.

McNab's physician, Dr. Alfredo Rathermann, called the Bears' ownership "poor sportsmen" and pointed out that since McNab will not be playing, his presence will not break the NFL's controversial new policy.

"Besides," said McNab at a hastily-called press conference,

"I'm still the same 183-pound 57-year-old man I was last week. How can sharing the late Dr. Hawking's brain pose a threat to the Bears? Do I look like a Monster of the Midway?"

COURT RULES FOR McNAB

January 28, 2038 (UPI) The U.S. District Court ruled that Coach Terry McNab's presence will not conflict with stated NFL policy, and that he will be allowed on the field when his Alaskan Malamutes, who are 53-point underdogs, meet the Chicago Bears in tomorrow's Super Bowl.

MALAMUTES UPSET BEARS, 7—3

January 29, 2938 (AP) In one of the great upsets of all time, the Alaskan Malamutes beat the Chicago Bears 7–3 in Super Bowl LXXIII.

Using unorthodox formations and attacking from strange angles, the Malamutes' new "Vector Defense" smothered the supposedly-unstoppable Bears' running game. Quarterback Pedro Cordero hit tight end Bennie Philander with a 9-yard touchdown pass at 3:12 of the fourth quarter for the winning score.

When asked how his defense managed to penetrate the vaunted Bears' line, Coach Terry McNab's only comment was "E z MC^2"

MAJOR OVERHAUL FOR BEARS

February 19, 2038 (UPI) In the wake of their devastating defeat in the Super Bowl, the Chicago Bears have fired Coach Rattler Renfro, and given unconditional releases to linesmen Jumbo Smith, Willie "The Whale" McPherson, Hannibal Cohen, Mountain O'Mara, and Tiny Tackenheim.

All five players expressed hope that they could start new careers in the World Wrestling Federation.

DREAMS
▼▼▼

F. PAUL WILSON

THE nightmare again.

I almost dread falling asleep. Always the same, and yet never quite the same. The events differ dream to dream, yet always I am in a stranger's body, a huge, monstrous, patchwork contraption that reels through the darkness in such ungainly fashion. And it's always dark in the dream, for I seem to be a creature of the night, forever in hiding.

And I can't remember my name.

The dreams are well-formed now. My head has cleared in them. So unlike the early dreams, which I can barely remember. They are no more than a montage of blurred images now— a lightning-drenched laboratory, a whip-wielding hunchback, *fear*, a stone-walled cell, chains, *loneliness*, a little girl drowning among floating blossoms, a woman in a wedding gown, townsfolk with torches, fire, a burning windmill, *pain, rage, PAIN!*

But I'm all right now. Scarred but healing. And my mind is clear. The pain from the fire burned away the mists. I remember things from dream to dream, and more and more bits and pieces from long ago.

But what is my name?

I know I must stay out of sight. I don't want to be burned again. That's why I spend the daylight hours hiding here in the loft of this abandoned stable on the outskirts of Goldstadt. I sleep most of the day. But at night I wander. Always into town. Always to the area around the Goldstadt Medical College. I seem to be attracted to the medical college. The reason rests here in my brain, but it scampers beyond my grasp whenever I reach for it. One day I'll catch it and then I'll know.

So many unanswered questions in these dreams. But aren't dreams supposed to be that way? Don't they pose more questions than they answer?

My belly is full now. I broke into a pastry shop and gorged myself on the sweets left over from yesterday, and now I'm wandering the back alleys, drinking from rain barrels, peering from the shadows into the lighted windows I pass. There's a warm resonance within when I see a family together by a fire. Once I must have had a life like that. But the warmth warps into rage if I watch too long, because I know such a scene will never be mine again.

I know it's only a dream. But the rage is so real.

As I pass the rear of a tavern, the side door opens and two men step out. I stumble further back into the shadows, wanting to run but knowing I'd make a terrible racket. No one must see me. No one must know I'm alive. So I stay perfectly still, waiting for them to leave.

That's when I hear the voice. The deep, delicious voice of a handsome young man with curly blond hair and fresh clear skin. I know this without seeing him. I even know his name.

Karl.

I lean to my right and peer down the alley. My heart leaps at the sight of him. It's not *my* heart; it's the huge, ponderous heart of a stranger, but it responds nonetheless, thudding madly in my chest. I listen to his clear, rich laughter as he waves good-bye to his friend and strolls away toward the street.

Karl.

I follow. I know it's dangerous but I must. But I don't go down the alley after him. Instead I lumber along in the back alleys, splattering through puddles, scattering rats, dodging stinking piles of trash as I keep pace with him, catching sight of his golden-haired form between buildings as he strides along the pavement.

He's not heading for home. Somewhere in my head I know where he lives and he's headed in the wrong direction. I follow him to a cottage at the north end of Goldstadt, watch him knock, watch a raven-haired beauty open the door and leap into his arms, watch them disappear inside. I know her too.

Maria.

The rage spewing up in me is nearly as uncontrollable as it is unexplainable. It's all I can do to keep myself from bursting through that door and tearing them both apart.

Why? What are these emotions? Who are these people? And why do I know their names and not my own?

I cool. I wait. But Karl doesn't appear. The sky lightens and still no Karl. I must leave before I am seen. As I head back toward the stable that has become my nest, my rage is gone, replaced by a cold black despair. Before I climb to the loft I pause to relieve myself. As I lower my heavy, crudely stitched pants I pray that it will be different this dream, but there it is—that long, thick, slack member hanging between my legs. It repulses me. I try to relieve myself without touching it.

I am a woman. Why do these dreams place me in the body of a man?

▼▼▼

Awake again.

I've spent the day talking, laughing, discussing the wisdom of the ages. Such a relief to be back to reality, back in my own body—young, lithe, smaller, smoother, with slim legs, dainty fingers, and firm, compact breats. So good to be a woman again.

But my waking hours aren't completely free from confusion. I'm not sure where I am. I do know that it's warm and beautiful. Grassy knolls flow green through the golden sunshine toward the majestic amethyst-hued mountains that tower in the distance. Sweet little birds dart about in the hazy spring air.

And at least when I'm awake I know my name: Eva. Eva Rucker.

I just wish I knew why I was here. Don't misunderstand. I love it here. It's everything I've ever wanted. Friendly people wandering the hills, wise men stopping by to discuss the great philosophies of the ages. It's like the Elysian Fields I read about in Greek mythology, except I'm alive and this is all real. I simply don't know what I've done to deserve this.

I have a sense that I was brought here as compensation for an unpleasantness in my past. I seem to remember some recent ugliness in which I was unwittingly involved, unjustly accused, something so darkly traumatic that my mind shies from the memory of it. But the wrong was righted and I've been sent here to recuperate.

I think of Karl and how he became part of my dream last night. Karl . . . so handsome, so brilliant, so dashing. I haven't thought of him since I arrived here. How could I forget the man I love?

A cloud passes across the sun as my thoughts darken with the memory of the dream-Karl in the dream-Maria's arms. Maria is Karl's sister! They would *never*!

How perverse these nightmares! I shouldn't let them upset me.

The sun reemerges as I push the memory away. It's wonderful here. I never want to leave. But I'm tired now. The golden wine I had with dinner has made me drowsy. I'll just lie back and rest my eyes for a moment . . .

▼▼▼

Oh, no! The dream again!

I'm in that horrid body, stumbling through the night. Can't I close my eyes even for a few seconds without falling into this nightmare? I want to scream, to burst from this cocoon of dream and return to my golden-lit fields. But the nightmare tightens its steely grip on me and I lurch on.

I stop at a school house. I'm hungry but there's something more important than food inside. I break down the door and enter the single classroom with its rows of tiny desks. I rip the top off one desk after the other and carry it to the shafts of moonlight pouring through the windows until I find the paper and pencil I seek. I bring them to the teacher's desk. I'm too large to seat myself, so I kneel beside the desk and force my huge ungainly fingers to grasp the pencil and write.

I know this is a dream, but still I feel compelled to let Karl know that even though my body has metamorphosed into this huge ungainly monstrosity, his Eva still cares for him.

After many tries, I manage a legible note:

KARL

I LOVE YOU

YOUR EVA

I fold the sheet and take it with me. At Karl's uncle's house—where Karl lives—I slip it under the door, then I stand back in the shadows and wait. And as I wait, I remember more and more about Karl.

We met near the University of Goldstadt where Karl was a

student at the Medical College. That was in my real life. I assume he remains a student in my dreams. I so wanted to attend the University but the Regents wouldn't hear of it. They were scandalized by my application. No women in the College of Arts and Sciences, and especially in the Medical College. *Especially* not a poor farm girl.

So I'd hide in the rear of the lecture halls and listen to Dr. Waldman's lectures on anatomy and physiology. Karl found me there but kept my secret and let me stay. I fell in love with him immediately. I remember that. I remember all our secret meetings, in fields, in lofts. He'd teach me what he learned in class. And then he'd teach me other things. We became lovers. I'd never given myself to any man before. Karl was the first, and I swear he'll be the only one. I don't remember how we became separated. I—

Here he comes. Oh, look at him! I want to run to him but I couldn't bear for him to see me like this. What torture this nightmare is!

I watch him enter his uncle's house, see him light the candles in the entryway. I move closer as he picks up my note and reads it. But no loving smile lights his features. Instead, his face blanches and he totters back against the wall. Then he's out the door and running, flying through the streets, my note clutched in his hand. I follow him as best I can but he outdistances me. No matter. I know the route. I sense where he's going.

When I arrive at Maria's house he's already inside. I lurch to a lighted window and peer within. Karl stands in the center of the room, his eyes wild, the ruddy color still gone from his cheeks. Maria has her arms around his waist. She's smiling as she comforts him.

"—only a joke," she says. "Can't you see that, my love? Someone's trying to play a trick on you!"

"Then it's a damn good trick!" Karl says, holding my note before her eyes. "This is how she always signed her notes—'Your

Eva.' No one else knew that. Not even you. And I burned all those letters."

"So what are you telling me?" Maria says with a laugh. "That Eva wrote you this note? That's certainly not her handwriting."

"True, but—"

"Eva is dead, my love."

The words strike like hammerblows to my brain. I want to shout that I'm here, alive, transformed into this creature. But I keep silent. I have no workable voice. And after all, this is only a dream. I must keep telling myself that.

Only a dream.

Nothing here is true and therefore none of it matters.

Yet I find a horrid fascination in it.

"They hanged her," Maria is saying. "I know because I went and watched. You couldn't stomach it but I went to see for myself." Her smile fades as an ugly light grows in her eyes. "They hanged her, Karl. Hanged her till she stopped kicking and swung limp in the breeze. Then they cut her down and took her off to the Medical College just as she requested. The noble little thing: wanted her body donated to science. Well, by now she's in a thousand little pieces."

"I know," Karl says. His color is returning, but his flush seems more a shade of guilt than good health. "I saw her brain, Maria. Eva's brain! Dr. Waldman kept it in a glass jar on one of the lab tables as an example of an abnormal brain. 'Dysfunctio Cerebri' his label said, right next to a supposedly normal brain. I had to sit there during all his lectures and stare at it, knowing the whole time who it had belonged to, and that it was not abnormal in the least."

"It should have been labeled a 'stupid' brain," Maria laughs. "She believed you loved her. She thought I was your sister. She believed everything we told her, and so she wound up taking the blame for your uncle's murder. As a result, you're rich and you don't ever have to think about her again. She's gone."

"Her brain's gone too. I so was glad when pranksters stole it and I no longer had to look at it."

"Now you can look at me," Maria says.

She steps back and unbuttons her blouse, baring her breasts. As Karl locks her in an embrace, I reel away from the window, sobbing, retching, running blindly for the stables I call home.

▼▼▼

Awake again.

Back in my Elysian fields, but still I cannot shake off the effects of that horrid dream. The dream-Maria's words have roused memories in my waking mind. They are partly true.

How could I have forgotten?

There was a murder. Karl's rich uncle. And I was accused. I remember now . . . remember that night. I was supposed to meet Karl at the house. He was going to introduce me to his uncle and bring our love out into the open at last. But when I got there, the door was open and a portly old man lay on the floor, bleeding, dying. I tried to help him but he had lost too much blood. And then the Burgomaster's men arrived and found me with the slain man's blood on my hands and the knife that had killed him at my feet.

And Karl was nowhere to be found.

I never saw Karl again. He never came to visit me. Never answered my notes. In fact, his barrister came to the jail and told me to stop writing to Karl—that Karl didn't know who I was and wanted nothing to do with the murderer of his uncle.

No one believed that I knew Karl. No one but his sister Maria had ever seen us together, and Maria said I was a complete stranger. I remember the final shock when I was told that Maria wasn't his sister at all.

After that the heart went out of me. I gave up. I lost the will to defend myself. I let them do with me as they wished. My only request was that my body be given to the Medical College. That was my private joke on the Regents—I would be attending the University after all.

I remember walking to the gallows. I remember the rope going around my neck. After that . . .

. . . I was here. So I was saved from execution. If only I could remember how. No matter. It will come. What does matter is that since arriving here my life has been a succession of one blissful day after another. Perfect . . .

Except for the dreams.

But now there are clouds gathering over my Elysian fields as I remember Karl's betrayal. I'd thought he avoided me in order to protect his family name, but the dream-Maria's words have not only awakened my memory, they've shed new light on all the things that happened to me after that night I went to Karl's uncle's house.

The clouds darken and thunder rumbles through the distant mountain passes as my anger and suspicion grow. I don't know if Karl lied and betrayed me as the dream-Maria said, and I don't know if he was the one who killed his uncle, but I do know that he deserted me in my hour of most dire need. And for that I will never forgive him.

The clouds obscure the sun and darken the sky, the storm threatens but it doesn't rain. Not yet.

▼▼▼

The nightmare again.

Only this time I don't fight it. I'm actually glad to be in this monstrous body. It's a curious thing, this body. Not a seamless creature, but a quilt of human parts. And powerful. So very powerful. My years of farm work left me strong for a girl, but I never had strength like this. Strength to lift a horse or knock down a tree. It feels *good* to be so strong.

I head for Maria's cottage.

She's home. She's alone. Karl is nowhere about. I don't

bother knocking. I knock down the door and step inside. Maria
starts to scream but I grab her by the throat with one of my long-
fingered hands and choke off all sound. She laughed at me last
night, called me stupid. I feel the anger surge and I squeeze
tighter, watching her face purple. I straighten my arm and lift her
feet off the floor, let them kick the empty air, just as she said
mine did in the dream-death she watched. I squeeze and squeeze
and *squeeze*, watching the blood vessels burst in her eyes and
face, watching her tongue protrude and turn dusky until she hangs
in my hands like a doll. I loosen my grip and shake her but she
remains limp.

What have I done?

I stand there, shocked at the rage within me, at the violence
it makes me capable of. For a moment I grieve for Maria, for
myself, then I shake it off.

This is a dream. A *dream!* It isn't real. I can do anything in
this nightmare body and it doesn't matter. Because it's only hap-
pening in my sleeping mind.

The realization is a dazzling white light in my brain. I can
do anything I wish in my dream-life. *Anything!* I can vent any
emotion, give in to any whim, any desire or impulse, no matter
how violent or outrageous.

And I will do just that. No restraint while I'm dreaming.
Unlike my waking life, I will act without hesitation on whatever
occurs to me. I'll lead a dream-life untempered by sympathy,
empathy, or any other sane consideration.

Why not? It's only a dream.

I look down and see the note I wrote Karl in last night's
dream. It lies crumpled on the floor. I look at Maria, hanging
limp from my hand. I remember her derisive laughter at how I'd
donated my body for the furtherance of science, her glee at the
thought of my being dissected into a thousand pieces.

And suddenly I have an idea. If I could laugh, I would.

After I'm finished with her, I set the door back on its hinges and wait beside it. I do not have to wait long.

Karl arrives and knocks. When no one answers, he pushes on the door. It falls inward and he sees his lover, Maria . . . all over the room . . . in a thousand pieces. He cries out hoarsely and turns to flee. But I am there, blocking the way.

Karl staggers back when I sees me, his face working in horror. He tries to run but I grab him by the arm and hold him.

"You! Good Lord, they said you'd burned up in the mill fire! Please don't hurt me! I never harmed you!"

What a wonder it is to have a physical power over a man. I never realized until this instant how fear has influenced my day-to-day dealings with men. True, they run the world, they have the power of influence—but they have *physical* power as well. Somewhere in the depths of my mind, running as a steady under-current, has been the realization that almost any man could physically overpower me at will. Although I never before recognized its existence, I see now how it has colored my waking life.

But in my dream I am no longer the weaker sex.

I do not hurt Karl. I merely want him to know who I am. I hold up the note from last night and press it against my heart.

"What?" he cries hoarsely. "What do you want of me?"

I show him the note again, and again I press it to my heart.

"What are you saying? That you're Eva? That's impossible. Eva's dead! You're Henry Frankenstein's creature."

Henry Frankenstein? The baron's son? I've heard of him—one of Dr. Waldman's former students, supposedly brilliant but highly unorthodox. What has he to do with any of this?

I growl and shake my head as I rattle the paper and tighten my grip on his arm.

He winces. "Look at you! How could you be Eva? You're fashioned out of different parts from different bodies! You're— " Karl's eyes widen, his face slackens. "The brain! Sweet Lord, Eva's brain! It was stolen shortly before you appeared!"

I am amazed at the logical consistency of my nightmare. In real life I donated my body to the Medical College, and here in my dream my brain has been placed in another body, a patchwork fashioned by Baron Frankenstein's son from discarded bits and pieces. How inventive I am!

I smile.

"Oh, my *God!*" Karl wails. His words begin to trip over each other in their hurry to escape. "It can't be! Oh, Eva, Eva, Eva, I'm so sorry! I didn't want to do it but Maria put me up to it. I didn't want to kill my uncle but she kept pushing me. It was her idea to have you blamed, not mine!"

As I stare at him in horror, I feel the rage burst in my heart like a rocket. So! He *did* conspire to hang me! A crimson haze blossoms about me as I take his head between my hands. I squeeze with all the strength I possess and don't stop until I hear a wet crunching noise, feel hot liquid running between my fingers.

And then I'm sobbing, huge alien sounds rumbling from my chest as I clutch Karl's limp form against me. It's only a dream, I know, but still I hurt inside. I stand there for a long time. Until I hear a voice behind me.

"Hello? What's happened here?"

I turn and see one of the townsfolk approaching. The sight of him makes my blood boil. He and his kind chased me to that mill on the hill and tried to burn me alive. I toss Karl's remains aside and charge after him. He is too fast for me and runs screaming down the street.

Afraid that he'll return with his neighbors, I flee. But not before setting fire to Maria's cottage. I watch it burn a moment, then head into the countryside, into the friendly darkness.

▼▼▼

Awake once more.

I have spent the entire day thinking about last night's dream. I see no reason to skulk around in the darkness any longer when

I'm dreaming. Why should I? The townsfolk realize by now that I'm still alive. Good. Let all those good citizens know that I am back and that they must deal with me again—not as poor Eva Rucker, but as the patchwork creature from Henry Frankenstein's crazed experiments. And I will *not* be mistreated any more. I will *not* be looked down on and have doors shut in my face simply because I am a farm girl. No one will say no to me ever again!

I will be back. Tomorrow night, and every night thereafter. But I shall no longer wander aimlessly. I will have a purpose in my dreams. I will start by taking my dream-revenge on the University Regents who denied me admission to the Medical College. I shall spend my waking hours devising elaborate ways for them to die, and in my dreams I shall execute those plans.

It will be fun. Harmless fun to kill them off one by one in my dreams.

I'm beginning to truly enjoy the dreams. It's so wonderful to be powerful and not recognize any limits. It's such an invigorating release.

I can't wait to sleep again.

EVIL, BE MY GOOD
▼▼▼

PHILIP JOSÉ FARMER

To Herr Professor Doktor Waldman,
University of Ingolstadt,
Grand Duchy of Bavaria

7 October, A.D. 1784

MY Esteemed and Worthy Colleague:

This is indeed a letter from one whom you must long have believed dead and entombed. I, Herr Professor Doktor Krempe, your colleague for many years, am not as dead as you have thought. Bear with me. Do not reject this letter as the product of a crazed mind. Read it to its end, and consider well what is herein.

Though I am dictating this letter, the hands which are writing this letter are huge and clumsy, not my own small and artistic hands. Moreover, they are freezing, and so is the ink in the pot. The supply of writing materials is nonexistent in this Godforsaken and icy desolation. The very limited amount available to me was brought from an icebound ship. Thus, I cannot give a detailed account of what happened to me since the time I was placed in my tomb.

Yes, this is, in a figurative sense, the voice of one everybody has assumed to be dead. It will be a shock, and it will seem to be an affront to both commonsense and logic. Only a professor of natural philosophy could possibly believe this narrative. I say "possibly" because even you, the most open-minded and liberal man I know, perhaps too much so, will find it difficult to put credence in it.

I repeat, please do not shred this letter because you believe that it is both fraudulent and written by a maniac. One item which will make you believe that this is an insane prank is the handwriting. You will compare it to the samples of my penmanship which are in your files, and you will readily see that the letter is not in my hand.

It is not. Yet, it is. Please keep reading. I will explain, though perhaps not to your satisfaction.

I am sending this by a native on skis from this utterly wretched Russian outpost east of Archangel. I have grave doubts that it will ever reach you. However, you are the only person who might think that my story could have some semblance of reality. I cannot send it to my wife. She would not understand anything in it; she would think it a cruel joke if it was explained to her.

Moreover, she has probably remarried. I must confess—a scandal no longer matters and you will keep it to yourself—that we did not, to put it mildly, care for each other.

To the breach, to my tale! Withhold your sense of disbelief until you have read the entire missive. Perhaps, then . . . but no, I doubt you will ever receive this.

The first stroke of lightning paralyzed me. That occurrence, as you know, was in September, 1780, on the grounds of our great university.

The second stroke of lightning, in November, of which you know nothing, freed me.

Yet, in many senses, the succeeding bolt put me in a prison far worse than the first. I could walk and talk after that stroke of hell's energy from the heavens. At the same time, I could not walk and talk. Another creature was walking and talking for me, though I did not want him to act as he acted.

(You are no doubt asking yourself, What second lightning stroke? Be patient. This and other matters will be explained soon.)

For many weeks after the first lightning bolt mummified me, as it were, I was faithfully attended by my wife, the nurses, and the best doctors in Ingolstadt. "Best" is only a relative ranking. All the physicians were quacks. They could have made some simple tests to ascertain if I was conscious and aware despite the fact that I could not move a muscle. But they assumed, in their ignorance and arrogance, that I was in a coma. And, to try to cure me, they bled me and, thus, assured that I did become unconscious from the loss of blood until my body restored the lost fluid!

May they all go to hell! And may that consist of being unable forever to move even their eyelids while they hear their wives, relatives, nurses, and attending quacks talk about them as if they were in their coffins! That condition, you stupid, lackwitted, and pompous practitioners of the unhealing arts, bringers of death to those whom Nature might have healed, would make you painfully aware of what your supposedly caring nurses and loving wives and servants really think of you!

I suffered more agonies than even the cruellest and most savage are doomed to endure forever. Murderers, mutilators, cannibals, blasphemers, freemasons, physicians, lawyers, bankers, and sodomists! You who have gone to hell and are destined to go! You will know little of real pain in that place! The tortures of the damned dead pale beside the tortures of the innocents who must live in the hell of the totally paralyzed!

I, Herr Professor Doktor Krempe, twice dead though not really dead, am come back from two tombs, to write this! Yet, it is not my hand that moves the pen!

I owe all of my second hell to my student in natural philosophy, the ever-egregious, hubris-swollen, and morally unprincipled Victor Frankenstein. I knew what his private opinion of me was because another student reported it to me. Frankenstein, that smug, self-centered, self-righteous, utterly irresponsible, and totally spoiled infant in a man's body, that overbearing and utterly snotty student, said that I was short and squat and the repulsiveness of my hoarse voice was only exceeded by that of my face. Also, he told my informer that only the mercy of God kept my stupidity from being fatal to me. So enraged was I on hearing this from my informant on that dismal October evening that I ignored the cold and driving rain and the perils of the ravening night skies to venture forth on foot to confront the slanderous scoundrel in his own quarters. And I was struck down by a lightning bolt en route to Frankenstein's quarters to confront him. Is there Justice? Is there a God Who believes in Justice?

Later, I was able to revenge myself upon him, though it was done through a very strange vicar, satisfyingly savage. What was not satisfying, I must admit, was my revenge. OUR revenge, I should say, and you will soon know what I mean by OUR! Nothing that could be done to Frankenstein on Earth or in hell would transform the fire in my bosom to sweetness and light, for which seemingly un-Christian statement I am fully justified.

Yet, according to the word of God as printed in the Holy Bible, I must forgive even my worst enemy. Otherwise, I go to hell, too. Is it worth it? I ponder this question often. My chief thoughts revolve around one possible solution to my dilemma. Did Frankenstein commit an unforgivable sin? The particular sin he committed is certainly not listed in the Holy Book. That unique offense against God, I suppose, would also make his sin an original sin. Thus, there are two more grave questions to concern the theologians, and God knows they have enough now that they cannot answer. Are there two unforgivable sins? Are there two original sins?

Unfortunately, or fortunately, they will not have to concern themselves with these matters. No one will ever know about the pair of double sins unless this account gets to a civilized nation. Or unless somebody else writes a book about the monstrous Frankenstein and his monstrous creation. That seems very unlikely. And it would, if it were written, probably be printed as a romantic novel, a fiction. Who among the unenlightened public, the ignorant masses, would believe it if it were presented as fact? For that matter, what learned man would put credence in it?

The day came that I died. That is, the purulent frauds attending me declared me dead. You can imagine, though the mental picture must be only a shadow of the real horror, how I felt! I strove to protest, to cry out aloud that I was still alive! I struggled so violently within myself, though in vain, that it was a wonder I did not have a genuine stroke! I was taken to the undertakers for the washing of my body, dressing me in my best suit, and obscene joking about the size of my genitals. I did manage, finally, to flutter my eyelids. Those drunken incompetents never noticed! Afterwards, while lying in state and listening to the comments about me from those hypocrites, my wife and relatives, I fought once more to blink. But, this time, I failed.

Fortunately for me, the practice among the English wealthy of embalming the body had not become as yet popular in Ingolstadt. Even if it had, my wife would not have permitted it because of the expense. As a result, I lived, though I can truly say that I wished it had been otherwise. I dehydrated, of course, while lying in state, two states, in fact. The other was the state of hell on Earth.

My dear colleague, put it in your will that a knife be driven into your heart before you are buried! Make sure that you are indeed dead before being buried!

The funeral was held—no doubt, you were there—and then the coffin was closed. Immediately thereafter, I was placed in the tomb. I expected to die quickly though horribly when the air in my coffin was used up. But my very shallow breathing made the oxygen last longer. Then, just as I was about to perish, the coffin lid was raised.

You must have already guessed, from my previous remarks, whose face I saw by the light of the torch in his hand. Young Victor Frankenstein, of course!

With him were two scroungy and scurvy fellows he had hired to assist him. They lifted me from the coffin and wrapped me in an oiled cloth enclosing ice chunks and put me in a wagon. In bright daylight! But my tomb was in a remote section of the cemetery, and he was in a desperate haste.

When the cloth was unrolled, I found myself in a filthy and cluttered room. His quarters off campus, I assumed. It looked like the typical degenerate student's room except for the great quantity of expensive scientific equipment. The usual stench of unwashed body and unemptied chamber pot was overriden by the odor of decaying flesh. I cannot go into detail about what followed because of the limited supply of paper and the increasingly wretched penmanship of the creature who is writing this. His hands are getting colder and colder, so I must not indulge myself any more. I must compress this incredible narrative as much as possible.

To be brief, Frankenstein dared to believe that he could make an artificial man out of dead bone and tissue and give the assemblage life! He would do a second time what God had done first! Man, the created, would become a creator! His creature was not visible since it was in a wooden box packed with ice and some preservative that he had discovered through his chemical researches.

I had believed and still believe that this scion of an aristocratic family was the acme of arrogance, stupidity, and selfishness. But God, for some unknown reason, had endowed this detestable being with the genius of Satan. The youth knew what he doing or he blundered into success, probably the latter.

Yes, success!

He placed me in a box filled with ice, sprayed me with some substance I cannot identify, and then proceeded to saw my skull open. I fainted from the horror and the pain, though the cutting was not as painful as I had anticipated.

What happened when I began bleeding, I do not know. I can only surmise that he knew then that I was still living. But, instead of making efforts to revive me, he continued his blasphemous and murderous work. I had known that he despised me, but I had not fathomed the depths of both his hatred of me and his relentless and conscienceless pursuit of a goal only a madman would desire or attempt to achieve.

I awoke late at night. The lightning stroke which he had drawn down from the storm clouds by means of a rod had revivified the body in which I found myself. Its body lived, and so did its brain.

However, that brain was mine!

How that fool of an inexperienced student had managed to connect the encephalic nerves to the others is beyond me. I would not have attempted it despite my deep knowledge of anatomy.

Though I am well-known for my mastery of language, I do not have the words to describe the sensations of being only a brain installed in vitro in an alien body. And what a body! As I was to discover later, it was eight feet in stature and was a disparate assemblage of human and animal parts. As the workmen say, built from scratch.

Of course, I did not know at the moment of awakening that I was not in my own fleshly shell. But it did not take me long to realize the true state of location when the monster lifted my hands. MY hands! They were a giant's, yet they had to be mine! Slowly and clumsily, I rose from the huge table on which I—no, not I, he—had been placed before Frankenstein pulled down the blazing vital fluid from the sky. I was aware not only of my own sensations but of the creature's. This was very confusing and continued to be so for some time before I was able to adapt myself to the unnatural situation.

I said that his sensations were also mine. His thoughts, feeble and chaotic though they were in their beginning, were perceived by me. Integrated by me would be a better description. And, perhaps, I should not describe the thoughts as such. The monster had no language, thus, no words with which to think. He did have the power of using mental icons—I suppose even a dog has that—and his emotions were quite humanlike. But he had no store of images in his brain, which was a veritable *tabula rasa*. Everything that he first saw, smelled, touched, and heard was new to him and impossible for him to interpret. Even the first time he experienced bowel rumblings, he was astonished and frightened, and, if you will pardon the indelicacy, his morning erections disturbed him almost as much as they disturbed me.

How am I to express comprehensibly the relationship of his brain to mine? In the first place, why should his brain be a blank tablet when he was brought to life? (It was, in reality, my brain, but I shall henceforth refer to that portion of my brain used by him as being his own brain.) His own brain should, on revivification, have contained all that it possessed before I died. It did not. Something, shock or some unknown biological or even spiritual mechanism wiped it clean. Or pushed the contents so deep that the creature had no access to them.

If part of the brain was scoured clean, why did a part remain untouched? Why was my consciousness pushed into a corner or, as it were, under the cerebrumic rug? I have no explanation for this phenomenon. The process of creation should not have been like God creating Adam but like God bringing Adam back to life after his longevity of nine hundred and thirty years. Adam would have remembered the events of his stay on Earth.

Our mental connection was, however, a one-way route. I was aware of all he felt and thought. He was totally unaware that a part of him was not he. I could not communicate with him, strive though I did to send some sort of mental semaphore signal to him. I was a passenger in a carriage the driver of which knew nothing of horses or the road he was on or why he was holding the reins. Unlike the passenger in this example, who could at least jump out of the vehicle, I could do nothing about my plight. I was even more helpless and frustrated than when I had been paralyzed by the first stroke of lightning. I was also more frightened and despairing than when in that "coma." That was a natural and not unheard-of situation. This was unnatural and unique.

I saw through the monster's eyes. (These, by the way, were long-sighted. Frankenstein had botched the selection of the visual orbs just as he botched everything else, though he desired to make a perfect human being. Why, in the name of God and all His angels, did Frankenstein build an eight-foot high man? Was that his idea of a being who would not stand out in a crowd?)

As I said, I saw through the eyes of this blasphemy in flesh. Though they needed glasses for reading, their deficiencies were not responsible for the peculiarity of my visual acuity. I saw as if I were peering through the big end of a telescope. What the creature saw as normal-sized, I assume, I saw as if reduced in size. At the same time, the images I received were as if the large end of the telescope were dipped just below the surface of a pond of clear water. The intersection of instrument and fluid made for a peculiar and somewhat blurry picture.

This distortion extended to my hearing also. Thus, the construction of the eyes was not the cause of this irritating phenomenon. It must have been the construction of the brain or, perhaps, a faulty connection between him and me that interfered with proper reception by me. Or perhaps that was the manner in which the creature saw and heard.

Great God! How I do run on! I know that both my time and the quantity of paper are limited. One may give out before the other does. Yet I, always noted for the clarity, conciseness, and absolute relevancy to the subject of my lectures to the benighted, apathetic, and thick-headed students of our university, am as silly and talkative as any one of the hundred passengers on Sebastian Brant's Ship of Fools. Forgive me. I have so many statements to make so that you will understand the story of Frankenstein, his monster, and myself.

Just now, the monster, despite my mental urgings, faltered in his copying of my mental dictation. It is not the cold in this shack which contributes to his weakness. It is the frigid finger of death touching him and, hence, me. I must hurry, must compress. However, as you must realize, you would not be reading this if I had not been successful in reactivating him into continuing the task I have set him without his knowing what he is doing or the reason for it.

He is falling apart, literally. It is my belief that he would have done so much sooner if Frankenstein, that unhappy combination of fool and genius, had not injected some chemical in him to prevent his organs, collected from different individuals and even different species, from reacting poisonously upon each other. The chemicals used to effect this have, however, dissipated their strength.

Yesterday, his right ear fell off. The day before, his left leg swelled up and is turning black. A week ago, he vomited all the polar bear meat and seal blubber that have been his—our—main ingredients of diet. He has been unable to keep much down since then. Most of his teeth are rotting.

Let us hope that I can keep pushing him until he hands over this letter to the messenger.

That hopelessly irresponsible Frankenstein was so horrified when his creation became alive that he ran away, leaving the monster, innocent as a baby and as full of potential good—and evil—as an infant, to his own devices.

I could do nothing but go along with the monster in his pathetic efforts to understand the world into which he had been involuntarily thrust. All of us, of course, had no say about our entering this harsh and indifferent universe. But most babies have someone to take care of their needs, to love them, and to educate them. This creature was, of all mankind, and it was human despite the doubts of itself and its maker, the most forlorn infant of all. Though I at first loathed him, I came to sympathize with him, indeed, to identify with him. Why not? Is not he myself, and is not myself he?

Onward more swiftly. As the end of his—our—lifespan approaches, so must the end of this letter be hastened.

No time for details, no matter how much they demand to be illuminated and explained.

The creature fled from Ingolstadt to the mountain forests nearby. He learned much about himself and the world and the people in this area. He longed for acceptance and love. He did not get either. He learned how to make and use fire. He approached a village in peace and was injured by the stones cast at him. He took refuge in an unused part of a cottage and spied upon the occupants, once-wealthy French aristocrats exiled and now living in poverty.

His eavesdropping enabled him to learn how to speak French. Part of that was my doing. I had by then managed to send him some messages of which he was not conscious. These were not commands which he obeyed or anything making him conscious of my presence, but the information stored in my brain, which included an excellent knowledge of French, oozed through to him.

(Incidentally, I discovered the most intimate details of the electrical, chemical, and neural constructions and functions of the human brain. Alas! No time to impart this stupendously vital information which would propel our knowledge of the brain to the high stage which I imagine the citizens of the twentieth century will enjoy. But I cannot resist informing you that the treelike organization of the nerves is a delight to the explorer. My travels up and down its trunks, branches, and twigs were the only joy I have had during my incarceration in the monster's body. I was, in a sense, a great ape swinging from branch to branch in the orderly jungle of the neural system, learning as I traveled. I discovered that the splanchnic nerve is actually three nerves and all control the visceral functions in various manners. I call them the Great, the Lesser, and the Least. I especially loved the Least Splanchnic Nerve, a modest, unassuming, and yet somewhat cheeky transmitter with unexpected aftereffects, a rosy glow, in fact.)

The creature—it has never had a name, a lack which has greatly depressed its self-esteem but heightened its fury and its lust for revenge: you have no idea what being nameless does to a human being—finally revealed himself to the occupants of the cottage. He expected compassion; he got repulsion and horror. The occupants fled. He burned down the cottage and then wandered aimlessly around. He rescued a girl from drowning and was wounded by a gun for his heroic deed. This ingratitude intensified his hurt and rage, of course. Then he came to Geneva, Frankenstein's native city.

Here he murdered Victor's brother, the child William. While he was doing this, I screamed at him, if a voiceless being can be said to scream. No use. The monster's hands—my hands—choked the life out of the infant.

The man-made thing encountered his maker and got him to

promise to make a female for him. Victor went to the Orkney Islands and did as promised. But, disgusted, suffering from Welt-schmerz—with which the monster was also afflicted—Victor destroyed the female, which was as huge and ugly as her male counterpart.

Oh, the catalog of horrors! The ravening creature murdered Henry Clerval, Victor's best friend. He raped and murdered Victor's bride on their wedding night. After that hideous deed, he declared that evil would henceforth become his good. He was sincere when he said that. But the words were not his in origin even if they were his in spirit. They were a paraphrase of Satan's defiant statement in Milton's *Paradise Lost.* "Evil, by thou my good."

Yes, the monster had read that noble work. It contains, as you know, some of the greatest lines in poetry. However, there are boring passages which stretch their dryness to an intolerable length. The reader feels as if he were a parched traveller lost in a Sahara of iambic pentameter.

I was the unwilling actor in a tragedy which was real, not Miltonic. You cannot imagine the agony and the shame I experienced while the monster was performing his ritual of lust and murder upon Elizabeth, Frankenstein's bride. Yet, I must confess that I also shared the ecstasy of his orgasm; though, soon after I was transported, I loathed myself.

Frankenstein, after he was put in prison because he went temporarily mad—temporarily?—after his father's death, began to track down his creation in order to slay him. After much time and many wanderings, both Frankenstein and his creature were in the Arctic, traveling on dogsleds. Victor became very sick but took refuge on an icebound ship. After telling his story to an Englishman aboard the vessel, he died.

Meanwhile, the ice pack broke up. The passage to warmer climes was open. But the monster came aboard just after his creator died. He had by then been stricken with the pangs of conscience, perhaps because he felt dimly my own reactions to his satanic deeds, though I was as eager as he to slay Victor, and these, in a twisted way, caused the monster to repent.

I do not think that he had sufficient reason because of this to decide to kill himself. He was far more the injured of the two. What did Frankenstein expect? That the creature, like a true Christian, would turn the other cheek? He had not been in- structed in Christianity and, anyway, how many of those so instructed would have forgiven such great evils done to them?

In fact, that the monster did have a conscience so tender and highly ethical trumpets forth his innate goodness.

But it may be that my mental urgings were by then influenc- ing him, however small their voices. I had been trying to get him to kill himself, for his sake and, I have to admit, for my own. What a miserable life I had been leading! Starving and freezing with him, hurt with him, sick with fury and desire for revenge with him. I wanted our lives—actually, a single life—to end.

One of the unforgivable sins is suicide. But I was not killing myself through my direct action. The nameless and pitiful unnat- ural creature would be doing it. My hands were clean; his would be dirty. But he would not have to burn in hell for that deed. He had no soul. Nor would I burn. I had died once and should have gone to Heaven. Instead, Frankenstein, the foul incarna- tion of the archdemon, had brought me back to life. For that blasphemous crime, Frankenstein would exist forever after death as a shade on the plain of burning sands in the seventh circle of Hell. There, an eternal rain of fire would fall on him. There, according to the great Italian poet, Dante, are the blasphemers and the sodomites, the violent against God, which Frankenstein certainly was. There also are the usurers, that is, the violent against Art. Frankenstein belongs in their ranks. He violated God's Art by making the monster. Thrice accursed, thrice tortured!

His monster finally forgave him, but I cannot do that. Thus,

the monster is more Christian than I. Theological and philosophical question for you, colleague. Does that indicate that God
should or must endow the monster with a soul? If He does, to
whom belongs the brain of that soul? What is my brain is his
brain and always the twain shall be one. The implications are
staggering. A whole college of St. Aquinases could consider that
one question for aeons.

To resume. The creature—and myself—declared to the
Englishman on the ship where Frankenstein died that he would
build a funeral pyre and lie down upon it until his loathsome
body was burned to ashes. Of course, you will find this ridiculous.
Where, in this Arctic wasteland, could he find a single branch
for fuel?

Then he boarded a large piece of ice and floated away. During
the interval before the ice island came to land, I managed
finally to communicate with the other part of my brain. It was
a one-way form, that is, I could impart some of my mental
suggestions or commands to him, though he was not aware of
my presence or of the command. I do not know how I finally
did it. I believe that it was his weakening state of health, his
decaying flesh, that enabled me to overcome whatever obstacle
had previously existed.

He—we—wandered over the snow-and-ice-covered land until
we came to this remote outpost inhabited by a few miserable
natives. We were given food, disgusting fare but nutritious, and
a shelter scarcely worthy of the name. Now, I could transmit my
commands, though they became distorted in the passage as if they
were flags manipulated by a drunken semaphorist. No doubt, this
was because of the rapidly decaying state of the monster's neural
system. Of course, that affected me, and my transmissions may
also have been at fault.

The main problem is that, the weaker and more disorganized
the creature's brain becomes, the easier it is for me to influence

him but that very removal of mental obstacles decreases the monster's efficiency in carrying out my messages.

To put it in the colloquial, you pay for what you get. Also, the more progress you make in solving a problem, the more problems you encounter.

I really cannot see now how legible the handwriting is. The objects I observe through his eyes are getting smaller and smaller. And the watery veil now seems to have swirling particles in it. These are becoming more numerous. It may not belong bfore them coleisce to from a seemerly slodid well.

Ferwale . . . is end . . . Dog forgove . . . menster. Me too . . . evn fregiv his creatr . . . Farknesten . . . Dog . . . nod Dog . . . min, God . . . God . . . furgiv . . . nodpar . . . pardin . . . pardon . . . fregiv . . . all . . . rwesched . . . humn . . . beins . . . evn monster . . . humn too . . . iverbudy . . . for!gev . . . all . . . Gd . . . God . . . fregiv me

A WRIT OF
HABEAS CORPUS
▼▼▼

CHELSEA QUINN YARBRO

IT was difficult writing with a crayon. His big, spatulate fingers were too awkward to manage more than a few dozen scrawled words on every page. He had asked for a pen, but they had not given him one, of course.

The other men in the psychiatric prison stayed away from him, except for Rowell, who made a point of not being frightened of anything. Occasionally he would swagger up to the large man and catch him with a hard look; he did that now, knowing that several of the other prisoners were watching.

"Whatcha doing, Frank?" Rowell asked while Frank struggled with the crayon. "Drawing a picture? What kinda picture?"

"Writing a letter," said Frank, every word coming out slowly and precisely, sounding like he was recovering from a stroke. When he was caught up in a different task, speech became an ordeal for him.

"Uh-huh," said Rowell, doing his best to read the red marks on the yellow paper upside down. "Who to?"

"A lawyer," said Frank. He leaned forward on the table and had the satisfaction of seeing Rowell take a step backward.

"Another try at getting out," said Rowell with certainty. "Man, they're never going to let you out. Never happen. Get that straight. Outside they think you're dead. No one knows you're alive, and that's the way they want it. You're here for forever." He smiled his dazzled, manic smile and struck the table with his fist. "You get that!"

"Leave me alone, Rowell," said Frank patiently, doing his best to write *sympathize* on one line. The *z* was getting away from him and he bit the tip of his tongue in concentration.

"You're a freak, that's what you are. You think you're such a genius, but you're a freak. Freak Frank, that's it!" He struck the table again, and hastily retreated as if he expected to be caught and punished for his audacity. "Freak!"

"You're probably right," said Frank as he went on with his letter. It covered five pages now, and would probably take another five, but that was no deterrent. He had learned that persistence paid; he kept at his task.

When he was finished, some four hours later, he read over the fruits of his labor:

Dear Mister Gregory Hartford:

Please excuse the way this looks and bear with me. I am in the psychiatric ward of Senzono State Prison and we are not permitted to use pens, pencils or type-writers, and I have some disability directly related to my case.

I would be most grateful if you could be willing to review my case. I have no money and can offer you very little in the way of a fee. But I believe that my case is sufficiently unique that you might decide to take it for the notoriety it could cause.

My case records can be put at your disposal if you would like to review them before speaking with me. After you have seen these I would hope you would sympathize with my predicament and be willing to file a writ of habeas corpus on behalf of my body. As you will discover in my records, there are reasonable legal grounds for such a request.

No matter what your decision, I thank you, Mister Hartford, for your attention.

> *Most sincerely,*
> *#5598735-PS14*
> *Frank Einstein*

The night staff physician addressed the envelope for Frank, and gave him the stamp to post it. "Good luck," he said to Frank as a matter of form. This was the fifteenth such letter Prisoner #5598735-PS14 had written and so far he had received no answers; none were expected. Prisoner #5598735-PS14 was one of those invisible inmates who had no family, no visitors, no contact with the world on the other side of the walls beyond what they saw on the evening news.

"Thanks," said Frank, and trudged back through the recreation room to his cell. Some of the others were watching television, but Frank was not a mingler and did not want to see *Stagecoach* for the fifth time. Old movies held little interest for him these days; they reminded him too much of the past.

▼▼▼

The envelope was as much a surprise to Frank as it was to the guard who brought it to him. Gregory Hartford had responded with a promptness that was as suspicious as it was gratifying; Frank opened the letter with many doubts possessing him.

Dear Mister Einstein;

Your letter surprised me, as I had been informed some time ago that you were dead. Yes, I am aware of your case and I think you may have a workable approach to your problem. I believe you are correct in calling your predicament legally unique.

You may be aware that my great-uncle was Spencer Dare; he followed your case with a great deal of interest, an interest I have come to share. It would please him if he knew that one of the family was acting on your behalf.

At present I am making arrangements to visit you next month. I hope this will be convenient.

Sincerely,
Gregory S. Hartford

Frank read the letter three times before he believed it, and even when his incredulity was gone, the notion had not yet sunk in. Someone was actually willing to review his case; Gregory Spencer Hartford was going to confer with him. In all the time he had been locked up he had never felt so vindicated as he did that afternoon.

He went for his weekly injection that was supposed to keep him calm, though both he and the chief surgeon knew that it had no effect on him whatsoever. For once he was annoyed at the farce of it all. "Let's get this over with," he told the surgeon, and then startled both of them by telling him about the response to his letter.

"Well, you must feel pretty good, I guess," said Doc Reginald when Frank finished.

"I don't know what I feel. I mean that, Doc. All the other letters—nothing. I wasn't expecting . . . this," said Frank, watching the needle sink into his arm just above the cicatrix. "It takes some getting used to."

"I guess it does," said Doc Reginald.

"I'm not getting my hopes up," Frank told him, anticipating just such a warning.

"I hate to say it, but much better not to, Frank. It's hard to take, I know." He patted Frank's huge shoulder. "You've got pretty good sense most of the time. Don't forget that now."

Frank nodded out of habit, then said, "But it is the first encouragement I've had. That's important, isn't it."

Doc Reginald considered his answer. "Encouragement is one thing, if you don't let it get its hooks in you. You've been inside a long time, and getting out isn't easy when you've been here so long. You don't know what you're getting into. That's what you've got to watch, making sure you don't expect much."

"That way I won't be disappointed?" Frank said, and nodded before Doc Reginald could answer.

▼▼▼

Gregory Hartford was small and wiry and incapable of holding still for more than three seconds at a stretch. He paced the interview room as he waited for Frank Einstein, his greenish eyes alight with the fire of battle. For once he was being offered a real challenge, something he could sink his teeth into; at thirty-six, he was primed and ready. And it was a case that Great-Uncle Spencer had followed. Great-Uncle Spencer said that the Einstein case had been a great miscarriage of justice, and the movie hadn't helped. Frank Einstein shouldn't be held responsible for what his brother did. Hartford almost rubbed his hands in anticipation. What could be better than that? He turned abruptly as Frank Einstein was ushered into the stark, dreary interview room.

"Mister Hartford?" said Frank, holding out his huge hand.

Although Hartford thought he was prepared for this moment, he goggled at the sight of Frank Einstein. He had not realized the size of the man, or the harshness of his scars. The one across his forehead was about the worst of the lot, Hartford decided, unable to keep from staring. It was wide and white and the suture marks straddled it in a series of deep puckers. No wonder there had been no doubts about his identification from witnesses. That face would linger in nightmares for years. "Mister . . . Mister Einstein." He had to steel himself for the grip of his hand.

"I'm very grateful to you for coming," said Frank, stepping back. He had seen that expression before and knew that he had to put some distance between himself and Hartford.

"Yes. Well. Glad to do it. It's an interesting case; you could say it's without precedent." He glanced once at the door, then made himself look at Frank again. His ten years of courtroom experience helped him keep his voice steady as he regarded the man who wanted to be his client. "Yes. Very interesting."

"You've gone over the records, then," said Frank, choosing the only wooden chair in the room to sit on; the plastic ones on the metal frames did not look sturdy enough for his bulk.

"Most of them. I've read the arrest records and the various psychiatric evaluations, as well as the press coverage at the time of the . . . uh . . . the events." He pointed out his briefcase. "I've got more material in there. I've gone over the basics, of course. Reviewed your trial transcript, the charges, and all that."

"Good," said Frank, clasping his hands together. "That means you know about the killings. Don't you." He did not expect a response. "I'm supposed to have killed Victor, and that kid by the lake, at least according to the charges."

"The arrest reports are pretty detailed. The case against you is definite, as far as it goes," said Hartford, his tone suggesting that Frank offer no excuses.

"As far as it goes. That's the trouble. You see, I know I was there. I don't really remember anything specific. It's almost as if it happened to someone else. That's the part that bothers me, that it seemed to be someone else. In a way, I guess I did those things. My hands seem to remember being around Victor's throat. But—" He lifted his hand and indicated the terrible scar on his forehead. "This makes a difference. Doesn't it? The brain, and the hands, I mean. Isn't it diminished capacity if it isn't your own brain?"

"That's for the jury to decide, if we can get you another trial." He made himself look at the scars without flinching. "Victor did that to you, didn't he?" Hartford asked, making himself take a sensible attitude toward this grotesque figure.

"Oh, yes. I'm his . . . brainchild." There was no mirth in the tight smile that accompanied his ironic joke.

"There was no question of complicity, was there? You weren't part of a conspiracy. You didn't plan it in advance. You didn't know he was going to do this to you." He folded his arms, then unfolded them for fear he might look too pugnacious. He did not want to do anything that could be interpreted as a challenge, not to someone who looked like *that*.

"No, I wasn't. Or I don't think I was. Maybe some part of me agreed, but not my mind. And I mean my mind, *mine*, not the brain in here now. I never knew what he was up to, I'm certain of that. I don't think he cared whether I agreed or not. I was Victor's lab animal, his experiment." He sighed. "Some people infect lab animals with anthrax. Victor infected me with life. And he did it with this brain and that machine of his."

"It *isn't* your brain, is it?" He fought down a sudden impulse to laugh at the bizarre question. "Or is it?"

"As much as my hands are, I suppose," said Frank. "Neither one is the one I was born with." He slumped and succeeded in looking even more like something chiseled out of granite.

"Without your permission." He paced in a circle at the part of the room that was farthest from Frank.

"What permission would that be? How would anyone give

permission for something like this? Certainly I would have refused him, if he'd asked me. I might not remember, but I *know* I'd never consent to something like this. Who would? He never inquired anything of this brain he stuck me with. I'm certain of that much. He was caught up in his experiment, don't you see? The rest didn't matter. First, last and always was his experiment." He made no attempt to disguise the depth of bitterness he felt.

"And so he exhumed you without your permission?" Hartford persisted. "The . . . main part of you?"

"That's what I told the police. That's what I told the judge at the hearing. They never found anything that said I was part of it, not in my will, not in Victor's papers. It's in the record." He stared down at his feet. "I tried to tell them everything, but it didn't do much good. I don't think they believed me, not until they found Victor's lab notes."

"Tell me." Hartford pounced on the words. "Tell me all of it. Start from the beginning."

"Again?" asked Frank. He looked up at Hartford and saw him nod eagerly. "All right. Again." He paused as he cast his mind—if it was his mind—back. "My brother, Doctor Victor Frankenstein assembled me from . . . bits and pieces. He called me Frank Einstein as a joke, I think. Einstein for genius, and Frank so he wouldn't have to remember my name. That much even the cops accept. The psychiatrist who examined me was pretty confused about my identity. He wasn't sure what part of me was me, and who the me was. If it's any answer, most of this body was taken out of his brother's coffin."

"And do you think you're his *brother*? After all this?" Hartford demanded.

"From my neck to my knees I am, and down my arms. My hands, my calves and feet, my head all belong to other people."

"Good Lord," said Hartford. "They didn't mention about you being his brother."

"Partly his brother," Frank corrected him. "The court suppressed that information. It was considered too shocking for the case, and for the trial. They said that the press would make too much of it. They claimed it would be too prejudicial." He looked at Hartford. "They took it out of my records too, I guess."

"I didn't find any specific mention of it," said Hartford carefully, unwilling to accuse the authorities of deliberate tampering. "They might have buried it somewhere I haven't looked yet."

Frank shrugged. "Would it make any difference? I don't know what Victor expected. I wouldn't, would I, not with Sacton's brain. Sacton didn't know a thing about it." He made himself not sigh. "I found out about Sacton a few years ago. They hushed up everything about him, too."

"You can't blame them. Elihu Sacton's brain. No wonder you've had trouble." Hartford was pacing again, still keeping his distance from Frank. "How many personalities did they think he had?"

"A dozen or so," said Frank patiently. "I haven't noticed them, really, but sometimes I think one or two of them must be around."

"Why is that?" asked Hartford. In spite of his best intentions, he was fascinated.

"Well, there are gaps in my memory." He went on with care. "I know these hands strangled Victor, but whether the hands did it, or one of those other personalities in Sacton's brain caused it, I can't be sure. What part of me is responsible for what happened? I haven't found out whose hands these are. He must have been a big son-of-a-bitch, judging by their size."

"That answers the question about Victor." He stopped a moment. "And the little girl. Do you remember anything about her?"

Frank shook his head, looking directly at Hartford. "I think I can remember meeting her, but it's . . . fuzzy. I think she might have given me a flower. I have an image of a little girl with a flower, anyway. The rest . . . I don't know."

"She was beaten and drowned," said Hartford with deliberate bluntness.

"I know. I heard all about it at the trial. It was awful." He looked down at his enormous hands. "I suppose I could have done it. I'm strong enough, God knows. But I don't think I'm capable of it, not I as I am now. I can't answer for then, or for the brain that did it."

"It's the brain in your skull, isn't it?" He made this an accusation.

"Yes, but it's not like it used to be. Over the years I've gotten . . . better integrated. Learning to talk again helped. I still feel . . . alien, but not internally hostile, the way I did at first, when all these . . . these parts"—he held up his hands as examples— "were not working together."

Hartford halted for an instant, then moved again. "But you have reason to think that you are not technically responsible for the murders."

"Well, the body isn't, I don't think." He followed Hartford with his eyes. "It could be the hands, but I suspect the brain was. It's different now."

"Are you certain of that? Are you confident you could never murder again?"

"Sacton's brain might want to, but the body wouldn't. We're in better balance now. I'm not Elihu Sacton, not any of his personalities. In a very real sense, I never was."

"Elihu Sacton's brain," said Hartford, in order to be certain.

"Yes. At least there are some records of his personalities. Three of them were . . . maybe still could be homicidal. That would be the issue now, wouldn't it? I think the court determined he might still be capable of killing, didn't it?" He tried to smile but his mouth never did it right.

"According to the records," said Hartford very carefully. "His case was one of the first. We don't know how to evaluate some of the results: there wasn't a good enough methodology then, and now . . ."

"Now it isn't really possible, is it?" said Frank quietly.

Hartford paused and shook his head. "No. I guess not."

▼▼▼

Doc Reginald scowled at the test results. "I'm sorry, Frank, but they're inconclusive. I don't know what to make of them, and that's the truth." He looked down at his patient, strapped to the scan platform, and regarded the machine tracings once more. "The trouble is, how much of this interference is due to brain transplant and how much of it is multiple personality echo? I don't know if we can differentiate one from the other."

Frank closed his eyes in resignation. "You do notice something that shouldn't be there, something that is . . . foreign?"

"Oh, yeah, so far as it goes, it's clear that the brain isn't behaving normally. There are lines here I've never seen before and it's anybody's guess what they mean." Doc Reginald patted Frank on the shoulder. "I'll hand this over to your attorney, of course, but what it does about your Habeas Corpus I'm damned if I know."

"Well, I don't know that much about it myself," said Frank, doing his best to make light of the situation. "Are you going to run any more scans, or is this it?"

"We'd better get another set, for comparison to the first two. We don't have a good enough sample of variations yet. There's too much irregularity from one to the other." He touched the operating lever. "You don't mind going back in, do you?"

"Not really," said Frank, though he found the narrow confines of the scanner upsetting. "Let's get it over with."

"Right you are," said Doc Reginald, and prepared to run the scans again.

Gregory Hartford pored over the test results and scribbled notes in the margins of the analysis Doc Reginald had offered. He paid little heed to Frank, who sat on the other side of the battered table, waiting to answer questions. "I won't be much longer. Sorry to keep you waiting."

"I don't have anything else going on," said Frank mildly. A new inmate had arrived the day before and Frank wanted to keep away from him, knowing how many of the other prisoners represented him as the terror of the institution. As much as he tried to be unmoved by this, it always bothered him.

"Doc Reginald has volunteered to be a witness for you, did you hear about that?" said Hartford as he folded the tests and slipped them into a file folder.

"He didn't mention it, no," said Frank. "That's very kind of him."

"He seems to think you got a raw deal. He thinks you've become someone who's a mixture, and that having Sacton's brain doesn't make you Sacton." He leaned back in his chair, balancing precariously on the back legs. "He said that it doesn't make any sense to keep you locked up this way."

"What way does he think I should be locked up?" asked Frank, watching Hartford with curiosity.

"Hey!" Hartford came back down on all four chairlegs. "What makes you say that?"

Frank regarded Hartford without blinking. "He's not going to recommend someone like me be turned loose, is he? He couldn't do that. Where would I work? Who would hire me? What would I do? Look at me. All the rehabilitation in the world isn't going to change this." He indicated the scars on his face and neck.

"That's probably true, and you can bet there are people who have used the way you look as an excuse to keep you locked up in this prison. Well, we've got laws against that now, and you've been kept here without a trial when you are obviously capable of appearing in court. It's time the people who put you here answer for it," said Hartford. He shifted in his chair. "Because you sure as hell shouldn't be here. You're right about that. And we're going to get you out." He drew himself closer to the table. "And speaking of getting you out of here, I have filed a writ of habeas corpus on your behalf, along with a motion for trial, on the grounds that not all the pertinent facts in the case were presented at the time your trial was waived. Once we get the body out, the next thing to do is to erase the mark against the mind. We've got a ton of material to present if they'll let us. I don't know how far we'll get with it, but it's worth a try, and it tells them that we're serious about the habeas corpus."

"What happens if they say yes?" asked Frank, startled at the zeal of his attorney. "I've been inside a long time. It might be easier if—"

"We get you out and we get you a proper trial. That's just for starters. We make sure we have expert testimony, the kind of thing you were deprived of before. We get information about brain transplants into the record—if there's anyone who knows enough about it to give the court the right information—and we push the medical ethics of your case for all we're worth. We show that you are the victim just as much as that little girl was. Maybe more the victim, because you were taken advantage of by your own brother and turned into—"

"A monster?" Frank suggested. "Won't I be that, still?"

"Not when I'm through with it. I can show that you were not responsible for anything that occurred after the surgery, that you were made the scapegoat for what Victor did. We can work every angle on this, from the advances in medicine since your operation to the social pressure you had to endure. I've been boning up on things. We've got precedent-setting issues here with you." His eyes brightened at the prospect. "If we handle this right, it could go all the way to the Supreme Court."

"In other words, we try Victor *in absentia*," said Frank.

"Something like that," said Hartford. "If nothing else, we should be able to establish much more than a reasonable doubt in regard to your legal responsibilities in the murder case, and your entitlement to compensation for your imprisonment and suffering. That last is a little chancy," he added, "but I think we can try for it. With any kind of jury, we should be able to get you everything you want, and then some." He slapped his hands onto the table. "That's the first step."

"The first step? And then what?" Frank asked. It sounded like something out of a movie, not anything that could happen to him.

"Yes. After we get your release we make sure that everyone in the country knows what's going on. Look, you're potentially a hot guy. I've seen the demographics on medical fuck-ups, and they're very favorable for you. So far they make media stars out of heart transplants, and most of those guys don't live long enough to tell about it. You had a brain transplant long before anyone else thought about it, and it *took*. That's the really big news, since no one else has been able to do it since, even with all the improvements in surgery." He made a sweeping gesture. "Think about it. You have another man's brain, another man's hands and feet, and from everything in your tests, you had no trouble with tissue rejection. That's nothing short of amazing. We can use that to the hilt."

"Use it how?" asked Frank apprehensively.

"Look, you can't turn back now. If you do, with the kind of questions I've been asking, the government'll be down on you, and God alone knows what they'll do."

"They haven't done anything so far," said Frank, his certainty faltering.

"That's because they'd forgotten about you. You can't count on that continuing, not after what we've started. You stick with me. We'll make sure you're protected, don't worry about that. We'll find a way to keep you from being a guinea pig ever again." He clapped his hands together, his face shining with purpose. "We get your story on every television broadcast from Maine to San Diego, we make sure every paper in the country covers your retrial." He was so enthusiastic that he got up and paced. "That way they won't dare to sweep you under the rug, or cart you off to some government installation. And there are side-benefits you can get out of this. I've been looking into selling your story to one of the big magazines or book publishers. You can get real money out of a deal like that. Who knows, your case is odd enough that there might even be a movie deal in it. Maybe Nick Nolte could play you—what do you think?"

Frank look baffled. "Movie deal? They made a deal already, before."

"Never mind that," said Hartford. "That's in the past. It doesn't mean anything. We work out a deal to do the story again, and this time, we make it about you, about what was done to you, not that crazy brother of yours."

"How . . ." He tried to order his jumbled thoughts. "This isn't possible, really, is it? I can't see how you could . . . It's unreal."

"That's because you're in here. You don't know how the world's changed out there. It doesn't matter what you see on TV, the real world will blow your mind." He stopped and looked chagrined. "I didn't mean that the way it came out. It's just that everything is so much more exciting than it was when you were locked up here. We're going to change that. The world is full of possibilities you've never dreamed of."

For an instant, the vision that filled Frank's thoughts was terrifying. He dreaded that world outside, the one he longed for. "But—"

Hartford waved his panic away. "If we work this out, you can come out of this with a nice little nest egg and the chance for some privacy as well, if that's what you want. But you might like being a star." He grinned. "I've been thinking it over and I can see lots of ways this is going to pay off. Aside from the movie and the book, there are going to be lots of medical facilities all over the country that will want to study you. Think about it. You can insist on grants and per diem payments every step of the way. You can protect yourself from getting rooked into anything clandestine. I'll handle all that stuff for you, every step of the way." He stopped and perched on the edge of the table. "I think you've suffered a real injustice, no doubt about that. But that's the key."

"I don't understand." Frank started to get up, but Hartford put his hand on his shoulder.

"You're the victim of injustice. You deserve a break or two. That's what's going to get you all the goodies." This time his grin was anticipatory. "You might not think so now, but a year from today, you're going to be famous."

The word all but stuck in his throat. "Famous?" repeated Frank, appalled.

"Damn right. Once we get you out of here, there'll be no stopping you. Us." Hartford chuckled. "I bet you never thought that would happen."

"No," said Frank quietly, "I didn't."

"All this from one writ of habeas corpus," Hartford went on, very satisfied with himself. His mind was brimming with possibilities that he could hardly wait to explore. "Just wait. You can't imagine what's going to happen to you now."

Frank shook his head. "No."

▼▼▼

A silver-grey limousine was waiting in front of the prison gate ten days later when Frank was released. Gregory Hartford was standing by the door, grinning. "I got a bottle of champagne and a deli picnic waiting," he said as he ushered Frank into the back of the splendid vehicle. "I bet you've never traveled in one of these before."

"Not that I know of," said Frank, looking around in awe. He felt out of place here. His new clothes did not quite fit and he was aware the world he was entering was not the one he left when the prison doors closed behind him all those years ago. He hunkered his bulk down into one of the plush-covered seats.

"This"—Hartford indicated the limousine as he got in and closed the door—"was provided by Gargantuan Films. They're the ones who won the auction for the film rights to your story. They're working out a publicity tour for you now with Eureka Books, so that the book and film can get publicity at the same time. I wish you could have been there when I sent out all the information on you. They just about bounced off the ceiling." He tapped on the chauffeur's shoulder. "You might as well get moving, Blake."

"Yes, Mister Hartford," said the chauffeur as he set the limousine in motion.

Hartford leaned back on the soft cushions. "I know this probably isn't the way Spencer Dare would have handled it, but back in his day, you couldn't do deals like this." Belatedly he reached for the champagne. "Let me pour you a glass. We can celebrate the freeing of your body."

Frank turned and stared out the tinted window at the psychiatric-prison walls, and for a moment wondered if he had perhaps been freer there than he was now.

"We've got dinner reservations in Manhattan at eight. We'll

be joining the president of Eureka Books and Samuel Flannagan, who's going to be your collaborator in the book. They're very anxious to meet you. I've got them champing at the bit." The champagne cork popped and Hartford offered Frank the first glass he filled. "Been a while since you've had any of this."

It took both hands for Frank to keep from spilling the wine. He watched it, following the lines of bubbles marching to the top of the flute. "I . . . don't know if I've ever had it. I don't remember." There was so much he didn't remember. In prison it had hardly mattered, but out here, he felt vulnerable, exposed.

"Well, that doesn't matter now; get used to it." He touched the rim of his glass to Frank's. "This is the life you're going to have. Enjoy it. You've earned it. You're not in prison any more."

There was a strange light in Frank's eyes, and his voice, when he answered, hardly seemed to belong to him. "No," he said to Hartford as the limousine sped away into the brilliant afternoon light, "I suppose not."

THE STATE
VERSUS
ADAM SHELLEY
▼▼▼

BENJAMIN M. SCHUTZ

FORENSIC EVALUATION

THIS is the report of the evaluation conducted by the forensic team of the behavorial sciences division at Goldstadt Medical Center on Adam Shelley (DOB 10/31/92).

Social History

Adam's mother was Mary W. Shelley, age 19 and a college freshman. She sought genetic screening of a possible pregnancy and was informed that unusual chromosomal defects were identified. She then filed for an abortion under the rape exemption. Her request was denied because the rape was not reported within the 7-day state guidelines for the exemption to be valid. As assault report had been filed with local police but there was no mention of a rape. Subsequent to the rejection of her request she apparently sought out an illegal abortionist in the city of Charlotte. She was arrested for fetal endangerment as part of the "sting" operation of the Department of Health and Welfare, which had established "apparently" illegal abortion shops across the state. A Sanctity Of Life motion was filed by the Fetal Defense League and Miss Shelley was committed to the Jesse Helms Memorial Reproduction Center for the duration of her pregnancy.

While in the center Miss Shelley suffered serious head trauma from either a fall or a possible suicide attempt. She was placed under the care of Dr. Henry Frankenstein of the neonatal intensive care unit. Although she was brain-dead, Dr. Frankenstein was able to sustain Miss Shelley as a viable carrier for the fetus. In fact it was during this case that Dr. Frankenstein developed many of the techniques now used in the induced coma treatment for chronic miscarriage, prematurity and pre-partum agitation in committed patients.

Subsequent to the birth of her child, Miss Shelley was maintained on life support systems and then transferred to the Raleigh-Durham Neurovegetative Center where she is still a resident. No father was ever named.

The child was named Adam Shelley by his legal guardians, the State Department of Social Services Child Protection Unit. He was raised in the pediatrics unit of the Helms Center until the age of seven. This was occasioned by the severity of his medical needs. (See findings under Physical/Medical Information.)

At age seven he was placed in long-term foster care with the DeLacey family in Winston-Salem. This was felt to be an appropriate placement, as the father was blind and the family already had a disabled daughter, Agatha, in addition to a son Felix. The placement seemed to go well and there was discussion of legal adoption by the DeLacey family. Unfortunately an incident occurred with a young friend of Agatha's. The child, Marian Ludwigsdottir, was two years younger than Adam. One afternoon she came to visit the children who were under the care of Mrs. DeLacey. She called them all in for a snack and, when Marian did not come in, she went out and found her dead in the family's above-ground swimming pool. The death was formally ruled accidental and no evidence linked Adam with the death, but the DeLaceys asked that he be returned to the care of the State.

At age nine Adam was placed outside the Helms Center for a second time. This placement was with the Sweet Love of Jesus Youth Home run by the television ministry of Billy Ray Washburn. Adam was there for almost two years. During that time he made several suicide attempts, including one near-fatal laceration through the large vein in his eyestalk. There was some consideration that this was an expression of guilt over the death of the Ludwigsdottir girl; however, Adam never expressed any knowledge of her death.

Unfortunately this home was raided by the police in the summer of 2005 when it was discovered that certain of the children were being selected out by the staff and housed in a separate building for use as sex partners by Reverend Washburn and members of his ministry board of directors. There was no evidence uncovered that Adam Shelley was abused in this fashion. However, there were unconfirmed reports from other children that Adam was physically abused by a staff member named Fritz Harmann, and that videotapes of his abuse were shown to stimulate some of the men before they molested other children. No copies of the videotapes were ever found. What cannot be disputed is that at the time of the raid by the State Police the body of Fritz Harmann was found hanging in his room, dead of a broken neck. It is also a fact that Adam Shelley was a resident of this special ward.

Brief attempts were made to place Adam in residential schools where he could receive multi-modal therapy for his disabilities. Because of his history, age and appearance it was determined that family placement was entirely out of the question. No matter where he was placed Adam was not welcome. He was tormented by other students, no matter what their disabilities. Ultimately he was returned to the Helms Center's Adolescent and Youth Services.

While a resident there he became aware of the connection between his birth and Dr. Frankenstein. Another resident showed him the *People* Magazine article about Dr. Frankenstein's work that made reference to his early discoveries and his original ground-breaking work on Mary Shelley and the birth of her son Adam.

Adam showed little overt interest in Dr. Frankenstein or his birth. Pediatric records show that he entered puberty rather late, around thirteen. Shortly thereafter, violent outbursts against staff and other residents increased. Adam was placed in solitary confinement and was so secluded when he made his escape from the Helms Center and went on his rampage.

Physical/Medical Examination

Adam Shelley is a well-nourished fourteen-year-old white male. He stands 6'7" and weighs 274 pounds. Whether his unusual size is part of his condition or a separate distinguishing feature is impossible to say.

Adam presents a mixed picture of various congenital Dysostoses, including Cleidocranial, Craniofacial (Crouzon's Disease) and Mandibulofacial (Treacher-Collins Disease or Franchescetti's Syndrome). Such a combination raises the possibility of exposure by the mother to mutagenic agents such as toxic waste or radiation. Mother's medical record however does not show similar symptoms.

EEG and CAT-scan were conducted while sedated, so the

results are not definitive. Adam refused to cooperate with the medical examination and so had to be tranquilized by use of a dart gun and then placed in restraints. No idiopathic or otherwise unusual brain activity was noted, nor were there lesions or tumors. The history for epileptiform seizures is negative.

Visually Adam presents with acrocephaly or tower skull, enlarged parietal and frontal areas of the skull and extremely exophthalmic eyes, actually sitting on soft stalklike protrusions. Stereoscopic vision is very poor and may well contribute to his general clumsiness and problems with gross motor articulation.

External ears are malformed; the growth of and enfolding of extraneous tissue interferes with proper reception of sound. The tissue should be considered tumorlike and surgical procedures are tantamount to pruning with rapid reappearance of the tissues.

Nostrils and sinus cavities are incomplete and not fully separated. Sense of smell is rudimentary. Highly arched cleft palate and defective dentition makes articulation extremely poor.

Early medical records show 27 separate surgeries to repair defects or halt worsening conditions. Present appearance represents maximal improvement. Rapid growth as an adolescent threatens to create further difficulties. In light of the current situation it should be pointed out that it is unusual for such an individual to live to his current age, and maximum expected lifespan would surely not be past early twenties.

Although Adam's size is very unusual, he does not seem to suffer from Giantism. Testosterone levels are normal and genital size and structure are normal and proportionate. Neither is he abnormally hirsute. Endocrine explanations for his behavior do not seem warranted nor would hormonal treatments such as chemical castration be effective.

Development other than the massive, congenital and irreversible craniofacial deformities seems within normal limits.

Psychological Functioning

Attempts at formal psychological testing with Adam were unsuccessful. He was presented with the Wechsler Intelligence Scale for Children–Revised (WISC-R), the Rorschach using the Exner Method and the Millon Adolescent Personality Inventory (MAPI), and destroyed the materials. Menacing gestures towards the staff psychologist led to a termination of the testing.

Structured interviews were attempted with Adam on one side of a shatterproof plexiglass barrier. Due to the constant mucosal drip from the incomplete sinuses into the throat and other dental and palate deformities, articulation of words is extremely poor and verbal communication quite limited. A review of early school records showed at at least average academic performance. In fact an early administration of the WISC-R, adapted for written responses, at age 7, just prior to the placement with the DeLacey family showed a verbal IQ of 107, Performance IQ 111, Full Scale 109, well within normal limits. There is no evidence available to us that Adam did not possess the requisite cognitive abilities to understand the consequences of his actions.

Adam was monitored by videocameras during his entire stay at Goldstadt Medical Center. Detailed analysis of vocalizations and movements showed no pattern of responses to internally generated stimuli, either as visual hallucinations or auditory command hallucinations. Instead he roamed his cell in repetitive movements much like any other higher-order zoological specimen is apt to do. Attempts to dislodge window bars or to bend the bars of his door have been unsuccessful and have decreased during his incarceration. Most of the time he sits on the floor in the far distant corner of his cell. He either cries or raps his head against the wall. Recently he has begun to pluck obsessively at his garments. No suicidal behavior has been noted but because of his early history it cannot be discounted. Constant video surveillance and the spartan nature of his quarters mean that a successful attempt is highly unlikely.

There has never been any observed history of the use of drugs or alcohol. Blood work taken when he was apprehended showed not even trace elements of any psychoactive drugs either prescribed or illegal. A claim of diminished capacity is not supported by any evidence.

We are not privy to much of Adam Shelley's psychological make-up. This has always been the case and it is even more so now that he actively refuses to cooperate with our evaluation. No content analysis of his fantasies is possible.

His appearance has set him apart from others since birth. The lack of a stable, consistent and nurturing maternal relationship has probably impaired his capacity for all subsequent object relations. His history shows greater and greater isolation, dating from the failure of the DeLacey placement. His possible involvement in the death of the neighbor girl raises the question of early impulsivity and poor self-control even within a familial setting. That loss may have been the cause of the suicide attempts he later made. This would point to the inner experience of guilt, loss, depression and some rudimentary capacity to empathize and identify with other people. He has seriously limited ability and almost no experience in developing required social skills.

He probably experienced some degree of object hunger and experienced the end of those relationships as a loss and some depression and guilt as an expression of personal responsibility. Unfortunately his behavior since then does not point to the continued existence of such internal structures or capacities. The death of Fritz Harmann may be explained as retribution for the abuse he inflicted; however, the records at The Helms Center show no remorse, guilt or affect of any kind at the event. Indeed Adam has steadfastly refused to ever discuss anything about his stay at the Sweet Love of Jesus Youth Home.

I think it would be appropriate to consider Adam as at least an antisocial personality disorder (DSM III-R 301.70) with very limited capacity to connect or empathize with others. Previous therapy attempts with Adam have been uniformly unsuccessful. Initial attempts foundered on his sensitivity to the reactions of the therapist to his appearance. He would test these therapists by getting very close to them, opening his mouth, and exposing his rhinolaryngeal cavity to them. Eventually, he gave up on therapy and refused to participate. His condition at this time should be considered permanent and not subject to remediation. The prognosis of coerced psychotherapy is notoriously poor.

Violence Assessment

This assessment will utilize a combined clinical and actuarial prediction model. Current data sources cannot be used, as Adam Shelley has refused to co-operate with the evaluation. We must rely upon interpretation of the evidence compiled by the police during their investigation.

Actuarial Variables

Age: Currently Adam is fourteen. While at one time this would have been considered early onset of a history of violence, this is no longer the case. What is of more importance is whether to date the first violent episode to the death of Marian Ludwigsdottir at age 7 or the death of Fritz Harmann at age 12. The evidence in these matters is highly equivocal. A cautious interpretation, attempting to minimize the probability of a false negative, would use the age of onset as 7. This is still statistically rare and an ominous prognostic sign.

Sex: Male. Unremarkable. The finding that at least 90% of all violent episodes are male activities has been a durable one.

Race: Caucasian. This factor weighs against a prediction of risk. Statistically, in the United States more violence is committed by minority group members. What is consistent with previous race studies is that both offender and victim(s) were of the same racial group.

Socio-economic Status: As an adolescent it is premature to definitely assign Adam Shelley to a particular social class. However, based on other highly correlated factors, a reasonable predicition can be made. 1. Family of Origin—Adam has been raised, with brief interludes, as a ward of the state and in institutional settings. Ultimate social class attainment for adults with this background correlates very highly with the distribution for children of single-parent unskilled labor families. 2. Educational/Occupational Level—Adam has never attended public schools. He has been educated as part of his treatment in residential hospital settings. Converting his current education achievements to public school equivalents, we believe him to be at least two years behind, possibly four. Likely occupational status is low. His lack of schooling, poor socialization and appearance would make it hard for him to work even on an assembly line. Due to his size and prodigious strength a case might be made for a higher standard of living in an isolated high-risk job such as a Game Warden in a sector with a high incidence of poaching and food hoarding.

Clinical Variables

History of Violence: Our approach relies upon a modified Kleinholz-Wessel Model. Case assumptions are that probability increases with each event, becoming a certainty at N5, and that the most important features of the pattern of events are: 1. Recency, 2. Severity, 3. Frequency, and an escalation in those features.

Most Recent Episode: The roots of the most recent episode of violence lay in a series of letters written by Adam Shelley to Dr. Henry Frankenstein. These letters were in the possession of Henry Clerval, Dr. Frankenstein's personal attorney. He informed the police that it was his advice to Dr. Frankenstein that he not reply to the letters because he felt that they were a precursor to a malpractice suit.

The essence of the letters (there were three) was Adam's belief that Dr. Frankenstein had an obligation to him to "locate and provide others of my kind" to ease the loneliness he felt due to repeated rejections by other people. The second letter contained vague threats against people in general but without any named victims. The last letter concluded with a vow to "ruin your life as you have ruined mine."

It was only three weeks after sending that letter that Adam Shelley escaped from the Helms Center. Dr. Frankenstein's home address was in the telephone book. It must be concluded that Adam made his way on foot that evening. There were no reports of anyone sighting him en route.

Dr. Frankenstein had just recently been married, for the first time, to Elizabeth Lavenza. His wife had been an intensive-care nurse at the hospital where Dr. Frankenstein was Chief of Neonatology.

In the home that evening were Dr. Frankenstein's younger brother, William, a close personal friend, Victor Moritz, who had been best man at the wedding, and his father, Alphonse Frankenstein.

▼▼▼

What follows is the official recreation of the crime scene by the police forensics experts. It is believed that Adam Shelley hid by the large bushes alongside the garage. When Victor Moritz opened the garage door to park the car he had borrowed, Adam Shelley slipped into the garage and hid in the shadows. Victor Moritz left the car and went into the house through the inside door. It was at that time that Adam Shelley gripped Victor Moritz from behind and strangled him with his bare hands.

Entering the house it appears that Adam Shelley was seen by William Frankenstein, who screamed and attempted to flee the house. He was caught by Adam Shelley who seized him by the neck with such force that while shaking him the spinal cord was severed and the spine itself broken at the topmost cervix. The boy's body was flung into the fireplace.

Williams' father Alphonse, apparently awakened by the sounds of the struggle, came upon the scene of his sons being murdered and suffered a sudden, massive and fatal heart attack.

Dr. Frankenstein and his wife were last seen leaving a party at 10:30 P.M. They probably arrived home around 10:50 P.M. Adam Shelley made no effort to hide the bodies and apparently waited for them in the darkened living room.

When Dr. Frankenstein entered the house, he was struck a blow on the side of the head and knocked unconscious. What follows is from the final statements by Dr. Frankenstein before his death en route to the hospital.

Dr. Frankenstein and his wife, who had passed out, were carried upstairs to their bedroom. Mrs. Frankenstein was placed on the bed and the Doctor bound to his desk chair with his neckties.

When he came to, he found Adam Shelley stroking the breast of his still unconscious wife. He demanded that he stop, and the boy laughed at him. He reminded the Doctor of his request that he provide him with others like himself and that he hadn't even bothered to respond. He said that he had originally planned to come to the house and kill Dr. Frankenstein for "forcing life upon me, a life beyond the reach of love," but now he had fashioned a more fitting revenge. He would let Dr. Frankenstein live but would take his wife and make her his own. He intended to make her pregnant and thereby create a family for himself in his own image, children to love and be loved by in return. Obviously Adam's plan was doomed. He had no appreciation of how hard it would be to create another like him even if he were the father.

Adam Shelley then proceeded to rape Elizabeth Lavenza Frankenstein in front of her husband. While this was going on

Dr. Frankenstein managed to work free from his bonds and threw himself at Adam Shelley. They struggled and Adam hoisted the Doctor overhead and threw him down the flight of stairs, where he suffered major cranial trauma.

Elizabeth Frankenstein attempted to flee out an upstairs window, but was caught by Adam Shelley. Leaving the house, with Mrs. Frankenstein over his shoulder, he stopped and dipped his fingers in Henry Frankenstein's blood and left a message on the mirror by the front door: "If not love, then fear me."

He then fled into the rapidly falling December snow. Henry Frankenstein managed to drag himself out of the front door of the house, where he was seen by a neighbor across the street who called the police.

Adam Shelley became the immediate object of an intensive statewide manhunt. The next day he was cornered in a nearby barn and captured. Before he surrendered, he held the body of Elizabeth Frankenstein overhead and broke her neck.

Prediction of Future Violence

Drawing on the psychological and medical findings, the social history and the recreation of the most recent violent episode, we offer the following predictions.

Violence exists as a potential within us all. There is a constant dynamic flux between those forces that inhibit its expression and those motives that it expresses. Violence occurs when a particular external situation or set of relationships destabilizes the balance of forces within an individual. A prediction of future violence must attempt to describe those forces, the stability of their balance, and what the likelihood is of a provocative situation occurring.

Adam Shelley is a permanently disfigured young man who interprets the reactions of others to his appearance as rejection. Although at one point in time that rejection may have resulted in hurt and sadness, it now sparks anger and rage. Adam's appearance is not alterable. Frankly, it is unlikely that the response to him by others can be altered either. Therefore social interactions pose a constant risk of provocation. Therapy to alter his responses to others is unlikely to be successful.

None of the emotions of "conscience" seem to operate within Adam Shelley at this time. He has shown no remorse or guilt over any of his actions. Whatever rudimentary capacity for empathy he may have had now seems gone. He views himself as something other than a human being, reducing his capacity to identify with them. Fear of retribution does not seem to motivate him. Indeed, it may be argued that he would seek out and welcome retaliation as an indirect form of suicide.

Adam's history of violence shows an increase in recency, severity and frequency. One may characterize the early episodes as accidental or retributive, but the deaths of William Frankenstein and Victor Moritz were merely expedient as means to his end, and that of Elizabeth Lavenza Frankenstein lapsed into the sadistic.

Conclusions

In sum, Adam Shelley seems a boy lacking in internalized inhibitors to violence, likely to run into many provocative situations, and now with a history that makes it almost certain that he will resort to violence again. Technically, the crimes that Adam Shelley are charged with constitute a mass murder, although his transportation of Elizabeth Lavenza Frankenstein argues for a classification as a spree killer. It is the opinion of this team that if allowed to return to society Adam Shelley would pose a constant high risk to kill again.

A number of mitigating conditions were explored in regards to criminal intent. No unusual brain pathology was noted, nor any neuro-hormonal disorders. Diminished capacity due to substance abuse, intentional or otherwise, was ruled out. Intelligence was deemed adequate to distinguish right from wrong. There was no evidence of psychotic process or command hallucinations. The crimes in question cannot be deemed to have arisen from an irresistible impulse. The original threat occurred in a letter mailed three weeks prior to the attack. There is clear evidence of planning and intentionality. During the crime, Adam Shelley reiterated his motive when he wrote in Henry Frankenstein's blood, "If not love, then fear me."

Recommendations

Reviewing the evidence accumulated by this team we must conclude that Adam Shelley was criminally responsible for the deaths of William, Alphonse, Elizabeth and Henry Frankenstein and Victor Moritz. We also conclude that he poses a constant high risk to kill again if released into society.

Despite his age, we cannot find any reason to reduce his sentence or grant a stay of execution.

M. Waldman, M.D., Ph.D.
Chief, Forensic Services
Behavioral Sciences Division
Goldstadt Medical Center

CHUI CHAI
▼▼▼

S.P. SOMTOW

THE living dead are not as you imagine them. There are no dangling innards, no dripping slime. They carry their guts and gore inside them, as do you and I. In the right light they can be beautiful, as when they stand in a doorway caught between cross-shafts of contrasting neon. Fueled by the right fantasy, they become indistinguishable from us. Listen. I know. I've touched them.

In the 80s I used to go to Bangkok a lot. The brokerage I worked for had a lot of business there, some of it shady, some not. The flight of money from Hong Kong had begun and our company, vulture that it was, was staking out its share of the loot. Bangkok was booming like there was no tomorrow. It made Los Angeles seem like Peoria. It was wild and fast and frantic and frustrating. It had temples and buildings shaped like giant robots. Its skyline was a cross between Shangri-La and Manhattan. For a dapper yuppie executive like me there were always meetings to be taken, faxes to fax, traffic to be sat in, credit cards to burn. There was also sex.

There was Patpong.

I was addicted. Days, after hours of high-level talks and poring over papers and banquets that lasted from the close of business until midnight, I stalked the crammed alleys of Patpong. The night smelled of sewage and jasmine. The heat seeped into everything. Each step I took was colored by a different neon sign. From half-open nightclub doorways buttocks bounced to jaunty soulless synthrock. Everything was for sale;; the women, the boys, the pirated software, the fake Rolexes. Everything sweated. I stalked the streets and sometimes at random took an entrance, took in a live show, women propelling ping-pong balls from their pussies, boys buttfucking on motorbikes. I was addicted. There were other entrances where I sat in waiting rooms, watched women with numbers around their necks through the one-way glass, soft, slender brown women. Picked a number. Fingered the American-made condoms in my pocket. Never buy the local ones, brother, they leak like a sieve.

I was addicted. I didn't know what I was looking for. But I knew it wasn't something you could find in Encino. I was a knight on a quest, but I didn't know that to find the holy grail is the worst thing that can possibly happen.

I first got a glimpse of the grail at Club Pagoda, which was near my hotel and which is where we often liked to take our clients. The club was on the very edge of Patpong, but it was respectable—the kind of place the serves up a plastic imitation of *The King and I*, which is, of course, a plastic imitation of life in ancient Siam . . . artifice imitating artifice, you see. Waiters crawled around in mediaeval uniforms, the guests sat on the floor, except there was a well under the table to accommodate the dangling legs of lumbering white people. The floor show was eminently sober . . . it was all classical Thai dances, women wearing those pagoda-shaped hats moving with painstaking grace and slowness to a tinkling, alien music. A good place to interview prospective grant recipients, because it tended to make them very nervous.

Dr. Frances Stone wasn't at all nervous, though. She was already there when I arrived. She was preoccupied with picking the peanuts out of her *gaeng massaman* and arranging them over her rice plate in such a way that they looked like little eyes, a nose, and a mouth.

"You like to play with your food?" I said, taking my shoes off at the edge of our private booth and sliding my legs under the table across from her.

"No," she said, "I just prefer them crushed rather than whole. The peanuts I mean. You must be Mr. Leibowitz."

"Russell."

"The man I'm supposed to charm out of a few million dollars." She was doing a sort of coquettish pout, not really the sort of thing I expected from someone in medical research. Her face was ravaged, but the way she smiled kindled the memory of youthful beauty. I wondered what had happened to change her so much; according to her dossier, she was only in her mid-forties.

"Mostly we're in town to take," I said, "not to give. R&D is not one of our strengths. You might want to go to Hoechst or Berli Jucker, Frances."

"But Russell . . ." She had not touched her curry, but the peanuts on the rice were now formed into a perfect human face, with a few strands of sauce for hair. "This is not exactly R&D. This is a discovery that's been around for almost a century and a half. My great-grandfather's paper—"

"For which he was booted out of the Austrian Academy? Yes, my dossier is pretty thorough, Dr. Stone; I know all about how he fled to America and changed his name."

She smiled. "And my dossier on you, Mr. Leibowitz, is pretty thorough too," she said, as she began removing a number of compromising photographs from her purse.

A gong sounded to announce the next dance. It was a solo. Fog roiled across the stage, and from it a woman emerged. Her clothes glittered with crystal beadwork, but her eyes outshone the yards of cubic zirconia. She looked at me and I felt the pangs of the addiction. She smiled and her lips seemed to glisten with lubricious moisture.

"You like what you see," Frances said softly.

"I—"

"The dance is called *Chui Chai*, the dance of transformation. In every Thai classical drama, there are transformations—a woman transforming herself into a rose, a spirit transforming itself into a human. After the character's metamorphosis, he performs a *Chui Chai* dance, exulting in the completeness and beauty of his transformed self."

I wasn't interested, but for some reason she insisted on giving me the entire story behind the dance. "This particular *Chui Chai* is called *Chui Chai Benjakai* . . . the demoness Banjakai has been despatched by the demon king, Thotsakanth, to seduce the hero Rama . . . disguised as the beautiful Sita, she will float down the river toward Rama's camp, trying to convince him that his beloved has died . . . only when she is placed on a funeral pyre, woken from her deathtrance by the flames, will she take on her demonic shape once more and fly away toward the dark kingdom of Lanka. But you're not listening."

How could I listen? She was the kind of woman that existed only in dreams, in poems. Slowly she moved against the tawdry backdrop, a faded painting of a palace with pointed eaves. Her feet barely touched the floor. Her arms undulated. And always her eyes held me. As though she were looking at me alone. Thai women can do things with their eyes that no other women can do. Their eyes have a secret language.

"Why are you looking at her so much?" said Frances. "She's just a Patpong bar girl . . . she moonlights here . . . classics in the evening, pussy after midnight."

"You know her?" I said.

"I have had some . . . dealings with her."

"Just what is it that you're doing research into, Dr. Stone?"

"The boundary between life and death," she said. She pointed to the photographs. Next to them was a contract, an R&D grant agreement of some kind. The print was blurry. "Oh, don't worry, it's only a couple of million dollars . . . your company won't even miss it . . . and you'll own the greatest secret of all . . . the tree of life and death . . . the apples of Eve. Besides, I know your price and I can meet it." And she looked at the dancing girl. "Her name is Keo. I don't mind procuring if it's in the name of science."

Suddenly I realized that Dr. Stone and I were the only customers in the Club Pagoda. Somehow I had been set up.

The woman continued to dance, faster now, her hands sweeping through the air in mysterious gestures. She never stopped looking at me. She *was* the character she was playing, seductive and diabolical. There was darkness in every look, every hand-movement. I downed the rest of my Kloster lager and beckoned for another. An erection strained against my pants.

The dance ended and she prostrated herself before the audience of two, pressing her palms together in a graceful *wai*. Her eyes downcast, she left the stage. I had signed the grant papers without even knowing it.

Dr. Stone said, "On your way to the upstairs toilet . . . take the second door on the left. She'll be waiting for you."

I drank another beer, and when I looked up she was gone. She hadn't eaten one bite. But the food on her plate had been sculpted into the face of a beautiful woman. It was so lifelike that . . . but no. It wasn't alive. It wasn't breathing.

▼▼▼

She was still in her dancing clothes when I went in. A little girl was carefully taking out the stitches with a seamripper. There was a pile of garments on the floor. In the glare of a naked bulb, the vestments of the goddess had little glamor. "They no have buttons on classical dance clothes," she said. "They just sew us into them. Cannot go pipi!" She giggled.

The little girl scooped up the pile and slipped away.

"You're . . . very beautiful," I said. "I don't understand why . . . I mean, why you *need* to . . ."

"I have problem," she said. "Expensive problem. Dr. Stone no tell you?"

"No." Her hands were coyly clasped across her bosom. Gently I pried them away.

"You want I dance for you?"

"Dance," I said. She was naked. The way she smelled was different from other women. It was like crushed flowers. Maybe a hint of decay in them. She shook her hair and it coiled across her breasts like a nest of black serpents. When I'd seen her on stage I'd been entertaining some kind of rape fantasy about her, but now I wanted to string it out for as long as I could. God, she was driving me mad.

"I see big emptiness inside you. Come to me. I fill you. We both empty people. Need filling up."

I started to protest. But I knew she had seen me for what I was. I had money coming out my ass, but I was one fucked-up yuppie. That was the root of my addiction.

Again she danced the dance of transforming, this time for me alone. Really for me alone. I mean, all the girls in Patpong have this way of making you think they love you. It's what gets you addicted. It's the only street in the world where you *can* buy love. But that's not how she was. When she touched me it was as though she reached out to me across an invisible barrier, an unbreachable gulf. Even when I entered her she was untouchable. We were from different worlds and neither of us ever left our private hells.

Not that there wasn't passion. She knew every position in the book. She knew them backwards and forwards. She kept me there all night and each act seemed as though it been freshly invented for the two of us. It was the last time I came that I felt I had glimpsed the grail. Her eyes, staring up into the naked bulb, brimmed with some remembered sadness. I loved her with all my might. Then I was seized with terror. She was a demon. Yellow-eyed, dragon-clawed. She was me, she was my insatiable hunger. I was fucking my own addiction. I think I sobbed. I accused her of lacing my drink with hallucinogens. I cried myself to sleep and then she left me.

I didn't notice the lumpy mattress or the peeling walls or the way the light bulb jiggled to the music from downstairs. I didn't notice the cockroaches.

I didn't notice until morning that I had forgotten to use my condoms.

▼▼▼

It was a productive trip but I didn't go back to Thailand for another two years. I was promoted off the traveling circuit, moved from Encino to Beverly Hills, got myself a newer, late-model wife, packed my kids off to a Swiss boarding school. I also found a new therapist and a new support group. I smothered the addiction in new addictions. My old therapist had been a strict Freudian. He'd tried to root out the cause from some childhood trauma—molestation, potty training, Oedipal games—he'd never been able to find anything. I'm good at blocking out memories. To the best of my knowledge, I popped into being around age eight or nine. My parents were dead but I had a trust fund.

My best friends in the support group were Janine, who'd had eight husbands, and Mike, a transvestite with a spectacular fro. The clinic was in Malibu so we could do the beach in between bouts of tearing ourselves apart. One day Thailand came up.

Mike said, "I knew this woman in Thailand. I had fun in Thailand, you know? R&R. Lot of transvestites there, hon. I'm not a fag, I just like lingerie. I met this girl." He rarely stuck to the point because he was always stoned. Our therapist, Glenda, had passed out in the redwood tub. The beach was deserted. "I knew this girl in Thailand, a dancer. She would change when she danced. I mean *change*. You shoulda seen her skin. Translucent. And she smelled different. Smelled of strange drugs."

You know I started shaking when he said that because I'd tried not to think of her all this time even though she came to me in dreams. Even before I'd start to dream, when I'd just closed my eyes, I'd hear the hollow tinkle of marimbas and see her eyes floating in the darkness.

"Sounds familiar," I said.

"Nah. There was nobody like this girl, hon, nobody. She danced in a classical dance show *and* she worked the whorehouses . . . had a day job too, working for a nutty professor woman . . . honky woman, withered face, glasses. Some kind of doctor, I think. Sleazy office in Patpong, gave the girls free V.D. drugs."

"Dr. Frances Stone." Was the company paying for a free V.D. clinic? What about the research into the secrets of the universe?

"Hey, how'd you know her name?"

"Did you have sex with her?" Suddenly I was trembling with rage. I don't know why. I mean, I knew what she did for a living.

"Did you?" Mike said. He was all nervous. He inched away from me, rolling a joint with one hand and scootching along the redwood deck with the other.

"I asked first," I shouted, thinking, Jesus, I sound like a ten-year-old kid.

"Of *course* not! She had problems, all right? Expensive problems. But she was beautiful, mm-mm, good enough to eat."

I looked wildly around. Mr. Therapist was still dozing—fabulous way to earn a thousand bucks an hour—and the others had broken up into little groups. Janine was sort of listening, but she was more interested in getting her suntan lotion on evenly.

"I want to go back," I said. "I want to see Keo again."

"Totally, like, bullshit," she said, sidling up to me. "You're just, like, externalizing the interior hurt onto a fantasy-object. Like, you need to be in touch with your child, know what I mean?"

"You're getting your support groups muddled up, hon," Mike said edgily.

"Hey, Russ, instead of, like, projecting on some past-forgettable female two years back and ten thousand miles away, why don't you, like, fixate on someone a little closer to home? I mean, I've been *looking* at you. I only joined this support group cause like, support groups are the only place you can find like *sensitive* guys."

"Janine, I'm married."

"So let's have an affair."

I liked the idea. My marriage to Trisha had mostly been a joke: I'd needed a fresh ornament for cocktail parties and openings; she needed security. We hadn't had much sex; how could we? I was hooked on memory. Perhaps this woman would cure me. And I wanted to be cured so badly because Mike's story had jolted me out of the fantasy that Keo had existed only for me.

By now it was the 90s, so Janine insisted on a blood test before we did anything. I tested positive. I was scared shitless. Because the only time I'd ever been so careless as to forget to use a condom was . . . that night. And we'd done everything. Plumbed every orifice. Shared every fluid.

It had been a dance of transformation all right.

▼▼▼

I had nothing to lose. I divorced my wife and sent my kids to an even more expensive school in Connecticut. I was feeling fine. Maybe I'd never come down with anything. I read all the books and articles about it. I didn't tell anyone. I packed a couple of suits and some casual clothes and a supply of bootleg AZT. I was feeling fine. Fine, I told myself. Fine.

I took the next flight to Bangkok.

The company was surprised to see me, but I was such a big executive by now they assumed I was doing some kind of internal troubleshooting. They put me up at the Oriental. They gave me a 10,000 baht per diem. In Bangkok you can buy a lot for four hundred bucks. I told them to leave me alone. The investigation didn't concern them. They didn't know what I was investigating, so they feared the worst.

I went to Silom Road, where Club Pagoda had stood. It was gone. In its stead stood a brand new McDonalds and an airline ticket office. Perhaps Keo was already dead. Wasn't that what I had smelled on her? The odor or crushed flowers, wilting . . . the smell of coming death? And the passion with which she made love. I understood it now. It was the passion of the damned. She had reached out to me from a place between life and death. She had sucked the life from me and given me the virus as a gift of love.

I strolled through Patpong. Hustlers tugged at my elbows. Fake Rolexes were flashed in my face. It was useless to ask for Keo. There are a million women named Keo. Keo means jewel. It also means glass. In Thai there are many words that are used indiscriminately for reality and artifice. I didn't have a photograph and Keo's beauty was hard to describe. And every girl in Patpong is beautiful. Every night, parading before me in the neon labyrinth, a thousand pairs of lips and eyes, sensuous and infinitely giving. The wrong lips, the wrong eyes.

There are only a few city blocks in Patpong, but to trudge up and down them in the searing heat, questioning, observing every face for a trace of the remembered grail . . . it can age you. I stopped shaving and took recreational drugs. What did it matter anyway?

But I was still fine, I wasn't coming down with anything.
I was fine. Fine!

And then, one day, while paying for a Big Mac, I saw her hands. I was looking down at the counter counting out the money. I heard the computer beep of the cash register and then I saw them: proffering the hamburger in both hands, palms up, like an offering to the gods. The fingers arched upwards, just so, with delicacy and hidden strength. God, I knew those hands. Their delicacy as they skimmed my shoulder blades, as they glided across my testicles just a hair's breadth away from touching. Their strength when she balled up her fist and shoved it into my rectum. Jesus, we'd done everything that night. I dropped my wallet on the counter, I seized those hands and gripped them, burger and all, and I felt the familiar response. Oh, God, I ached.

"Mister, you want a blowjob?"

It wasn't her voice. I looked up. It wasn't even a woman.

I looked back down at the hands. I looked up at the face. They didn't even belong together. It was a pockmarked boy and when he talked to me he stared off into space. There was no relation between the vacuity of his expression and the passion with which those hands caressed my hands.

"I don't like to do such thing," he said, "but I'm a poor college student and I needing money. So you can come back after 5 p.m. You not be disappointed."

The fingers kneaded my wrists with the familiarity of one who has touched every part of your body, who has memorized the varicose veins in your left leg and the mole on your right testicle.

It was obscene. I wrenched my own hands free. I barely remembered to retrieve my wallet before I ran out into the street.

▼▼▼

I had been trying to find Dr. Frances Stone since I arrived, looking through the files at the corporate headquarters, screaming at secretaries. Although the corporation had funded Dr. Stone's project, the records seemed to have been spirited away.

At last I realized that that was the wrong way to go about it. I remembered what Mike had told me, so the day after the encounter with Keo's hands, I was back in Patpong, asking around for a good V.D. clinic. The most highly regarded one of all turned out to be at the corner of Patpong and Soi Cowboy, above a store that sold pirated software and videotapes.

I walked up a steep staircase into a tiny room without windows, with a ceiling fan moving the same sweaty air around and around. A receptionist smiled at me. Her eyes had the same vacuity that the boy at McDonalds had possessed. I sat in an unraveling rattan chair and waited, and Dr. Stone summoned me into her office.

"You've done something with her," I said.

"Yes." She was shuffling a stack of papers. She had a window; she had an airconditioner blasting away in the direction of all the computers. I was still drenched with sweat.

The phone rang and she had a brief conversation in Thai that I couldn't catch. "You're angry, of course," she said, putting down the phone. "But it was better than nothing. Better than the cold emptiness of the earth. And she had nothing to lose."

"She was dying of AIDS! And now *I* have it!" It was the first time I'd allowed the word to cross my lips. "You *killed* me!"

Frances laughed. "My," she said, "aren't we being a little melodramatic? You have the virus, but you haven't actually come down with anything."

"I'm fine. Fine."

"Well, why don't you sit down. I'll order up some food. We'll talk."

She had really gone native. In Thailand it's rude to talk business without ordering up food. Sullenly I sat down while she opened a window and yelled out an order to one of the street vendors.

"To be honest, Mr. Leibowitz," she said, "we really could use another grant. We had to spend *so* much of the last one on cloak-and-dagger nonsense, security, bribes, and so on; so little could be spared for research itself . . . I mean, look around you . . . I'm not exactly wasting money on luxurious office space, am I?"

"I saw her hands."

"Very effective, wasn't it?" The food arrived. It was some kind of noodle thing wrapped in banana leaves and groaning from the weight of chili peppers. She did not eat; instead, she amused herself by rearranging the peppers in the shape of . . . "The hands, I mean. Beautiful as ever. Vibrant. Sensual. My first breakthrough."

I started shaking again. I'd read about Dr. Stone's great-grand-father and his graverobbing experiments. Jigsaw corpses brought to life with bolts of lightning. Not life. A simulacrum of life. Could this have happened to Keo? But she was dying. Perhaps it was better than nothing. Perhaps . . .

"Anyhow. I was hoping you'd arrive soon, Mr. Leibowitz. Because we've made up another grant proposal. I have the papers here. I know that you've become so important now that your signature alone will suffice to bring us ten times the amount you authorized two years ago."

"I want to see her."

"Would you like to dance with her? Would you like to see her in the *Chui Chai* one more time?"

▼▼▼

She led me down a different stairwell. Many flights. I was sure we were below ground level. I knew we were getting nearer to Keo because there was a hint of that rotting flower fragrance in the air. We descended. There was an unnatural chill.

And then, at last, we reached the laboratory. No shambling Igors or bubbling retorts. Just a clean, well-lit basement room. Cold, like the vault of a morgue. Walls of white tile; ceiling of stucco; fluorescent lamps; the pervasive smell of the not-quite-dead.

Perspex tanks lined the walls. They were full of fluid and body parts. Arms and legs floating past me. Torsos twirled. A woman's breast peered from between a child's thighs. In another tank, human hearts swirled, each neatly severed at the aorta. There was a tank of eyes. Another of genitalia. A necklace of tongues hung suspended in a third. A mass of intestines writhed in a fourth. Computers drew intricate charts on a bank of monitors. Oscilloscopes beeped. A pet gibbon was chained to a post topped by a human skull. There was something so outlandishly antiseptic about this spectacle that I couldn't feel the horror.

"I'm sorry about the décor, Russell, but you see, we've had to forgo the usual decoration allowance." The one attempt at dressing up the place was a frayed poster of *Young Frankenstein* tacked to the far wall. "Please don't be upset at all the body parts," she added. "It's all very macabre, but one gets inured to it in med school; if you feel like losing your lunch, there's a small restroom on your left . . . yes, between the eyes and the tongues." I did not feel sick. I was feeling . . . excited. It was the odor. I knew I was getting closer to Keo.

She unlocked another door. We stepped into an inner room.

Keo was there. A cloth was draped over her, but seeing her face after all these years made my heart almost stop beating. The eyes. The parted lips. The hair, streaming upward toward a source of blue light . . . although I felt no wind in the room. "It is an electron wind," said Dr. Stone. "No more waiting for the monsoon lightning. We can get more power from a wall socket than great-grandfather Victor could ever dream of stealing from the sky."

And she laughed the laughter of mad scientists.

I saw the boy from McDonalds sitting in a chair. The hands reached out toward me. There were electrodes fastened to his temples. He was naked now, and I saw the scars where the hands had been joined at the wrists to someone else's arms. I saw a woman with Keo's breasts, wired to a pillar of glass, straining, heaving while jags of blue lightning danced about her bonds. I saw her vagina stitched onto the pubis of a dwarf, who lay twitching at the foot of the pillar. Her feet were fastened to the body of a five-year-old boy, transforming their grace to ungainliness as he stomped in circles around the pillar.

"Jigsaw people!" I said.

"Of course!" said Dr. Stone. "Do you think I would be so foolish as to bring back people whole? Do you not realize what the consequences would be? The legal redefinition of life and death . . . wills declared void, humans made subservient to walking corpses . . . I'm a scientist, not a philosopher."

"But who are they now?"

"They were nobody before. Street kids. Prostitutes. They were dying, Mr. Leibowitz, dying! They were glad to will their bodies to me. And now they're more than human. They're many persons in many bodies. A gestalt. I can shuffle them and put them back together, oh, so many different ways . . . and the beautiful Keo. Oh, she wept when she came to me. When she found out she had given you the virus. She loved you. You were the last person she ever loved. I saved her for you. She's been sleeping here, waiting to dance for you, since the day she died. Oh, let us not say *died*. The day she . . . she . . . I am no poet, Mr. Leibowitz. Just a scientist."

I didn't want to listen to her. All I could see was Keo's face. It all came back to me. Everything we had done. I wanted to relive it. I didn't care if she was dead or undead. I wanted to seize the grail and clutch it in my hands and own it.

Frances threw a switch. The music started. the shrilling of the *pinai*, the pounding of the *taphon*, the tinkling of marimbas and xylophones rang in the *Chui Chai* music. Then she slipped away unobtrusively. I heard a key turn in a lock. She had left the grant contract lying on the floor. I was alone with all the parts of the woman I'd loved. Slowly I walked toward the draped head. The electron wind surged; the cold blue light intensified. Her eyes opened. Her lips moved as though discovering speech for the first time. . . .

"Rus . . . sell."

On the pizzafaced boy, the hands stirred of their own accord. He turned his head from side to side and the hands groped the air, straining to touch my face. Keo's lips were dry. I put my arms around the drape-shrouded body and kissed the dead mouth. I could feel my hair stand on end.

"I see big emptiness inside you. Come to me. I fill you. We both empty people. Need filling up."

"Yes. Jesus, yes."

I hugged her to me. What I embraced was cold and prickly. I whisked away the drape. There was no body. Only a framework of wires and transistors and circuit boards and tubes that fed flasks of flaming reagents.

"I dance for you now."

I turned. The hands of the McDonald's boy twisted into graceful patterns. The feet of the child moved in syncopation to the music, dragging the rest of the body with them. The breasts of the chained woman stood firm, waiting for my touch. The music welled up. A contralto voice spun plaintive melismas over the interlocking rhythms of wood and metal. I kissed her. I kissed that severed head and lent my warmth to the cold tongue, awakened passion in her. I kissed her. I could hear chains breaking and wires slithering along the floortiles. There were hands pressed into my spine, rubbing my neck, unfastening my belt. A breast touched my left buttock and a foot trod lightly on my right. I didn't care that these parts were attached to other bodies. They were hers. She was loving me all over. The dwarf that wore her pudenda was climbing up my leg. Every part of her was in love with me. Oh, she danced. We danced together. I was the epicenter of their passion. We were empty people but now we drank our fill. Oh, God, we danced. Oh, it was a grave music, but it contented us.

And I signed everything, even the codicil.

▼▼▼

Today I am in the AIDS ward of a Beverly Hills hospital. I don't have long to wait. Soon the codicil will come into effect, and my body will be preserved in liquid nitrogen and shipped to Patpong.

The nurses hate to look at me. They come at me with rubber gloves on so I won't contaminate them, even though they should know better. My insurance policy has disowned me. My children no longer write me letters, though I've paid for them to go to Ivy League colleges. Trisha comes by sometimes. She is happy that we rarely made love.

One day I will close my eyes and wake up in a dozen other bodies. I will be closer to her than I could ever be in life. In life we are all islands. Only in Dr. Stone's laboratory can we know true intimacy, the mind of one commanding the muscles of another and causing the nerves of a third to tingle with unnamable desires. I hope I shall die soon.

The living dead are not as you imagine them. There are no dangling innards, no dripping slime. They carry their guts and gore inside them, as do you and I. In the right light they can be beautiful, as when they stand in the cold luminescence of a basement laboratory, waiting for an electron stream to lend them the illusion of life. Fueled by the right fantasy, they become indistinguishable from us.

Listen. I know. I've loved them.

I, MONSTER
▼▼▼

LOREN D. ESTLEMAN

I shall ascend my funeral pile triumphantly,
and exult in the agony of the torturing flames.

—The Monster

IT was all so deadly familiar.

The farmers and innkeepers and harness-makers and their mad
wives armed with torches and pitchforks, yammering like red Indi-
ans in the demented courage of the pack, the great wrinkled baying hounds loping clumsily, black lips skinned back from
parchment-colored fangs as they tore at my tendons, drawing
blood on every third lunge, the onlookers too cowardly even to
join the mob shrieking orgasmically for my eyes and entrails;
and I, the fistulous towering ogre of the collective carnal nightmare, lashed to a great makeshift wooden cross like some
mutant Christ, borne straining and bellowing and pitching on
a hydrophobic sea toward my fate in the puddle of light in the
center of the arena.

Really, things were getting out of hand. The dogs at least

would have to go. Most of the profits were tied up in bandages and iodine.

▼▼▼

I didn't build a pyre.

Those who have read Robert Walton's letters to his sister recounting details of the polar voyage that brought him into contact with Victor Frankenstein, published as *Frankenstein, or The Modern Prometheus*, will recall that I took my leave of the explorer, and of Frankenstein's corpse still warm upon the deck, with a pledge to remove myself from this plane through a conflagration. I did not lie, but neither did I carry out that design.

So efficient was the process of thought in the brain which my mortal creator in his fiendish perfectionism had selected, that I had decided against death by fire almost before I left that ice-locked vessel. What was burning but ordinary destruction for the most hideously extraordinary being in the history of the world? Had I journeyed all this way to the earth's ceiling in search of a venue unlike all others only to end my wretched existence in the same manner that fishwives employed to dispose of their kitchen refuse? The answer, shouted back at me mockingly by the frozen cliffs, was a resounding negative.

I know not how many bleak days I wandered through the eternal twilight, tormented by the certainty that I could not end my torment. I gave no thought to food, nor to the hell-cold that lay like a gun barrel along my spine and made flatirons of my feet; until the very deadness of my extremities revealed to me in a flash—oh, ecstatic bolt!—that I need take no action whatsoever, that by doing nothing, nothing at all, I would invite the elements and my own poor clay to render me extinct.

I walked.

Walked as the cold clawed at my flesh, walked as hunger

shredded my stomach like blind worms. I fancied I headed north, away from the cities of men and the treacherous warmth and sustenance that only pretended to nurture as they preserved this wretch for fresh cruelties, greater injustices, world without end; but in truth I had no instruments to point the way, and at least once in my delirium I was convinced that each step drew me nearer to that nightmare country, my own instincts having forsaken me as surely as had my creator. My ears and nose lost sensation, my lips cracked and bled, the blood crystallizing the instant it touched the air—contributing, no doubt, to my fearsome configuration. And yet I walked still.

Whether I plunged in actuality through a sheet of ice imperfectly formed into the numbing black waters, or whether it was a wishful hallucination, I shall never know. I do not remember the precise moment when tortured *beingness* became kind oblivion. My last clear memory was the sight, scores of leagues away on a great floe, of a solitary white bear standing on its hind legs to defend itself from a ring of huge shaggy wolves, and of a deep emotion, so alien to my tragic uniqueness, of pride of kinship when the besieged brute lashed out with one enormous paw and slapped a pouncing wolf to the ground. Blood sprayed, the would-be attacker's agonized yelp echoed off the ice peaks, a pretty fugue. Then darkness, utter and profound. (I have since come to discount the vision of the siege, for the polar bear's range is not shared by wolves; but the pleasure-memory is no less great for that.)

My next emotion was rage.

That I should live to experience the emotion at all, that was its cause.

Alive still! How many more brief slumbers must I endure before the endless sleep?

You must understand that I had no way of determining at the time that I had slumbered for two hundred years.

▼▼▼

I heard before I saw.

The steady whine of a great engine, like Frankenstein's dynamoes at my first awakening.

My confusion was complete. Was this, then, Hell for a synthetic man? Was it my fate, alone among all others, to relive again and again my awful span, with the additional refinement of foreknowledge? For is not the ability to know what is to come any man's—and certainly any monster's—definition of Hades? The rage came then, with the scarlet blinding purity of the one I had known when my depraved God slashed to pieces the mate he had created for me before my very eyes. Had I a legion of Lucifer's faithful before me at that moment I would have slaughtered them all, and laughed at the demonic blood staining me from neck to heels. But I could not move.

Something held me pinioned in the supine position. I sensed without investigating that it was stronger than I. Not organic then, for no mere creature was a match for this thing pieced together from gigantic cadavers and imbued with alchemy. A mechanical device, encasing my body and leaving only my head free to turn so I could observe—

Nothing.

Hollow sky beyond a small thick window level with my eyes, above and below. What I assumed at first to be Arctic floes were in fact clouds viewed from above. I was no longer chained to the earth I despised.

Heaven, then! And all the blather I had read in both Testaments and dusty theological tracts about the immortality only of God and the Soul of Man was but ignorant fustian. Whatever Life Force Frankenstein had harnessed was worthy of the Eternal. What a supreme joke! But what was its point? Would I not be as much an outsider among angels as I had been among men? If thus, by what right was this called Paradise?

I had little time to ponder, for a stirring of the air told me
that I was no longer in solitude. The angle of my repose did not
allow me to observe my new company, but I heard two distinct
voices in conversation. As to their subject I remained unaware,
for although they spoke English it was in a strange, flat accent
that I knew instinctively was not Continental, and many of their
words were foreign: *okay, software, head honcho, megabucks*—it
may as well have been the language of Cathay for all I compre-
hended. A match was struck, I smelled tobacco burning, and the
exchange that followed was as much as I understood from that
first encounter with my captors:

"Jesus, Hal! You know what the old man said about smoking
in here."

"Relax, the old man's snoozing. I'll put it out the minute
Godzilla there complains."

Several minutes of indecipherables ensued, then a door
opened and shut and I was again alone. Sometime later someone
entered who I sensed had not been in the earlier party, walked
directly up to where I lay, and placed his fingers on my neck,
the first time since my brief and poignant acquaintance with the
saintly Dr. Lacey, so very long ago—just *how* long I did not then
know—that a human being had touched me willingly. Through
my veiling lashes I observed the surprise on his spare old clean-
shaven features.

"A pulse!" he whispered, in an intonation which I recognized
at once as German. "*Du lieber Gott*! It lives!"

"I live," I then affirmed, in a voice that creaked as if dust
were flaking off the cords. "Who so exclaims?"

Whereupon his ancient jaw dropped, revealing to me that the
craft of making dentures had advanced far since my time; he
clutched his breast beneath the white smock he wore and fell out
of my line of vision. That, I was to learn, would be my sole
meeting before death claimed him at age seventy-six of Dwight
Laemmle, Professor of Anthropology and the senior academician

with the famed 1988 Arctic expedition sponsored by the University
of Michigan College of Arts and Sciences.

▼▼▼

I had placed myself in jeopardy through foolhardiness. Fortune
had spared me.

When at length the professor's corpse was discovered, I
resolved not to give myself away twice, at least until such time
as I was free of restraint; for although I craved immolation as
much as ever, my hatred of man, surpassing my loathing of life
itself, would not allow me to surrender my fate to my age-old
tormentors. Happily, excitement and consternation over the eminent researcher's death (apoplexy was the cause) diverted attention
from the inert thing sharing his quarter, so that I was able to
feign dissolution for the remainder of the flight.

For flight it was. By now I had divined that this was no
celestial chariot, but an earthly craft, and that somehow during
my time in the North, that accursed Science that was Frankenstein's only altar had mastered the art that Nature had intended
for birds as thoroughly as he himself had usurped the Power of
Life. I knew then the first feeble stirrings of the Great Truth
whose full disclosure was yet to come, along with its horror.

Much time would pass before I would learn of the discovery
Professor Laemmle had made in a glacier: of a man, physically
gargantuan and Neanderthal in appearance but wearing clothing
associated with early polar explorers in the eighteenth century,
preserved exactly as he was in life; of his removal under a blanket
of secrecy to the team's "airbase," where the outer jacket of ice
was thawed slowly away and its prisoner transferred to a portable
climate-controlled chamber of the professor's own devising,
intended for the preservation of specimens as large as a saber-
toothed cat, whose acquisition in pristine state was his great
dream.

I know now that following the removal on *terra firma* of the professor's remains, the "specimen"—myself—still in its shining cylinder, was unloaded with considerably less ceremony into the rear of a four-wheeled contrivance called a van and whisked northward from a thing termed an airport in a place called Detroit in a region known as Michigan in the United States of America, that former British colony of which I had heard much in times past, though its celebrated status as an egalitarian haven was but a mockery to me, for it was populated by men. Our destination was the city of Flint and research facilities maintained there by the university. At the time, of course, it was all a dazzling jumble of lights and noise and that distressingly coded English, and I reverted to my first conclusion that I had awakened in Hell. It was as if Frankenstein had only counterfeited death and lived to breed a community of students of the forbidden arts. By then I was beginning to realize that I had done more than nod off after the episode of the bear.

A detour was taken, whether because of an accident or the ubiquitous construction by which this bizarre culture was constantly uprooting itself and rebuilding, I cannot say even now. Abruptly my view through the windows shifted from directional markers and broad colored placards bearing cryptic legends— MORE TASTE/LESS FILLING, SID'S REPTILE CITY, FOOD FOLKS AND FUN—to evergreens, and the surface over which we traveled became rough. The cigar-shaped chamber in which I was confined, unsecured, and rocked from side to side. I aided it. Left, right, left, right, gaining momentum with each roll, until one violent lurch brought it up against the side of the vehicle with a bang that shook my entrails. When I recovered I could move my left arm.

Although I had gained but an inch, it was evident something had been jarred loose, some clamp or latch. With my new lever-age I flexed and strained, and it seemed to me that something was yielding. For the next half hour, possibly longer, I struggled, resting only when my heartbeat and respiration grew so loud I really feared they would be overheard. A last, desperate, frustrated heave, and the cylinder popped open in two halves like an egg. Needles pricked my extremities as circulation returned. Then like the ambulatory corpse I was I stepped from my coffin.

At that moment the van braked. Either we had reached our terminus or my movements had been felt in the front seat. Footsteps crunched in gravel, someone passed between a window and the light, heading for the doors in back. I waited until the latch clicked, then hurled myself at both doors with all my strength.

They flew apart with no resistance, one of them striking my visitor and laying him horizontal. I nearly landed on him, caught my balance on the roadbed, and was looking around for bearings when a second man appeared from the other side of the van.

"Clive, what's—"

A pudgy, balding young man wearing an odd quilted coat, he broke off when he saw me standing over the limp form of his companion. I recognized his voice immediately as one of those I had overheard in the air. I raised my arm to club him, but at the sight of me he made a choking noise, wheeled, and ran up the road, pumping his arms and legs awkwardly. I made a contemptuous gesture in his direction and plunged off into the thick wood.

It was, I found out later, state-owned land and largely undeveloped, reminding me no little of the Swiss countryside where I had been brought to life. A thin sheet of snow covered the ground, but I was accustomed to far worse cold, and in fact abandoned the heavy fleece-lined oilskin I had worn at the pole. I have since decided that the time was late November. I was approaching a birthday.

For two days I wandered that sylvan country, avoiding roads and marveling at the constant hum of motor traffic that penetrated the deepest forest. The first time a jet-powered aircraft shrieked overhead I dove in terror for cover, but as this became a regular occurrence with no apparent threat to me, I recorded it in my mental roster of the complexities of this strange new land.

Early on the second day I encountered my first human being since the incident at the van. This one was armed.

We entered a clearing at the same time from opposite sides. He was clad entirely in luminescent orange from cap to boots, a sight to startle the ages. When he saw me he stiffened, paused, then raised a rifle to his shoulder. But I had anticipated the maneuver, and in the flick of an eyelash I crossed the acre that separated us, tore the weapon from his grip just as knee. I flung away the pieces and was prepared to do the same to his pathetic body when he fainted.

Bewildered by what I had seen of the principles of self-preservation in this place, I left him where he lay. Many weeks later I would see his likeness on the front page of a garish periodical under the declaration:

TERRIFIED HUNTER REPORTS: I ESCAPED BIGFOOT!

I was ravenously hungry. Forgetting in my confusion my vow to starve, I slew and ate a deer, leaving only the hooves, hide, and antlers. It failed to satisfy me after two centuries of total abstinence.

At length I came upon a dwelling on a wooded hill, which I at first took for a church: a three-story triangle of wood and glass, its shingled roof extending almost to the ground, it suggested nothing so much as a steeple fashioned after the letter A. Although the front door was locked, the knob twisted free with ridiculous ease and I entered, ready to throttle whatever occupants I found, for where there was civilization there was sustenance.

No one accosted me. I was alone in a house whose stale air

informed me that it had not been inhabited for some time. Empty
of heart, I ignored the sitting-room furniture and strange contriv-
ances that surrounded me and made my way to what seemed to
be a pantry, furnished with a table and chairs, a waist-high bench
with a basin built into it, more odd devices, and an upright chest
made of enameled metal. I opened the chest. The frigid air that
came out startled me. When I recovered, I examined the packages
I found inside and identified them as frozen meat, although by
what witchcraft its owner had managed to harness the Arctic air
and bring it back for preservation in this moderate climate, I could
not fathom. I pulled out all the packages and left them on the
floor to thaw while I looked elsewhere for immediate gratification.

In a cupboard I found scores of airtight metal containers with
labels bearing likenesses of fruits and vegetables. The seams
opened with little effort and I gorged myself until I realized that
with judicious rationing, I could survive on the stores of the house
indefinitely while I contemplated my next maneuver. I thereupon
returned the meat to the chest lest it spoil.

I shall not tax the reader's patience with my reaction to the
miracles that revealed themselves to me in those early days. Electric light, appliances large and small, an instrument on a wall
which when manipulated brought forth a rumble from below and
filled the house with heat, a vessel that was clearly a chamber
pot, but which emptied and cleansed itself with water at a flick
of a lever—how my creator would have reveled in it! But the box
in the ground-floor sitting-room was the greatest of all. The first
time a small man appeared in its illuminated window and fired
a tiny pistol at me through the glass, I very nearly destroyed the
box in self-defense. Imagine, then, my dumbfoundment when,
days after I switched it on—it had been operating continuously,
for my fascination with it was inexhaustible—the name *Frankenstein* issued from the speaker.

It was a cable hook-up, of course, and I had happened upon

a channel that played old movies twenty-four hours a day. During the classic horror-film retrospective that ran all that week I saw *Frankenstein, The Bride of Frankenstein, The Son of Frankenstein, The Ghost of Frankenstein,* and *Frankenstein Meets the Wolf Man,* some of them several times as the features were repeated. I learned from the parade of unctuous hosts who introduced the films that the tale of the scientist and his creation had been told by Mary Shelley from Robert Walton's letters and brought to the screen by Hollywood a century later, becoming a part of the popular culture, which little suspected its truth.

The motion pictures were remarkable. Jack Pierce, Universal's make-up genius, had added to the synthetic man a pair of electrodes protruding from the neck and a curious flattening of the top of the skull; in every other particular, save clothing and scars that seemed never to heal, he had transformed actor Boris Karloff into an eerie replica of my own tragic self. Further, Karloff (and, to a lesser extent, the other performers who assayed the role in the final two films), endeavored to portray the creature sympathetically, with an understanding of his plight. This was vindication; and more than once, having fallen asleep in front of my magic window, I awakened with the grim certainty that I had dreamt it all, and expected to find myself still awaiting death on the roof of the world.

However, my education did not stop there. Through the news channels I learned of test-tube babies, cloning, genetic engineering, and other incidents of science's quest for the Secret of Life, no longer a blasphemy but a revered pursuit funded by government and carried out not in dreary farmhouses and deserted watchtowers but in fully-equipped laboratories under the glare of public scrutiny. And like those primitive organisms assuming shape and symmetry in petri dishes and on glass slides, an awareness stirred and began to grow deep in my borrowed brain that I was no longer Alone.

Such was my state, shaken by these astounding conclusions, that I was more curious than wary when the door to my private sanctuary opened unexpectedly and I found myself face to face with my landlord.

I knew by the key in his hand, which he had found unnecessary because of the forced lock, that he was the owner. A thickset, solidly built man in his middle years, he wore a hat with a soft brim and a dark coat with a fur collar over a gray suit of clothes, odd attire for the country. Seeing me towering there he hesitated, but the look in his eyes was more caution than fear.

Said I finally, "Do not be alarmed. When I came here I sought merely food and shelter."

"Uh-huh," he grunted. "And now?"

"I know not. But I shall leave if you will stand aside."

His eyes evaluated me. "Are you as strong as you look?"

For no reason that I can ascertain I stooped and lifted the twelve-foot leather sofa by one leg, holding it level with my shoulder. Then I replaced it. He nodded, as if he had expected nothing less. "I think we can work something out." He opened his coat.

Fearing a weapon, I moved toward him, but he extended nothing more lethal than a small white pasteboard. At length I took it and read the legend printed on one side:

CLARK FLOREY
President, W.W.G.

I read the initials aloud. They meant nothing to me.

"World Wrestling Guild," he explained. "I'm a promoter."

▼▼▼

The dogs would definitely have to go. Despite the rehearsed histrionics of the hired "peasants" and the cheering and catcalls of the crowd, I made a mental note to talk to Clark about it after the bout.

It was a small enough complaint. I had no conflict with the new haircut that created the illusion my head was flat on top, nor with the plastic electrodes secured to my neck by a flesh-colored collar, although the latter sometimes gave me a rash in auditoriums that lacked air conditioning, but I would not be mauled by animals before I had even set foot in the ring.

The auditorium in this case was in Cleveland, and my opponent, waiting patiently on the ropes while I worked up the crowd with some convincing bellowing prior to bursting free of the bonds that held me to the cross, was Sloan Van Whale, the Dutch Terrorist, with whom I was to wrestle two falls out of three, no disqualifications, in a classic Texas Cage match for the World Wrestling Guild heavyweight championship. The house was sold out, with a ten percent cut of the gate guaranteed to me under my contract with Clark and a commercial endorsement deal in the works if the network approved of the ratings from the night's telecast. I had already appeared on the cover of *Abs and Pecs*, and there was talk *TV Guide* wanted to interview me for an article it was preparing on the resurgence in popularity of professional wrestling. And why not? I was largely responsible.

I was billed as *Frankenstein*. Father would be so proud.

THIS ICY REGION
MY HEART ENCIRCLES
▼▼▼

STEVE RASNIC TEM

AND

MELANIE TEM

HE had come back. She had always known he would, because she had imagined it so.

She had imagined his form: moving slowly from shadow to shadow, as one with the weathered faces of the brick and stone, at times almost indistinguishable from pillar or hitching post. Sleeping in an abandoned stable space or beneath a tree in Hyde Park.

Once she had imagined his face, too, but she could not re-imagine it now. She could be sure only that, as always, it was a live visage properly dead. A too-vivid dream. Once before she had dreamed such a thing: that her firstborn and first-dead babe had come back to life, that the sweet little thing had been only cold, that she and Shelley had rubbed it before the fire, and it had lived. But when she'd awakened there had been no baby; her Mary Jane was still dead.

How was it she had so long survived this beautiful and monstrous Imagination, when with regularity it repulsed and wounded her? Her own dear Shelley had not survived. It seemed to her now that he had been little but Imagination in its purest, most beautiful, most dangerous form, inspiration for both Victor Frankenstein and the Monster, neither of them wholly recognizable after all these years.

Shelley's features would not have been recognizable, either, that July day on the beach off Via Reggio. They had tried to keep the details from her, but she had persisted. There had been his green jacket, and in the pockets his volumes of Keats and Sophocles. His beautiful face had been bloated and pulled apart by the dark sea. But she would have recognized him by his form, by the shadow his soul had cast.

During the past few days she had glimpsed such a shadow stretched out across a neighboring rooftop on Chester Square, and once in a distant garden stiff and erect as a giant scarecrow. This shadow was soulless, and she knew at once who cast it. She almost welcomed him, although she was so afraid.

He had come back, and with him he'd brought some of the icy regions of his exile. The weather was extraordinarily cold. She had lain down in January, and now she thought February must be fast approaching. She had always disliked the English climate, but she could not remember a London January ever quite so cold.

But why call this creature a "he," unless this was, indeed, Shelley returning to her, making his way back out of the icy emptiness, the wasteland beyond passion and poetry? Such thoughts filled her with guilt, as if she were the abomination. She was a foolish old woman.

The Monster wrapped the cold about itself like a winding sheet, as if for protection. She had touched the window glass once but could touch it no more; the distant shadow beyond it had burned her fingers with its ice. The air in the street appeared

solid, full of light, and much too cold to breathe. She wanted to
warn her son Percy not to go out but could not quite manage it.
She had never been able to keep her children safe.

Birds froze on the branches. Their dark bodies littered the
pavement. Each day the dark form seemed closer. She wondered
if she should warn the Queen, Buckingham Palace being only a
short distance away. But even if she could, what might she say?
She could talk to her of Shelley, but not of this other bringing
its ice deep into the heart and soul of England. Victoria's strong
affection for her Albert was widely known, but what did the
Queen understand of spirit and Imagination?

Out in the square dogs grew heavy with sheaths of ice and
collapsed into their fur. Mary saw that the glass in the window
had begun to crack, the fissures so crisp and definite that she
wondered if they might lie across her eyeballs instead. Warm, wet
fingers tracked the cold of her throat. What could it want?

"What do you want?"

Outside her window, ice thundered and moaned with the
Monster's cries, and London paid no heed.

The Monster had come for Shelley's heart. It was hers. She
would not give it up.

Mary knew her husband's heart more intimately now than
ever when he was alive. It was as though, without referent during
the more than twenty-eight years since Shelley's drowning, she
had recreated his heart for herself, endowed it with a new kind
of life.

Imagination, Mary thought, and, although her body ached
with new pain and her spirit with old, "the beaming face of
Imagination peeped in, and the weight of deadly woe was lightened." She smiled. Some twenty years ago, when she'd written
those words, she'd been amazed and distressed to discover even
moments of happiness, and she'd thought she knew everything
about both woe and Imagination. How strange, she thought now

as she'd thought all her life, how strange a thing her life had been!

Kind, gloomy Edward Trelawney had first presented Shelley's heart to Leigh Hunt, snatched unconsumed from the flames of the beach pyre which Mary had been unable to bring herself to attend. She'd been told, and had not been surprised, that the body had been slow to burn, had finally separated after three hours, the unusually large heart apparently impregnable to the fire. Again and again her Imagination had conjured vivid, not entirely unwelcome visions of the scene: hand bandaged, eyes glistening with tears from smoke and grief and pain, Trelawney saying nothing as he passed Shelley's heart to another, though far lesser, poet.

At last Shelley's heart had been returned to Mary, and she had kept it with her all these years. She had wrapped it in linen and in the lines of his poem *"Adonais,"* and—although written as an elegy to a man he had not much liked—they had come to speak to her as if they'd always been closest to her beloved's heart:

I am borne darkly, fearfully, afar!

In the miserable little house at Pisa, always so vulnerable to floodwaters and now suddenly and permanently flooded by Shelley's absence, the heart had been as agitated as she was, had never been able to find a place. It had rested briefly on table, shelf, rain-grayed corner of the floor, for Mary had been unwilling to believe any surface capable of supporting it for long and had worried that the baby would somehow stumble on it and would know what it was, or, equally horrible, would not know.

At Albaro, her dreadful first home alone, the wrapped heart had reposed on her desk. His heart, then, had occupied very nearly the same space as her own while she set about what was to have been her one life-task: commemorating the only creature worth loving and living for, the essential being who had been both trapped and enshrined in a fragile image, now shattered, now freed, while she was left to go on as best she could.

But with each move thereafter, the package containing Shelley's heart had become simply a part of the household furnishings. In all the London flats—Speldhurst Street, Somerset Street, Park Street—in Putney, now here at 24 Chester Square, it had been scarcely more remarkable to her than this mirror or that chair. And yet still his words would come back to her, as if the pressure of his heart had rubbed them from the manuscript and launched them into the air:

> . . . *a grave among the eternal* . . .

The words came into her like a whisper from his heart. Sometimes it seemed a desecration to her, and dangerous, that Shelley's heart had not been burned, sometimes a miracle.

Waking from dreams she could remember if she wanted to, Mary found herself staring at the cold mantel where, in this room, the heart package had always sat. Her own habitual unmindfulness of it disgusted her, and she said aloud, "Monster." It was a name she'd often used for herself in the journals no one would ever see, and now, halfway to the grave, she dared say it aloud: "Monster!"

As if in reply there was a shifting outside her window, a shadowy fall of snow, a cracking as of long-unused limbs bending and seeking purchase on the outer walls. It had come back. Fear had descended now into weariness, and Mary rolled over, away from the mantel and the window and the heart, and thought to go back to sleep, for there would be nothing again today worth waking to.

Something was in her bed, something small and solid and very still at about the level of her waist. Mary reached down among the bedclothes and touched the object, gasped and pulled her hands back, forced herself to find the thing again and extract it and hold it up. With great effort of will she did not drop it, held it at arm's length and stared. Mary Jane, dead in her bed again. Her baby girl, dead.

The baby was not really there. Mary's hands were empty. Trembling, she lay back on her pillow and thought how alone she was, how alone she'd always been, estranged from her fellows and estranged from herself. Those who accused her of having a cold heart were wrong: her heart was hot, searing, but the core of her was protected by layers and layers of ice that had allowed her to survive.

Outside her window the city cracked beneath the weight of ice, and a hungry, half-imagined shadow made its way awkwardly toward her room. Shelley's words provided no comfort:

He had adorned and hid the coming bulk of Death.

Mary struggled out of bed and crossed the few steps to her window. The sun had risen into a painful glaring of snow-filled sky, turned the room and her white nightgown gray. The birds were silent, their beaks packed with ice. Toward her from among the skeletal trees was coming a very small figure, with the wide-legged toddle of a child just learning to walk. As Mary watched, mesmerized by a horrible and impossible hope, the sun rose another sliver and illuminated the child's face. Mary's throat constricted as though a hand had closed around it. "Clara!" she cried aloud. Her little girl—dead these thirty years, her health sacrificed for her father's who had died anyway—looked up at the sound of her name, and Mary, though unable to move, was frantically thinking how she might open the window and climb out and run across the cold blanket of sunrise and this time save her daughter, when the child was gone.

But another child was there. Older, sturdier, closer to her, blond hair glinting in the early sun. William. Willmouse. Willy Blue-Eyes. His death foretold by three years in the book of the Monster: *William is dead! That sweet child, whose smiles delighted and warmed my heart, who was so gentle, yet so gay. Victor, he is murdered.* And foretold, too, the mother's culpability, inescapable no matter what the circumstances of her child's death: *"Oh, God. I have murdered my child!"*

Mary was not surprised to see William after the others. But her heart stopped at the sight of him, long enough for her vision to fill in with blackness as though the sun had never risen, would never rise again, or as though its rising made no difference anymore. What cruelty was this that sent her dead children to her now, to remind her that she had taken for herself, however unwillingly, years and years of life that should have been theirs? To remind her, too, monstrously, that she would sacrifice them all again, even darling William, for one more day with Shelley. She managed to get the window open, skinning her knuckles on the ridge of ice, and to thrust both hands out into the frigid air, but her gesture sent William away again and she was alone.

. .. *earth's shadows fly* . . .

Shelley's heart had known it all.

She was not alone. When she turned and staggered toward her bed—thinking she might sleep at least until her surviving son and his wife began to stir and she must accept another day for living—her bed was already occupied. A female figure, head thrown back halfway off the mattress, black mouth open and marked throat exposed, features blurred and mingled, skin yellowed and taut in the slanting light so that Mary said aloud, "Fanny!" and then, "Harriet!" and knew that it was both. Her love for Shelley and his for her had murdered them both; the marks of her hands and his were on both their hearts, and, given the choice, she would without hesitation do it again.

From where she stood with her back chilled by the icy breeze from the half-open window, the bed was between her and the door. At the foot of the bed was a space just wide enough for her to pass through sideways. She pressed herself against the wall and began to sidle along it, hoping she could escape from this room with the specter in the bed, into the early-morning liveliness of her son's family, which was as bright and open and unencumbered by genius and shadows as he was.

But the figure reached for her. "Fiend!" Mary shrieked. "Leave me alone!"

The face was a monstrous composite of the women Mary had killed—her sister, Shelley's first wife, and someone else she could not quite name. "You will always be alone," the woman murmured, "until you take me in."

The woman was holding her hands out palms up, obviously in supplication. The woman wanted something from her, and Mary was moved to a primal kind of pity, but horror and revulsion were stronger and she took a few more steps along the wall toward the door.

"Don't deny me, Mary."

Her breath already short and wheezing, Mary bolted. Too soon, though, or too late, because the woman slipped between her and the door, like a shadow when the light has shifted. Arms encircled her waist. Hot breath like smoke, sweet as the grave, misted her eyes and took her own breath away. There was an explosion inside her head, a burst of exquisite color and then the rush of darkness, and in that moment she saw who the woman was. "Mother!" she cried.

Her mother, whose life and very name she had taken for her own, embraced her so tightly that Mary felt her heart and her skull split open. Her mother rushed into her mind and body and reclaimed them. "You created me!" her mother was whispering, but of course that wasn't true; Mary was her mother's creature, given life and then abandoned.

Mary fell sideways and struck her temple on the corner of the bed. Thinking there must be blood, she meant to raise a hand to the wound, and discovered she could not. She managed to drag herself up onto the bed and turn herself over so that she could breathe. Her entire left side was paralyzed. The apparition was gone, and she was alone in the room, hearing the household waking around her and knowing it had nothing to do with her anymore, staring quite without intention at the packaged heart on the mantel over no fire.

Once, very young, she had come upon a gray cat nibbling yellow roses. "Shelley!" she had called in delight to her not-yet-husband. "Here is a cat eating roses! She will turn into a woman!" And Shelley, charmed, had written it down.

Mary tried to sit up, and found she could not. She could not reach the wrapped heart on the mantel, and could lift only one hand to press on her own heart which was, remarkably, still beating. She had lived with Shelley—breathed the same air, dreaded and courted the same shadows, watched the same cat eating the same roses—for a brief, whole lifetime; she had lived without him nearly four times as long, a lifetime that was not yet finished. She suspected that, by now, he was more real and present to her in his absence than he'd ever been while physically alive in this corporeal world.

Now as she was preparing at last to join him, Mary thought she should unwrap the linen and, for what would be the last time, encounter Shelley's heart directly. Touch it. Smell it. Take measure of what remained of it. Observe its color and shape. Hold it against her breast (her nipple an eye that had so frightened him at Diodati, seeing the future, suckling the past) until her own heart stilled. She did not think she had much time.

She could not reach the "Adonais" with Shelley wrapped at its heart. She could not get out of bed; the mere thought of trying to move all those muscles in concert and sequence was ludicrous. She thought to summon Percy or his Lady Jane to fetch the heart for her, but the bell had been placed on the table at her left side, where last night it had been perfectly accessible, and now she couldn't raise or lower her fingers to ring it.

Someone came anyway. There were purposeful footsteps and harsh, rapid breathing. Mary tried to speak her relief and gratitude, and to tell what it was she wanted. For some reason, she was afraid. For some reason, she was weeping, and she herself could scarcely make sense of the guttural sounds that came from her throat.

It was not kind Jane come to do her bidding, nor her son. It was not Shelley at her door, inside her cold room with the sunrise, at her deathbed, although she had more than half expected him as guide. It was not any of the spectral women who had appeared to her earlier. She knew, suddenly, who it was.

"Monster!" she whispered, and knew that no one listening would comprehend the greeting.

It was her Monster, first given form in that long-ago, tumultuous, companionable summer at Diodati when everything had seemed possible if only fate could be avoided. Death and grief, then, had been mere words, with no true echo in her heart, although she, like the others, had thought she knew all the grand emotions of the world. After the first nightmare and the subsequent fugue-like fever of creation, Mary had come to think of the Monster as idle, foolish fancy, nothing more than a toy of a girl's Imagination. Now here it was, more real than she was; she was aware of an odd tingling sensation in the parts of her body that had been paralyzed by the touch of her mother's shade, and of a terrifying warmth in the icy region around her heart.

The Monster made as if to touch her, to caress or attack. Mary tried to shrink away, but the Monster was very close, as if their feet were attached, or the tops of their heads, or—like the infant Siamese twins she and Shelley had seen in a traveling freakshow one autumn in Genoa—their breastbones, sharing one swollen heart.

Mary rubbed her eyes with her right fist and tried clumsily to shake her head. Although the light in the room was steadily growing brighter as the sun rose over ice, she could hardly see. But the peculiar and oddly familiar odor of the Monster overlay the old-woman's-sickroom smell, a mix of acrid human sweat and chemical bitterness unexpectedly, disorientingly, lightened by a flowery fragrance.

She stared, and the Monster took form before her. The boundaries of her body were no longer clear. The Monster was so near to her now that it might have been inside her.

As always, the limbs of the Monster were perfectly proportioned, the features beautiful. Cumbersomely, Mary surveyed her own body and visualized her own face, first as in a mirror and then from the inside out. She had always thought of herself as plain, and years without Shelley had made her ugly; although she could not specify an appendage or a feature out of place, she had long thought of herself as deformed.

The pearly yellow skin of the Monster lightly, almost delicately covered the network underneath of muscles and arteries. Mary was able to lift her right hand enough to inspect it. Her own skin was grayish, wrinkled, mottled, stretched too tightly in some spots and hanging loosely in others; the underlying bone structure and pattern of blood vessels looked wrong, as though they could not possibly function, and, indeed, on the other, distant side of her body they no longer did.

The creature's hair was lustrous black, and flowing. Mary twisted her head crookedly on the hot pillow, and remembered that her own hair was tangled, dirty, dulled by age and sickness and too much sorrow.

All these characteristics of the Monster were familiar to her. She remembered dreaming them, imagining them, writing them down, reading them aloud to her appreciative if somewhat distracted first audience. But there was something new this time. Creation, once turned loose upon her chaos, had not stopped. Horror had vivified. During its ice-bound exile the Monster had changed much as she had changed; its long period of corruption had dropped its disguise and exposed an entirely new face. The mask of the Monster had rotted away. Shelley's heart must have always known:

. . . he hath awakened from the dream of life . . .

Now she knew what had always been true: her Monster was female. She had not created the pendulous breasts, the delicate hands, the shadowy and concave region between the thighs; she would never have been able to bring herself to allow such thoughts into her mind, much less to set them down on paper or, dear God, read them aloud to the three intense young men who had not in the first place truly regarded women as real. But her Monster was and had always been female, a woman like herself, and Mary did not know how she could bear this revelation.

And she knew why the Monster had come to her now. If she did not somehow protect Shelley's heart, the Monster—her own orphaned creation, the one so long denied—would discover and devour it, would claim it as her own. But how could one protect a heart?

"Go away from me!" It was more a wail than a shout, more a plea than a command.

The Monster drew back a little, her beautiful face contorted with the bitterness of the eternal outcast. Mary had imagined that the Monster's face would look like that to Victor Frankenstein but she had never expected herself to be the agent of such unhappiness. She knew her own features were twisted, too, and she could not smooth them anymore.

"Why are you here? Why have you come to me now?" It was a senseless question, for she knew the answer, but she held her breath painfully for the other's reply.

"You summoned me," the creature said, and Mary recognized the voice as more like hers than hers was now.

She did not deny it. "Go away, then. I have changed my mind."

"I have nowhere else to go. I belong to you. I am your creature. No one else will have me."

"I will not have you, either, you hideous thing." Her own
cruelty amazed her and was, she saw, utterly ineffectual.

"I am your creature." The Monster pounded her chest. "And
I am empty. I am in need of . . ." She stopped, her neck turning
awkwardly as she gazed about Mary's room.

Mary stopped herself from finishing the plea, and said instead,
audaciously, "Bring me that bound poem on the mantel, then.
There is a linen-wrapped parcel inside. Bring me my husband's
heart."

Her Monster smiled in childlike pleasure at being asked to do
something for her, and Mary's stomach turned. The Monster did
not seem surprised by the request, or in the least confused. She
turned stiffly and made her way directly to the mantel, her strides
much longer than Mary's would have been so that she crossed
the room in two steps. Her hands around the bundle were steady;
Mary could hardly bear to see them there and, indeed, could see
only their outline in the icy brightness of the room.

The Monster lifted the package from the mantel, pivoted, and
brought it to her. Mary could raise only one hand to take it and
the Monster would not release it to her, as if knowing she would
drop it and the contents would spill. She bent from the waist and
set the bundle on Mary's lap. It was remarkably light. That was
distressing. Poems should be heavy, Mary thought, and Imagination. Shelley's heart should be heaviest of all.

My spirit's bark is driven far from the shore . . .

Mary fumbled with the brittle pages of the "Adonais." The
beautiful lines tore beneath her trembling fingers and she wept.

. . . fed with true love tears instead of dew . . .

The linen bindings were stiff and tight from the years, and
with only one hand she had no hope of manipulating them.

One with trembling hands clasps his cold head . . .

The Monster put her hand over Mary's and Mary recoiled, but she was held fast, and the Monster's longer, stronger fingers pried apart the linen, carrying Mary's fingers with them like shadows.

A tear some dream has loosened from his brain.

Mary could not see inside the stiff old cloth. Its shadows had deepened, its wrinkles roughened. Her probing fingers felt nothing but grit and dust. She looked at her Monster, and for a long moment they were both motionless and silent.

Grief returns with the revolving year . . .

Mary cried out. The Monster cried out. The cloth was empty. Shelley's heart was gone.

Mary scrambled for an explanation. Perhaps the heart had never been there. Perhaps Hunt, aided by her own mad fantasies, had tricked her, or Trelawney been crazed by his own grief; perhaps all these years she had kept herself in the unmindful presence of an empty piece of cloth.

More likely, the heart had simply disintegrated. Like everything else in her life, it had likely faded away from her, been reclaimed, altered its form and substance so thoroughly that she couldn't recognize it anymore. The Monster was weeping, her hot tears melting Mary's flesh.

Or someone had taken it.

Mary and her Monster shrieked at each other at the same time, "You have stolen the heart!"

The Monster's hands came around Mary's throat. The powerful thumbs pressed into her vocal chords so that she had no hope of crying out. The Monster's frenzied thoughts exploded in her own brain, and her whole body was paralyzed now, although she seemed to be moving very fast. Her heart was being consumed by the Monster's flame, as Shelley's had not been; there was a curious sensation of wholeness and warmth. As she hurtled into the dark caverns of this new journey, her Monster came with her, holding high the torch.

▼▼▼

*Mary Wollstonecraft Godwin Shelley died in her London residence
on the first day of February, 1851. Paralysis had set in during the
last month of her illness. She was buried at St. Peter's Church,
Bournemouth, in a tomb with her father William Godwin, her
mother Mary Wollstonecraft Godwin, and Shelley's heart.*

MAD AT THE ACADEMY
▼▼▼

ESTHER M. FRIESNER

IT was, as it had to be, a dark and stormy night. Somewhere, anyway. But the California skies over Forest Lawn Cemetery were clear and the moon would not be hurried to fullness, no matter what the darkly evil doings and despite the demands of artistic necessity. A myopic crescent squinted down over the tombs, and almost missed sight of the lithe figure in ninja garb presently stealing from one shadowy mausoleum to the next.

Even without it being stormy, the night was dark. They generally are. And so a flashlight beam bobbed and wavered just ahead of the midnight creeper. The pencil-thin lance of light picked out the crushed gravel paths, the carved sleeping lions, the weeping angels and assorted other funereal bric-a-brac guarding the eternal rest of those who had left life, joy, and good taste behind them.

All at once, the way became a smidgen more jungly. The flashlight snared mountains of flowers in its beam: gardenias by the acre, massed flocks of white orchids, ghastly sheaves of ashy roses, lashed to wire forms. So much horticultural overstatement could only indicate a recent burial. One blanket arrangement used marigolds to spell out: ROBERT, WE WILL ALWAYS

LOVE YOU. The "i" in "Will" was dotted with a heart of bachelor's buttons that contained a Smiley Face picked out in pink rosebuds. The comma was candytufts.

The flashlight paused, then clicked off. "This must be the place," said its owner. The voice sounded feminine, but that was just a best-guess. Whoever this untimely caller was, the ninja mask he, she, or it wore did much to garble and disguise voice and words as well as face.

"Time to get to work." Talking to oneself is an excusable aberration if the conversation takes place among the dead, notoriously poor raconteurs all. The flashlight was holstered, a small but useful-looking crowbar drawn. Beyond the heaps of vegetation, the door of the tomb beckoned. It looked almost impossible to reach without running a combine harvester across that miniature ocean of flowers. Difficult? For some. But the catlike grace of the ninja is legendary. Not a petal would be out of place to mark the fact that someone had paid a clandestine visit to this grim monument.

The catlike grace of anyone with the bucks to buy a cheap knockoff ninja suit is a wild variable. Mask or no mask, the words, "Oh, sweet green bloody *damn!*" were perfectly audible as a freestanding wreath of silvery dahlias pulled a sneaky blindside maneuver, deliberately stuck out one easel-leg where some people wanted to walk, and flung itself on top of its prey when they both went toppling down the tomb steps together.

"Shit, I broke a nail." This time both voice and subject-matter conspired to leave no doubt: that was no ninja, that was a lady. She crawled out from amid the flowers, brushed her black p.j.'s clean of clinging petals, and assaulted the tomb once more. It was easier now. If one wreath was fallen, why stop there? Her eager hands chucked aside all the other floral tributes to dear Robert's memory while she hummed the song about jump down, spin around, pick a bale o' cotton.

Breaching the mausoleum door was a piece of cake. Inside, she was pleased to discover that she didn't need her flashlight. Robert's executor had sprung for an anemic eternal light, a fan of Vaselined orange glass lit from behind by as big a dimbulb as good old Robert had been. Not much light, but enough to see her way clear.

The coffin lid decided to teach her the moral lesson that we must strive mightily to reach our desires. It wouldn't open. It laughed at her crowbar. This would have been good if it were not a mere figure of speech although, come to think of it, Robert too had always managed to laugh between tightly clenched lips. An open-mouthed guffaw would have revealed his fillings. For an actor, visible cavities meant they docked you so many Physical Perfection Points, with a corresponding drop in salary.

Cursing, she gave the crowbar one more stiff-armed downward shove. Something gave. The coffin lid popped up like well-done toast. "About fucking time," she observed, and tilted the lid back all the way.

Death and the Make-Up Department had been very good to Robert. Gazing down on him like this—his limbs composed, his face serene—it was hard to call up a vision of him in earthly sleep—belly down, rump up, nose squashed, gaping mouth drooling into the pillow, one hand invariably tucked underneath himself in case some cat burglar broke in who'd want to steal the family jewels.

Which word, "jewels"—in the concrete and not the slang sense—brought her back to the matter at hand. So to speak. Really, Robert's executor had been niggardly, even for a lawyer. Only three rings decorated each hand, and none of them bearing top-seeded gems. At least the corpse still wore the gold neck-chains that had been his hallmark in life. People would have expected to see them at the viewing, and the *paparazzi* needed to catch the glitter of real gold in their lenses when they took their bon voyage shots of the dead celeb. Whether or not Robert's attorney had planned to return the next day and strip off the goodies, they had to stay put for the funeral. In Hollywood there was a name for folks who denied the expectations of the Press: dogmeat.

"I'm just saving him the trouble, that's all," she murmured, trying to keep her hands from shaking as she reached behind his neck for the clasps. She wore gloves, but it was hard not to imagine an unearthly cold penetrating the thin black cotton if she accidentally touched Robert's flesh. She worked quickly, eager to be the hell out of there.

She got four chains off and had only three to go when a clasp stuck. She had done this enough times before to know that graverobbing is never without its little glitches. The secret is not to panic, as she reminded herself. Then the clasp got caught on her cuff and Robert's head lolled into the crook of her arm and something went wrong with whatever mortuary magic was used to keep his mouth shut and his jaw dropped and she saw all those fillings winking up at her again and she screamed.

"Allow me."

Fat, capable hands reached over the lip of the casket to undo the golden snare. She was free to fall back a few steps and get a good look at the little black gun levelled at her chest.

"You'd better explain," said the little man whose little gun it was. "But first you'd better take off that mask."

She did, without demur. You don't argue with firearms, even if they are in the power of a small, bald, plump individual in laboratory whites who must be the evil twin brother of the Pillsbury Doughboy. As she pulled the ninja hood away, she tossed the freed masses of her auburn hair just the way she'd done in *Amazons in Leather Cages.* If you can make your captor want to have sex with you, she reasoned, he won't kill you.

Then again, considering where she'd just met this one, maybe that wasn't such a sure bet. Forest Lawn was her answer to Tiffany's; what if it was this bozo's answer to a dating service? Some like it hot only when they can get it cold.

"Speak up, my dear," he said. "Who are you? What are you doing here? And be honest. I loathe liars."

All right, she told herself. So he's not in show business. Aloud she asked, "Are you—are you a guard?"

"A guard? Me?" He threw his head back and laughed. He had more cavities than Robert, all of his filled with gold. His Klondike mouth closed with a startling snap. "Yes, I am a guard: Guard and guardian of the secrets of life itself! Warder of the mysteries behind the divine spark of human mortality. Orphic visionary who dares to trace backwards the dark path that leads every man from the light of existence into the grim shades of the grave. They dare to call me mad—mad, do you hear? Ha, those fools! Mad! Me! I! I, Dr. Godwin Shelley, mad—!" A peal of maniacal, spittle-dotted laughter echoed within the tomb.

"Oh," she said.

Strange to say, she was not afraid. A bright hope dawned in her heart, a stainless, innocent hope like that of a child who has gone astray in a dark and sinister shopping mall, only to find the rest rooms at last. She knew what he was talking about. She thought he was off his nut, but speaking the same language as an armed-and-dangerous wacko meant you were halfway to *disarming* him. And she certainly knew this language, all righty. Hadn't she lost her virginity in Devoe Jenkins' pickup truck during the Halloween marathon showing of *Frankenstein, Son of Franken-stein, Revenge of Frankenstein,* and *Frankenstein Meets the Wolf Man* at the Yellow Rose Drive-In in Eastland? Some things stay with you.

"Pleased to meet you, Doctor. My name is Polly Doree. I'm an actress and part-time model." She took the little pouch from her waist and poured its glittering contents onto the floor between them. "I also rob the dead." She gave him her best Penetrating

Sincerity stare, only used once in *Swordswoman of Venus*, a movie famous for its amount of sincere penetration. "Can we talk?"

"You fool! That was his brain you dropped!"

"Oh, put a sock in it, Doc. He's going to be an actor. It's not like he needs one."

Time passed. Things happened.

"The next asshole who calls me Igor," she said, "I kill."

Dr. Shelley leaned across the monster to pat his assistant's nylon-sheathed knee (in a strictly professional manner, of course) and reminded her, "They can call you anything they like, Polly my dear, so long as they call United Press first and give us more of that lovely, bankable, free publicity." His hand remained where it was, although with the monster's considerable bulk intervening it couldn't have been a comfortable position for the good doctor to maintain.

Polly crossed her legs abruptly, jerking temptation out from under her employer's sweaty palm. Her full, red lips jutted out in a pout that had caused more than a few casting directors to lose their heads but not, unfortunately, all the really juicy movie and TV roles in their keeping. Seductive lips and a dollar twenty-five will get you a cup of coffee in Malibu when the aforesaid lips are incapable of delivering lines more complex than, "Look out, Steve! He's got a chainsaw! EEEEEEE!"

"The press are all jackals anyway," Dr. Shelley continued. "How appropriate, therefore, that they take this tasty little morsel in their teeth and run with it." The streetlights slipped glimmering over his thick rimless glasses and hairless pate. When he smiled, his spit-slick teeth reflected the passing multicolored neon flow outside the speeding limousine.

"I don't care." Polly crossed her arms under her sequin-encrusted breasts. "I had just as much of a hand in this as you did. You even said you couldn't have done it without me! So why aren't I getting any of the upfront credit, huh?"

"My dear," Dr. Shelley purred. "You shall have this and more upfront, I promise you. In the meanwhile, remember what all this publicity will do for your own career."

Polly remained unmollified. "Publicity, sure, only these dumb fucks act like you did the whole thing and all I did was hump around your la-*bore*-atory drooling, 'Yessss, mawster. Igor go get brain now, mawster.' "

"Igor *drop* brain, too." Dr. Shelley chuckled and leaned forward to open a fresh bottle of champagne from the in-limo bar. He passed Polly a crystal flute of Moet et Chandon and tried to make light of her complaints.

"My precious girl, no one appreciates your help more than I. The advice you offered me, based on your—aha—intimate knowledge of so many, so *very* many of Hollywood's brightest stars, was irreplaceable when it came to selecting which specific physical attributes my creation should—hrrum—annex from which sources."

Polly glowered. "Are you calling me a bimbo, too?"

"Not in the strictly pejorative sense." He raised his glass in a toast to Word Power while she struggled to figure out whether or not she'd been insulted.

"This has not been an easy project for either of us," he went on. "Science demands her sacrifices. Proper credit is the least of it, be assured. Have I not endured the gibes and sneers of my fellow academics? The short-sighted fools. They could not see the magnitude of what I dared, what I had undertaken in the name of humanity! They called me mad—mad, do you hear? They dared to laugh at me! To snicker up their sleeves, to chuckle in their chairs, to titter behind their test tubes! Well, we shall see who laughs last. I swore I would make them pay, pay dearly, and now that my hour of triumph is at hand—ha! Hahahahahaha!"

"You're foaming at the mouth again." Polly passed him a handkerchief the size of a pillowcase. "Don't worry, your old ivy-covered buddies are paying plenty dear to keep up with your shenanigans, Doc. Have you seen the price of movie tickets lately?"

"Yes, yes; just so." Dr. Shelley looked sheepish as he wiped away generous dollops of frothy slaver. He sipped his champagne and tried to recapture his air of pseudo-European urbanity. "I beg your pardon; I do tend to get carried away by the Muses at times."

"Great, as long as the Muses remember to bring a strait-jacket," Polly muttered. "You miserable, patronizing, stuffed-shirt loon, *I'll* show you publicity. Just let us get there and I'll show you more than you bargained for."

"Did you say something, Polly?"

"Nothing, Dr. Shelley." She drained her champagne.

The limo took a sharp right turn and sent its three passengers canting violently left. The doctor gave a horrified squawk as the full weight of the monster's body fell heavily on top of him.

"Off! Get him off me! Off, off, off!" His incongruously dainty feet in their patent leather evening shoes kicked like a baby's.

"Yes, Dr. Shelley." Polly sighed and reached into her rhine-stoned purse for the one instrument capable of controlling the monster.

Four and a half choruses of the Oscar Mayer Weiner song later, just when Polly thought she was about to blow her brains out through the red plastic kazoo, the monster responded. Rubbing his eyes to clear them of sleep, he inquired, "Are we there yet?"

"Soon. Meanwhile, get the hell off Dr. Shelley."

"Ohhhh." the monster's soulful blue eyes widened. "I am sorry. I'll just move then, shall I?"

"Mn'nghah!" Dr. Shelley concurred.

Very slowly, yet with a peculiar agility partially his own, the monster levered himself upright. Dr. Shelley's glasses were twisted a quarter-turn around his head, his tuxedo was the worse for wear, his shirt front awash with bubbly, but on the whole he was glad to be back among the air-breathers.

"Next time I make a creature, I'm going to use track-star parts where it counts," he huffed, adjusting his spectacles. "Why can't you move any faster?"

The monster bowed his head with the fabled little-boy charm that had made its former owner big box-office. "Sorry." Polly knew how readily those tears now rising in the monster's eyes would spill over. Hadn't she insisted that Dr. Shelley "shop" for eyes and tear-ducts separately? Much more microsurgery, but oh, how it paid off! Those baby blues were gorgeous on their own; combined with weeping capabilities "borrowed" from a long-gone actor synonymous with male sensitivity, they were wide-screen dynamite.

"Ach, don't cry, don't cry! Save it for the press, damn it!" Dr. Shelley urged his own huge handkerchief into the monster's hand. "You don't want to look bad on camera."

The monster shuddered. "Camera . . . camera *bad*."

Polly gave him a fast elbow to the ribs. His entire thoracic region had been—Polly liked the term "appropriated for the Ages"—from a late twentieth-century muscleman famous for massacre-your-way-to-Justice movies. She and the doctor had been damned lucky to find enough cultivable tissue in that one's tomb to grow back a mass so big. It would take a piledriver to make any impact on that barricade of beef, but the monster flinched at her touch anyway.

"Cut that 'Camera bad' retro-crap," she snapped. "Camera *good*. Camera, just fucking *mah*-vellous, got it? No camera, no movies; no movies, no money; no money, and you might as well be dead, in this town."

"I know." the monster's wonderful eyes started shipping on water again.

"Now cool down—" her voice dropped to a whisper "—and remember what we planned."

"Look! Look! There it is!" Dr. Shelley exclaimed suddenly. He pointed at a blur of brighter light ahead, just barely visible through the double barrier of smoked glass windshield and plastic partition separating passengers from chauffeur. Traffic thickened. The limo fed itself into a parade of its peers. Classic black, sheik-of-Araby white, flashy silver, trashy gold, and a slew of Caribbean Sunset pastels, the limousines nudged their way forward, an automotive species motoring upstream to spawn.

There was a lengthy bout of stop-and-go as they waited their turn; then the moment Polly had dreamed of every time she went to the movies, including all the heels-high screenings she'd attended with Devoe Jenkins: the door beside her was opened; the first battery of flashbulbs set off their dazzling barrage; the uniformed security troops strained to keep the crowds of celebrity-stalkers from surging forward as Polly Doree stepped out onto the plush red carpet leading in to the Academy Awards.

Only they're not here to see you, said a still, small voice inside her. *Bites, don't it?* It was a major-league snotty, still, small, voice.

Up yours, she informed it. *Pretty soon I'm gonna be the* only *one they'll want to see.*

Cameras clicked, more flashes strobed off her rigid smile. Microphones bobbed in her face until her canine teeth threatened to snag on the foam head-covers. They were all around her, the hungry little mediacrats, faces upturned to receive any sacramental sound-bites she might choose to let fall. Power. Dear God, yes, it *was* better than sex.

Over just about as fast, too. The monster emerged, Dr. Shelley hanging on his arm, and Polly Doree turned invisible in front of an audience of millions. She didn't like it one damned bit.

That's all right, she told herself. *I can wait.*

Inside, the hall was a buzz and a murmur, a huge shell containing hundreds of excited conversations. The general hubbub effect was like listening in on a school of piranhas chowing down. As the three of them made their way to their table past rows of staring eyes, Polly picked up various snips of malicious chatter:

"—lower budget than my kid's *bar mitzvah* video."

"You're surprised? They were lucky even to find a cheap producer who'd take the chance. You know how hard it is getting insurance on a corpse?"

"Uh-huh, but if he gets the Oscar, they'll be standing in line to offer him jobs and kiss his dead ass."

"Whose ever *that* used to be."

"Hey! think he still gotta pay taxes?"

"—heard of voting the graveyard, but this—!"

"Whaddaya expect? You can always count on the Academy to put up at least one sympathy nominee."

"Yeah, sure, but that's only supposed to be for some old-timer who's as good as dead."

"As good as? Baby, this guy goes it one better."

A woman shrieked with laughter. "—know how they love showing support for comebacks."

"—acts about as well as he did before."

"Whatcha mean *he*? Don'tcha mean *they*?"

"—see how I've got a chance at the Oscar when I'm up against a one-man fucking *ensemble*."

The crowd settled down. The camera-ready smiles were strapped in place. The ceremonies began. At the monster's side, Polly checked the contents of her evening bag and almost panicked when she couldn't find the papers. She dumped the entire contents onto the table before breathing a sigh of relief: there they were. She only had time to tuck them away before the Best Actor category came up and every television camera in the house swivelled on her table.

He won. There had never been any doubt of it. Polly over-heard one or two bushels of sour grapes behind her:

"Sure, they voted for him: professional courtesy. I always said the Academy was a bunch of old stiffs!"

"Now, now, maybe they just did it so no one could accuse them of prejudice against a minority group."

"Since when are the dead a minority?"

"Listen, you—" An immense wave of applause crested and broke, drowning out all further comments.

"O.K., babe; *now*." Polly stuck her arm through the monster's and stood, beaming at the audience. In full control, she steered him towards the stage.

Dr. Shelley scuttled after. "Stop! Stop! What are you doing? We agreed that I was to accompany him to accept the award! I warn you, Polly—!"

She looked at him briefly, over one shoulder. "And I'm warn-ing *you*, Fatso: the game's changed. Clear off. Now."

But he didn't. He followed them all the way up onto the platform, yapping like a Yorkie on speed. He even grabbed hold of the monster's other arm and hung on. The creature gave him a pained look, but kept walking.

The glittery guest-emcees at the podium were showbiz veter-ans, hardtimers from the trenches of Tinseltown. They held their ground at the monster's approach, although the keener cameras focused on the lady's knuckles turning white as she clutched the Oscar and the gentleman's teeth beginning to splinter under the pressure of his forced smile. The statuette was nearly dropped during the hand-off as they skittered rapidly away into the wings.

The monster stood at the podium, Polly on his left arm, Dr. Shelley on his right. In his hands the Oscar gleamed. "I—uh—I want to thank everyone who made this possible."

"Don't you mean every*body*?" someone shouted from the audience.

The monster blinked, flustered. Dr. Shelley saw his chance and lunged, seizing the statuette. "Thank you, thank you all for this vote of confidence in my great work. And I want to assure you that, although the newspapers have made an unnecessary to-do over the exact post-mortem legal rights to which my—ah—creation is entitled, I will do everything in my power to safeguard his interests in all future cinematic projects we undertake—"

"That's the right word!"

"—on his behalf. It is the least I can do for a being whose very existence serves as living proof that my theories are viable. Now let them scoff at me! I spit upon their smug preconceptions! They called me mad—mad, do you hear! But I showed them; I showed them all! I—!"

"I married him," said Polly, very softly, right into the other microphone.

Cameras zoomed in, newshounds swooped, Dr. Shelley suffered a temporary loss of eyesight when he made the mistake of looking directly into all the flashes that went off, illuminating the Las Vegas marriage license and wedding photographs Polly produced from her handbag. She took the opportunity to relieve him of the Oscar.

"Vegas? you took him to *Vegas?*" the doctor wailed, hands groping wildly for her throat. "You said you were just going out to see if his legs could still breakdance after you dropped his brain!"

"I lied," Polly said too quietly even for the mike to pick up. In a much louder voice she added, "Look out! He's got a chainsaw! EEEEEEE!" and booted Dr. Shelley off the stage onto a table of screenwriters. They kept drinking.

She put her arm back around her new-to-slightly-used hubby and prepared to field questions from the press. Her lashes were demurely lowered, as much for stage effect as to preserve her own eyesight from the neverending photographic flares from over twoscore sensationalism-crazed shutterbugs. She had just revealed that the terms of her hard/soft book deal prevented her from describing the honeymoon when a loud, throaty growl rent the air.

"Camera *bad*! Camera *bad*!" the monster thundered. He flailed his arms at the encroaching media.

"Darling, please—" Polly went unheard. The monster swiped the Oscar and laid about him, smashing every camera he could reach. "Oh, crap." She sighed. "Now I'll probably have to wish I were an Oscar Mayer wiener *six* times before he calms down." She dove into her purse for the kazoo.

Which wasn't there. If the flashbulbs had allowed, she might have seen it 'way back on the table, where she'd left the other contents of her purse while searching for her wedding evidence. In desperation, she tried singing the magical control-song, but it wasn't the same.

"Camera *bad*! Camera *bad*! Camera always get my bad side! You know what that does to a guy in this business? Camera *bad*!" Six more Nikons bit the dust. Polly grabbed him by the elbow; she didn't even slow him down. And then, when she imagined she saw her whole dubious career going down the sure-enough toilet, things did what they have a habit of doing when it seems they can't get any worse:

They got worse.

"Conrad! Baby!" A starlet in blue bugle beads leaped onstage, seizing the moment and the creature's other arm.

"Eric! Honey!" A second chit, this one hermetically sealed in mauve satin, followed suit, glomming onto the monster's right knee.

"Brad, how could you? After all we meant to each other! After all the time we lived together!" This little bonbon lost half her green lamé minidress in a heroic slide for the ankles.

It was pretty obvious what was going down. *You're not the*

only bimbo in this burg who knows a great PR gimmick when it leaps out of the grave at you, the still, small voice gloated. *How many different—um—contributors did you and old Doc Shelley use to make this patchwork prima donald?*

What the hell does that matter?

Well, honey, it looks like each of your pieces had a past, and here they all come back atcha!

"Somebody get these bimbos out of here!" Polly screamed. Whether she hoped to outshout that annoying inner voice or she really thought she'd get some help, she failed. A fourth young-and-tender female sprang out from the wings, a fifth from behind the curtained backdrop, a sixth and a seventh staged a photo-finish race for the podium and latched onto their chosen portions of the creature like suction cups to wet glass. More followed. The monster staggered, dripping with women like a raw corn-dog with batter. He dropped the Oscar. It landed on Dr. Shelley's head, splattering it open like the soft-boiled egg it resembled and giving one of the screenwriters a great idea for a new script.

And on the stage, the starlets kept coming. Every one called the monster by a different name, every one had some claim to make on some part or portion of his being, every one held fast to whichever prime cut she viewed as her lawful property and every one had no trouble at all pronouncing the words "sue," "lawyer" and "palimony." It was bad.

Then the agents joined them and it was all over.

Something had to give, and it did. There was a moist, meaty, tearing sound. The arm in Polly's grip went suddenly limp, and then she was falling backwards, the combined weight of the creature and all his components' Significant Others avalanching down on top of her. The last thought that went through her mind before the lights went out for good was, *I told* him *to double stitch the seams, but would he listen?* Noooooo!

She really should have known. Planned. Anticipated what is

common knowledge. You see, the thing about Hollywood is this: You get the smallest sliver of success under your skin and the next thing you know, everybody wants a piece of you.

They'll get it, too.

That's showbiz.

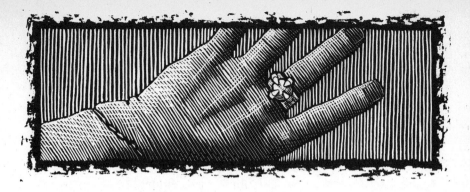

LAST CALL FOR
THE SONS OF SHOCK
▼▼▼

DAVID J. SCHOW

BLANK Frank notches down the Cramps, keeping an eye on the blue LED bars of the equalizer. He likes the light.

"Creature from the Black Leather Lagoon" calms.

The club is called Un/Dead. The sound system is from the guts of the old Tropicana, LA's altar of mud wrestling, foxy boxing, and the cock-tease unto physical pain. Its specs are for metal, loud, lots of it. The punch of the subwoofers is a lot like getting jabbed in the sternum by a big velvet piston.

Blank Frank likes the power. Whenever he thinks of getting physical, he thinks of the Vise Grip.

He perches a case of Stoli on one big shoulder and tucks another of Beam under his arm. After this he is done replenishing the bar. To survive the weekend crush, you've gotta arm. Blank Frank can lug a five-case stack without using a dolly. He has to duck to clear the lintel. The passage back to the phones and bathrooms is tricked out to resemble a bank vault door, with tumblers and cranks. It is up past six-six. Not enough for Blank Frank, who still has to stoop.

Two hours till doors open.

Blank Frank enjoys his quiet time. He has not forgotten the date. He grins at the movie poster framed next to the backbar register. He scored it at a Hollywood memorabilia shop for an obscene price even though he got a professional discount. He had it mounted on foamcore to flatten the creases. He does not permit dust to accrete on the glass. The poster is duotone, with lurid lettering. His first feature film. Every so often some Un/Dead patron with cash to burn will make an exorbitant offer to buy it. Blank Frank always says no with a smile . . . and usually spots a drink on the house for those who ask.

He nudges the volume back up for Bauhaus, doing "Bela Lugosi's Dead," extended mix.

The staff sticks to coffee and iced tea. Blank Frank prefers a nonalcoholic concoction of his own devising, which he has christened a Blind Hermit. He rustles up one, now, in a chromium blender, one hand idly on his plasma globe. Michelle gave it to him about four years back, when they first became affordably popular. Touch the exterior and the purple veins of electricity follow your fingertips. Knobs permit you to fiddle with density and amplitude, letting you master the power, feel like Tesla showing off.

Blank Frank likes the writhing electricity.

By now he carries many tattoos. But the one on the back of his left hand—the hand toying with the globe—is his favorite: a stylized planet Earth, with a tiny propellored aircraft circling it. It is old enough that the cobalt-colored dermal ink has begun to blur.

Blank Frank has been utterly bald for three decades. A tiny wisp of hair issues from his occipital. He keeps it in a neat braid, clipped to six inches. It is dead white. Sometimes, when he drinks, the braid darkens briefly. He doesn't know why.

Michelle used to be a stripper, before management got busted, the club got sold, and Un/Dead was born of the ashes. She likes being a waitress and she likes Blank Frank. She calls him "big guy." Half the regulars think Blank Frank and Michelle have something steamy going. They don't. But the fantasy detours them around a lot of potential problems, especially on weekend nights. Blank Frank has learned that people often need fantasies to *seem* superficially true, whether they really are or not.

Blank Frank dusts. If only the bikers could see him now, being dainty and attentive. Puttering.

Blank Frank rarely has to play bouncer whenever some booze-fueled trouble sets to brewing inside Un/Dead. Mostly, he just strolls up behind the perp and waits for him or her to turn around and apologize. Blank Frank's muscle duties generally consist of just *looming*.

If not, he thinks with a smile, there's always the Vise Grip.

The video monitor shows a Red Top taxicab parking outside the employee entrance. Blank Frank is pleased. This arrival coincides exactly with his finish-up on the bartop, which now gleams like onyx. He taps up the slide pot controlling the mike volume on the door's security system. There will come three knocks.

Blank Frank likes all this gadgetry. Cameras and shotgun mikes, amps and strobes and strong, clean alternating current to web it all in concert with maestro surety. Blank Frank loves the switches and toggles and running lights. But most of all, he loves the power.

Tap-tap-tap. Precisely. Always three knocks.

"Good," he says to himself, drawing out the vowel. As he hastens to the door, the song ends and the club fills with the empowered hiss of electrified dead air.

▼▼▼

Out by limo. In by cab. One of those eternally bedamned scheduling glitches.

The Count overtips the cabbie because his habit is to deal only in round sums. He never takes . . . change. The Count has never paid taxes. He has cleared forty-three million large in the past year, most of it safely banked in bullion, out-of-country, after overhead and laundering.

The Count raps smartly with his umbrella on the service door of Un/Dead. Blank Frank never makes him knock twice.

It is a pleasure to see Blank Frank's face overloading the tiny security window; his huge form filling the threshold. The Count enjoys Blank Frank despite his limitations when it comes to social intercourse. It is relaxing to appreciate Blank Frank's condition-less loyalty, the innate tidal pull of honor and raw justice that seems programmed into the big fellow. Soothing, it is, to sit and drink and chat lightweight chat with him, in the autopilot way normals told their normal acquaintances where they'd gone and what they'd done since their last visit. Venomless niceties.

None of the buildings in Los Angeles has been standing as long as the Count and Blank Frank have been alive.

Alive. Now there's a word that begs a few new comprehensive, enumerated definitions in the dictionary. Scholars could quibble, but the Count and Blank Frank and Larry were definitely alive. As in "living"—*especially* Larry. Robots, zombies and the walking dead in general could never get misty about such traditions as this threesome's annual conclaves at Un/Dead.

The Count's face is mappy, the wrinkles in his flesh rice-paper fine. Not creases of age, but tributaries of usage, like the creeks and streams of palmistry. His pallor, as always, tends toward blue. He wears dark shades with faceted, lozenge-shaped lenses of apache tear; mineral crystal stained bloody-black. Behind them, his eyes, bright blue like a husky's. He forever maintains his hair wet and backswept, what Larry has called his "renegade opera conductor coif." Dramatic threads of pure cobalt-black streak backward from the snow-white crown and temples. His lips are as thin and bloodless as two slices of smoked liver. His diet does not render him robustly sanguine; it merely sustains him, these days. It bores him.

Before Blank Frank can get the door open, the Count fires up a handrolled cigarette of coca paste and drags the milky smoke deep. It mingles with the dope already loitering in his metabolism and perks him to.

The cab hisses away into the wet night. Rain on the way.

Blank Frank is holding the door for him, grandly, playing butler.

The Count's brow is overcast. "Have you forgotten so soon, my friend?" Only a ghost of his old, marble-mouthed, middle-Euro accent lingers. It is a trait that the Count has fought for long years to master, and he is justly proud that he is intelligible. Occasionally, someone asks if he is from Canada.

Blank Frank pulls the exaggerated face of a child committing a big boo-boo. "Oops, sorry." He clears his throat. "Will you come in?"

Equally theatrically, the Count nods and walks several thousand worth of Armani double-breasted into the cool, dim retreat of the bar. It is *nicer* when you're invited, anyway.

"Larry?" says the Count.

"Not yet," says Blank Frank. "You know Larry—tardy is his twin. There's real time and Larry time. Celebrities *expect* you to expect them to be late." He points toward the backbar clock, as if that explains everything.

The Count can see perfectly in the dark, even with his murky glasses. As he strips them, Blank Frank notices the silver crucifix dangling from his left earlobe, upside-down.

"You into metal?"

"I like the ornamentation," says the Count. "I was never too big on jewelry; greedy people try to dig you up and steal it if they know you're wearing it; just ask Larry. The sort of people who would come to thieve from the dead in the middle of the night are not the class one would choose for friendly diversion."

Blank Frank conducts the Count to three highback Victorian chairs he has dragged in from the lounge and positioned around a cocktail table. The grouping is directly beneath a pinlight spot, intentionally theatrical.

"Impressive." The Count's gaze flickers toward the bar. Blank Frank is way ahead of him.

The Count sits, continuing: "I once knew a woman who was beleaguered by a devastating allergy to cats. And this was a person who felt some deep emotional communion with that species. Then one day, poof! She no longer sneezed; her eyes no longer watered. She could stop taking medications that made her drowsy. She had forced herself to be around cats so much that her body chemistry adapted. The allergy receded." He fingers the silver cross hanging from his ear, a double threat, once upon a time. "I wear this as a reminder of how the body can triumph. Better living through chemistry."

"It was the same with me and fire." Blank Frank hands over a very potent mixed drink called a Gangbang. The Count sips, then presses his eyelids contentedly shut. Like a cat. The drink must be industrial strength. Controlled substances are the Count's lifeblood.

Blank Frank watches as the Count sucks out another long, deep, soul-drowning draught. "You know Larry's going to ask again, whether you're still doing . . . what you're doing."

"I brook no apologia or excuses." Nevertheless, Blank Frank sees him straighten in his chair, almost defensively. "I could say that you provide the same service in this place." With an outswept hand, he indicates the bar. If nothing else remains recognizable, the Count's gesticulations remain grandiose: physical exclamation points.

"It's legal. Food. Drink. Some smoke."

"Oh, yes, there's the rub." The Count pinches the bridge of his nose. He consumes commercial decongestants ceaselessly. Blank Frank expects him to pop a few pills, but instead the Count lays out a scoop of toot inside his mandarin pinky fingernail, which is lacquered ebony, elongated, a talon. Capacious. Blank Frank knows from experience that the hair and nails continue growing long after death. The Count inhales the equivalent of a pretty good dinner at Spago. Capuccino included.

"There is no place in the world I have not lived," says the Count. "Even the Arctic. The Australian outback. The Kenyan sedge. Siberia. I walk unharmed through fire-fight zones, through sectors of strife. You learn so much when you observe people at war. I've survived holocausts, conflagration, even a low-yield one-megaton test, once, just to see if I could do it. Sue me; I was high. But wherever I venture, whatever phylum of human beings I encounter, they all have one thing in common."

"The red stuff." Blank Frank half-jests; he dislikes it when the mood grows too grim.

"No. It is their need to be narcotized." The Count will not be swerved. "With television. Sex. Coffee. Power. Fast cars and sado-games. Emotional encumbrances. More than anything else, with *chemicals*. All drugs are like instant coffee. The fast purchase of a feeling. You *buy* the feeling, instead of earning it. You want to relax, go up or go down, get strong or get stupid? You simply swallow or snort or inject, and the world changes because of you. The most lucrative commercial enterprises are those with the most undeniable core simplicity; just look at prostitution. Blood, bodies, armaments, position—all commodities. Human beings want so *much* out of life."

The Count smiles, sips. He knows that the end of life is only the beginning. Today is the first day of the rest of your death.

"I do apologize, my old friend, for coming on so aggressively.

I've rationalized my calling, you see, to the point where it is a speech of lists; I make my case with demographics. Rarely do I find anyone who cares to suffer the speech."

"You've been rehearsing." Blank Frank recognizes the bold streak the Count gets in his voice when declaiming. Blank Frank has himself been jammed with so many hypos in the past few centuries that he has run out of free veins. He has sampled the Count's root-canal quality coke; it made him irritable and sneezy. The only drugs that still seem to work on him unfailingly are extremely powerful sedatives in large, near-toxic dosages. And those never last long. "Tell me. The drugs. Do they have any effect on *you?*"

He sees the Count pondering how much honesty is too much. Then the tiny, knowing smile flits past again, a wraith between old comrades.

"I employ various palliatives. I'll tell you the absolute truth: mostly it is an affectation, something to occupy my hands. Human habits—vices, for that matter—go a long way toward putting my customers at ease when I am closing negotiations."

"Now you're thinking like a merchant," says Blank Frank. "No royalty left in you?"

"A figurehead gig." The Count frowns. "Over whom, my good friend, would I hold illimitable dominion? Rock stars. Thrill junkies. Corporate monsters. No percentage in flaunting your lineage there. No. I occupy my time much as a fashion designer does. I concentrate on next season's line. I brought cocaine out of its Vin Mariani limbo and helped repopularize it in the Eighties. Then crank, then crack, then ice. Designer dope. You've heard of Ecstasy. You haven't heard of Chrome yet. Or Amp. But you will."

Suddenly a loud booming rattles the big main door, as though the entire DEA is hazarding a spot raid. Blank Frank and the Count are both twisted around in surprise. Blank Frank catches a glimpse of the enormous Browning Hi-Power holstered in the Count's left armpit.

It's probably just for the image, Blank Frank reminds himself.

The commotion sounds as though some absolute lunatic is kicking the door and baying at the moon. Blank Frank hurries over, his pulse relaxing as his pace quickens.

It has to be Larry.

▼▼▼

"Gah-DAMN it's peachy to see ya, ya big dead dimwit!" Larry is a foot shorter than Blank Frank. Nonetheless, he bounds in, pounces, and suffocates his amigo in a big wolfy bear hug.

Larry is almost too much to take in with a single pair of eyes.

His skintight red Spandex tights are festooned with spangles and fringe that snake, at knee level, into golden cowboy boots. Glittering spurs on the boots. An embossed belt buckle the size of the grille on a Rolls. Larry is into ornaments, including a feathered earring with a skull of sterling, about a hundred metalzoid bracelets, and a three-finger rap ring of slush-cast 24K that spells out AWOO. His massive, pumped chest fairly bursts from a bright silver Daytona racing jacket, snapped at the waist but not zipped, so the world can see his collarless muscle tee in neon scarlet, featuring his caricature in yellow. Fiery letters on the shirt scream about THE REAL WOLF MAN. Larry is wearing his Ray-Bans at night and jingles a lot whenever he walks.

"Where's ole Bat Man? Yo! I *see* you skulking in the dark!" Larry whacks Blank Frank on the biceps, then lopes to catch the Count. With the Count, it is always a normal handshake—dry, firm, businesslike. "Off thy bunnage, fang-dude; the party has *arriiiived*!!"

"Nothing like having a real celebrity in our midst," says Blank Frank. "But jeez—what the hell is this *'Real'* Wolf Man crap?"

Larry grimaces as if from a gas pain, showing teeth. "A slight

little ole matter of copyrights, trademarks, eminent domain . . .
and some fuckstick who *registered* himself with the World Wrestling Federation as 'The Wolfman.' Turns out to be a guy I bit,
my ownself, a couple of decades ago. So I have to be 'The Real.'
We did a tag-team thing, last Wrestlemania. But we can't think
of a good team name."

"Runts of the Litter," opines the Count. Droll.

"Hellpups," says Blank Frank.

"Fuck ya both extremely much." Larry grins his trademark
grin. Still showing teeth. He snaps off his shades and scans Un/
Dead. "What's to quaff in this pit? Hell, what *town* is this,
anywho?"

"On tour?" Blank Frank plays host.

"Yep. Gotta kick Jake the Snake's ass in Atlanta next Friday.
Gonna strangle him with Damien, if the python'll put up with
it. Wouldn't want to hurt him for real but might have ole Jake
pissing blood for a day, if you know what I mean."

Blank Frank grins; he knows what Larry means. He makes a
fist with his left hand, then squeezes his left wrist tightly with his
right hand. "Vise Grip him."

Larry is the inventor of the Vise Grip, second only to the
Sleeper Hold in wrestling infamy. The Vise Grip has done Blank
Frank a few favors with rowdies in the past. Larry owns the move,
and is entitled to wax proud.

"I mean pissing *pure* blood!" Larry enthuses.

"Ecch," says the Count. "Please."

"Sorry, oh cloakless one. Hey! Remember that brewery, made
about three commercials with the Beer Wolf before *that* campaign
croaked and ate dirt? That was me!"

Blank Frank hoists his Blind Hermit. "Here's to the Beer
Wolf, then. Long may he howl."

"*Prost,*" says the Count.

"Fuckin A." Larry downs his entire mugfull of draft in one

slam-dunk. He belches, wipes foam from his mouth and lets go with a lupine *yee-hah*.

The Count dabs his lips with a cocktail napkin.

Blank Frank watches Larry do his thing and a stiff chaser of memory quenches his brain. That snout, the bicuspids, and those beady, ball-bearing eyes will always give Larry away. His eyebrows ran together; that was supposed to be a classic clue in the good old days. Otherwise, Larry was not so hirsute. In human form, at least. The hair on his forearms was very fine tan down. Pumping iron and beating up people for a living has bulked out his shoulders. He usually wears his shirts open-necked. T-shirts, he tears the throats out. He is all piston-muscles and zero flab. He is able to squeeze a full beer can in one fist and pop the top with a gunshot bang. His hands are callused and wily. The pentagram on his right palm is barely visible. It has faded, like Blank Frank's tattoo.

"Cool," Larry says of the Count's crucifix.

"Aren't *you* wearing a touch as well?" The Count points at Larry's skull earring. "Or is it the light?"

Larry's fingers touch the silver. "Yeah. Guilty. Guess we haven't had to fret that movieland spunk for quite a piece, now."

"I had fun." Blank Frank exhibits his tat. "It was good."

"*Goood*," Larry and the Count say together, funning their friend.

All three envision the tiny plane in growly flight, circling a black and white world, forever.

"How long have you *had* that?" Larry is already on his second mug, foaming at the mouth.

Blank Frank's pupils widen, filling with his skin illustration. He does not remember.

"At least forty years ago," says the Count. "They'd changed the logo by the time he'd committed to getting the tattoo."

"Maybe that was why I did it." Blank Frank is still a bit lost.

He touches the tattoo as though it will lead to a swirl dissolve and an expository flashback.

"Hey, we *saved* that fuckin studio from bankruptcy." Larry bristles. "Us and A&C."

"They were shown the door, too." To this day, the Count is understandably piqued about the copyright snafu involving the use of his image. He sees his face everywhere, and does not rate compensation. This abrades his business instinct for the jugular. He understands too well why there must be a Real Wolf Man. "Bud and Lou and you and me and the big guy all went out with the dishwater of the Second World War."

"*I* was at Lou's funeral," says Larry. "You were lurking the Carpathians." He turned to Blank Frank. "And *you* didn't even know about it."

"I loved Lou," says Blank Frank. "Did I ever tell you the story of how I popped him by accident on the set of—"

"*Yes.*" The Count and Larry speak in unison. This breaks the tension of remembrance tainted by the unfeeling court intrigue of studios. Recall the people, not the things.

Blank Frank tries to remember some of the others. He returns to the bar to rinse his glass. The plasma globe zizzes and snaps calmly, a man-made tempest inside clear glass.

"I heard ole Ace got himself a job at the Museum of Natural History." Larry refers to Ace Bandage; he has nicknames like this for everybody.

"The Prince," the Count corrects, "still guards the Princess. She's on display in the Egyptology section. The Prince cut a deal with museum security. He prowls the graveyard shift; guards the bone rooms. They've got him on a synthetic of tana leaves. It calmed him down. Like methadone."

"A night watchman gig," says Larry, obviously thinking of the low pay scale. But what in hell would the Prince need human coin for, anyway? "Hard to picture."

"Try looking in a mirror, yourself," says the Count.

Larry blows a raspberry. "Jealous."

It is very easy for Blank Frank to visualize the Prince, gliding through the silent, cavernous corridors in the wee hours. The museum is, after all, just one giant tomb.

Larry is fairly certain ole Fish Face—another nickname—escaped from a mad scientist in San Francisco and butterfly-stroked south, probably to wind up in bayou country. He and Larry had shared a solid mammal-to-amphibian simpatico. He and Larry had been the most physically violent of the old crew. Larry still entertained the notion of talking his scaly pal into doing a bout for pay-per-view. He has never been able to work out the logistics of a steel fishtank match, however.

"Griffin?" says the Count.

"Who can say?" Blank Frank shrugs. "He could be standing right here and we wouldn't know it unless he started singing 'Nuts in May.' "

"He was a misanthrope," says Larry. "His crazy kid, too. That's what using drugs will get you."

This last is a veiled stab at the Count's calling. The Count expects this from Larry, and stays venomless. The last thing he wants this evening is a conflict over the morality of substance use.

"I dream, sometimes, of those days," says Blank Frank. "Then I see the films again. The dreams are literalized. It's scary."

"Before *this* century," says the Count, "I never had to worry that anyone would stockpile my past." Of the three, he is the most paranoid where personal privacy is concerned.

"You're a romantic." Larry will only toss an accusation like this in special company. "It was important to a lot of people that we *be* monsters. You can't deny what's nailed down there in black and white. There was a time when the world *needed* monsters like that."

They each considered their current occupations, and found that they did indeed still fit into the world.

"Nobody's gonna pester you now," Larry presses on. "Don't bother to revise your past—today, your past is public record, and waiting to contradict you. We did our jobs. How many people become mythologically legendary for just doing their jobs?"

"Mythologically legendary?" mimicks the Count. "You'll grow hair on your hands from using all those big words."

"Bite this." Larry offers the unilateral peace symbol.

"No, thank you; I've already dined. But I have brought something for you. For both of you."

Blank Frank and Larry both notice the Count is now speaking as though a big Mitchell camera is grinding away, somewhere just beyond the grasp of sight. He produces a small pair of wrapped gifts, and hands them over.

Larry wastes no time ripping into his. "Weighs a ton."

Nestled in styro popcorn is a wolf's head—savage, streamlined, snarling. The gracile canine neck is socketed.

"It's from the walking stick," says the Count. "All that was left."

"No kidding." Larry's voice grows small for the first time this evening. The wolf's head seems to gain weight in his grasp. Two beats of his powerful heart later, his eyes seem a bit wet.

Blank Frank's gift is much smaller and lighter.

"You were a conundrum," says the Count. He enjoys playing emcee. "So many choices, yet never easy to buy for. Some soil from Transylvania? Water from Loch Ness? A chunk of some appropriate ruined castle?"

What Blank Frank unwraps is a ring. Old gold, worn smooth of its subtler filigree. A small ruby set in the grip of a talon. He holds it to the light.

"As nearly as I could discover, that ring once belonged to a man named Ernst Volmer Klumpf."

"Whoa," says Larry. Weird name.

Blank Frank puzzles it. He holds it toward the Count, like a lens.

"Klumpf died a long time ago," says the Count. "Died and was buried. Then he was disinterred. Then a few of his choicer parts were recycled by a skillful surgeon of our mutual acquaintance."

Blank Frank stops looking so blank.

"In fact, part of Ernst Volmer Klumpf is still walking around today . . . tending bar for his friends, among other things."

The new expression on Blank Frank's face pleases the Count. The ring just barely squeezes onto the big guy's left pinky—his smallest finger.

Larry, to avoid choking up, decides to make noise. Showing off, he vaults the bartop and draws his own refill. "This calls for a toast." He hoists his beer high, slopping the head. "To dead friends. Meaning us."

The Count pops several capsules from an ornate tin and washes them down with the last of his Gangbang. Blank Frank murders his Blind Hermit.

"Don't even think of the bill," says Blank Frank, who knows of the Count's habit of paying for everything. The Count smiles and nods graciously. In his mind, the critical thing is to keep the tab straight. Blank Frank pats the Count on the shoulder, hale and brotherly, since Larry is out of reach. The Count dislikes physical contact but permits this because it is, after all, Blank Frank.

"Shit man, we could make our own comeback sequel, with all the talent in this room," Larry says. "Maybe hook up with some of those new guys. Do a monster rally."

It could happen. They all look significantly at each other. A brief stink of guilt, of culpability, like a sneaky fart in a dimly lit chamber.

Make that dimly-lit *torture dungeon*, thinks Blank Frank, who never forgets the importance of staying in character.

Blank Frank thinks about sequels. About how studios had once jerked their marionette strings, compelling them to come lurching back for more, again and again, adding monsters when the brew ran weak, until they had all been bled dry of revenue potential and dumped at a bus stop to commence the long deathwatch that had made them nostalgia.

It was like living death, in its way.

And these gatherings, year upon year, had become sequels in their own right.

The realization is depressing. It sort of breaks the back of the evening for Blank Frank. He stands friendly and remains as chatty as he ever gets. But the emotion has soured.

Larry chugs so much that he has grown a touch bombed. The Count's chemicals intermix and buzz; he seems to sink into the depths of his coat, his chin ever-closer to the butt of the gun he carries. Larry drinks deep, then howls. The Count plugs one ear with a finger on his free hand. "I wish he wouldn't *do* that," he says in a proscenium-arch *sotto voce* that indicates his annoyance is mostly token.

When Larry tries to hurdle the bar again, moving exaggeratedly as he almost always does, he manages to plant his big wrestler's elbow right into the glass on Blank Frank's framed movie poster. It dents inward with a sharp crack, cobwebbing into a snap puzzle of fracture curves. Larry swears, instantly chagrined. Then, lamely, he offers to pay for the damage.

The Count, not unexpectedly, counter-offers to buy the poster, now that it's damaged.

Blank Frank shakes his massive square head at both of his friends. So many years, among them. "It's just glass. I can replace it. It wouldn't be the first time."

The thought that he has done this before depresses him further. He sees the reflection of his face, divided into staggered components in the broken glass, and past that, the lurid illustration. Him then. Him now.

Blank Frank touches his face as though it is someone else's.

His fingernails have always been black. Now they are merely fashionable.

Larry remains embarrassed about the accidental damage and the Count begins spot-checking his Rolex every five minutes or so, as though he is pressing the envelope on an urgent appointment. Something has spoiled the whole mood of their reunion, and Blank Frank is angry that he can't quite pinpoint the cause. When he is angry, his temper froths quickly.

The Count is the first to rise. Decorum is all. Larry tries one more time to apologize. Blank Frank stays cordial, but is overpowered by the sudden strong need to get them the hell out of Un/Dead.

The Count bows stiffly. His limo manifests precisely on schedule. Larry gives Blank Frank a hug. His arms can reach all the way 'round.

"*Au revoir*," says the Count.

"Stay dangerous," says Larry.

Blank Frank closes and locks the service door. He monitors, via the tiny security window, the silent, gliding departure of the Count's limousine, the fading of Larry's spangles into the night.

Still half an hour till opening. The action at Un/Dead doesn't really crank until midnight anyway, so there's very little chance that some bystander will get hurt.

Blank Frank bumps up the volume and taps his club foot. A eulogy with a beat. He loves Larry and the Count in his massive, broad, uncompromisingly loyal way, and hopes they will understand his actions. He hopes that his two closest friends are perceptive enough, in the years to come, to know that he is not crazy.

Not crazy, and certainly not a monster.

While the music plays, he fetches two economy-sized plastic bottles of lantern kerosene, which he ploshes liberally around the bar, saturating the old wood trim. Arsonists call such flammable liquids "accelerator."

In the scripts, it was always an overturned lantern, or a flung torch from a mob of villagers, that touched off the conclusive inferno. Mansions, mad labs, even stone fortresses burned and blew up, eliminating monster menaces until they were needed again.

Dark threads snake through the tiny warrior braid at the back of Blank Frank's skull. All those Blind Hermits.

The purple electricity arcs toward his finger and trails it loyally. He unplugs the plasma globe and cradles it beneath one giant forearm. The movie poster, he leaves hanging in its smashed frame.

He snaps the sulphur match with one black thumbnail. Ignition craters and blackens the head, eating it with a sharp hiss. Un/Dead's PA throbs with the bass line of "D.O.A." Phosphorus tangs the unmoving air. The match fires orange to yellow to a steady blue. The flamepoint reflects from Blank Frank's large black pupils. He can see himself, as if by candlelight, fragmented by broken picture glass. The past. In his grasp is the plasma globe, unblemished, pristine, awaiting a new charge. The future.

He recalls all of his past experiences with fire. He drops the match into the thin pool of accelerator glistening on the bartop. The flame grows quietly.

Good.

Light springs up, hard white, behind him as he exits and locks the door. The night is cool, near foggy. Condensation mists the plasma globe as he strolls away, pausing beneath a streetlamp to appreciate the ring on his little finger. He doesn't need to eat or sleep. He'll miss Michelle and the rest of the Un/Dead folks. But he is not like them; he has all the time he'll ever need, and friends who will be around forever.

Blank Frank likes the power.

VICTOR
▼▼▼

KAREN HABER

THE man feels his body dying by inches. His toes are like wood. His lower legs are without feeling. He is alone in the icy wastes, unattended. As the numbing spreads upward through his chest he is surprised by the gentle warmth that accompanies it. He sinks gratefully into that warmth, draws it up around him as he would thick bedcovers. Yes, he is safe in a snug bed. It is the house around him that is cold. And he is not young. He is old, old and weary. The space around his cot is crowded by his memories, by the sepia-toned shades that stalk, transparent, before him over the hard wooden floor.

▼▼▼

Justine swings like a pendulum, like a clapper inside a bell, slowly, back and forth, hanging by the neck from the rope that has killed her. Her skin is pale, almost white. A trickle of red blood seeps from her slack, open mouth.

"Oh, God," Elizabeth cries. "It's terrible. Why didn't you save her?" She turns from the high window in their hideaway and her eyes are dark with revulsion. "They hanged her for you. For your crimes. I know that now."

"No," he says. "I'm innocent. I meant no harm, ever. Should I have turned myself in? Would you have me stripped and dead before that howling mob?"

Elizabeth is unrelenting. His beloved bride is judge and jury. "Better that you did and saved your immortal soul. What evil did Justine commit? Her only mistake was in being born, in living with us, working for us. And in caring for poor William. You killed her. You and your morbid, damned creature."

"No," he says. "Wait, Elizabeth. Don't go."

But she is gone, like the rest of them. Killed by his ambition. The wind rushes in through the open window and the sound of its passage is like that of a soul in agony. He is alone in the darkness.

▼▼▼

Sinews like pink cords, like the strings of an instrument. Pluck them and they echo the theme of life. Victor leans over the cadaver on the dissection table, fascinated. He is skilled with the knife, and he cuts here, cuts there. He will learn the secrets of the body, and science will empower him to use them.

Red stains climb up his gloves and sleeves as he works within the body cavity and the damp cloth clings to him like a clammy second skin. He ignores it. He will do great things with what he learns. The name of Frankenstein will be added to the scientific and medical brotherhood, to the great pantheon of knowledge.

Determined, he pursues nature. But not through wooded glen and sunlit meadow. The fascination resides for him in the charnel house, the graveyard.

"Still chopping and probing?" Henry Cherval asks. He is peering around the door, his nose wrinkling at the sour smell of formaldehyde. "Whew! What a horrid odor. Come out into the daylight and sniff the sweet air."

"Later, Henry."

"You're as fixed on this as you were on Cornelius Agrippa and Paracelsus." Henry shakes his head. "Professor Waldman has diverted you from philosophy into necrology."

"He showed me that philosophy dealt merely with words," Victor says. "But science contains the essence of life. Not death, Henry. Life."

"There's a letter from Elizabeth on the table."

"Later."

▼▼▼

He tries to lift numbed arms, raise his numb head. So warm. He lies back upon his deathbed, waiting patiently. He knows that if he is too eager, death may elude him. He has chased this quarry for years, knows its moods and caprices. He has learned not to be eager.

No pills, razors, rope. Best to lie here, eyes closed and sunken in huge sockets. Quiet, yes. It will be drawn to him by the ease, by the quiet. A shy rabbit, death. He chuckles at the thought. Oh, he'd trapped it once or twice. Or so he'd imagined. But always, always, death had escaped him. Danced away maddeningly, just out of reach. The brush of a whisker, the touch of a cottony tail as it went past him. "Wait for me," he'd cried, as tearful as any Alice, out of wind and running hard. "Oh, please, wait."

All his life, he had run fast, had run hard to catch up, to catch it and beat it. Dry laughter rattles in his thin, dry throat. To win against death. To turn it back as though it were a soft cotton blanket fresh from the laundry and not a filthy, web-like shroud. He chuckles again. So young and arrogant. How good to have been that, to have had that angry impatience, once, long ago. Before the reckless flight to the Northern ice to evade his nemesis.

▼▼▼

Geneva glistens in the summer sunlight, a jewel-like city with neat, clean streets and busy, good-natured citizens. Victor has grown up there, the scion of a distinguished family deeply rooted in service to the community. In Geneva, the name of Frankenstein is synonymous with men of law. His father had married, late, the daughter of an old friend. Their eldest son, Victor, has inherited his mother's determination and his father's love of knowledge.

"Victor thinks that the world is a secret which only he can discover," his father says.

"Give him time, then, and opportunity," says his mother. "And when he's ready, give him his cousin Elizabeth as a bride."

His youngest brother William, pampered favorite of the household, with plump pink cheeks and golden hair like silk to the touch. Waiting by the door, jigging up and down, and tugging at Victor's jacket.

"Where are you going?"

"To the Academy."

"Take me. Take me along, please." The blue eyes shine with adoration at the older brother.

Victor is accustomed to the childish worship and careless of it. "Don't you want to go see what Nanny's about?"

"Nanny takes care of babies. I want to go with you."

He smiles sadly. "When you're older, perhaps."

"Now." The lower lip juts out in playful petulance.

Victor pats the child on the shoulder. Pushes him away. "Perhaps when you're older."

In the sitting room, Victor's mother turns to his father. "Victor is like a second father to that boy."

"Yes," says the older man, almost napping in his chair. "I daresay he will take responsibility for him, someday."

▼▼▼

William. Justine. Elizabeth. Bones rattling in cold boxes. Spectres 'round my bed. He has killed you all. Driven a dagger at my heart through you.

▼▼▼

The room is dark, illuminated by a single source. Victor is sweating, bent over the surgical table working hard, carving and sewing, mating tissues, furiously trying to effect another dark miracle.

"A companion," the creature says. "You will give me a woman." His voice is thick, nearly incoherent. "I must have a mate. Am I to wander alone while all else in nature is paired?"

"You are not of nature," Victor says, and his voice shakes with fear.

"You have created me. You will create my woman."

Throughout the hot night Victor toils. The creature withdraws to brood in solitude.

Near dawn, a bird fills the air with trilling song.

Victor pauses in his desperate labors, wipes his brow. He has engendered one abomination. Is that not enough? What has he learned? Too much. He pulls back from the table and the torso lying there. He puts down the knife.

"If I must be alone, so will you be," the creature says. "I am in your mirror, your dim reflection. And I will be with you on your wedding night."

▼▼▼

The philosopher's stone. The elixir of life. Better if I never learned of those fanciful imaginings. Father, why did you not tell me that other, better investigations had already borne fruit? The clean rationality of chemistry would had drawn me, surely. I curse that day in the inn when I came upon Agrippa's work. I curse you, Father. All fathers. All men and all their offspring.

He stretches a wooden toe and for a moment the warmth recedes. The room dims, fades, replaced by blinding whiteness.

Henry, he thinks. Dear Henry, favorite friend of childhood. And Father. Brave, loving man. Gone. All I ever loved. Fitting payment. But not enough.

For poor Henry alone surely he will go to hell, and he welcomes the journey. A hot red space filled with chittering, buzzing horrors: birds with jagged teeth and clamshell wings, swollen nightmares with spindly legs, cloven hooves, and hairy, piglike hides cleft to reveal gelatinous eggs filled with staring yellow eyes? What awaits? Has a special torment been devised for me?

Victor chuckles.

Such arrogance. Even after so many years, he has not completely outgrown that dangerous, insolent pride. The thought almost gives him pleasure. He leans back upon his pillow. Even his head feels numb, warm.

▼▼▼

William has been missing all day and into the night. With growing fear, the family and servants search. The maid Justine is distraught at the news of the young boy's disappearance. She delays her return to town, searching each hayloft, each milkshed she passes.

"William," she calls, and the echoes fade to nothing. "Sweet boy, come to me."

She lingers too long in the fields—perhaps he has fallen asleep under a berry bush, foolish child—and the thick town gates are locked against her now. The night is short and sleepless, save for a strange dream in which she sees some monstrous shadow looming above her and feels the touch of strange hands pulling at her apron.

In the morning, she stumbles back to Geneva, exhausted, disheartened. Her brown hair is matted, her eyes dull.

"Justine," Elizabeth cries. "Where have you been?"

"Out all night, looking for young Will. Has he returned?"

Elizabeth's eyes glisten with tears. "They found him early this morning."

"Good, then. I'll go to him."

A hand on her shoulder stops her. "His neck was broken. Some fiend did it and stole the jeweled locket I'd given him to wear."

"Dead?" Justine staggers back against the wall. Is this a nightmare, too? Her hands begin to pick nervously about her person, straightening a sleeve, flipping up a collar, reaching into a pocket of her apron to close upon an unfamiliar object. She draws it forth, holds it up to the light. Gasps in disbelief.

Upon her open palm rests a jewel-encrusted golden locket threaded upon a broken velvet ribbon.

▼▼▼

Clever madman. The diseased imagination and cruelty of the thing. To murder first the beloved younger brother, then to implicate an innocent family maid. Stripping the tree bare with relentless malice. Oh, clever, brutal monster.

▼▼▼

Elizabeth, his bride, lies upon the bed like a discarded doll, her arms at strange angles, her head bent horribly back. Her eyes stare at him, accusing, empty.

And Henry, good Henry, is found strangled in the snow.

His father, bowed down by too many tragedies, succumbs to sorrow.

Victor is alone. But that noise, what is that noise? Death approaching? No, he is too anxious, breathing too hard. He will scare away that black rabbit. Calm, he must be calm.

Those sounds, like the groan of stairs under a heavy foot. Surely not death coming.

The space around his bed is crowded by his memories. But one is missing. One alone of that ghostly crew who may yet survive his creator. Coming now, tracking him, to find him and finish the job death has abandoned?

▼▼▼

By late November he has done it. The object of two years' work lies shuddering upon a stained pallet and opens dull amber eyes. The grotesque mouth stretches in what might become a smile. A misshapen hand reaches out. And Victor knows that he has failed.

He has attempted pure science, that most sacred of religions. So pure, so certain. And he knows with cold clarity that he will be called a blasphemer. His name will be whispered to children as a threat. His ambition will be cursed.

The creature rises up, mutters something guttural. The grasping hand comes nearer.

"No!"

Victor pulls back, slams the door behind him, and bolts it. Will the thing rise up to pound and smash its way to freedom? He pauses. Curious sounds issue from the locked chamber. High, keening. Almost like that of a crying child.

▼▼▼

The creature. Even now, Victor cannot restrain a shiver of dread. He had tried to love it. But the hideous countenance, more awful than any mummy reanimated, recalled to life. His own guilt and fear had become too great, the noise of the mob too loud. The thing at first had not been evil. How can the dead be evil? If, through clean and pitiless science they are reborn, must they then put on that stain of Christian guilt and wretched responsibility as though donning rusty old clothing? No. No.

Again the heavy footfall. It is the monster—coming to finish him. Here at last.

A huge hand grabs him roughly by the shoulder.

"Sit up," the creature says. "Face your death."

"I am ready."

"Are you?" The creature leans back and the seamed face contorts with strange mirth. "I do not think so." The awful hands reach for him.

Despite his resolve, Victor feels a faint stab of fear, of defiance. "Wait," he says. "You cannot be so completely evil."

"Evil?" The monster pauses as though surprised. "I am not the evil one. It is you. Your guilt. Your will."

"But the murders . . ."

"Committed by you through me."

"How dare you. I am innocent of any killing."

"You are not innocent. You made me. Repudiated me. Pretended to know nothing as all around you were destroyed. I have made no pretense, ever, as to my true nature. But you, you have remained silent while others were slain in your place. You are the monster. And there will be no peace for you."

Victor meets the gaze of those dead amber eyes and understands. Death will not end it, will not be the safe hiding place he has imagined. Merely a tunnel, rather, a conduit to the hell of rebirth. He will become the creature. He must, as penance. And the monster will midwife his rebirth after death, the creator recreated, the creation the father. He will become the reflection of his own creature.

He wants to weep. Oh gods, he thinks, will his be the first face I see when I awaken? And what shall I call him? Father? Brother?

Powerful hands close upon his throat. The pressure is unbearable. The monster's face is close to his. In the moment of extremis, Victor closes his eyes.

The creature vanishes. The walls of the room melt and disappear.

Victor is lying in the snow, alone.

He looks around. Gone, he thinks. No one is there, no one at all. A delusion brought on by the cold.

I must get up. I must find shelter.

Clumsily he rises to his knees, forces deadened legs to bear his weight. He pauses, takes a step. Then another. But his legs are too weak, too numb. He falls hard against the snowpack and stays there, eyes closed against the brilliant whiteness.

Behind him in the wasteland he hears a sound. The unmistakable crunch of snow being compressed by slow, deliberate footsteps. As he listens, the wind dies to a whisper.

The steps grow louder.

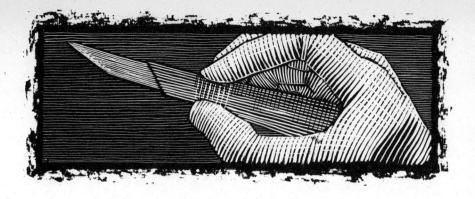

PART FIVE
▼▼▼

GARFIELD REEVES-STEVENS

T HEY remind one of fires, do they not?"

Samantha Grant glanced away from the night and the deep and glittering vista sweeping out beneath the Hollywood Hills. She had been thinking of the part. She hadn't heard what her host had said.

"I beg your pardon?" she asked.

"Fires," her host repeated, as if caught up in distant memories. "Torches, really. Like vast parades of people carrying torches."

"Oh," Samantha said. "The lights." She looked back through the floor-to-ceiling windows, trying not to think of the hundred-and-twenty foot drop down the sheer side of the lot off Mulholland. As was Warren Beatty's estate to the east, and Marlon Brando's compound to the west, so too was this house as secluded and unassailable as any medieval castle.

Yet the house was not isolated. Past the black silhouettes of the trees below, Los Angeles was defined as uncountable shimmering sparks of light, strung out along the streets and highways like dew on a spider's web. *And I'm here, where I'm supposed to be*, Samantha told herself, *right in the middle of it for as long as I live. The city at my feet, the studios in the valley behind me. Right in the center of the web.*

She took a breath and the cool air of the house caressed her as gently as the silk she wore beneath the tightly draped black jersey of her Azzedine Alaïa dress. She had rented it from Dressed to Kill. Three hundred dollars for the evening. But if she got the part, then the extravagance would be worth not eating for the next few weeks.

"Yes, they do," Samantha said. She turned again to her host. "Very hot fires."

Edward Styles had stopped watching the city. He was watching his guest, as if she were no less magnificent than the view his house possessed.

Samantha Grant had seen that look before. And she had been in town long enough to know how to handle it.

That's right, she thought as she caught Edward's gaze and held it. *I know this town, I know how this business works.* His sparkling gray eyes flickered lightly to her lips. She could still feel the thick covering of her lipstick there and she knew it would be glistening moistly in the candlelight that filled the expansive circular living room. *Use it, use it*, she told herself—the mantra of the unemployed actor. *Seven hundred dollars' worth of Dr. Morely's collagen injections in these lips. They're* meant *to be looked at.* Then, calculatingly, she bit in ever so lightly on her lower lip, knowing that in class her scene partner would be proud of the subtle innocence that expression conveyed. Michelle Pfeiffer had nothing on her.

Edward's eyes came back to her own, with no indication that he might have detected any artifice in her mood. He spoke in the portentous language of Hollywood. "The city is like that, at times. Hot." His eyes dropped from her face, alighting gently on the low and taut neckline of her dress.

And look at those, too, Samantha thought. *Thirty-five hundred a pair.* Everything she had earned from her one week of work on the USA Network made-for. At twenty-three, she had not required augmentation—she planned on that later, when she had moved past her prime in this town, perhaps twenty-eight, certainly by thirty. For now, Dr. Morely had persuaded her that all she required had been a careful tuck of skin, and a subtle lift and minor recontouring with the fat cells which had been carefully vacuumed from her inner thighs. *Go ahead and look,* she thought. *That's what they're there for. That's why this body is the way it is, the way I made it. So that you'll want to look, so they'll all want to look, to see me spread across a sixty-foot expanse of reflective theater screen. To have me in the privacy of their televisions and VCRs.* She thought of the part. It was all for the part and the rewards it would bring her.

Edward's gaze swept over the rest of her and—always the gentleman—met her eyes again, apparently oblivious to her green-tinted contacts and the small folds that hid the thin scars of an ever-so-slight rearrangement of her lids. Big eyes were in this year, Dr. Morely had assured her.

"We find it quite passionate," Edward continued, and Samantha had talked with him long enough this evening to realize that when he said "we" he meant only himself. "This city. The heat and . . . excitement of it." Edward lifted the thin Steuben flute of champagne to his lips and drank from it as softly as a kiss.

Samantha did the same, holding his gaze, and realizing as the Dom's bubbles lightly cascaded across her tongue that the other guest would not be coming this evening. That sudden knowledge did not upset her. It did not even surprise her. This was Hollywood and the rules of conduct were as simple and as brutal as those in any other jungle. As far as Samantha Grant was concerned, if that was the way her host had chosen to play the game tonight, then she was prepared to go eye to eye with him. And with that decision she knew she had moved another step closer to getting what she wanted. What she needed. What she lived for.

Edward put his champagne glass on a small, black marble cube by the window, then checked his watch. Even five feet away, Samantha could see the gleaming profile of Mickey Mouse on the watch's face, set out in platinum and gold. There were only ten of those watches in existence and Edward Styles had received his personally from Michael Eisner the day *Stardreamers* had grossed $100 million, less than two weeks after its opening. At a hundred mill a watch, by rights Edward Styles should have three of them for that one movie alone—the first film to have outgrossed *Home Alone* in the domestic market despite more than three years of decreasing box office and a faltering economy. But unlike most other producers, Edward surprisingly had refrained from self-promotion, avoided the media, and waited quietly in the Hollywood Hills until almost all outside the business had moved on to the movies of the next season and forgotten about him.

Until now. Until the inevitable.

Stardreamers II.

Edward smiled at Samantha as if apologizing that he had done something as mundane as look at his watch. "We believe it is time," he said, then gestured elegantly away from the windows.

Samantha played the part she knew was expected of her. "Won't Steven be joining us?" Her reading of the line was perfect. She sounded as if she honestly believed that Spielberg would be arriving at any moment.

Edward responded with equal sincerity, making a face of benign disappointment. "Alas, he's been held up and asked us to continue without him." Edward winked conspiratorially. "Apparently, he's reediting the ending of *Close Encounters of the Fourth Kind*. Again."

Samantha placed her glass beside Edward's, reflexively tugging down on her dress's hemline which had been precariously drawn up by even that simple movement. "Isn't it supposed to open next month?"

"Exactly," Edward agreed. "That Steven, too much the perfectionist. But then, he does earn his keep."

Edward's laugh was unexpected and Samantha was surprised to see how that expression transformed her host's face, bringing back to it an essence of youthfulness she had assumed was long gone. Not that Edward had let youth go without a fight. Her own experience with the science and art of face and body resculpting had taught her the telltale signs to watch for.

To the untrained eye, Edward Styles was a healthy and fit fifty-year-old, casually but fashionably attired in a loose ivory silk shirt buttoned to the neck, and draped linen trousers that spilled easily onto twelve-hundred dollar slip-ons from Fred Segal. Like Steve Martin, his conservatively cut hair was brilliant white so it did not age him as much as make his appearance memorable. The corners of his eyes were accented with creases which an aging generation of baby-boomers insisted on calling smile lines, not wrinkles. But despite those signs of age and experience, his lids were tight and his brow taut, leading Samantha to suspect that hidden somewhere in his transplanted hairline there would be a fine white scar from at least one facelift.

The flesh around Edward's jaw was also tight; no doubt a sagging half-inch of skin had been removed to smooth the neck and define the bone. Or perhaps the clean and sculpted planes of his cheekbones were the result of implants which had served to return the tautness of youth to flesh worn out through decades of battling gravity. Dr. Morely had suggested a similar procedure to build up Samantha's face, but in the end, they both had decided that her cheekbones were fine as they were for now, requiring only the removal of her two rearmost wisdom teeth to allow her cheeks to draw in and accentuate the leanness of her youth.

Samantha was impressed by what she saw in Edward. Here was a man who cared about himself and his appearance as much as she did about hers. She wondered who his doctor was, though that was a question that would have to wait for later. Some people were uncomfortable with the topic. Samantha knew that she would be uneasy discussing her various procedures with someone she did not know well. Though according to the evening's undercurrents, she suspected that she would not be uncomfortable with her host much longer. Once the part was hers, of course.

Edward picked up what appeared to be a black remote control wand for a television or stereo system, and pressed one of its dozens of studs without looking. Samantha heard a muted electric whir and turned her head in time to see a full curved wall panel of tan suede smoothly roll away to expose an intimate dining alcove at the side of the circular room. Edward gestured to it with the remote and a dozen tiny halogen spotlights came to life to illuminate all within it.

Samantha followed her host to the elevated alcove where a small circular granite table and two intricately carved wooden chairs had been placed to allow both diners to continue to savor the view through the sweeping windows. From the size and the shape of the rest of the circular room, she guessed that there could be as many as five more alcoves hidden behind the curved wall panels. Cynically, she wondered which one would contain the bed.

In the dining alcove, the dark stone tabletop was strewn with pale yellow curls of flower petals and set with irregularly shaped black porcelain plates artfully decorated with salads and edged with gold. Beside them, a full complement of bronze utensils was assembled, twisted in shapes that owed as much to Giger as they did to notions of utility. And rising like crystal flowers from the table, more delicate Steuben flutes and goblets rose up, glittering beneath the pinpoint spots that lit the alcove like the stage it was.

Probably had a set decorator from the studio arrange this, Samantha thought. She wondered how much longer she would have to wait before she could command such indulgences. Julia Roberts had achieved it in three movies. Samantha wanted to set a new record.

Edward pulled out Samantha's chair for her, then slipped her so easily toward the table that she was surprised by his strength. For a moment, she grew concerned that it might make a difference to how the evening would be played out. Force was against the rules, but it happened. Samantha would regret it if she would have to respond in kind, which she was fully capable of doing. She held her hands beneath the table and checked the alignment of the silver blocks on her ring and bracelet. Unlike her dress, her jewellery was her own, a century-old, heavy European design which had almost become fashionable again, with clever insets of silver which could be snapped out to provide studded cutting surfaces for self-defense. Samantha had yet to use the jewellery as it had been intended, but there was always a first time. She brought her hands back to the tabletop as she waited to see which direction the negotiations would take.

Edward sat gracefully in the chair opposite her. To his right a hammered copper sphere held a second bottle of champagne. The roughly textured metal globe, eighteen inches at its equator and sliced off at an angle through its northern hemisphere, rested atop a glass cylinder like an egg in a cup. Samantha had seen the piece in *Connoisseur*. It was worth more than the BMW convertible she had rented for the evening, maxing her Mastercard so she wouldn't have to park her six-year-old Civic on Edward's multi-million dollar driveway.

But Samantha kept her face composed and paid no special attention to the sphere, as if she were exposed to such opulence every day. She could not appear to be hungry for what Edward could offer her. That wasn't the way negotiations for parts were typically conducted in this town. But it was the way she was determined to behave.

Edward took the champagne bottle from its ice, wrapped a small linen cloth over its cork and twisted slightly until there was a small hiss. When he took the linen away, a pale exhalation of vapor cascaded from the bottle's open neck.

"Perfect," Samantha said. There was an appreciative flicker of response in Edward's eyes as he reached across the table to pour the pale liquid into her glass. The champagne frothed up within the narrow flute but not as robustly as the first bottle he had poured by the windows. Samantha decided to let her host determine if the bottle was off. She lifted her glass by its delicate stem and waited for Edward to have the first taste.

"To Hollywood," Edward said. "Where all things are possible, and beauty is everywhere." He sipped his champagne as another smile blossomed on his face. "And always at reasonable prices," he added with self-amusement.

Ah well, Samantha thought, *money does not necessarily imply taste—in champagne or wit.* "To Hollywood," she said, then returned her host's smile and sipped at her own glass. Unlike the first bottle, this champagne was only passable.

"We meant it about finding beauty everywhere," Edward said to the tabletop as he carefully replaced his champagne glass and picked up the smallest of three oddly bent forks. He looked up suddenly. "You are a very beautiful woman, Samantha."

For an awkward moment, Samantha lost the flow of their conversation, as if Edward had jumped ahead a page in the script they were supposed to follow. The scene that line led to properly belonged after dinner, with cognac, after the part at least had been mentioned in passing. She took another quick swallow of champagne to give herself time to recover.

"Why, thank you, Edward." *Totally banal*, she thought in distress. But he had sprung the compliment on her so unexpectedly that she had nothing to work with. She tried to think what her acting coach would suggest or where her scene partner might take the dialogue in an improv class. *Work with it. Work with it.*

"Oh, my dear, *we* are not the one to thank." Edward narrowed his eyes an instant, cutting them off from the sparkling highlights of the glass and gleaming black porcelain, making shadows form beneath his brow as black as the silhouettes outside his window. Samantha felt he had something more to say, but had changed his mind. Then his brow lifted again and his suddenly visible eyes once more filled with light, like the candles beyond them in the living room, like the fires that sparkled in the night outside the windows.

Before Samantha could reply, or even think of a reply, Edward spoke again. "Tell me about yourself."

That line Samantha was prepared for. She speared a piece of roasted red pepper with her fork. "I'm an actor."

Edward waited for elaboration but none came. "My dear, we are all actors."

"Even you?" Samantha asked, crumbling a small piece of chèvre with her salad knife.

Edward sat back in his chair and reached for his champagne again. "To be a producer of motion pictures is to be many things to many people. So yes, even we have been, and perhaps still are, an actor."

"Then you know everything you have to know about me," Samantha said. The past was the past and she was not inclined to discuss it. Perhaps, when it became absolutely necessary, something appropriate could be created for *People* and *Premiere*. But for now, all that mattered was her talent, her skill, and her appearance. She wanted to make it in this town on her own, not because of her carefully hidden connection to the business.

Samantha could feel Edward studying her as she concentrated on her salad. She wondered who had prepared it. She wondered if there were anyone in the house now, or if Edward had arranged for complete privacy. Sending the help away was not a good sign. Samantha felt comforted by the weight of her jewellery.

"Perhaps we do . . . ," Edward said at last.

Samantha looked up from her plate. Edward's eyes were firmly locked on hers.

". . . know all we need to know about you," he concluded. "A woman without a past, without connections. How charmingly enigmatic." He removed the champagne bottle from its copper sphere once more. "How . . . Hollywood."

Samantha heard more than a note of criticism in Edward's voice as he drew out the last word he had spoken. She decided that she should try to explain her position, to soften it, at least.

"Does it really matter how I spent my summer vacation when I was fifteen?" she asked, trying to keep her voice light. She held the stem of her glass as Edward filled it again. *One more sip,* she cautioned herself, *and that's all. Until the negotiations are concluded.*

"Matter in what way, my dear?" Edward finished topping up Samantha's glass, then returned the bottle to the ice without adding to his own.

He's watching what he's drinking, too, Samantha noted. *He knows this is a business meeting.*

"In what we're discussing," Samantha answered.

Edward placed his hands on the table to either side of his place setting. "And what might that be?"

Samantha felt that the script had been changed on her again—that Edward's business manager had misrepresented her presence at this dinner, that she was expected to be just another starlet *du jour,* good for an evening of sexual aerobics at a producer's house in exchange for a non-speaking, topless walk-on in a direct-to-video feature. She made up her mind to leave. And then she saw the briefest flicker of a smile on Edward's face.

"Forgive me," he said warmly. "You were about to depart, weren't you?"

Samantha thought for a moment, then decided not to answer.

Edward's smile grew even broader. "*Now* we know all we need to know about you. Principles are so rare to find in this town. And so refreshing." He picked up his glass and nodded to her. "We are here to discuss *Stardreamers II*."

Samantha took a small sip of champagne to ease the sudden dryness in her throat.

"So let us begin. What do you know about it?" Edward asked. He returned to his salad.

"That you feel it's time for the continuation of the Stardreamers' story to be told," Samantha said.

Edward nodded.

"That you have a script that Spielberg likes."

Another nod.

"That having Jacqueline Eight die at the end of the first movie was a terrible mistake and that you will need a new love interest for Austin Three in the sequel."

Edward waved his hand in polite protest. "Jacqueline's death was not a mistake. We had no choice. Demi Moore was most adamant about not doing a sequel. It was never in her contract."

"Really?" Samantha asked, truly surprised. "But . . . sequels are money in the bank. People love sequels."

Edward looked dubious. "Even though most sequels never do as well as the first of a series?" He spoke as if he were extending an invitation to a debate.

Samantha leaned forward. "But what about *Godfather II*?"

Edward shook his head. "What about *Ghostbusters II*?"

"*Aliens*," Samantha said.

"*Back to the Future II*," Edward countered.

Samantha gestured forcefully with her fork. "That was a marketing mistake. They had a classic second act problem, no resolution, just like . . . like *The Empire Strikes Back*." She could hear the excitement in her own voice. She loved the business. She wanted in. She needed that part. "But at least people knew that with *Empire*, they'd still have to wait a few more years for *Jedi*. With *Back to the Future III* coming out just a few months later, the audience for *II* didn't take it seriously. They . . ." Samantha felt something sticking in her throat and had to stop to cough. She covered her mouth but nothing was dislodged. She coughed again. Edward held out her champagne glass and she put her fork down to take it. Surprisingly, the liquid was almost flat, but it soothed the irritation. Unfortunately, she had lost the momentum of her argument.

"I'm sorry," she said apologetically, "I forgot what I was saying." She could feel her cheeks redden. She was an actor. How could she not remember her lines?

"Quite all right," Edward said, topping up her glass again. "You were saying that some sequels do end up being better than the originals."

"Do you believe that, too?" Samantha asked.

"Ah, my dear, we are living proof of it." Edward laughed and Samantha joined him uncertainly.

"Have you produced other sequels?" she asked. She had called up everything she could about her host on the Baseline computer service. Until *Stardreamers*, Edward Styles's credit list as producer had been as lowkey and unassuming as her own as an actor. *But he said he had been an actor, too,* Samantha reminded herself. *Maybe that's what he meant about sequels. Or maybe he directed one when he was starting out.*

"Other sequels?" Edward repeated. "Not in Hollywood." He held up a finger to forestall her next question. "And certainly not in your lifetime, my dear." He turned his knife and fork over on his plate. "Our past has little to do with our present. Even less to do with our future. Just the same as you, my dear. We are what we are, are we not? We live just for the moment. And what better place to be for that than here—a town with no memory for the past, no thoughts of the future, only an eternal present where appearance is all."

"I can understand that," Samantha said. At least, she hoped she could. That last swallow of champagne had put her on the brink of her limit and she felt she was in danger of having the room suddenly start spinning out of control.

"Of course you can, my dear. You are everything this city holds sacred. Beautiful, driven, without a past, and . . ." He reached across the table to take her hand in his. ". . . prepared to do whatever you have to do to get whatever you want." He lightly danced his fingers across the heavy silver ring she wore.

"What do you mean?" Samantha tried to pull away but Edward's hand felt warm and oddly soothing on her own.

"Your ring, dear Samantha. And your bracelet. I recognize them. A deFontaine design. Paris. 1880s. Monsieur deFontaine produced gentlemen's canes with daggers. Ladies' brooches and jewellery with secret catches for . . . self-defense. The Bijan of his day, no doubt."

Samantha's hand refused to move from beneath Edward's. *He's so strong*, she remembered. But she couldn't feel any pressure, any sense that she was being held against her will. Only warmth.

"Just as you were prepared to leave when you thought we might try to . . . what's the properly cinematic phrase to use here . . . have our way with you? And you were also prepared to use this ring and bracelet on us if you didn't get what you wanted. Were you not?"

Samantha watched Edward quickly remove her jewellery as

if she were watching dailies. There she was up on the screen, but there was nothing she could do to affect the outcome of the take.

"I wouldn't have . . ." she said slowly. The warmth in her hand was also spreading in other regions of her body. "I only wanted the part."

Edward stood and slipped the jewellery into his pants pocket. "Well, in that, at least, we are different." He walked around the table to stand at her side. "You wanted one part, whereas we want them all."

Samantha felt herself being pulled out from beneath the table and spun around to view the living room again. Beyond the windows, the city's web of lights danced and blurred as if the torches were combining to form one hellish conflagration, blazing with the heat that coursed through her body, a frightening magnification of the comforting glow that spreads so wonderfully from a single sip of . . .

"Champagne," Samantha said. Her mouth felt thick and slow and detached, as if Dr. Morely had overinjected her lips, making them swell hopelessly beyond any useful size.

Edward stepped down from the dining alcove to stand before her with the remote control wand in his hand. "Never drink champagne with salad," he said. "The dressing makes it impossible to truly appreciate the subtle nuances of flavor, or to identify the presence of methoprominol." Edward's smile was broad and winning as he held the remote over his shoulder and pressed a stud. Behind him, a cloud of bundled fabric descended over the panoramic windows like a theater curtain coming down at the end of the final reel.

"What are you doing?" Samantha had to struggle to form the words. Despite the disorientation she felt in her mind, she was still sitting upright in the chair, without slumping, as if she were slowly losing control over her body.

"Why, we thought you knew," Edward said kindly. He aimed his remote at a series of points along the curved wall opposite the now covered windows. Samantha heard more muffled electric motors as the suede wall panels rolled aside. "I'm preparing for my next production."

Samantha slowly turned her head to see more shadowed alcoves revealed by the moving wall panels. Five of them, just as she had suspected. She had terrible visions of there being movie equipment hidden in them, so that Edward could film her drugged body committing unspeakable acts. *And if he ever releases the stills,* she thought in her growing delirium, *my career will be ruined.*

Then Edward pressed the stud that turned on the lights in the first alcove and Samantha saw that things were even worse than she had imagined. Quite possibly worse than David Cronenberg could imagine as well.

There was a body in the alcove: a more than middle-aged man in a bright blue suit with wide lapels and flared trousers. His tie was a screaming mixture of orange and lime green flowers. His face was sunken, like a carved and hollow rotting pumpkin falling in on itself. He was obviously dead, strapped to a flat wooden angled panel like an insane hunter's trophy.

"Who . . . who . . ." It was all Samantha could manage to say.

"This is Bernie," Edward answered helpfully, guessing her question. He looked at Samantha with concern. "We don't think you'd know him. So few people did. Television producer. Did a lot of co-productions in the late sixties, but nothing big. Nothing . . . notable." He walked over to the body. "And after a good twenty years of nothing remarkable, Bernie left town the same month that we . . . arrived."

Edward held up his arms in an exuberant shrug. "*Quelle coincidence, n'est-ce pas?*"

Samantha tried to shake her head but that act was beyond her. All she could do was say, "I don't understand."

Edward pursed his lips, then activated the lights in the next alcove.

Samantha moaned. There was another body, strapped to another angled panel, also male, also dead.

"Now this is Harold," Edward said as he walked over to the second alcove. He spoke as clearly and as matter-of-factly as if he were doing a voiceover for a National Geographic special. "He ended up in television, just like Bernie. That's where they met, actually."

Harold had short-cropped hair atop his caved-in head and wore a grey suit with a thin black tie. The once-white shirt beneath that tie was stained with something dark and sludgelike that had run around Harold's neck from behind.

"Harold started out in radio," Edward continued. "In New York. That's where all the action was back after the war. Radio turning into television. Lots of people breaking into the business. No one could keep track of them all. Easy to make good money and keep a low profile at the same time." Edward looked sadly at Samantha. "That's why they could be older, you see. Being unknown was more common back then. Not like now. To find someone with a low profile today means to find someone young. *And* with principles. Just like you, to be precise."

Samantha moaned again and Edward frowned.

"You shouldn't have any control left over your voluntary nervous system," he said. "Can you talk?"

Samantha concentrated. "Did . . . you kill them . . . ?"

Edward nodded apologetically. "Eventually, more or less."

He's insane, Samantha thought, her sudden panic making her unexpectedly lucid. "Will you . . . kill me . . . too?"

Edward looked thoughtfully at the ceiling. "Yes and no," he

said at last, then met her eyes again. "Some might h.
of a philosophical debate."

Completely insane. Samantha put everything she had into
effort to stand up but all she did was rock forward an inch. The
back again.

Edward glanced at his watch and Mickey's ear-capped outline
gleamed for an instant, leaving a dark afterimage in Samantha's
vision. "You *are* a fighter, aren't you," he said. "A few more
minutes then." He aimed the remote and the third alcove lit up.

Samantha moaned and felt her few mouthfuls of salad churn
within her.

The third body on display wore a dust-covered suit of thick
brown fabric. Its pants were belted around its sternum and the
diamond-shaped tie it wore barely reached from its neck to the
belt buckle. Samantha tried to concentrate on the buckle. Or the
neck. Anywhere but on the head. Or where the head should be.

What was left above the shoulders of the third body was something fissured and scooped out, as if the dead man's head had
been cut and emptied like the doctored champagne's hammered
sphere of copper.

"We know what you mean," Edward said consolingly. "Quite
crude. Technical problems still to be worked out. Burned note-
books to be reconstructed." He turned away from the ruined body.
"His name was Ollie. Came over from the old country . . . years
ago. Did a lot of live radio though his name, alas, appears
nowhere today. The nature of the business, we're afraid. Quite
ephemeral. Though that's not necessarily bad for those in . . .
our position."

Edward turned away from Ollie's body and walked back to
Samantha. She could feel herself covered in cold sweat, but
whether it was from fear or the chemical he had made her drink,
she could not be sure. She watched as Edward leaned down to
look at her closely. She didn't understand the concern she saw in

his eyes. Then he moved behind her and she couldn't turn to see where he was going or what he was doing.

"It was a much simpler time back then," he said behind her. "Everything was so new. Nothing was understood." Something tapped against Samantha's forehead and she jerked back a full half-inch in horror. Her vision went white for an instant. She made a dry, gagging sound deep in her throat. Then she realized that Edward was only dabbing at her sweat-covered face with a linen napkin from the table. "Just trying to make you more comfortable, my dear."

He kept dabbing and Samantha had the terribly disjointed impression that he was trying not to disturb her make-up.

"You see, dear Samantha, back then, in the beginning, the twenties, the thirties, after the war and almost all the time since then, it was so easy to hide, to stay unknown . . . ."

Has he been killing people that long? Samantha thought. *But he can't have been. He's not old enough. I mean, his plastic surgeon is good . . .*

"But no longer, we're afraid." Edward stepped back to study Samantha's face as if he had just finished painting on it. "One tries to do one's work, staying in the background, never suspecting that one day one might produce a little movie that would become the industry's largest-grossing film of all time." Edward dropped his voice to a whisper, as if passing on an important secret. "*Stardreamers* was all right as far as such movies go, but honestly, it wasn't *that* good."

Samantha could only blink her eyes in confusion.

"But then," Edward continued, checking his watch again, "who can ever know what it is that the movie-going public wants to see?" He tapped his hand to his chest. "Do you suppose we might have found our calling?"

Samantha forced more words from her throat with a dry and gasping shudder. Deep inside, she knew the negotiations were at an end and that she was finished in this town. She couldn't even invoke her uncle, the television director's name to help her, though she had sworn to herself never to do that so she could make it here on her own, without the taint of being given work for her uncle's sake. But all of that planning and dreaming was over. The script had been totally abandoned and she had nothing left within herself to use in improvisation. She could only ask the most basic of questions now. Why him? Why her? Why anything?

". . . why . . . are you here . . ." The words burned like fire as they left her.

Edward smiled sadly. "Why, my dear, what better place could there be for us?" He pressed the button that lit the fourth alcove, then stepped aside. And even if Samantha could have moved, she doubted she would have, so great was her shock at seeing the fourth body.

It was improbably tall and grey-skinned and clothed in black with a long grim face topped by a longer forehead, ringed by the heavy stitches of century-old surgery. There was no tie around its neck, no collar. Only the dull gleam from twin metallic bolts imbedded on either side.

The fourth body's skull was empty, too.

"You see, my dear," Edward explained, "we're a bit of a sequel ourselves."

The savage scream of unbearable terror that grew in Samantha emerged only as a slowly dying rasp. *He didn't kill those people . . .*

"We never could remember what our name had been," Edward mused, lost in thought. "So this one we just call . . . Frank."

. . . he was those people. And now . . . and now . . .

Edward walked over to Samantha and effortlessly picked her up from her chair. "And now we've waited long enough. Disney is most insistent about starting pre-production on *Stardreamers II*, so it is time for Edward Styles to take his leave."

He carried her past the bodies, all of them with their empty heads—holders for the one part that had lived in them all, and then passed on to the next and the next and the . . .

Edward paused by the fifth alcove. Samantha could feel him fiddling with the remote as he held her. The lights came on. Brilliant, blinding against immaculate tiled white surfaces, the gleam of chrome, the scent of antiseptic. The glitter of surgical tools laid out so neatly, so professionally. Samantha wondered who could help him. *If* anyone could help him.

There were two beds in the alcove and Edward put her on the one with the heavy straps. When he had finished binding her in place, he allowed his hands to slide along the swell of her dress's neckline, almost with respect. "We've often wondered what these might feel like . . . from the inside," he said with a gentle smile.

Samantha's scream was only a whisper. A dying whisper which cried a final question.

Edward leaned forward to his guest with a look of genuine curiosity. "We beg your pardon, my dear. What was that you asked?"

Samantha stared into Edward's eyes, saw his face in gleaming detail. She could see it now, the thin white scar she had guessed lay near his hairline. Though now she knew it was not the scar of a facelift.

She opened her mouth to try and ask her question again, only then becoming aware of a movement to her side. *We're not alone!* she thought. *Someone else is here! Someone else who can—*

"Did you ask, why you?" Edward said. "Is that it? Why did we choose you?"

In her sudden hopeful excitement, Samantha was able to nod her head a fraction of an inch. That was exactly what she had asked. But now she didn't care. Now all she wanted to know was who else was with them. Who else was there who could help her.

"Well, you know what this town is like," Edward said with a genial laugh. "Despite all the glamour and all the stories that are told, Hollywood really is just one big small town."

Samantha felt Edward pat her shoulder as he straightened up above her. Then the second figure leaned in closer, and just before his rubber-gloved hands pulled up his surgical mask and the glittering scalpel began its descent, Samantha realized she knew who it was.

Edward's voice came from far away. "We have a friend in common, my dear. Someone who knows all the best parts in town. . . ."

Then Dr. Morely's scalpel began its work. The pain reminded Samantha of the fire from a thousand torches, and for as long as she lived, she was right in the middle of it.

FRANKIE BABY
▼▼▼

JOYCE HARRINGTON

I am forcing myself to write this. It's not a pleasant task. It makes me think about all the things I could have done, should have done, to prevent the tragedy. But I didn't know, dear God, I had no idea what Francesca had in mind, or what strange roads she had traveled in her researches into the origins and creation of life.

The creation of life. That's a joke. And a very bad one, at that. Whatever she created, it was not life. And it resulted in the destruction of the single human being that both she and I loved best in the world.

But I'm getting ahead of myself. Let me try to start at the beginning.

I suppose it all began with two little girls, close friends from the day they met in kindergarten. Francesca, whose parents, Dr. and Mrs. Howard Stein, made a singularly unfortunate choice in the naming of their shy, withdrawn, only daughter, and Johanna, golden-haired, blue-eyed, cute-as-a-button Johanna who grew up to become my wife.

Almost from the time we met, Johanna told me stories of her

brilliant friend. Of how Francesca had excelled in everything in their school days, and how her achievements were always tainted by the cruel teasing of the other children. With her unmanageable curly dark hair, her piercing dark eyes, and her evocative name, it was perhaps, inevitable that she would become known as Frankie Stein, "The Bride of Frankenstein."

Johanna was her defender and champion in those days, and her only friend. I wish I had known Johanna as a child. I can almost see her battling playground injustices on behalf of one who could not defend herself. When I met her, she had recently graduated from law school and was working on poverty cases for the Legal Aid Society.

At that time, Francesca was still in medical school in another state, and I didn't meet her until she came to our wedding a few years later. She was Johanna's maid of honor, looking stiff and unnatural in her ruffled gown. I got the sense that she felt betrayed by Johanna's marriage. She barely spoke to me, and not at all to the other wedding guests. Johanna, however, was not disturbed by her friend's ungracious behavior. She merely said, "Well, that's Frankie. We made some silly childish vow years ago never to marry or have children. I guess she still lives by it and thinks I should have, too. She'll get over it."

I didn't really care whether or not Francesca got over it. Johanna and I set about living our lives together. Like many of our acquaintances, we agreed to put off having children until our careers were established. Johanna decided to specialize in child abuse cases, not the best-paying kind of law practice but enormously fulfilling to her. I earned my half of our bed and board as a newspaper reporter while brooding over the novel I would write some day.

The city we lived in was small enough for civility and large enough to support a real newspaper. Not that we didn't have our share of modern urban woes. I wrote about muggings, drug busts, corrupt politicians, and thieving company officers almost every day, with the occasional heinous murder thrown in just to prove that our town was holding its own in the rising violent crime statistics. Johanna saw the other side of the statistics, the human side, the bruised and battered children, the raped babies, too frightened or too young to speak of the crimes committed against them.

The months and years went by. We both felt we were doing important work. We bought a house, nothing grand, but it had a couple of extra bedrooms that we used "temporarily" as our studies, one for each of us. Our work schedules were crazy, so we usually grabbed something to eat whenever and wherever we could. But once or twice a week, we managed to have dinner together. And I became inordinately proud of my Sunday brunches. My pecan waffles were my masterpiece.

It was a very ordinary life. And we loved it, and each other, very much.

During those years, we saw nothing of Dr. Francesca Stein. Johanna had an occasional brief note, usually a notification of a new research grant or one of the many honors that began to be heaped upon her head. Once in a while, I'd come across a wire service story that mentioned her name, but these gee-whiz "science of the future" accounts seldom gave more than a brief sketch of what she was up to, something to do with genetic research.

Then suddenly one day, Johanna heard the alarm go off in her biological clock. "I don't want to be an old bag with a kid in high school," was the way she put it.

"You're only 37," I reassured her. "Old is 90. And you'll never be a bag, old, young, or in-between."

"You do understand what I'm saying, don't you?" she asked in her best "you're-so-stupid-but-I'm-willing-to-be-patient" courtroom manner. "I want to have a baby. Now."

"Now is impossible," I told her. And before she could mount

her high horse, I added, "How about nine months from now?" Truth is I had been wondering for some time how to broach the subject myself. I'd graduated to syndicated columnist of the liberal-satirical persuasion, taking on everything from killer bees to gun control, and I had a bit more time to consider the really important things, like the propagation of the species. My own personal species. I thought I'd make a pretty good father.

Did I say that Johanna was efficient? Efficiency is not the most endearing virtue in the world, but with Johanna it all seemed so effortless and she never used it to make fools of the rest of us bumblers. Nine months to the day, she produced a squalling eight-pound bundle of female energy, which she promptly named Francesca.

"Are you sure about that?" I asked her. "It's not as if Dr. Frankie is likely to be flattered or put herself out for the kid."

"You got any alternatives in mind?" she asked. "How about naming her after your mother? Or mine?"

"Francesca's fine with me," I said. The two grannies are Edwina and Gertrude, respectively.

Dr. Frankie sent no baby gift but wrote that she had established a trust fund, payable on Francesca's eighteenth birthday, to finance her education, providing she agreed to study some form of science. Johanna said, "Well, that's pretty nice. Frankie wouldn't know how to buy baby goodies and now the kid's got an option on the future."

"What if she wants to be a lawyer or a writer or a beach bunny?" I asked.

"She'll be whatever she wants to be," Johanna replied, "but if she wants to be another Frankie, she's got the choice. It wasn't easy scrimping through law school."

"Okay," I muttered, "but I don't like it. And I don't want her to know about it. A choice is a choice is a choice, but not if one of them is prepaid."

"Are you feeling just a teeny bit usurped? Don't worry. I won't tell her. I won't steer her. And eighteen is a long way off."

We forgot about Dr. Frankie's trust fund in the sheer joy of watching this perfect infant creature burp and gurgle and grow. And, yes, I changed diapers. Not as neatly as Johanna did, but adequately enough to do the job. By then, I was working at home. My columns were being picked up by more and more newspapers every week, and I was being invited to speak at journalism schools and all kinds of industry conventions. It was heady stuff for an ex-crime-beat reporter, and my prevailing attitude was "Russell Baker, watch out!"

It was, perhaps, inevitable that our daughter should become Frankie Baby. Especially when Dr. Frankie called to announce her intention of paying us a visit. Not us exactly. She'd been asked to consult on some work being done at a nearby research center, but she wanted to spend all her free time with us. Our Francesca was then three years old, precocious, of course, and in our eyes the most beautiful little girl in the world. She looked more like Johanna than like me, but she seemed to be developing my long, skinny legs and ironic outlook on life. She flatly refused to watch Mr. Rogers on TV, and thought Big Bird would make a nice Thanksgiving dinner. Johanna accused me of influencing her opinions. Well, maybe I did. A little.

Dr. Frankie appeared on schedule, with a gray streak neatly dividing the front of her mountain of bristly curls. It was all I could do to restrain myself from remarking on her uncanny resemblance to Elsa Lanchester. In private, I asked Johanna, "Do you think she does it on purpose?" Johanna pretended not to know what I was talking about.

By then, Johanna's study had been turned into a bright, primary-colored sleeping and playing room for Frankie Baby. No pink ruffles for our little tigress. There was a day bed for sleepover baby-sitters, and that's where we stashed Dr. Frankie for the three days she was spending with us. There was nowhere else to put her. I needed my own study for the churning out of columns, and I often worked late into the night.

Frankie Baby took to her namesake like a noodle to chicken soup, and—surprise, surprise—the attraction was mutual. The weird doctor patiently answered all her questions, pertinent and impertinent, and took her along to meetings with the local Dr. Frankie groupies. Excuse me, I mean her fellow research scientists.

The three days passed quickly and pleasantly enough. Dr. Frankie even admitted to reading my column occasionally, although she disagreed with everything I wrote. Just as a lark, her kind of lark, she persuaded Johanna and me to contribute to a gene bank she was establishing. "You're both fine specimens," was the way she put it. "I'd like to have your samples in storage." How could we refuse such a gracious request?

A week after Dr. Frankie left, Frankie Baby died. There's no other way to say it but straightforward and blunt. It was sudden. It was terrifying. And it had all the doctors baffled. One day, a healthy, active, obstreperous little girl. The next, a pain-wracked, fevered, tormented young animal. There was no medical miracle for Francesca; all they could do was keep her sedated while they frantically tried to diagnose what was killing her. It was all over in twenty-four hours. A weary doctor told me, "It was as if all her systems turned toxic on her and then shut down. I've never seen anything like it before."

Johanna. How can I describe her grief? She raged. She brooded. She cried enough to irrigate the Sahara. She refused to let me comfort her, and she took to sleeping in Frankie Baby's room. She even neglected her law practice. "How can I deal with those kids?" she wailed. "At least they're alive." Nothing on earth, it seemed, would console her. Through all of this, there was no word from Dr. Frankie.

Finally, after about six months during which Johanna flatly refused any kind of psychiatric help, I called the doctor. It was a desperate move, but I was afraid that Johanna was beginning to think about suicide. It was nothing she said—she barely spoke except about the most ordinary things—but she had developed a kind of morbid detachment, as if she were contemplating eternity. If anyone could shake Johanna out of it, the cranky Dr. Frankie probably could.

"Yes," she said. "I'll come. Everything is ready."

"What's ready?" I asked her.

Dr. Frankie turned uncharacteristically coy. "You'll see when I get there," she said. "Expect me in two days. And don't tell Johanna."

How could I not tell Johanna? We'd always told each other everything. At least, until Johanna had turned silent and withdrawn. But, I told myself, Dr. Frankie obviously had some kind of surprise in store. If it was a surprise that would restore Johanna to me and to herself, then it was worth keeping my mouth shut. Two days wasn't long to keep a secret.

I started waiting for the doorbell to ring as soon as I got up on the second day. Johanna usually slept late, curled up in Frankie Baby's youth bed. I looked in on her, said good morning, asked her if she wanted a cup of coffee. As usual, there was no answer. As usual, I touched her arm, made sure she was breathing. Still sleeping, she flinched away from my touch. Sure, it hurt. But what could I do about it? Except that on that day, I could hope that Dr. Frankie would work some miracle.

It was a long day. I tried to work, but the words on my computer screen didn't make much sense. Johanna got up around noon, picked at the breakfast I made for her, and then watched television. It didn't seem to matter to her what she watched. She just sat there, glassy-eyed. I switched channels a few times. She kept on watching. When I turned the set off, she moaned softly until I turned it back on. It was the worst she'd been in all these long months. If I hadn't been expecting Dr. Frankie any minute, I think I probably would have bundled her up and packed her off to a psych ranch.

All through the afternoon of soap operas, reruns, and kid shows, she sat there, my beautiful, intelligent, sarcastic wife. I couldn't bear to watch her and I couldn't bear to leave her alone for more than five minutes. Three times, I tried to call Dr. Frankie to see if maybe her plans had changed and she'd forgotten to let me know. All I got was her voice on an answering machine telling me that she was not available. I left no messages. What could I say? "I'm waiting here for you to save my wife?"

At last, when the six o'clock news came on, Johanna got up and turned the set off. "Tired," she murmured. "So tired." I followed her into the kitchen, where she peered into the refrigerator, opened and closed all the cupboards and drawers, and then stood by the back door with her face pressed up against its window.

"What are you looking for?" I asked her.

She ignored me. I might as well not have been there. I tried to put my arms around her. She shook me off impatiently. Then quite deliberately, she went to the knife drawer, took out the first knife that came to hand, a small paring knife, and held it to her throat. I leaped to stop her, but before I could, she threw the knife down and collapsed onto the floor, sobbing convulsively.

At that moment, the doorbell rang.

I picked Johanna up and carried her back into the living room. She was so light, so fragile, and her poor, sad face was streaked with tears. I laid her on the couch and covered her with an afghan. The doorbell rang again.

"We have company," I told Johanna. She stared at me without comprehension.

"I'm going to open the door now. Will you be all right?"

She closed her eyes.

I backed across the room and into the small foyer, watching her for any sign that she might try to repeat her knife trick. I jerked the front door open without looking to see who was there. And I didn't look until I heard a familiar voice cry, "Daddy!"

She leaped into my arms just the way she used to, wrapping her legs around my waist and snuggling her face into my neck. I stared over her golden curls into Dr. Frankie's triumphant grin.

"I've brought you your daughter," she announced. "Your genetically perfect daughter."

The child, whoever she was, scrambled down from my arms and ran across the room to Johanna. "Mommy! Mommy!" she yelled. "Get up, Mommy! I'm hungry."

And there was my miracle. Johanna, her face bright, her eyes shining, stood up and, as if nothing in the world had happened, took the child's hand and said, "Well, let's get you something to eat."

I glared at Dr. Frankie. "What is it?" I demanded. And then, without waiting for an answer, I followed my wife and the child who was an exact replica of our dead daughter into the kitchen.

Johanna was making a peanut butter sandwich. The girl was sitting at the kitchen table, in Frankie Baby's favorite chair, drinking a glass of milk.

"Wait a minute," I said, grabbing Johanna's hand. "Who do you think that is?"

"My baby's come back. Isn't it wonderful?" she replied. She wrenched her hand out of mine to go on with her sandwich-making, and I wound up with peanut butter on my thumb. Thoughtfully, I licked it off. On the plus side, Johanna had snapped out of her funk. I'd been ready to mortgage my soul to achieve that. But there were too many minuses connected with this incredible recovery, no doubt some I didn't even know about. Yet.

Confident that, in her present state of euphoria, I could leave her alone, I went back into the living room. Dr. Frankie was ready and waiting for me.

"I know you have questions," she said. "I wish you didn't. I wish you could just accept this the way Johanna has."

"Who is she? She's not my daughter. Where did you find her?"

"She's as much your daughter as the one who died. Let's just say she's an improved version of the original."

I couldn't believe what I was hearing. Yet the proof was sitting there in the kitchen, eating a peanut butter sandwich. "Improved? How?"

Dr. Frankie grinned. "She has my intelligence. She's my daughter, as well as yours. Remember those gene samples? I took some from Frankie Baby, too. Weeded out the imperfections, added more of your better characteristics and Johanna's, and crowned the mix with my own mental capacity. You're going to be very proud of your daughter."

"All that in six months?"

"More than six years. I've been working on this project for a long time. But I needed to get it out of the lab and into a real world situation. Yours was the ideal case."

"We're not a case and she's not my daughter," I insisted. "My daughter died."

"And now she's alive again." Johanna had come into the living room. "Frankie, do you know what she said to me? She said, 'Mommy, I want to be just like Auntie Fran when I grow up. With lots and lots of babies.' How many babies do you have, Frankie?"

"Quite a few. They're all part of the project. And they're all more or less perfect."

"And do they all look like this one?"

"No. Not all of them. This one is the best of the Francesca lot."

Johanna absorbed that information, mulling it over and staring at her friend. I kept my peace, waiting to see what she would do.

She moved closer to Dr. Frankie, her eyes intense, her shoulders squared. I'd seen her like that before, when she described the most horrendous of her cases, and I didn't envy Dr. Frankie one little bit. Johanna could be scathing.

"Frankie, she's perfect. But there's something a little odd about her."

"You'll get used to it," Dr. Frankie said complacently.

"I don't know that I will," Johanna said. "Let me tell you why. She had to go to the bathroom, and, of course, I went with her. I didn't want to lose sight of her for a moment. And here's the funny thing, Frankie. She hasn't got a belly button. Have you ever seen a child without a belly button?"

"I didn't think that mattered, Johanna. It would serve no useful purpose." Dr. Frankie was beginning to look a little nervous.

"Oh, it matters, all right. But you wouldn't understand it. It's the connection. The physical evidence that the child and the mother were once connected. Its absence made me think straight for the first time in months. It was no coincidence that my baby died a week after you left, was it, Frankie? You killed her, didn't you? You injected her with some damned slow-acting virus, something the doctors couldn't cure. You killed her so you could replace her with this creation of yours. You may be a brilliant scientist, Frankie, but you know zilch about people. Do you deny any of this?"

"No. Why should I? You should be grateful to me for bringing her back better than before. This one will never be sick. She's genetically immune to every known disease. She's going to live a long time and contribute enormously to mankind."

"I'm afraid she won't," said Johanna. "She wasn't immune to this."

There was the knife again, blood-stained and quivering in Johanna's hand. I lurched toward her, trying to grab her arm.

But before I could reach her, Dr. Frankie had produced a gun and fired. Johanna fell to the floor. I bent to pick up the knife. The doctor fired again, barely missing my head. I let fly with the knife, that little paring knife. It caught the doctor in the throat. She gasped and dropped the gun.

"I was ready," she whispered. "To protect my child. You don't understand." And then she toppled over.

Johanna was dead, shot through the heart. In the bathroom, Dr. Frankie's creation was dead. And Dr. Frankie was bleeding to death on my living room rug. I called the police.

There was nothing they could charge me with. Dr. Frankie lived to stand trial for murder. She got off on self-defense. Mercifully, no one seemed to know what to do about the dead child with no navel except give it a decent burial. It was not mentioned at the trial. Johanna went to her grave under the stigma of mental imbalance. Someday, I'll set that right.

I still don't know if Johanna's final accusation was correct. Chances are I'll never know. But I do know that Dr. Francesca Stein killed my wife, and that she's back in her remote Rocky Mountain lab creating more perfect little pseudo-humans.

And me? Well, I still churn out my columns. But I do it now from a lonely mountain cabin overlooking Dr. Frankie's place. And my favorite fantasy is blowing the lab and everything in it sky-high. Maybe someday, it'll be more than a fantasy. On that day, I'll write my final column. Watch your local newspaper.

PITY THE MONSTERS
▼▼▼

CHARLES DE LINT

> We are standing in the storm
> Of our own being.

> —Michael Ventura

"**I** was a beauty once," the old woman said. "The neighbourhood boys were forever standing outside my parents' home, hoping for a word, a smile, a kiss, as though somehow my unearned beauty gave me an intrinsic worth that far overshadowed Emma's cleverness with her schoolwork, or Betsy's gift for music. It always seemed unfair to me. My value was based on an accident of birth; theirs was earned."

The monster made no reply.

"I would have given anything to be clever or to have had some artistic ability," the old woman added. "Those are assets with which a body can grow old."

She drew her tattery shawl closer, hunching her thin shoulders against the cold. Her gaze went to her companion. The monster was looking at the blank expanse of wall above her head, eyes unfocused, scars almost invisible in the dim light.

"Yes, well," she said. "I suppose we all have our own cross to bear. At least I have good memories to go with the bad."

▼▼▼

The snow was coming down so thickly that visibility had already become all but impossible. The fat wet flakes whirled and spun in dervishing clouds, clogging the sidewalks and streets, snarling traffic, making the simple act of walking an epic adventure. One could be anywhere, anywhen. The familiar was suddenly strange; the city transformed. The wind and the snow made even the most common landmarks unrecognizable.

If she hadn't already been so bloody late, Harriet Pierson would have simply walked her mountain bike through the storm. She only lived a mile or so from the library and the trip wouldn't have taken *that* long by foot. But she was late, desperately late, and being sensible had never been her forte, so there she was, pedaling like a madwoman in her highest gear, the wheels skidding and sliding for purchase on the slippery street as she biked along the narrow passageway between the curb and the crawling traffic.

The so-called waterproof boots that she'd bought on sale last week were already soaked, as were the bottoms of her jeans. Her old camel-hair coat was standing up to the cold, however, and her earmuffs kept her ears warm. The same couldn't be said for her hands and face. The wind bit straight through her thin woolen mittens, her cheeks were red with the cold, while her long brown hair, bound up in a vague bun on the top of her head, was covered with an inch of snow that was already leaking its wet chill into her scalp.

Why did I move to this bloody country? she thought. *It's too hot in the summer, too cold in the winter. . . .*

England looked very good right at that moment, but it hadn't always been so. England hadn't had Brian whom she'd met while on holiday here in Newford three years ago, Brian who'd been just as eager for her to come as she had been to emigrate, Brian who walked out on her not two months after she'd arrived and they had gotten an apartment together. She'd refused to go back. Deciding to make the best of her new homeland, she had stuck it out surprisingly well, not so much because she led such an ordered existence, as that she'd refused to run back home and have her mother tell her, ever so patronizingly, "Well, I told you so, dear."

She had a good job, if not a great one, a lovely little flat that was all her own, a fairly busy social life—that admittedly contained more friends than it did romantic interests—and liked everything about her new home. Except for the weather.

She turned off Yoors Street onto Kelly, navigating more by instinct than vision, and was just starting to congratulate herself on having completed her journey all in one piece, with time to spare, when a tall shape loomed suddenly up out of the whirling snow in front of her. Trying to avoid a collision, she turned the handlebars too quickly—and the wrong way.

Her front wheel hit the curb and she sailed over the handlebars, one more white airborne object defying gravity, except that unlike the lighter snowflakes with which she momentarily shared the sky, her weight brought her immediately down with a jarring impact against a heap of refuse that someone had set out in anticipation of tomorrow's garbage pickup.

She rose spluttering snow and staggered back towards her bike, disoriented, the suddenness of her accident not yet having sunk in. She knelt beside the bike and stared with dismay at the bent wheel rim. Then she remembered what had caused her to veer in the first place.

Her gaze went to the street, but then traveled up, and up, to the face of the tall shape that stood by the curb. The man was a giant. At five-one, Harriet wasn't tall, and perhaps it had something to do with her low perspective, but he seemed to be at least seven feet high. And yet it wasn't his size that brought the small gasp to her lips.

That face . . .

It was set in a squarish head which was itself perched on thick broad shoulders. The big nose was bent, the left eye was slightly higher than the right, the ears were like huge cauliflowers, the hairline high and square. Thick white scars criss-crossed his features, giving the impression that he'd been sewn together by some untalented seamstress who was too deep in her cups to do a proper job. An icon from an old horror movie flashed in Harriet's mind and she found herself looking for the bolts in the man's neck before she even knew what she was doing.

Of course they weren't there, but the size of the man and the way he was just standing there, staring at her, made Harriet unaccountably nervous as though this really was Victor Frankenstein's creation standing over her in the storm. She stood quickly, wanting to lessen the discrepancy of their heights. The sudden movement woke a wave of dizziness.

"I'm dreadfully sorry," she meants to say, but the words slurred, turning to mush in her mouth and what came out was, "Redfolly shurry."

Vertigo jellied her legs and made the street underfoot so wobbly that she couldn't keep her balance. The giant took a quick step towards her, huge hands outstretched, as a black wave swept over her and she pitched forward.

Bloody hell, she had time to think. I'm going all faint. . . .

▼▼▼

Water bubbled merrily in the tin can that sat on the Coleman stove's burner. The old woman leaned forward and dropped in a tea bag, then moved the can from the heat with a mittened hand.

Only two more bags left, she thought.

She held her hands out to the stove and savored the warmth.

"I married for money, not love," she told her companion. "My Henry was not a handsome man."

The monster gaze focused and tracked down to her face.

"But I grew to love him. Not for his money, nor for the comfort of his home and the safety it offered to a young woman whose future, for all her beauty, looked to take her no further than the tenements in which she was born and bred."

The monster made a querulous noise, no more than a grunt, but the old woman could hear the question in it. They'd been together for so long that she could read him easily, without his needing to speak.

"It was for his kindness," she said.

▼▼▼

Harriet woke to the cold. Shivering, she sat up to find herself in an unfamiliar room, enwrapped in a nest of blankets that carried a pungent, musty odor in their folds. The room itself appeared to be part of some abandoned building. The walls were unadorned except for their chipped paint and plaster and a cheerful bit of graffiti suggesting that the reader of it do something that Harriet didn't think was anatomically possible.

There were no furnishings at all. The only light came from a short, fat candle which sat on the windowsill in a puddle of cooled wax. Outside, the wind howled. In the room, in the building itself, all was still. But as she cocked her head to listen, she could just faintly make out a low murmur of conversation. It appeared to be a monologue, for it was simply one voice, droning on.

She remembered her accident and the seven-foot tall giant as though they were only something she'd experienced in a dream. The vague sense of dislocation she'd felt upon awakening had grown into a dreamy kind of muddled feeling. She was somewhat concerned over her whereabouts, but not in any sort of a pressing way. Her mind seemed to be in a fog.

Getting up, she hesitated for a moment, then wrapped one of the smelly blankets about her shoulders like a shawl against the cold and crossed the room to its one doorway. Stepping outside, she found herself in a hall as disrepaired and empty as the room she'd just quit. The murmuring voice led her down the length of the hall into what proved to be a foyer. Leaning against the last bit of wall, there where the hallway opened up into the larger space, she studied the odd scene before her.

Seven candles sat in their wax on wooden orange crates that were arranged in a half circle around an old woman. She had her back to the wall, legs tucked up under what appeared to be a half-dozen skirts. A ratty shawl covered her grey hair and hung down over her shoulders. Her face was a spiderweb of lines, all pinched and thin. Water steamed in a large tin can on a Coleman stove that stood on the floor in front of her. She had another, smaller tin can in her hand filled with, judging by the smell that filled the room, some kind of herbal tea. She was talking softly to no one that Harriet could see.

The old woman looked up just as Harriet was trying to decide how to approach her. The candlelight woke an odd glimmer in the woman's eyes, a reflective quality that reminded Harriet of a cat's gaze caught in a car's headbeams.

"And who are you, dear?" the woman asked.

"I . . . my name's Harriet. Harriet Pierson." She got the odd feeling that she should curtsy as she introduced herself.

"You may call me Flora," the old woman said. "My name's actually Anne Boddeker, but I prefer Flora."

Harriet nodded absently. Under the muddle of her thoughts, the first sharp wedge of concern was beginning to surface. She remembered taking a fall from her bike . . . had she hit her head?

"What am I doing here?" she asked.

The old woman's eyes twinkled with humour. "Now how would I know?"

"But . . ." The fuzz in Harriet's head seemed to thicken. She blinked a couple of times and then cleared her throat. "Where are we?" she tried.

"North of Gracie Street," Flora replied, "in that part of town that, I believe, people your age refer to as Squatland. I'm afraid I don't know the exact address. Vandals have played havoc with the street signs, as I'm sure you know, but I believe we're not far from the corner of Flood and MacNeil where I grew up."

Harriet's heart sank. She was in The Tombs, an area of Newford that had once been a developer's bright dream. The old, tired blocks of tenements, office buildings and factories were to be transformed into a yuppie paradise and work had already begun on tearing down the existing structures when a sudden lack of backing had left the developer scrambling for solvency. All that remained now of the bright dream was block upon block of abandoned buildings and rubble-strewn lots generally referred to as The Tombs. It was home to runaways, the homeless, derelicts, bikers, drug addicts and the like who squatted in its buildings.

It was also probably one of the most dangerous parts of Newford.

"I . . . how did I get here?" Harriet tried again.

"What do you remember?" Flora said.

"I was biking home from work," Harriet began and then proceeded to relate what she remembered of the storm, the giant who'd loomed up so suddenly out of the snow, her accident. . . . "And then I suppose I must have fainted."

She lifted a hand to her head and searched about for a tender spot, but couldn't find a lump or a bruise.

"Did he speak to you?" Flora asked. "The . . . man who startled you?"

Harriet shook her head.

"Then it was Frank. He must have brought you here."

Harriet thought about what the old woman had just said.

"Does that mean there's more than one of him?" she asked.
She had the feeling that her memory was playing tricks on her
when she tried to call up the giant's scarred and misshapen features. She couldn't imagine there being more than one of him.

"In a way," Flora said.

"You're not being very clear."

"I'm sorry."

But she didn't appear to be, Harriet realized.

"So . . . he, this Frank . . . he's mute?" she asked.

"Terrible, isn't it?" Flora said. "A great big strapping lad like
that."

Harriet nodded in agreement. "But that doesn't explain what
you meant by there being more than one of him. Does he have
a brother?"

"He . . ." The old woman hesitated. "Perhaps you should ask
him yourself."

"But you just said that he was a mute."

"I think he's down that hall," Flora said, ignoring Harriet's
question. She pointed to a doorway opposite from the one that
Harriet had used to enter the foyer. "That's usually where he goes
to play."

Harriet stood there for a long moment, just looking at the old
woman. Flora, Anne, whatever her name was—she was obviously
senile. That had to explain her odd manner.

Harriet lifted her gaze to look in the direction Flora had
pointed. Her thoughts still felt muddy. She found standing as
long as she had been was far more tiring than it should have
been, and her tongue felt all fuzzy.

All she wanted to do was to go home. But if this *was* the
Tombs, then she'd need directions. Perhaps even protection from

some of the more feral characters who were said to inhabit these abandoned buildings. Unless, she thought glumly, this "Frank" was the danger himself. . . .

She looked back at Flora, but the old woman was ignoring her. Flora drew her shawl more tightly around her shoulders and took a sip of tea from her tin can.

Bother, Harriet thought and started across the foyer.

Halfway down the new hallway, she heard a child's voice singing softly. She couldn't make out the words until she'd reached the end of the hall where yet another candlelit room offered up a view of its bizarre occupant.

Frank was sitting cross-legged in the middle of the room, the contents of Harriet's purse scattered on the floor by his knees. Her purse itself had been tossed into a corner. Harriet would have backed right out of the room before Frank looked up except that she was frozen in place by the singing. The child's voice came from Frank's twisted lips—a high, impossibly sweet sound. It was a little girl's voice, singing a skipping song:

> *Frank and Harriet, sitting in a tree*
> *K-I-S-S-I-N-G*
> *First comes love, then comes marriage*
> *Here comes Frank with a baby's carriage.*

Frank's features seemed more monstrous than ever with that sweet child's voice issuing from his throat. He tossed the contents of Harriet's wallet into the air, juggling them. Her ID, a credit card, some photos from back home, scraps of paper with addresses or phone numbers on them, paper money, her bank card, all did a fluttering fandango as he sang, the movement of his hands oddly graceful for all the scarred squat bulk of his fingers. Her make-up, keys and loose change were lined up in rows like toy soldiers on parade in front of him. A half-burned ten dollar bill lay beside a candle on the wooden crate to his right. On the crate to his left lay a dead cat, curled up as though it was only sleeping, but the glassy dead eyes and swollen tongue that pushed open its jaws gave lie to the pretense.

Harriet felt a scream build up in her throat. She tried to back away, but bumped into the wall. The child's voice went still and Frank looked up. Photos, paper money, paper scraps and all flittered down upon his knees. His gaze locked on hers.

For one moment, Harriet was sure it was a child's eyes that regarded her from that ruined face. They carried a look of pure, absolute innocence, utterly at odds with the misshapen flesh and scars that surrounded them. But then they changed, gaining a feral, dark intelligence.

Frank scattered the scraps of paper and money in front of him away with a sweep of his hands.

"Mine," he cried in a deep, booming voice. "Girl is mine!"

As he lurched to his feet, Harriet fled back the way she'd come.

▼▼▼

"The hardest thing," the old woman said, "is watching everybody die. One by one, they all die: your parents, your friends, your family. . . ."

Her voice trailed off, rheumy eyes going sad. The monster merely regarded her.

"It was hardest when Julie died," she went on after a moment. There was a hitch in her voice as she spoke her daughter's name. "It's not right that parents should outlive their children." Her gaze settled on the monster's face. "But then you'll never know that particular pain, will you?"

The monster threw back his head and a soundless howl tore from his throat.

▼▼▼

As Harriet ran back into the room where she'd left Flora, she saw that the old woman was gone. Her candles, the crates and stove remained. The tin can half full of tea sat warming on the edge of the stove, not quite on the lit burner.

Harriet looked back down the hall where Frank's shambling bulk stumbled towards her.

She had to get out of this place. Never mind the storm still howling outside the building, never mind the confusing maze of abandoned buildings and refuse-choked streets of The Tombs. She just had to—

"There you are," a voice said from directly behind her.

Harriet's heart skipped a beat. A sharp, small inadvertent squeak escaped her lips as she flung herself to one side and then backed quickly away from the shadows by the door from which the voice had come. When she realized it was only the old woman, she kept right on backing up. Whoever, whatever, Flora was, it wasn't her friend.

Frank shambled into the foyer then, the queer lopsided set of his gaze fixed hungrily upon her. Harriet's heartbeat kicked into double-time. Her throat went dry. The muscles of her chest tightened, squeezing her lungs so that she found it hard to breathe.

Oh god, she thought. *Get out of here while you can.*

But she couldn't seem to move. Her limbs were deadened weights and she was starting to feel faint again.

"Now, now," the old woman said. "Don't carry on so, Samson, or you'll frighten her to death."

The monster obediently stopped in the doorway, but his hungry gaze never left Harriet.

"Sam-samson?" Harriet asked in a weak voice.

"Oh, there's all sorts of bits and pieces of people inside that poor ugly head," Flora replied. "Comes from traumas he suffered as a child. He suffers from—what was it that Dr. Adams called it? Dissociation. I think, before the accident, the doctor had documented seventeen people inside him. Some are harmless, such as Frank and little Bessie. Others, like Samson, have an unfortunate capacity for violence when they can't have their way."

"Doctor?" Harriet asked. All she seemed capable of was catching a word from the woman's explanations and repeating it as a question.

"Yes, he was institutionalized as a young boy. The odd thing is that he's somewhat aware of all the different people living inside him. He thinks that when his father sewed him back together, he used parts of all sorts of different people to do so and those bits of alien skin and tissue took hold of his mind and borrowed parts of it for their own use."

"That . . ." Harriet cleared her throat. "That was the . . . accident?"

"Oh, it wasn't any accident," Flora said. "And don't let anyone try to tell you different. His father knew exactly what he was doing when he threw him through that plate-glass window."

"But . . ."

"Of course, the father was too poor to be able to afford medical attention for the boy, so he patched him up on his own."

Harriet stared at the monstrous figure with growing horror.

"This . . . none of this can be true," she finally managed.

"It's all documented at the institution," Flora told her. "His father made a full confession before they locked him away. Poor Frank, though. It was too late to do anything to help him by that point, so he ended up being put away as well, for all that his only crime was the misfortune of being born the son of a lunatic."

Harriet tore her gaze from Frank's scarred features and turned to the old woman.

"How do you know all of this?" she asked.

"Why, I lived there as well," Flora said. "Didn't I tell you?"

"No. No, you didn't."

Flora shrugged. "It's old history. Mind you, when you get to be my age, everything's old history."

Harriet wanted to ask why Flora had been in the institution herself, but couldn't find the courage to do so. She wasn't even sure she *wanted* to know. But there was something she had no choice but to ask. She hugged her blanket closer around her, no longer even aware of its smell, but the chill that was in her bones didn't come from the cold.

"What happens now?" she said.

"I'm not sure I understand the question," Flora replied with a sly smile in her eyes that said she understood all too well.

Harriet pressed forward. "What happens to me?"

"Well, now," Flora said. She shot the monster an affectionate look. "Frank wants to start a family."

Harriet shook her head. "No," she said, her voice sounding weak and effectual even to her own ears. "No way."

"You don't exactly have a say in the matter, dear. It's not as though there's anyone coming to rescue you—not in this storm. And even if someone did come searching, where would they look? People disappear in this city all of the time. It's a sad, but unavoidable fact in these trying times that we've brought upon ourselves."

Harriet was still shaking her head.

"Oh, think of someone else for a change," the old woman told her. "I know your type. You're filled with your own self-importance; the whole world revolves around you. It's a party here, an evening of dancing there, theatre, clubs, cabaret, with never a thought for those less fortunate. What would it hurt you to give a bit of love and affection to a poor, lonely monster?"

I've gone all demented, Harriet thought. All of this—the monster, the lunatic calm of the old woman—none of it was real. None of it *could* be real.

"Do you think he *likes* being this way?" Flora demanded.

Her voice grew sharp and the monster shifted nervously at the tone of anger, the way a dog might bristle, catching its master's mood.

"It's got nothing to do with me," Harriet said, surprising herself that she could still find the courage to stand up for herself. "I'm not like you think I am and I had nothing to do with what happened to that—to Frank."

"It's got everything to do with you," the old woman replied. "It's got to do with caring and family and good Samaritanism and decency and long, lasting relationships."

"You can't force a person into something like that," Harriet argued.

Flora sighed. "Sometimes, in *these* times, it's the only way. There's a sickness abroad in the world, child; your denial of what's right and true is as much a cause as a symptom."

"You're the one that's sick!" Harried cried.

She bolted for the building's front doors, praying they weren't locked. The monster was too far away and moved too slowly to stop her. The old woman was closer and quicker, but in her panic, Harriet found the strength to fling her bodily away. She raced for the glass doors that led out of the foyer and into the storm.

The wind almost drove her back inside when she finally got a door open, but she pressed against it, through the door and out onto the street. The whirling snow, driven by the mad, capricious wind, soon stole away all sense of direction, but she didn't dare stop. She plowed through drifts, blinded by the snow, head bent against the howling wind, determined to put as much distance between herself and what she fled.

Oh god, she thought at one point. My purse was back there. My ID. They know where I live. They can come and get me at home, or at work, anytime they want.

But mostly she fought the snow and wind. How long she fled

through the blizzard, she had no way of knowing. It might have been an hour, it might have been the whole night. She was shaking with cold and fear when she stumbled to the ground one last time and couldn't get up.

She lay there, a delicious sense of warmth enveloping her. All she had to do was let go, she realized. Just let go and she could drift away into that dark, warm place that beckoned to her. She rolled over on her side and stared up into the white sky. Snow immediately filmed her face. She rubbed it away with a mittened hand, half-frozen with the cold.

She was ready to let go. She was ready to just give up the struggle, because she was only so strong and she'd given it her all, hadn't she? She—

A tall dark figure loomed up suddenly, towering over her. Snow blurred her sight so that it was only a shape, an outline, against the white.

No, she pleaded. Don't take me back. I'd rather die than go back.

As the figure bent down beside her, she found the strength to beat at it with her frozen hands.

"Easy now," a kind voice said, blocking her weak blows. "We'll get you out of here."

She stopped trying to fight. It wasn't the monster, but a policeman. Somehow, in her aimless flight, she'd wandered out of The Tombs.

"What are you doing out here?" the policeman said.

Monster, she wanted to say. There's a monster. It attacked me. But all that came out from her frozen lips was, "Muh . . . tacked me. . . ."

"First we'll get you out of this weather," he told her, "then we'll deal with the man who assaulted you."

The hours that followed passed in a blur. She was in a hospital, being treated for frostbite. A detective interviewed her, calmly, patiently sifting through her mumbled replies for a description of what had happened to her, and then finally she was left alone.

At one point she came out of her dozing state and thought she saw two policemen standing at the end of her bed. She wasn't sure if they were actually present or not, but like Agathie Christie characters, gathered at the denouement of one of the great mystery writer's stories, their conversation conveniently filled in some details concerning her captors of which she hadn't been aware.

"Maybe it was before your time," one of the policemen was saying, "but that description she gave fits."

"No, I remember," the other replied. "They were residents in the Zeb's criminal ward and Cross killed their shrink during a power failure."

The first officer nodded. "I don't know which of them was worse: Cross with that monstrous face, or Boddeker."

"Poisoned her whole family, didn't she?"

"Yeah, but I remember seeing what Cross did to the shrink— just about tore the poor bastard in two."

"I heard that it was Boddeker who put him up to it. The poor geek doesn't have a mind of his own."

Vaguely, as though observing the action from a vast distance, Harriet could sense the first officer looking in her direction.

"She's lucky she's still alive," he added, looking back at his companion.

In the days that followed, researching old newspapers at the library, Harriet found out that all that the two men had said, or that she'd dreamed they had said, was true, but she couldn't absorb any of it at the moment. For now she just drifted away once more, entering a troubled sleep that was plagued with dreams of ghosts and monsters. The latter wore masks to hide the horror inside them, and they were the worst of all.

She woke much later, desperately needing to pee. It was still dark in her room. Outside she could hear the wind howling.

She fumbled her way into the bathroom and did her business, then stared into the mirror after she'd flushed. There was barely enough light for the mirror to show her reflection. What looked back at her from the glass was a ghostly face that she almost didn't recognize.

"Monsters," she said softly, not sure if what she felt was pity or fear, not sure if she recognized one in herself, or if it was just the old woman's lunatic calm still pointing an accusing finger.

She stared at that spectral reflection for a very long time before she finally went back to bed.

▼▼▼

"We'll find you another," the old woman said.

Her tea had gone cold but she was too tired to relight the stove and make herself another cup. Her hands were folded on her lap, her gaze fixed on the tin can of cold water that still sat on the stove. A film of ice was forming on the water.

"You'll see," she added. "We'll find another, but this time we'll put her together ourselves, just the way your father did with you. We'll take a bit from one and a bit from another and we'll make you the perfect mate, just see if we don't. I always was a fair hand with a needle and thread, you know—a necessary quality for a wife in my time. Of course everything's different now, every-thing's changed. Sometimes I wonder why we bother to go on. . . ."

The monster stared out the window to where the snow still fell, quietly now, the blizzard having moved on leaving only this calm memory of its storm winds in its wake. He gave no indica-tion that he was listening to the old woman, but she went on talking all the same.

THE LAST SUPPER AND A
FALAFFEL TO GO
▼▼▼

BY GEORGE ALEC EFFINGER

IT was a brisk, mid-November, frost-on-the-pumpkin night
when two men in the front seats of an Arbier Parish Sheriff's
patrolcar broke off an argument about who'd they'd rather nail,
Michelle Pfeiffer or Kim Basinger. The bigger of the two said he
wouldn't have Kim Basinger on a bet, but he wouldn't mind
getting close to Uma Thurman. The smaller patrolman started to
say that he'd never even heard of Uma Thurman, but they both
shut up at the same moment because they saw something in
the chilly darkness that shouldn't have been there. They were
parked at the foot of the levee, and they were there to chase
down high school kids who liked to wind out their dads' cars
on the crushed-shell roadway at the top of the embankment.
Laying rubber on the levee was desperately illegal in Arbier
Parish, though no one could say why, least of all Officer Kasparian or Officer Block in the patrolcar.

Fortunately for the patrolmen, who were relieved to curtail
their everlasting debates concerning either unobtainable women

or the true meaning of the Arbier Parish Legal Code, all Officers Kasparian and Block saw through their windshield was a guy. A damn big guy. He was seven feet tall without half trying, and he was just standing in the Johnson grass about halfway up the levee, a kind of confused expression on his Mary, Mother of God ugly face.

"That's one ugly son of a bitch," said Officer Kasparian.

"We been trained for all sorts of eventualities," said Officer Block, slowly opening the car door. "But the resources of St. Didier Parish are pretty limited, as you and I both well know after the failure of the recent bond measures. So I think I'm right when I say I wasn't trained for no ugly. No ugly like this. God don't like no ugly."

"Let's not be putting words in the holy mouth of the Almighty, at least not yet," said Officer Kasparian. "You notice that the ugly guy has his head sewn on? Anything in any of those high-tech law enforcement seminars they send you to in Orleans Parish about dealing with sewn-on head perpetrators?"

"They talked about this guy once who had the end of his tongue ripped off and they raced him to the hospital and to this very day he's almost as functional as you or me. This is pretty much different, though."

"Uh huh," said Officer Kasparian, slowly getting out of the patrolcar on his side. Both cops had their nightsticks at the ready, but neither had drawn his sidearm.

Officer Block raised his hands above his head. "We mean you no harm. We are friends. We come in peace."

"Hey," called Officer Kasparian from the defensive position he'd taken beside the front left wheel well, "why are you treating him like some kind of alien invader from space or something?"

Officer Block turned and gave his partner an exasperated glare. "How many seven-foot-tall guys with their heads sewn on do we usually run into between the towns of Arbier and Linhart?"

"Not a lot," Officer Kasparian admitted.

"So let me try it my way, all right?" Officer Block stood in the damp weeds and waved his hands over his head some more, clearly forgetting what happened to everyone who tried that, in the 1953 movie classic, *The War of the Worlds*.

The damn big guy looked from Officer Block, who was practically hopping up and down trying to establish communication, and Officer Kasparian, who was still in his nearly invisible defensive position on the far side of the car. "Say," yelled the ugly giant, "can I help you guys out with something?"

Officer Block nodded to Officer Kasparian, who crawled carefully back into the patrolcar and called into the Sheriff's Office in Linhart. He gave the sergeant there all the particulars, and the ultimate decision was that the guy who'd just had his head sewn on was doing nothing especially illegal, but Officers Block and Kasparian were to transport the big mother to Mercy Lutheran in Linhart anyway, dump him on an emergency room nurse or doctor, and then get back to their position.

The two patrolmen had time to look at each other. Then Officer Block said, "Well, let's do it." He called out to the big mother. "We think we ought to run you by the hospital. Is that okay with you?"

"You bet," said the poor seven-foot-tall sucker. He got quietly into the back of the patrolcar, separated from the peace officers in front by a heavy steel cage. This was where the ugly giant's problems really began.

Officer Kasparian and Officer Block drove the big mother to Mercy Lutheran Hospital in the parish seat of Linhart. The cops handed the guy with the sewn-on head over to a nurse, accepted a scrawled release form in return, and gladly escaped back into the cool, clear evening.

The emergency room doctor had a lot of trouble getting information from the ugly giant, who couldn't remember his name, didn't know where he lived, and couldn't recall any friends or relatives who might come get him.

The doctor had the innocent sucker undress, and was astonished by the full catalogue of sewn-on parts—not just the head, but arms, legs, lesser appendages, and the top of the skull, where a sly and crafty surgeon could have stashed stolen jewels or strange and virulent poisons if there were no brains inside taking up the space. The doctor shrugged, hid the ugly giant in an out-of-the-way room, stuck him full of Thorazine, and kept him under observation.

Soon, the hospital realized it couldn't justify holding the big mother any longer, and its Social Services Department passed him along to the Hanson State Hospital for the Mentally Disabled, where a social worker steered the weird-looking bastard to a work-release program. They gave him a job and loaned him enough money to get a small apartment. That might have been the answer to all the poor sucker's problems, except when he reported to work the first day, his supervisor discovered the gruesome giant had no Social Security Number.

Without the number, the damn big ugly son of a bitch couldn't pay taxes and couldn't stay in the work-release program. The Social Security Department frowned to learn that the only information the innocent bastard could offer was a name, Victor Frankenstein, which was sewn on a label inside the big mother's sport jacket, which in the first place fit him like a junior miss sweater on the Goodyear blimp.

The dumb guy went from federal agencies to state agencies to local agencies, all promising in their titles to do their utmost with human resources and manpower and economic development. Even the Welfare Department threw the poor bastard out when he could answer only the first question on their evaluation sheet, and the Civil Rights people had a tough time deciding just how his rights were being abridged.

After being evicted from his apartment, he'd taken up residence in a large Maytag refrigerator carton on an upper floor of a burnt-out and abandoned tenement in a rubble-strewn neighborhood of Linhart. There were lots of other people huddled in their cartons in the same building, but they had little to say to each other. At night, in the cold darkness, the grotesque son of a bitch could hear the scamperings of little animal legs.

Days passed, and his frustration grew faster even than his physical hunger. He had no money. He hadn't eaten in days. Begging never even occurred to him, and after all, who would drop a dollar or a handful of loose change into the grotesque, deformed hands that showed every sign of coming from the same human-parts outlet store as his horrible sewn-on head?

The next morning was Thursday, and the big mother awoke to the sound of music. Friday he had an appointment to visit the Community Action Agency and check out their action, but today was free, though. He crawled out of the Maytag carton, stood, and stretched, listening idly to the far-off clashing of drums. He could hear a few other people nearby crunching shattered glass and broken brick, and he saw their shabby figures when they passed before a windowless opening that hadn't yet been boarded over. He stretched again, stared around defiantly in case anyone had designs on his Maytag carton, and climbed slowly down the foul-smelling staircase to the ground floor.

The sun was its ineffectual autumn self, hiding behind clouds that might rain or might snow or might just sit there in the same place in the sky until April. The air had gotten colder overnight, and the ugly bastard jammed his huge, misshapen hands into the sport jacket's pockets. He wished he owned gloves. Gloves were just another treasure he could acquire if he stumbled upon the secret of getting a Social Security Number.

The reedy blare of band music came to him, made discordant by distance. The sorry schmuck sat down on a low stone wall and glanced toward the sound. High above the barren, leafless autumn trees floated vast, fantastic figures, the inflated balloons of Linhart's annual Thanksgiving event. It wasn't New York and it wasn't Macy's, but Linhart, Louisiana took pride in its smaller version of the grand parade. The big mother with the sewn-on head was astonished.

The brain that had recently been crammed into his misfitted and still-sutured skull had not been created new, like a mass of blank and empty neural tissue receptive to every new experience. No, his brain had come from somewhere—from *someone*, it had to be admitted—and within it there were peculiar vestiges of knowledge and behavior. They explained his unfailing politeness and his grim acceptance in the face of one agency's failure to help after another.

Even more positive remnants were buried, though, in his dim and perplexed mind. One of these was a faint image of a Thanksgiving Day Parade, watched on television perhaps, or maybe in person, curbside in Linhart or New York or some city in-between. The ugly giant smiled slowly, and moved his arms clumsily in time with the music. He stood from the crumbling stone retaining wall and lurched unsteadily in the direction of the parade. "Music good," he said to himself in his rough, hoarse voice.

He walked for ten minutes, up a hill and down another, and then along an avenue that ran perpendicular to the street he was following. He looked down one side-street and saw, like a childhood miracle, a giant inflated balloon in the shape of a mighty rocket ship from a television show that had lasted only one TV season. A high school band marching in front of the balloon was tootling away on the TV show's nearly forgotten theme song.

The ignorant bastard hurried excitedly to the curbside, where he could hear the complaining of the band members. The air was cold, and the lower brass players were having trouble with their heavy metal mouthpieces. The woodwind players worked their fingers constantly to keep them limber. "Hey, man," yelled one snare drummer sourly, "what we doin' this for anyway, man? Nobody payin' us or *nothin'*." Despite the band members' ill humor, it was all more spectacular than anything the unlucky schmuck had ever seen. He turned his sewn-on head and bolted neck to catch a preview of what was coming next. It seemed to be a mass of cold, sullen young girls in pink suits with pointed hoods, carrying flags of blue and silver that they whipped through the air in something approaching precision.

"It's a sign," said the innocent bastard, "a terrible sign, that I woke up this morning in a Maytag carton in a burnt-out building and didn't even know that it was Thanksgiving. It is the perfect statement of my ultimate degradation." Yet the parade passed him by like a religious procession with additional clown units, and he began to feel a deep, overpowering emotion. It was stronger than anything the ugly giant had ever before experienced. It was a kind of cleansing, an absolution that began down at the most basic elements of his being. Witnessing the Thanksgiving Day Parade validated him as a person, even though the wary civil authorities would not take the initiative in their agencies and programs to help him. The big guy shrugged; all that was for the future. For the present, he was just like everyone else, standing on the edge of the street and thrilling at one astonishing marching unit after another.

The supreme magical moment came right at the end, as it always did. The float that closed the parade, the one that was more elaborate, more beautiful, with more sparkles and flocked snow, was the Santa Claus float. Santa Claus had arrived for the season in Linhart, Louisiana, through the auspices of the Sudarin-Cooke department store.

The ugly bastard with the sewn-on head stared up through the twinkling lights, and lithe young men and women dressed like Santa's helpers waved down to him. The concept, the firm belief in Santa already existed in the big mother's truncated awareness, and suddenly it occurred to him that if the government had set itself firmly upon a road to failure, then only magic had a chance to salvage the innocent sucker's desperate life.

"Here, Santa!" yelled the grotesque son of a bitch. "Here, Santa! Here, Santa!" He yelled and yelled until the Santa Claus on the sequined throne swiveled slowly from one side of the float to the other, and Santa's face turned down toward the eager throngs on the sidewalk. Santa's eyes locked with the damn big guy's for just a moment, and the ugly bastard was sure that for the briefest instant, wordless communication had passed between them. He knew it. He felt it. And just to be on the safe side, the big man began yelling, "My number! My number! My number!"

For his part, Santa stared tiredly and then looked away toward a shrieking young boy in a heavy, uncomfortable winter jacket. "Ho, ho, ho," said Santa, wheezing just a little after the long parade. The boy in the winter jacket just screamed and turned away.

The ugly bastard watched the Santa float move along the street, and he realized that the parade had passed and was over. His restructured chest was filled with hope and joy. Every bit of this day had been a new experience for him, and he wondered how much more blissful life could get, short of death and a return to the parts department.

The poor sucker wandered away from the avenue, back toward his own burnt-out tenement. He walked through a vacant lot, and three men and a woman were standing around a fire in a big old fifty-five gallon drum. They invited him to warm his hands by the fire, and he was so overwhelmed by their generosity that he could find nothing to say. He found himself weeping. Further up the street, a man sat on the front stoop of his apartment building with a tiny portable television. The man invited the dumb bastard to watch for a while, because one professional football team was threatening to do something offensive to the other. The big guy didn't know if he wanted to stand there and witness it. He was still feeling so wonderful from the parade and seeing Santa.

Before he could make a decision, a young woman with a clipboard came down the hill toward him. "Hello, sir," said the young woman. "Happy Thanksgiving."

The poor sucker had become fond of young women with clipboards. They were always so earnest. "Thanksgiving," he said, nodding. "Thanksgiving good."

"You haven't had Thanksgiving dinner yet?" said the woman. She smiled at the ugly son of a bitch. She took him by the arm, something few people had dared to do without a syringe full of Thorazine in the other hand.

"Dinner?" asked the big mother.

The young woman smiled. "Come with me. We have turkey and stuffing and mashed potatoes and cranberry sauce and pumpkin pie. All supplied by Linhart's united charities, under the direction of the sheriff's annual Feed the Homeless program." She began leading him down a long hill that curved to the left. The pavement was cracked and broken, and the windows in all the tenements had been boarded over with plywood, just like the one where he kept his Maytag carton.

"My name is Shanna," said the young woman. "We'll just go in here." She led the grotesque man into a large metal-sided building, which most of the year served as a parking area for the sheriff's various crime-fighting vehicles. These had all been moved elsewhere, and the dusty, chilly space inside the metal warehouse had been filled with collapsible metal tables and chairs.

There were hundreds of people just like the ugly bastard—well, like him in that they had nowhere else to go on Thanksgiving. And they were all sitting at the paper-covered tables, ravenously downing the miraculous holiday meal, served to them on plastic trays by sheriff's deputies and by older women active in charity functions.

Shanna took a seat at one of the tables and indicated that the innocent sucker sit beside her. "May I get your name, sir?" she asked, pencil and clipboard all ready for data entry.

"Victor," said the damn ugly man. He remembered that from his short stay in Mercy Lutheran hospital. "Victor, they told me. I remember. Victor something. Somethingstein. Rosenstein. No, that's not right. I used to know. I used to remember." It hadn't yet dawned on the big mother that he was going to get a tray of food to eat, too.

"Victor Rosenstein," said Shanna happily. "That'll do just fine. And do you live in this neighborhood?"

Just then, one of the deputies arrived with a pink tray that had seen its years of service. The deputy put the tray of food in front of the innocent son of a bitch, whose eyes opened wide, as if all the glorious bounties of the earth had been spread before him. "Happy Thanksgiving," said the deputy, and then he left to serve another person.

"For me?" asked the innocent guy.

"Enjoy it, Mr. Rosenstein," said Shanna. "You didn't answer my question. Do you live in this neighborhood?"

The easiest thing to grab first was a dinner roll, and the poor sucker had it completely crammed in his mouth, making talking difficult. "Yes," he said. "In a Maytag carton in one of these buildings."

Shanna nodded knowingly and wrote something on the clipboard. "Do you use intravenous drugs, Mr. Rosenstein?" she said casually.

He'd gotten rid of most of the dinner roll, but refilled his mouth with hot mashed potatoes. He chewed a little while. "Are those the good kind or the bad kind?" he asked.

"Well—"

"No drugs," he said definitely. "No food, no home, no drugs, no number." He cut up his turkey clumsily and shook his head. "My number. My life could be my own if they just gave me my number."

"But you wouldn't use intravenous drugs, would you, Mr. Rosenstein?" Shanna said with a forced laugh.

"No, of course not," said the ugly man. "Just say no. Many people just say no. To me."

Shanna stood beside him and covered one of his scarred hands with hers. "Yet here you sit, on Thanksgiving. You see, people *do* care. You should give thanks, Mr. Rosenstein, thanks to God for what you do have. Now, please excuse me, I have to go find someone else who hasn't had Thanksgiving dinner."

"Thank you, Shanna," said the big mother. "You have given me the courage to go on. Shanna friend. Friend good." Shanna gave his huge hand a squeeze with her little one, and walked away.

The food was good and hot, and the innocent sucker enjoyed every bit of it. When he was finished, he just sat at the paper-covered table until another sheriff's deputy led him gently by the arm out of the corrugated steel garage and back into the evening. It was getting dark, and it was getting colder, too. The big man shivered. He looked up and saw ragged tears among the clouds, where bright stars glittered like the cheap jewels on Santa's float. The poor schmuck had learned that there was nothing to do after dark, and the neighborhood got more dangerous the later it got, so he made his way slowly from the garage back up the hill to the particular building where he kept his Maytag carton. There were many vacant places on the rubble-strewn floors of the rows of tenements, and many unclaimed appliance cartons. But the big mother had come to think of his carton and his ruin of a building as "home." He never noticed the astonished and frightened looks the passers-by gave him as they met along the way.

There was enough light left when he arrived at his Maytag carton to do some housecleaning. He used his huge, booted foot to shove the fragments of brick and the sharp, many-colored shards of glass into a pile a few feet from the carton. He thought about a broom. With his number, with a job, with money, he could buy a broom and sweep the area around his carton perfectly clean. For now, though, that was only a dream, and he did the best he could.

He slept lightly in the cold, waking many times and covering himself with sheets of newspaper. He could see his breath in the chill, faintly-lighted air. In the morning he got up, remembering that he had appointments. First, though, he walked down the hill to the magic place where they had given him so much good food. He would ask them for more. It was morning now, and he was hungry.

The sheriff's deputies had taken down all the collapsible tables and chairs, and cleaned the place of garbage, which the city's refuse removal system had already taken far away somewhere. The big gates to the garage stood wide-open, but there was no sign anymore of young women with clipboards, or trays of food, or charity of any kind. Instead, the trucks and bulldozers and other heavy machinery of the parish had been driven back into place.

The big man stood at the gates, confused. "I want food!" he shouted.

A sheriff's deputy walked over slowly. "We ain't doin' that," he said calmly. "We did that yesterday, but we ain't doin' that today. You understand?"

The innocent sucker stood a moment in deep thought. "Food here yesterday," he said, "and Santa, and the Cowboys making the Redskins upset. Today—"

The deputy took a toothpick out of his mouth and examined it, but it looked just fine to him. "Now, as I was sayin'," he said—he had a reputation for getting along real well with junkies and winos and fruitcakes and whatever else wandered by—"we did food yesterday, but we ain't doin' food today? You got that?"

The grotesque son of a bitch nodded.

The deputy took a deep breath and let it out. "Now, Santa is something completely different. You want Santa, you got to go to the Suderin-Cooke Department Store. You can even get your picture taken and all. You know where that store is?"

"No, sir, I don't," said the poor bastard.

The deputy looked down at the ground and drew a line with the edge of his shoe. "You just follow this street along until you run into a big courthouse square. Then you ask somebody else. Got it?"

"I'm grateful for your help, officer," said the ugly schmuck.

"Never mind. You just say hello to Santa for me."

The damn big guy followed the street down into a shopping district, and found the department store after terrifying two frail ladies with blue-tinted hair and gloves. He giant with the sewn-on head went into the carefully decorated store and accomplished the next part of his chore merely by looming over men, women, or children and growling "Santa!" From then on, he just went in the direction of the points.

Suderin-Cooke's was Linhart's last local independent department store, and it tried to maintain a certain old-fashioned charm about itself. It worked very hard at not looking like the well-known national stores that had come to take over the shopping malls in recent years. It was quickly decided this Friday morning that essential to maintaining the store's hundred-and-ten-year image was the immediate removal of the seven-foot reconstructed man who was apparently disturbing customers already. From all outward appearances, the grotesque bastard didn't appear likely to open a new Suderin-Cooke charge account or use an old one. The department store's security personnel called the Linhart sheriff's office.

As luck would have it, it wasn't Officer Kasparian and Officer Block who picked up the big man from the department store. It was Officer Gautreaux and Officer Williams' call. Officer Gautreaux never said very much. Officer Williams' attitude toward life could be captured quickly enough. This is what he said to the innocent giant as he was bending him into the back of their patrolcar. "You think you big? You think you big, you son of a bitch? I got little girl cousins, they wearin' little pink K-Mart socks and jumpin' rope, they make you look like the old man, he be talkin' to himself sellin' tamales next to the drugstore. You think you big. And your head sewn-on. Listen, son of a bitch, where you be goin', they staple everything they can't just Velcro." The conversation in the patrolcar continued in exactly that tone of voice, from Officer Williams in solo, until they got to the sheriff's department.

The sergeant wanted to know what the problem was.

"Suderin-Cooke's say he cause a complaint," said Officer Williams.

The sergeant nodded.

"He was lookin' for Santa," said Officer Gautreaux.

The sergeant nodded. "He ain't done nothin'. Find out who he is, put him in the pit, and have somebody come get him. Them stitches got to be givin' him some grief. Goddamn department store calls us, this guy probably wasn't doin' nothin' but bein' tall."

Officer Williams laughed without humor. "Son of a bitch think he tall, huh?"

"My wife and I don't even go in that store no more," said Officer Gautreaux. "They treat you like you're trackin' germs across their china."

"Name?" asked the sergeant.

"Victor," said the ugly bastard. "Victor Rosen, um, stick."

"Victor Rosenstick, is that correct?"

"Yes, sir."

"Address?"

There was a long silence. "I don't know."

Officer Williams looked at Officer Gautreaux and rolled his eyes. "Here we go," he said.

They kept the innocent son of a bitch all day and overnight in the pit—what they called their holding cell—and then tried to get rid of him in the morning. The big mother didn't want to leave. The cot and mattress and hot food was the best treatment he'd had since Mercy Lutheran Hospital, although the sheriff's deputies couldn't give him any Thorazine. That was okay. He demanded in a loud voice to be put back in jail, but it got him nowhere. By unspoken agreement, they let Officer Williams be in charge of returning the poor sucker to society. "Hey, hey, hey," said Officer Williams, adjusting his sunglasses, "wait you see where I let you out the car. Say, boy, what color *are* you?"

It is not the world's way to let things go easier. The big man knew things would only get worse. He tried other meetings, other agencies, other sympathetic people who had never learned that their jobs didn't let them really kick a brick.

Finally, when he hadn't eaten in days, in absolute desperation, he saw a young girl with a falaffel sandwich in her hands. He didn't stop to reason. He grabbed the falaffel sandwich and ran with it. The girl's mother ran after him, and others followed in a maddened fury as the story spread, as the newcomers made it seem that he had done other, more horrible things to the young girl than just steal her sandwich. He ran toward his den, his Maytag carton high in its reeking, vagrant tenement building.

The afternoon began to grow darker as he ran, and slowly as the clock moved toward five the people of the city felt a change. They realized that something new, something unforgiveably innocent had entered their bewildering domain. With the scent of fresh blood in the air, it would take the groups and loners only a short time to track and hunt the poor mother back to his ruined and crumbling tenement, back to the sad shelter of his Maytag box.

Below, on the sidewalk, weapons and blazing torches in hand, they'd all at last give him his identity of sorts, and then—as ritual demanded—his final, fiery apotheosis.

FRANKENSTEIN
▼▼▼

A SELECTED FILMOGRAPHY

While Mary Shelley's tale of Frankenstein has not been so widely interpreted in the movies as Bram Stoker's Dracula, her creation story has achieved equally mythic proportions.

The fortunes of the story in the movies have varied, as the following filmography indicates, but whatever the incidental changes, two thematic elements in the story are always the same: (1) mankind has every reason to mistrust science and (2) a monster is someone who is both ugly and mateless. Everything else is annotation.

Now, the filmography, which is not meant to be either complete or a list of the best films on the Frankenstein theme. Rather, what follows is meant to display the range of treatments Mary Shelley's story has received in the movies.

FRANKENSTEIN
1931 (B & W)   U.S.A.   71 minutes
Universal Pictures
Director: James Whale
Producer: Carl Laemmle, Jr.
Screenplay: Garrett Fort, Francis Edward Faragoh, Robert Florey
Photography: Arthur Edeson
Cast: *Colin Clive, Boris Karloff, Mae Clark, John Boles, Edward Van Sloan*

This triumphant film, whose sixtieth birthday this book celebrates, gives us the creature (called the "Monster" in the film credits) as we have ever after seen him: tall, ill-clad, lumbering, with a square head and pegs sticking out from his neck. His face gaunt, his eyes baffled, he stands unsteadily with his arms upthrust toward the light which, with the innocence of the newborn, he tries to seize.

Despite Colin Clive's tortured and flaccid performance as Henry Frankenstein (Victor, in the novel) and a singularly helpless rendering of Elizabeth by Mae Clark, Whale's film achieves the stature of a masterpiece because Whale understood the innocence, the sexual frustration and the consequent baffled rage that are at the heart of Mary Shelley's story. Whale's direction is superbly sensitive and transforms what might have been simply another popular genre film into one with darkly tragic implications.

Whale had help. He found an actor, Boris Karloff, who did justice to his complex understanding of the role of the creature. Whale, too, was splendidly served by the makeup Jack Pierce created for Karloff and by Harry Strickfadden's stupendous special effects in the creation scene.

THE BRIDE OF FRANKENSTEIN
1935 (B & W)   U.S.A.   75 minutes
Production Company: Universal Pictures
Director: James Whale
Producer: Carl Laemmle
Screenplay: William Hurlbut and John L. Balderston
Photography: John Mescall
Special Effects: Jack Pierce and John P. Fulton
Cast: *Boris Karloff, Colin Clive, Valerie Hobson, Elsa Lanchester, Ernest Thesiger, Dwight Frye*

The Bride of Frankenstein is a phenomenon: a sequel film that surpasses in excellence the film that it follows. Called by many (and I concur) one of the greatest horror films of all times, it deserves all the praise ever heaped upon it. It has James Whale's continuingly sensitive direction and an eloquent screenplay in which the sexual implications of *Frankenstein* are fully developed. It has also superlative performances by everyone except the romantic leads, Colin Clive and Valerie Hobson, who are in any event expected only to register pain or fear at appropriate moments.

When those two are not turning the screen turgid we have Elsa Lanchester playing, deliciously, both Mary Shelley and the Bride; and Boris Karloff playing a more humanized (because vocal) creature who has been promised a laboratory-made bride, and Ernest Thesiger, in a jewel-like rendering of Dr. Pretorius, Henry's collaborator, one of the greatest comic-malevolent characters ever to appear on film. We have finally, a marriage-cum-cataclysm scene that is so physically destructive and erotic that it leaves filmgoers gasping.

THE SON OF FRANKENSTEIN
1939 (B & W)   U.S.A.   95 minutes
Production Company: Universal Pictures
Director: Rowland V. Lee
Producer: Rowland V. Lee
Screenplay: Willis Cooper
Photography: George Robinson
Cast: *Basil Rathbone, Boris Karloff, Bela Lugosi, Lionel Atwill, Josephine Hutchinson*

Son of Frankenstein, the third of the three impressive "Frankensteins" Universal Films made in the thirties is the one with the least symbolic depth, but its sprightly plot goes a long way to compensate for what it lacks in complexity.

Basil Rathbone is cast as Wolf von Frankenstein. Wolf, son of the Henry Frankenstein we have seen in the two previous films, is a research scientist in the United States when news is brought to him that he has inherited his father's estate. With his wife Elsa and his son Dieter in tow, he returns to the family's home in Germany where Ygor, a broken-necked criminal shepherd who has survived hanging, persuades him to revive the "sick" monster.

Wolf undertakes the task as a way to vindicate his maligned father. Ygor wants the resurrection so that he can use the creature to avenge himself on the jurors who sent him, Ygor, to the gallows.

The Son of Frankenstein is notable for several reasons: first, there are its sets, chiefly oversized, brooding stairways, vast halls with towering ceilings providing a natural habitat for dark and dreadful acts; then it has Bela Lugosi who with a hoarse voice and aura of sly intelligence is uncannily persuasive as Ygor; then it has Lionel Atwill playing the marvelously conceived Inspector Krogh who, we are told, lost an arm in a previous encounter with the creature and who, in this film, loses his artificial arm to him at a climactic moment. Atwill plays the German martinet police inspector with great style and with high good humor.

Sadly enough, though Karloff is still here, the zest with which he played the creature in the earlier two films is gone. The fault may lie with the screen play in which the creature is no longer presented as "more sinned against than sinning." As the critic, Phil Hardy (*The Encyclopedia of Horror Movies*) puts it, "The unmistakeable shift is from monster as victim to monster as demon." The result is that he rarely stirs compassion in us, and the film, for all its stylishness, feels flatter than its predecessors.

THE GHOST OF FRANKENSTEIN
1942, (B & W) U.S.A. 68 minutes
Universal Pictures
Director: Erle C. Kenton
Producer: George Waggner
Screenplay: W. Scott Darling
Photography: Milton Krasner
Cast: *Cedric Hardwicke, Ralph Bellamy*

The Ghost of Frankenstein, while it continues to exploit the by now coherent imagery of the *Frankenstein* myth shows a marked decline in Hollywood's ability to handle it. Lon Chaney Jr. behind *his* makeup simply cannot match Karloff as the creature. Still, it is pleasant to watch such seasoned inhabitants of scary movies as Lionel Atwill and Bela Lugosi at work again. Not a great film, but not quite dreary, either.

FRANKENSTEIN MEETS THE WOLF MAN
1943, (B & W) U.S.A. 74 minutes
Universal Pictures
Director: Roy William Neill
Producer: George Waggner
Screenplay: Curt Siodmak
Photography: George Robinson
Cast: *Lon Chaney Jr., Bela Lugosi, Lionel Atwill, Ilona Massey, Maria Ouspenskaya*

Here is a film that is important only because it marks the signal decline in film of the compelling *Frankenstein* idea. If the film proves anything it is that one cannot make a fine horror movie by simply throwing great old horror regulars together. Lugosi as the monster elicits pity, but only because his performance is so shabby. Nobody cares that Lon Chaney (as Laurence Talbot) wants medical help to escape the curse of werewolfism. Everybody is grateful when both monsters (so the law of sequels will permit) are destroyed at the end of film. That end comes none too soon.

ABBOTT AND COSTELLO MEET FRANKENSTEIN
1948 (B & W) U.S.A. 83 minutes
Universal Pictures
Director: Charles T. Barton
Producer: Robert Arthur
Screenplay: Robert Lees, Frederic Rinaldo, John Grant
Photography: Charles Van Enger
Cast: *Bud Abbott, Lou Costello, Bela Lugosi, Lon Chaney Jr., Glenn Strange, Lenore Aubert, Vincent Price*

*This review of *Frankenstein Meets the Wolf Man* appears also in the volume *The Ultimate Werewolf*.

Another *pot pourri* film in which Universal Pictures, acting on the principle that if one monster made for great box office then four would make even more money, gave us Dracula, the Frankenstein creature, the Wolfman and the Invisible Man, each of whom makes an appearance of longer or shorter duration. But the real fun in this film is the presence in it of Abbott and Costello, whose disingenuous high jinks turn what would otherwise be a sorry venture into quite a jolly eighty-three minutes of monster mash.

I WAS A TEENAGE FRANKENSTEIN
1958 (B & W)   U.S.A.   76 minutes
MGM
Director: Herbert L. Strock
Producer: Herman Cohen
Screenplay: Kenneth Langtry
Photography: Lothrop Worth
Cast: *Whit Bissell, Phyllis Coates, Robert Burton, Gary Conway,*
     George Lynn, John Cliff

This shabby sequel to *I Was a Teenage Werewolf* (1957), is important only as an example of the way Hollywood, in the fifties, was trying to address the newly discovered world of teen America.

The plot of the film, a sad parody of the 1931 film story of Frankenstein, has a visiting British scientist, a descendant of Baron Frankenstein, fulfilling his boast that he will make a human being. The creature he makes, though ugly, has sense enough to know that the scientist is evil and turns on him, to the eminent satisfaction of the crocodile that the scientist keeps in his basement.

THE CURSE OF FRANKENSTEIN
1957 (Color)   Great Britain   82 minutes
Hammer Films
Director: Terence Fisher
Producer: Anthony Hinds

Screenplay: Jimmy Sangster
Photography: Jack Asher
Cast: *Christopher Lee, Peter Cushing, Hazel Court, Robert
Urquhart, Valerie Gaunt, Noel Hood, Michael Mulcaster,
Patrick Troughton, Marjorie Hume*

This is the first of the great Hammer Films that revivified both the Dracula and the Frankenstein legends in the movies and is also the first Frankenstein film in color. Hammer's contribution to the genre was the formula it invented for its films: look expensive, sound intelligent, don't spare the sex. The result was a series of films whose sets had the look of luxurious elegance and whose ingenues radiated sensuality. Beyond that, the Hammer horror films have shrewd casting, brilliant direction and intelligent screenplays working for them.

Here, in *The Curse of Frankenstein*, Christopher Lee, playing the role of the creature, manages to convey through pounds of makeup the creature's isolation and dismay, while Peter Cushing is the glacial scientist who will not permit feelings to stand in the way of his research. Cushing and Lee would go on together gracing Hammer horror films for more than a decade after this notable beginning.

JESSE JAMES MEETS FRANKENSTEIN'S DAUGHTER
1965 (Color) U.S.A. 82 minutes
Circle Productions
Director: William Beaudine
Producer: Carroll Case
Screenplay: Carl K. Hittleman
Photography: Lothrop Worth

Surely, the two most obvious contenders for the title of the world's worst horror film are *Plan Nine From Outer Space* and

Jesse James Meets Frankenstein's Daughter. I suspect JJMFD would lose by a point or so because its outrageous plot and its ridiculous casting invest it with some vague aura of charm. Then, too, it is the vulgar twin of William Beaudine's *Billy the Kid Versus Dracula* and that should keep it from deserving a place at the bottom of the barrel—but only just.

The plot? Onyx, a granddaughter of Henry Frankenstein who finds herself in the American West, decides to follow in her ancestor's footsteps in the people-creating line by inserting an artificial brain into the skull of Jesse James' friend. The sutures on his skull when she is done look as if they were sewn with barbed wire. Everything else about this film is just as delicate.

FRANKENSTEIN CREATED WOMAN
1967 (Color)   Great Britain   92 minutes
Hammer Films
Director: Terence Fisher
Producer: Anthony Nelson Keys
Screenplay: John Elder (Anthony Hinds)
Photography: Arthur Grant
Cast: *Peter Cushing, Susan Denberg, Throley Walters, Duncan Lamont, Robert Morris, Peter Blythe*

Here is a breakthrough Frankenstein film, for two reasons: first, there is no home made male creature in it fresh from the laboratory and creating havoc; and second, it introduces such a bizarre sexual ambiguity into its plot that it adds fresh complexity to the Frankenstein idea.

This time Baron Frankenstein (Peter Cushing in a particularly fine performance) transplants the soul of a man decapitated for a crime he did not commit into the voluptuous body of a female suicide. The revived woman, with the man's soul guiding her, sets out to take vengeance on the people who contrived his execution. The result is something of a Hammer film festival as scenes of subtle sexual symbolism and ingenious revenge are played out for our delectation on the screen. The result, even without the presence of the tragically abused "monster," is a film that deserves to be taken seriously for its own quite satisfying sake.

YOUNG FRANKENSTEIN
1974 (B & W)   U.S.A.   108 minutes
Gruskoff Ventures/20th Century Fox
Director: Mel Brooks
Producer: Michael Gruskoff
Screenplay: Gene Wilder and Mel Brooks
Photography: Gerald Hirshfield
Cast: *Gene Wilder, Peter Boyle, Marty Feldman, Madeline Kahn, Cloris Leachman, Terri Garr, Kenneth Mars, Gene Hackman*

The plot of this bubbly spoof of Frankenstein films is a crazy quilt of plots from the three great Universal *Frankenstein* films of the thirties. What makes this at once an enduring and an endearing film is that Mel Brooks and Gene Wilder respected the material at which they were poking fun. The result is that viewers experience two pleasures at once watching the film: frequent shocks of nostalgia as they recognize snippets or whole scenes from Frankenstein film lore; and the delight that comes from seeing those scenes distorted through the comic lenses provided by two of America's zaniest talents.

A caution: the film, hilarious and zestful as it is, is occasionally marred by macho sexual humor that, depending on the context, is either tasteless or coarse.